BYLINE
BUDAPEST

DIANE WAGNER

BYLINE BUDAPEST

This is a work of fiction. Names, characters, dialogue, events, places, public and private entities are the product of the author's imagination or are used fictitiously. Any resemblance to actual persons, living or deceased, is entirely coincidental.

Editor: Scott Driscoll
Copy Editor: Michael G. Ryan

Publishing Consultant: Geoff Affleck, AuthorPreneur Publishing Inc., authorpreneurbooks.com

Cover Designer: Zizi Iryaspraha Subiyarta
Interior Designer: Amit Dey—amitdey2528@gmail.com

Library of Congress #2025913909
ISBN 979-8-9993263-0-0 (paperback)
ISBN 979-8-9993263-2-4 (audiobook)
ISBN 979-8-9993263-1-7 (eBook)

For Jeff,
because you still make me laugh.

PROLOGUE

O n Oct. 23, 1956, students in Budapest sparked a revolution against Hungary's Kremlin-installed government. These students and the hundreds of thousands of Hungarians who joined them were called freedom fighters. Their chief demand: that Hungarians should run their own country for the benefit of Hungarians.

That spark was kindled in part by Radio Free Europe, a privately-owned American radio service set up in 1949 to broadcast a Western perspective on world affairs to listeners in the Soviet satellite states of Bulgaria, Czechoslovakia, Hungary, Poland, and Romania. Until 1972, Radio Free Europe claimed to be paid for by American citizens contributing "truth dollars" to fight the "big lie" of Communism: in reality, it was covertly funded by the Central Intelligence Agency. A sister station, Radio Liberty, broadcast similar material to the Soviet Union. Radio Free Europe and Radio Liberty merged in 1967, funded by the United States Agency for Global Media, an independent federal agency, overseen by the United States Congress.

In the months following the revolution, US Congressional and independent investigations documented the role Radio Free Europe's broadcasts played in encouraging and fostering the hopes and expectations of the freedom fighters. It wasn't that Radio Free Europe's programming ran counter to American policy: rather, Radio Free Europe did its job *too* well. Its promise that the entire Western world stood with Hungary left too much open to interpretation at a desperate time, with deadly consequences.

1

CHARLIE'S WAR

C harlie Atkins stood near the back of the truck, an inflated pillow-shaped balloon held taut between her fingertips. Thin, clear as glass, and nearly as tall as the twenty-three-year-old, five-foot-one Charlie, the balloon shimmered in the cold night air, bright as a mislaid star. It should have been airborne by now, one of thousands of balloons rising silently in the dark sky, floating invisibly eastward over neutral Austria toward communist Hungary.

Overhead, the spring moon glinted off scattered patches of late snow. Charlie—small-boned, slim, her white-blonde hair cut short—glanced at her watch. There was just enough light to see its face: It was nearly two A.M.

The signal to release the balloons was late.

Something is wrong. Charlie's warm breath turned to mist in the frosty air. She looked out at the clearing, carved only recently out of the old spruce and silver firs of the *Bayerischer Wald*, the low, thickly wooded forest that separated West Germany from Czechoslovakia and Austria. On any other night, these woods would be quiet, left to the grey wolves, black grouse, and red deer.

Not tonight.

Tonight, thirteen large silver trailer trucks ringed the clearing, parked tightly together. Their headlights blazed in the dark like unblinking, feral eyes. Light poured out from the backs of the trucks too, powered by the groaning *chugga-chugga-chugga* of gasoline-powered generators. A state-of-the-art meteorological weather station stood at the far edge of the clearing alongside a barracks, a mess hall, and a lab filled with the latest instruments for predicting and tracking the direction of the wind. More light streamed from every window.

Among the trucks, dozens of volunteers—East Europeans, West Germans, and Americans like Charlie—handed up sandwiches and hot mugs of coffee to the crews working inside. No one lingered; there was too much work to be done. Charlie's eyes caught a flash of light, a glint from one of the rifles carried by the guards patrolling the clearing's perimeter. The guards were on high alert for Kremlin saboteurs attempting to disrupt tonight's mission: launching weather balloons filled with messages intended for Hungarians trapped behind the Iron Curtain.

Four months into her job as Radio Free Europe's most junior copy girl, Charlie knew that everything about this night's operations—the newly built weather station, the rented trucks, even the coffee served by the volunteers—was only possible thanks to truth dollars donated by ordinary Americans. These funds, raised at bake sales and church bazaars or tossed in hats at patriotic public rallies, took aim at the 'big lie' of communism—that totalitarianism provided the same freedoms as democracy—by supporting Radio Free Europe's accurate, trustworthy broadcasts to listeners trapped behind the Iron Curtain. Just thinking about it made Charlie's heart nearly burst with pride: Even after two devastating world wars, Americans continued to back a free and democratic Europe, this time with a war of words. *Geographic borders aren't soundproof,* she thought with a gleam of satisfaction as she surveyed the clearing. *Too bad for the Reds.*

Despite the frigid air, sweat ran down her face, and her arms ached. For hours, she had stuffed balloons with leaflets printed in Hungarian on cheap, sepia-tinged newsprint. The leaflets carried messages of solidarity—*A Szabad Nyugat veled áll a zsarnokság ellen!* The Free West stands with you against tyranny! *Küzdj a szólásszabadságodért és a jogállamiságért!* Fight for your right to free speech and the rule of law! *Magyarországot magyaroknak kell irányítani!* Hungary must be ruled by Hungarians!—plus the shortwave frequencies where Radio Free Europe's forbidden-by-Moscow news and programming could be found. The leaflets, small enough to be quietly passed among friends, promised Hungarians that they were not alone.

Charlie wiped her face against her shirt sleeve and then tethered her balloon with half-a-dozen others; together, the balloons hung motionless in the night, a bouquet of huge, alien blossoms filled with lighter-than-air hydrogen glinting in the moonlight. The air stank: sweet, from the gasoline for the generators, and sour, from the raw cabbage funk of ethyl mercaptan, the sulfur compound added to make highly flammable hydrogen gas leaks easier to detect. She glanced up toward the forest's ridge line. The dark, jagged silhouettes of the trees stood still, like mute soldiers standing at attention: chin up, chest out, shoulders back, stomach in. Nothing moved; there was not the slightest hint of a breeze. Even the huge windsock mounted on the roof of the weather station drooped, limp as an empty sleeve. *No wonder the signal is late.*

"Wind—there will be plenty of wind tonight, you said." A furious voice exploded, loud enough to be heard over the noisy grind of the generators.

Charlie turned.

Ernie Owens—the editorial chief of Radio Free Europe's Central Newsroom and Charlie's boss—stood in the clearing. Owens—fifty-three, fireplug short and golf-ball round—jabbed his unlit cigar at the slight, balding man in front of him. "Where the hell is the wind you promised me?"

The meteorologist—*Richards, wasn't it?* Charlie thought—stared miserably at the ground, as though hoping it might open up and swallow him whole. Things had been different during the briefing Richards had given at Radio Free Europe's sprawling European headquarters in Munich, West Germany, two days earlier.

"Weather forecasting is part science, part technology, and part dark arts," Richards had told the assembled group. His voice brimmed with confidence. A sparse moustache drooped untrimmed over his upper lip, and his rumpled white cotton shirt badly needed ironing. "Napoleon used balloons for reconnaissance, did you folks know that? So did the Union Army, so they could see where the Confederate soldiers were hiding. In Korea, the Chinese and the North Koreans used 'em to deliver messages urging our boys to lay down their arms and come enjoy the good life under communism. Oh, yes," Richards said, his voice sounding gleeful, "balloons have a long and wicked history in warfare."

He held up a limp wisp of plastic, a single unfilled balloon spun from polystyrene as fine as spider's silk, and passed it to Charlie, who was sitting in the front row. She let it drape over her fingers, as sheer and filmy as a fresh cobweb. It weighed practically nothing at all yet once inflated with hydrogen, Richards told the group, each balloon would be light and strong enough to rise 40,000 feet—maybe more—into the stratosphere.

"These new balloons are state-of-the-art, designed specifically for you folks at Radio Free Europe. They can travel six hundred miles away from the launch site using only the direction and speed of the wind. We know this because these balloons have little bitty transmitters called radiosondes attached to 'em." Richards held up a small boxy instrument the size of a transistor radio. "Weighs about as much as a ping-pong ball. Once the balloons pop, gravity and wind do the rest of your work for you. Your leaflets will scatter everywhere, and I guarantee you there aren't enough soldiers in the entire Red Army to find and confiscate every single one."

Now, forty-eight hours later in this cold, dark West German forest clearing, Richards cowered in front of Owens. "Tonight's forecast says the wind is supposed to blow like the dickens—" he began, his voice quavering, but Owens cut him off.

"I don't give a damn about what the forecast is supposed to be. Do you have any idea how much it costs to put an operation like this together? You get your fanny over to that fancy-pants lab of yours and tell me how much longer it will be before we can launch."

Richards's head bobbed up and down. He turned and scampered across the clearing toward the weather station.

Owens turned around.

"And you," he growled catching sight of Charlie, his face still angry. "I already said no. You have a job. You clip wire copy. You file. You keep the coffee hot. End of discussion."

This time, Charlie was ready. Job openings on Radio Free Europe's news staff didn't open up very often, and she didn't want to let this chance get away. "I know, Mr. Owens. You've never hired a woman reporter before. But there is a first time for everything, right? All I want is a shot. If I can't write for beans, you'll be the first one to tell me. What have you got to lose?"

Owens took his cigar out of his mouth and looked at it sourly. There was no smoking allowed anywhere in the clearing tonight—not this close to the truckloads of hydrogen tanks required to fill the more than 3,000 balloons scheduled to launch tonight. "I don't get it, Atkins. What the hell are you doing here, anyway?"

Charlie's pulse quickened. She knew exactly why she was here, thousands of miles from the flat, hot lonesome farmlands of California's San Joaquin Valley where she grew up. At home, everyone she knew was getting on with their lives—going to work or college or getting married and having babies. Like Owens, the grandparents who had raised Charlie expected her to marry and take over the daily operations of running the family ranch. Her future was all mapped out—it just wasn't the future Charlie wanted.

She lifted her chin. "You know why I'm here, Mr. Owens. The last war changed everything for all of us. Nuclear war, if it comes, will be a million times worse. I want to help people understand the human cost of war—before it's too late."

Owens scowled. "If things escalate to nuclear war, there won't be anyone or anything left to care." His voice was sharp. "In the meantime, no editor worth his salt should consider hiring a girl for his news staff, let alone to write about something as complicated as war. You wouldn't last ten minutes if things got hot, and there would be hell to pay in the papers if anything happened to you."

"Not every war story happens on a battlefield," Charlie shot back, raising her voice to make sure he heard her over the noise of the generators. "There are casualties everywhere if only you look. Those are the war stories I want to write—about ordinary people whose lives are still blown apart."

Lives like hers. Her father, Captain A. J. Atkins, disappeared in the closing days of the war. The US Army's telex had been brief: A. J. died while serving his country, his body unrecoverable. Without the father she adored, Charlie's life had never been the same.

"Your time would be better spent looking for a husband." Owens pointed his unlit cigar at Charlie and then clamped it back between his teeth. "Wear a skirt for a change. Do something with your hair. Your chances might improve."

Charlie looked down. He wasn't wrong. She didn't dislike dresses—she just didn't find them practical. She preferred slacks like the ones she wore now, dark wool taken in to fit her tiny waist, paired with a white button-down cotton shirt, its long sleeves rolled partway up her arms. Yet even with her hair cut short, she stood out—blue-eyed and blonde, fresh as a Yankee Doodle daisy.

Charlie felt a light tickle of wind on the back of her neck. "You said anyone could apply for the job with a live news writing sample. Grace Kelly's wedding is Thursday, and I have an angle that is right for Radio Free Europe's listeners. I'll come in early and stay late as necessary, to make sure my usual work is done. I'll have it on your desk by the end of the day."

Owens was already shaking his head. "Grace Kelly is a second-rate actress, marrying a third-rate prince from a country the size of a postage stamp. Why should our listeners care about her when they are struggling to survive another day?" Behind him, the windsock on the weather station stirred, its tail lifting faintly with the breeze. "I refuse to give that damn wedding any more coverage than is absolutely required."

"But that's just it, Mr. Owens," Charlie said, her words tumbling out eagerly. "My story isn't about Grace Kelly but about what a wedding like hers means for women who aren't movie stars or princesses. It's about survival, resilience, and hope—"

"Hope has no place in a serious newsroom." Viktor Farkas, the youngest and most popular of Radio Free Europe's Hungarian commentators, cut Charlie's sentence off as he stepped out of the dark. He stood next to Owens, barely glancing at Charlie. "Even a news clerk should understand such things."

Charlie tried not to grimace. She did not like—or trust—Viktor. He wasn't much older than she was, but everything about him unnerved her: his blue eyes, as cold and hard as January ice, his cheekbones, as sharp as right angles, and his teeth, which were broken and jagged like rickrack. Even the way Viktor dressed unsettled Charlie: He wore the hand-me-down uniform of a refugee, mute reminders of a life forever disrupted. Viktor spoke with authority in a deep, rich baritone instantly recognizable to listeners of Radio Free Europe's Hungarian radio service, yet he easily dismissed anything outside his own worldview. Like the possibility that women could be reporters, let alone war correspondents, same as a man.

"If hope is so dangerous, then what are we all doing out here in the middle of nowhere?" Charlie tried to keep the annoyance she felt out of her voice. "What is the point of anything Radio Free Europe does, if not to give our listeners hope?"

Viktor turned on Charlie, his eyes locked on hers, intense and steady as a searchlight. "Giving hope to those who have none is a dangerous thing." His accented English, clipped and precise, sounded like typewriter keys striking paper. "It must be done carefully, by men with experience and judgment. Anything else is frivolous and only prolongs suffering. You are young, Miss Atkins, and raised in the freedom of the West. You will never be a serious journalist because you do not understand that false hope is worse than no hope at all."

"No one should live without hope."

"And yet many people do, Miss Atkins, and they are better off than waiting for something that never comes." Viktor turned to Owens. "We are ready to launch the balloons. We wait only for the signal."

Owens grunted. "Tell everyone to sit tight until the damn wind decides to blow."

Viktor nodded and turned away without so much as a backward glance at Charlie.

She watched him disappear among the trucks, past a clutch of tethered balloons. The balloons tugged at their strings, as if eager to be set free.

"You could learn something from Viktor," Owens said. He pushed his thick, black glasses back up his nose. "He knows firsthand what it costs to hope for better, only to lose everything—his family, his country, his friends, and years of his life, too, in prison."

"The tryout for the reporting staff, Mr. Owens." Charlie kept her voice level, refusing to let him change the subject. "All I am asking for is a chance to show you what I can do."

Exasperated, Owens inspected the plug end of his cigar. "Listen, Atkins, if you think you can make me care about Grace Kelly's wedding, go ahead. Write your damn story. But if you can't—" His eyes glittered—"then you and I agree to *never* discuss you applying for a reporter's job ever again." He replaced the cigar in his mouth. "That is our deal."

Owens's smirk told Charlie exactly what she needed to know: He didn't think she could do it.

"I'll take that deal," she said quickly before he could change his mind.

A shout. Richards ran toward them, waving his arms and shouting. "We have wind! Go! Go, go, go!"

Charlie and Owens looked up. Dark, patchy clouds raced across the star-filled sky as the trees swayed and bent along the ridgeline. The windsock on the meteorological station flew a full horizontal salute.

"Release the balloons!" Owens thundered, and suddenly, the first ones rose, surging upward from among the trucks, one gleaming, gossamer bubble after another.

Charlie ran back to where she had been working. With quick fingers, she unhooked all of the balloons. Each one hung motionless for an instant then caught a gust of air and whipped furiously into the air, translucent and luminous in the moonlight, soaring over the dark Austrian countryside, silent and unseen, toward Hungary. Even the mid-April air smelled different, crisp and expectant, like the coming of spring.

Charlie's heart soared, too. Owens's deal wasn't exactly a ringing endorsement, but she didn't care. She had her shot. Write a story that gave Radio Free Europe's listeners hope? Charlie intended to do just that, no matter what Owens or Viktor thought.

2
CHARLIE

On the bus ride back to Munich, Charlie, exhausted, was too excited to sleep.

With the rest of the volunteers, she had worked through the night and into the afternoon to make sure Radio Free Europe's 3,000 balloons were filled and released. By now, those balloons were floating east over the sharp peaks and ridges of the Austrian Alps and the quiet of its lowland villages. Not until the balloons reached Hungarian airspace more than three hundred miles away would they burst open and shower down the leaflets they carried. Charlie tried to picture that moment, when thousands of leaflets fluttered down from the sky unannounced to be picked up and read by welders in Győr's manufacturing plants in Hungary's west, professors at Szeged's universities in the south, Miskolc's coal miners in the northeast, railway workers in Kecskemét in central Hungary, and minor bureaucrats fifty-three miles north in Budapest, Hungary's capital. If the wind carried just right, the balloons and their cargo of leaflets might even make it as far east as Sátoraljaújhely, the last Hungarian town before Czechoslovakia. It had been tiring, repetitive work, but Charlie didn't mind. As the bus wound down through the mountains toward Munich, she closed her eyes and listened to the soft chatter of voices on the bus.

She had known from an early age that she wanted to tell war stories. Not the kind filled with battle tactics, body counts, or how many yards were lost or gained; she wanted to write about the people war left in its wake. Ordinary people, trying to make sense of the incomprehensible.

She was born in 1933 on her grandparents' ranch, the Double Aught, in California's agricultural bread basket, the oil-rich farmland of the San Joaquin Valley. Her mother died before Charlie formed a memory of her. Her father, Adolf Joseph—called A. J. by everyone, including Charlie—named her after Charlemagne, the Dark Ages king who united much of Europe. A. J. nicknamed her Charlie for short.

Life in the San Joaquin Valley—ringed by the snow-crested peaks of the Sierra Nevada Mountains to the east, the scrub and mist-covered Northern Coast Range to the west, and the woody, thick-leaf chaparral of the Tehachapis to the south—was hard. The Great Depression's perfect storm of bank failures, farm foreclosures, and factory closures left few households untouched. In California, Okies fleeing the black blizzards of West Texas and the Oklahoma Panhandle and *braceros* from Mexico flooded into the valley, competing for rock-bottom wages picking citrus or sugar beets or strawberries. With Charlie in the front seat, once a week, A. J. made the rounds of the shanty towns and the government camps where the farm workers lived, dropping off whatever extra produce the ranch could spare.

Charlie, tow-headed and barefoot, followed A. J. everywhere, padding after him down the Double Aught's long rows of almond and avocado trees, into the barn to fork hay for the horses, and out into the fields where A. J. picked or planted crops alongside the hired hands who kept the ranch running. She followed him into the cockpit of his old Curtiss Jenny, too, which A. J. bought to make extra money for the ranch by dusting crops up and down the valley. The Curtiss Jenny was Charlie's favorite place to sit with her father. "Flaps up for lift—that is what gets you up in the air," A. J. told her, his hand over hers as he showed her how the biplane's control stick worked. She loved the way his light tenor sounded warm and close in her ear. "Flaps down to slow your landing," he said, as he taught her how to glide the Curtiss Jenny down for a soft landing.

On Dec. 7, 1941, everything changed. The Japanese Imperial Navy attacked Pearl Harbor, and the United States hurtled into war, first with Japan and then days later with Germany and Italy. Eight-year-old Charlie's small world shattered.

The first casualty was Annie Ito, Charlie's first—and best—friend.

Executive Order 9066, signed by President Franklin D. Roosevelt on February 19, 1942, mandated the forced relocation of anyone with Japanese ancestry living on the Pacific Coast, whether born in the United States or not. They were to be sent away for the duration of the war—for their own protection against vigilantes seeking revenge for the attack on Pearl Harbor, President Roosevelt claimed, and to make sure no one sent secret messages about American troop readiness to military leaders in Japan.

A. J. drove eight-year-old Charlie into downtown Bakersfield, past Vest's Drug Store and the clock tower at 17th and Chester, to say goodbye to Annie.

They found her and her parents standing in the hard, bright April sun, at the front of a long line that started at the Kern County Courthouse and then snaked around the block. Like everyone else, the Itos were permitted to bring only bedrolls and one small suitcase apiece. Annie's mother clutched a handbag brimming with fresh bok choy and daikon from the family farm the Itos had sold days earlier for pennies on the dollar.

Charlie squatted down on the sidewalk next to Annie, who sat on the edge of her suitcase. "I brought you something." Charlie held out a dog-eared copy of the Nancy Drew book *The Whispering Statue*. "I thought you could read it on the bus."

Annie shook her head. Her straight black hair hung down her back in two neat braids. Like her parents, Annie wore a large white baggage tag pinned to her coat collar. Her name and housing assignment for Camp Manzanar—officially the Manzanar War Relocation Center three hours northeast of Bakersfield—was scrawled on the tag.

"But this one is our favorite, remember?" Charlie said uncertainly. Despite her father's best attempt to explain, Charlie was still trying to work out why Annie and her parents were leaving. "It's the one where Nancy meets Togo for the first time." Togo, Nancy's little wire-haired terrier, was the character Annie liked best.

Annie crossed her arms tightly over her chest and said nothing.

"When will you be back?"

"Why would we come back to a place where no one wants us?"

"What do you mean? This is your home."

Annie raised her head. Her eyes were red and swollen as she looked over Charlie's shoulder. "Not anymore."

Charlie turned to follow Annie's gaze. Miss Caroline, her Sunday school teacher, was across the street, one among a sea of familiar faces cheering and shouting. Charlie started to wave until she read the hand-lettered sign Miss Caroline held: "Dirty, stinkin' Japs go home, this is a white man's town."

Charlie whirled back to look at Annie, astonished. "But you have never even been to Japan."

Annie's face crumpled. She squeezed her eyes shut but not tight enough to keep the tears in. Charlie hugged Annie; she was crying, too.

A hiss of brakes, a screech of metal, and the door of a yellow school bus swung open at the curb. Mr. Beason, who picked up Charlie and Annie for school every morning and brought them home in the afternoon, was in the driver's seat. He nodded at Charlie. He didn't look at Annie.

Mr. Ito placed a hand on Annie's shoulder and nudged her gently up the steps. Charlie, not bothering to wipe away her tears, followed alongside the bus as Annie and her parents found seats inside. Charlie waved until the bus pulled away from the curb. Annie didn't wave back.

Charlie turned to her father. "I don't understand. Annie didn't do anything wrong."

A. J. scooped her up in his arms. "This is what fear and hate does, Charlie—it makes us turn on each other." His clearwater blue eyes mirrored her own. "Even though it's hard right now, in her heart, Annie knows you will be her friend always."

Charlie hoped her father was right.

The second casualty for her was a minor one, the shortage of the Hershey Milk Chocolate candy bars she loved as sugar-rationing took hold.

The third casualty was A. J.—whether he was called up for duty or volunteered, Charlie didn't know. The night before he left, he sat with her in the Curtiss Jenny looking out over the ranch one last time before he rolled the plane into the Double Aught's barn for storage.

"I am going to war to fight for what is good and right," he told her over the soft *plink-plink-plink* of nearby meadow toads looking for mates. "Seems to me the world is a whole lot better off when people live together as friends and neighbors, like you and Annie. Someday, when you grow up, I hope you will understand why this is important enough for me to leave you and the ranch."

Charlie leaned against her father, breathing in his familiar scent of sweat and woodsmoke. Fear and dread surged through her like the swell of a coming storm. She didn't understand, not one bit. "Why can't you do that here? Annie left, and she hasn't come back. Why do you have to go away, too?"

"Because away is where the war is. I'll write you all about it, every chance I get. I'll be back before you know it, Charlie."

A. J. carried her into the house and stayed with her until she fell asleep. In the morning, she awoke to find him gone.

Left in the care of her aging grandparents, her days on the Double Aught felt long. Before school, she fed the chickens or cut thick slabs of bread for her grandfather's breakfast. After school, she worked in the family's garden, bringing snap peas or collard greens to the kitchen for dinner. Her grandfather, Josef, a lanky, taciturn Prussian immigrant, made sure Charlie knew how to work with her hands and taught her the names of every tool in the barn in his native German: *Axt. Schaufel. Säge.* Axe. Shovel. Saw. Her Scotch-Irish grandmother, Iona Mae, showed Charlie how to keep the Double Aught's books: how much it cost to run the ranch and often how little was left over.

A. J. kept his word. He wrote often, his letters filled with funny pictures and stories about the people he met. He couldn't tell her where he was—that was a military secret, he joked—only that he was safe and couldn't wait to come home to her and the ranch. Once A. J. mentioned a friend he hoped would come visit the Double Aught once the war was over.

Even then, Charlie knew life on the ranch was not for her. At night, when her chores were done, she listened to the radio, eager for any snippet of news that might help her feel closer to A. J., wherever he was. She knew there was a bigger, wider world out there beyond the ranch. That world was at war, and it had taken her father from her. She wanted—needed—to see and understand it for herself.

She read, too, especially news stories and magazine spreads written by women war correspondents and photographers—Martha Gellhorn, Margaret Bourke-White, Ruth Cowan, Marguerite Higgins, and Lee Miller. They went to war, same as the men, but, barred by the US Army from frontline reporting, found their own ways to tell stories about what it all meant. They wrote about the silent, stoic faces of women—Czech, Polish, or French—watching fathers, sons, or husbands march off to war, the bewildered Nazi child soldiers left fatherless, leaderless, and adrift when the fighting finally stopped, and the thousand-yard stares of American boys in the Pacific Theater's evac hospitals, contemplating home. Most of all, they put a human face on war.

When the war ended, A. J. was not among the fathers, sons and brothers who found their way home. Months after V-E Day—May 8, 1945, Victory in Europe Day—a plain cardboard box labeled *Captain Adolf Joseph (A. J.) Atkins, Died in Service, No Remains Recovered*, arrived at the Double Aught. It held A. J.'s personal belongings, which included a wristwatch Charlie had never seen before but immediately claimed as her own. Its crisp white face sported art deco-styled black numerals and, just above the number six, a single red star, a pentagon, set with ruby-colored glass. It became the only piece of jewelry Charlie wore, a daily reminder of her father.

By the time she was a junior in high school, she thought she, too, could put a human face on war like the women journalists she admired. She introduced herself to Mike Harris, the managing editor of her hometown newspaper, the *Bakersfield Californian*, and told him that she wanted to be a war correspondent.

At sixty-four, Harris, who was too close to a forced retirement that he dreaded, liked Charlie's spunk. He took her under his wing and made a point of teaching her the basics of good journalism. "Write your stories the way you might tell your next-door neighbor the news," he told her. "Tell what happened to whom, and why it matters. Keep your sentences simple, like a conversation, and let each idea build on top of the one before it."

Charlie paid close attention. With Harris's coaching, she honed her eye for stories that tugged at the heart strings, like the quiet rituals of a family's graveside Father's Day visit. She racked up every byline she could. After high school, she tried her hand at community college but found herself restless for more. When a group of hometown Gold Star

Mothers organized a tour to visit the European graves of their fallen sons, Charlie proposed going along to write about their journeys of grief and remembrance. Harris gave her the assignment, and that night Charlie told her grandparents that she was leaving Double Aught. "I want to see the world," she said, "and as a reporter, I can help others see it, too."

Her grandfather scowled, his left hand cupped around his bad ear. "*Europa* is not *gut*," Josef said in his stiff, German-accented English. "*Zwischen immer und nie*. Between always and never. Always fighting, never at peace. Not *gut* for me. Not *gut* for your father, *Gott* rest his soul. Not *gut* for you either."

Instinctively, Charlie's fingers brushed against her father's watch, its brown leather band loose around her slim wrist. "A. J. never came home," she said. "Maybe I'll find out why."

#   #   #

Charlie found her grandfather was right about Europe: it roiled, restless and unmoored. Reminders of the war's destruction—the dead, the missing, the displaced, the ruined cities—hung like a shroud over everyday tasks: finding food, finding work, finding a place to live. So did nightmare visions of wars yet to come: nuclear war between the United States and the newly thermonuclear-armed Soviet Union, or the sinister, silent unleashing of chemical or biological weapons with the potential to kill millions. Nor were her hometown Gold Star Mothers alone in their journeys—in churchyards across Europe, they were joined by other mothers and fathers, also come to honor their dead.

Still, there were hopeful signs. Buoyed by the Marshall Plan's billions of dollars in American economic aid, Western Europe was rebuilding. In 1953, Soviet Premier Joseph Stalin died, and his replacement, Nikita Khrushchev, spoke of peaceful coexistence with the West and eased censorship and repression at home. In May 1955, West Germany joined the North Atlantic Treaty Organization (NATO), and Austria regained its sovereignty, declaring itself officially neutral between East and West. Charlie found it all intoxicating. When her assignment for the *Bakersfield Californian* ended, she counted up her savings, took a deep breath, and decided to stay in Europe. She found a job in Munich at Radio Free Europe as a news clerk. Not the reporter's job she hoped for, but it was a start.

#   #   #

As the bus neared Munich, its gears groaned and whined in the late afternoon traffic. Charlie opened her eyes. Her plan for tomorrow was simple. She would go in to Radio Free Europe as usual and start her daily routine: routing wire copy to the right editors, picking up or returning library materials, and distributing carbon copies of stories or internal memos. As soon as pictures of Grace Kelly's wedding came across the photo wire, she would leave for the one interview she intended to do for her story. Once it was done, she would write it up, leave it on Owens's desk, and then stay late to finish up whatever was left.

Charlie watched as the outskirts of the city rolled by outside her window. Although Dachau, the first of the Nazi's brutal, inhumane concentration camps, was only half an hour away by car, here Munich felt reborn. The city was nearly destroyed in the closing days of the war by Allied bombers, but one by one the ruined buildings were slowly disappearing, replaced by new apartments and shops. Munich's population was growing again, too, up to nearly a million residents, nearly what it had been in 1939 when *Führer* Adolf Hitler's invasion of Poland sparked World War II. Along the boulevards, young oak trees were being planted to replace those lost in the war, and the city's buses were running again with West German clockwork precision. *All of it, hopeful signs for a better future*, Charlie thought.

She glimpsed Radio Free Europe's familiar white stucco exterior just ahead. She sat forward on her seat, glad the long bus ride from the *Bayerischer Wald* to Munich was nearly over. *By this time tomorrow, Grace Kelly will be a princess, and maybe I will be on my way to a job on the news staff*, she thought.

Hopeful signs for a better future, indeed.

3
PAPER BULLETS

The next morning, Charlie hurried up the eight low, wide concrete steps at the front entrance to Radio Free Europe. It was ten minutes after nine: Grace Kelly and her six bridesmaids were not due at Monaco's Saint Nicholas Cathedral for another hour. Plenty of time, Charlie figured, to get started on her day's work before pictures of the wedding began to materialize on the Associated Press' wirephoto machine. So intent was Charlie on getting into the office that she was halfway across the lobby before Gerhard, the dour-faced clerk at the front desk, managed to flag her down.

"You are late for your appointment, *Fräulein* Atkins," Gerhard said, looking down his nose at her, disapproval lacing his terse, exacting English. With one long, knobby finger, he pointed at a man on the far side of the otherwise empty lobby, his back to the room as he bent over to study a scale model of one of Radio Free Europe's steel-and-guy-wired transmitter towers. "Your guest is waiting."

Charlie groaned. She had forgotten entirely. A routine request for a morning tour of Radio Free Europe had come in the week before, and Owens had kicked it downstairs to her.

Charlie shifted her canvas bag to her other shoulder, mustered up a smile, and mentally crossed her fingers that her visitor would not ask too many questions.

"Impressive, isn't it?" She kept her voice bright as she stepped up next to her guest. With her left hand, she tapped the top of the model's spire lightly with one finger. "These antennae are designed specifically for Radio Free Europe. They bounce our signals off the earth's upper atmosphere, the ionosphere. That's how our broadcasts are able to travel as far into Eastern Europe as they do."

She turned to introduce herself. Up close, the man was thin-boned and birdlike, nearly bald, with a sharp beak of a nose and piercing brown eyes. The fine lines around his eyes gave away his age—sixty at least—and he leaned heavily on a wooden cane. A white Roman clerical collar peeked out from his wool overcoat.

"Welcome to Radio Free Europe, Father," she said. "I'm Charlie Atkins."

"Daniel Popov." His eyes followed Charlie's wrist. "That is a most unusual watch you're wearing, Miss Atkins. May I take a closer look?"

Startled, Charlie turned her arm toward him. Father Popov pulled her wrist close and peered at the watch's face with its single ruby-red star. "I do believe that is a Kremlin star."

"A what?"

"A Kremlin star," Father Popov repeated. "There are stars just like this on top of the Kremlin's five main towers. They were Stalin's idea, to remind Russians of the power of the state. Each one is twelve feet high, and they light up at night so that they can be seen all over Moscow. May I ask how you came to own this particular watch?"

"It belonged to my father."

Father Popov cocked his head and peered at her, his eyes bright. "Oh? That must be quite a story."

"Maybe," Charlie said. Gently, she extricated her wrist. "I never got a chance to ask him."

Father Popov flushed. "My apologies."

"Shall we start our tour?" Charlie, eager to change the subject, pointed at the oversized wooden map of Eastern Europe and the Soviet Union mounted on the lobby wall. Each country nestled against its neighbors like the pieces of a giant jigsaw puzzle. The nations of the U.S.S.R. were colored blood red while the Soviet Socialist Republics—those countries with the geographic bad luck to provide a buffer zone for Russia's long, hard-to-defend western frontier— were a deep, rosy pink.

"Radio Free Europe's programming focuses on five of the Soviet Socialist Republics—Bulgaria, Czechoslovakia, Hungary, Poland, and Romania. Our sister organization, Radio Liberation, broadcasts to Russia and the fourteen republics that make up the U.S.S.R." Charlie ticked them off on her fingers in alphabetical order to make sure she got them all. "That's Armenia, Azerbaijan, Byelorussia, Estonia, Georgia, Kazakhstan, Kirgizia, Latvia, Lithuania, Moldavia, Tajikistan, Turkmenistan, Ukraine, and Uzbekistan."

Automatically, she started walking backward across the lobby, toward the thick white security door that led into the main part of the building. Giving tours like this one was part of her job as the most junior member of the staff, and most days she didn't mind. Today, however, she hoped to keep the tour short. The story she had pitched to Owens was due by the end of the day.

"After the war, Stalin made clear that he didn't want Western ideas about freedom or democracy to take hold in the countries he controlled," Charlie continued. "He closed borders across Eastern Europe and made sure all official communications—newspapers, radio stations, textbooks— followed the official Communist Party line. That worried a lot of Americans in government and business. They got together and founded the National Committee for a Free Europe in 1949 to promote democratic values. Radio Free Europe was one of the first projects they set up. Their idea was to use radio broadcasts to let listeners behind the Iron Curtain know they have not been forgotten, and to talk to them about alternatives to communism, like democracy. We think of ourselves as sort of a Marshall Plan of ideas—sharing what it's like to live in a free and open society."

Charlie pulled the security door open for Father Popov. Her heart sank as she watched him limp slowly toward her and the long central hallway that served as the building's spine, one careful step at a time. *So much for a quick tour,* she thought, dismayed. This one was going to take longer than usual, and she was already pressed for time.

#   #   #

Inside the central hallway, Radio Free Europe's main corridor echoed with quick footsteps and the bright chatter of half-a-dozen languages. Charlie stepped back to let two men arguing in animated Russian pass as she waited for Father Popov.

His eyes followed the men down the hallway. "Elvis Presley versus Frank Sinatra," he said, smiling in amusement as he translated their chatter for Charlie's benefit. "Russians will argue about anything."

Charlie stepped back to let the priest shuffle past her. "Radio Free Europe went on the air for the first time on Independence Day, July 4, 1950," she said, taking small steps to keep pace with him. "At first, all of our programs were recorded in New York and flown to Europe, but that meant the news was stale by the time it went on the air. If we wanted to provide useful news, we had to find a way to do it faster. We needed a European presence and the ability to hire émigrés with the language and journalistic skills to help us run our five individual radio services. That's why we built this facility in Munich—so that we could write, record, and transmit our programs faster. We have twenty-two broadcasting studios, six control rooms, plus editorial offices for each radio service. We even built this building in such a way that when the Cold War is over, the West Germans can use it use as a hospital."

"You think the Cold War is going to end, do you?"

"Don't you?" Charlie said. "The Soviets can't keep seventy million East Europeans captive forever—especially the more they hear from us about what it means to live in freedom. That is what makes our radio services so powerful."

"The Nazis believed in the power of radio, too," Father Popov said. His voice rasped, like the scrape of footsteps on dry gravel. "They made cheap radios, called *Volksempfänger*. Every time *Herr* Hitler gave a speech, everyone was expected to stop and listen. The radios were set up so that no foreign stations could be heard on them. Just official broadcasts. An effective strategy, as it turned out."

"Maybe," Charlie said, smiling, "but there is an important difference. Our broadcasts aren't propaganda. We work hard to get our facts right, and our stories are every bit as truthful as what you might hear from Walter Cronkite on CBS News.

We don't allow editorializing or opinions unless it's strictly labeled as commentary."

Father Popov stopped and thumped his cane. "Of course you broadcast propaganda. Even news that is fair and balanced is propaganda. Propaganda aims to persuade people to a certain point of view—democracy over communism—which is exactly what you people do."

"I guess that's true." Charlie eyed Father Popov. "You sound more like a college professor than a priest."

"Guilty as charged." Father Popov began to walk again, one halting step after another. "I did teach—one semester at the Army War College. Russian language studies and military history. That was in the spring of 1917, and the Great War was in full swing. When the United States joined on the side of the Allies, my students enlisted, and so did I. The war—" He gestured with his cane—"left me with a permanent reminder of what men are capable of doing to other men. While I recuperated, I had time to think about my future. Returning to my classroom seemed pointless. I found my way to seminary school, and eventually, to a job with the war department."

"The war department?" Charlie cocked her head as she looked at him. "That seems like a strange place for a priest."

"Does it?" Father Popov glanced at the black-and-white photographs showing Radio Free Europe's building under construction on the wall, but he kept moving. "I am of the opinion that the war department needs more men like me, men of peace, especially since the war to end all wars did not quite do the job. When World War II started, the war department sent me here to Munich, to help figure out how this time we might do a better job keeping the peace."

"And have you figured out how to keep the peace?"

"I regret to say that so far we have not." He smiled faintly. "Like any good bureaucracy, the war department spends too much time studying what went wrong the last time around. But you folks—maybe you are onto something. If we learn to fire only words at each other—paper bullets—maybe the outcome can be different. Not perfect, but better. Maybe there is hope after all that we can do a better job waging peace."

False hope is worse than no hope at all, Viktor had said. "Does hope have a place in war, even when all seems lost?" Charlie asked.

"In Romans Chapter 8, the apostle Paul tells us we are saved by hope but only when we cannot clearly see the outcome," Father Popov said. "His point is that hope gives us the strength to persevere, no matter how bad things are. So yes, I believe that hope has its place, even in war, maybe along with a healthy dose of realism."

"Hope with a dose of realism—I like that," Charlie said as she stopped in front of a thick blond wood door. "This is the first stop on our tour."

Charlie pulled the door open so that Father Popov could see inside. The cramped, noisy room was filled with rows of headset-wearing men and women, their faces fixed in concentration as they typed furiously on individual transcription machines. "This is our monitoring section, the 'ears' of Radio Free Europe. We record as much official news, speeches, and local radio programs as we can. Our transcribers translate and type up verbatim what is being broadcast. Those transcripts give us a good understanding of what people are being told by their governments day in, day out."

She pointed to the bank of reel-to-reel tape recorders lining the far wall, their large silver wheels turning like clockwork in slow, lazy loops. "Our tape recorders turn on at four in the morning and run until 1:00 A.M. We can have a full English language translation of a major speech within an hour, which allows us to respond quickly with fact-based rebuttals to—" She nearly said government propaganda—"what we believe to be misinformation."

One of the transcribers lifted her head. She was dark-haired and petite, and dwarfed by the man's grey wool cardigan she wore. Its long sleeves were folded back into thick cuffs that stretched halfway up her arms. She nodded and smiled at Charlie without slowing her pace.

Charlie waved back. "That is Mária Szabó, one of our Hungarian transcribers. She escaped from Budapest three years ago, after her husband died in prison. That is his sweater she's wearing. She says it helps to keep his memory alive." She closed the door to the monitoring section gently.

They moved down the corridor in slow lockstep, the tap of Father Popov's cane a faint counterpoint to their steps.

He said, "Americans are not known for their language skills unless you are lucky enough to grow up in an immigrant family like mine. I dreamed in Russian until I was ten or eleven years old." He craned his neck sideways to glance at Charlie. "Meanwhile, you folks hire mostly émigrés like your friend Mária. People who leave their countries sometimes have a certain way of looking at things. An agenda. Maybe old scores to settle. You folks worry about the wrong thing being said? Especially if you don't understand the languages of your listeners?"

"It's a fair question. We have strict editorial and policy guidelines. We can tell our listeners that we stand with them, but we can't promise them military support from the West to help them overthrow their government. We're not an official government station like the Voice of America—we're more like a home radio service. Our job is to ask the questions we think people would like to ask their own governments."

"You think you know here in Munich what a Pole in Warsaw or a Bulgarian in Sofia wants to ask their government?"

"Our broadcasts are illegal to listen to, so we can't do listener surveys. Instead, we interview as many cross-border travelers as we can for the latest news and whether they think our broadcasts are getting the facts right. We also know the Soviets work pretty hard to jam our signals, which we think is a good indication that our broadcasts are accurate. And—" Charlie stopped in front of a large glass window overlooking rows of shelves filled top to bottom with books—"we read."

She pointed through the window. "This is our reference library—books, government reports, speeches, magazines, and newspapers. We create detailed files on important topics—the economy, how this year's harvest is doing versus last year's, and how much things cost. We also keep files on government officials and key people—like factory bosses or party leaders—so that we can hold them accountable for what they say and do."

"The communists do the same sort of thing. Keep files on people."

"You are right—they do." Charlie's eye caught the clock on the library wall. It was nearly ten o'clock; Grace Kelly's wedding was about to get underway. She needed to keep Father Popov moving. "But there is a difference," she said as she started walking again. "Our files are based on the government's own records and published materials. No one is coerced or tortured into reporting on anyone else. And we use our files to fight lies with facts."

"Such as?"

"Well, suppose the president of Czechoslovakia gives a speech, saying that the standard of living for Czechs is going up, thanks to the communist system. Our job is to ask whether this is true. Are workers being paid more than they were two or three years ago? Can housewives find flour or eggs in the shops? Can families find a place to live and afford to heat it in the winter? We use the government's own facts and figures to check what they say."

"All the while feeding your listeners a steady diet about the good life in America. Supermarkets bursting with goods and open to all, brand-new cars rolling off Detroit's production lines, a chicken in every pot."

Charlie shifted her canvas bag to her other shoulder. "Is that a bad thing? My father used to say that most people want the same things—a good job, a safe place to live, a better life for their children."

"Your father sounds like a very smart man. Where did he serve?"

Charlie felt a familiar pang, the way she did when she thought about how little she knew about A. J. and what had happened to him after he left the Double Aught. "Honestly, I don't know, but I wish I did," she admitted. "I was eight when he left for boot camp, and his letters didn't say."

By the time Charlie and Father Popov reached the Central Newsroom, it was twenty minutes to eleven. Inside, a dozen reporters—all men in shirt sleeves—banged away on boxy grey Royal Standard typewriters, their desks shoved one against another in the middle of the small room to save space. Piles of wire copy and overflowing baskets of newsprint covered nearly every surface. Underneath it all was a nonstop staccato, the *tikka-tikka-tikka* of the wire service terminals—the Associated Press, United Press International, Reuters, TASS, the Soviet news feed, plus half a dozen more wire services from across Eastern Europe. The AP's wirephoto machine was running at full speed, too. *Wedding pictures*, Charlie thought eagerly. *Perfect timing.*

"This is where I work," Charlie said. It was her favorite part of the tour, a chance to show off how a round-the-clock newsroom operated. "We're the heartbeat of Radio Free Europe—we manage incoming news from all over the world. We select the stories we think listeners in Eastern Europe will care most about—new scientific and engineering developments, advances in agriculture or animal husbandry, economic news, announcements from the Vatican, military conflicts—and we route those stories on to the individual radio services to review, edit, translate, and air. We also write original stories—how American elections work, interviews with politicians or film stars or businessmen, or what music American teenagers are listening to right now. We operate twenty-four hours a day to keep our hourly news bulletins fresh and up to date."

Charlie pointed to the editorial budget—the list of stories planned for the day—scrawled on one of the room's blackboards. "All five language services run some of the same stories. Today it looks like that will include an update on Khrushchev's meetings in London with Prime Minister Eden and the new charter for an international agency to set guidelines for the peaceful use of the atom bomb. The stations choose the rest of their programming. They know best what their listeners are most interested in hearing about."

Charlie scanned the room. Owens was nowhere to be seen. *Good*, she thought. *No chance of being waylaid.* "If you will excuse me a minute," she said to Father Popov, "I just need to pull some pictures off the wirephoto machine."

She almost made it across the room.

"Red alert, Atkins!" Owens's voice boomed out from his office. "Coffee, stat!"

Charlie grimaced but hurried to the newsroom's small kitchen. She filled the percolator with water and ground coffee and plugged it in. As the coffee brewed, she checked the wirephoto machine. There, materializing on photographic paper wrapped around the machine's rotating drum, was the first picture of Grace Kelly. She emerged from a long, black limousine to take the arm of an older man in full morning dress—*her father*, Charlie figured—waiting to escort her into the grand white limestone cathedral.

Despite herself, Charlie caught her breath.

Metro-Goldwyn-Mayer, the studio where Kelly starred in *Mogambo*, *High Society*, and *The Country Girl*, for which she won an Academy Award for Best Actress, had put its wardrobe department to work on their star's behalf. Thirty seamstresses spent six weeks furiously creating her wedding dress. It was unlike anything else Charlie had ever seen: a delicate, sophisticated gown made with *peau de soie* silk and antique lace. The photographer had caught the actress' face as she prepared to take on the role of a lifetime: a real princess who was about to leave everything familiar behind. Was it a love match? Charlie hoped so. She scooped up the picture and slipped it into her canvas bag.

When the coffee was finished, Charlie poured it into a clean coffee mug and added a healthy dollop of cream. She carried it with both hands to Owens's office and placed it on his desk. He picked it up and began to drink it without so much as a thank you.

As Charlie rejoined Father Popov, a series of chiming bells came across the radio. Eleven A.M.

"That sound is the Liberty Bell," Charlie said. "It rings on the hour before every single newscast. And I am afraid it means our time is over."

#   #   #

In the front lobby before leaving, Father Popov paused.

"I'm retired now, but I still have friends in the war department who might be able to tell you more about where your father served," he said, leaning heavily on his cane. "I can ask around if you like—unofficially, of course. I would just need your father's full name."

"That is very kind of you," Charlie said, genuinely touched. "His name is Captain A. J.—for Adolf Joseph—Atkins. And yes, any information at all would be wonderful."

Father Popov nodded. "If I learn anything useful, I will be in touch. In the meantime, good luck to you. Take care of that watch."

As soon as Father Popov was out of sight, Charlie hurried back inside the building for the portable reel-to-reel tape recorder she had managed to borrow for her interview. She was already late, but Charlie knew that Sophie—her first and best friend in Munich and the woman whose story she planned to leave on Owens's desk that afternoon—would understand.

4
TRÜMMERFRAUEN

E ven Charlie's bus was running late.

It idled, steady as a ticking clock, as four women, their faces white with plaster dust, carried a large window across the street in front of the bus. They were *Trümmerfrauen*—rubble women—paid to salvage reuseable materials from bombed-out buildings because there were no men around to do the job. The *Trümmerfrauen* moved in rhythmic lockstep, calling out their steps as they moved: *eins, zwei, eins, zwei.* Under her breath, Charlie counted with them—*one, two, one, two*—as if she might help hurry them along. The *Trümmerfrauen* were nearly past the bus when the window shattered, sending shards of glass tinkling to the street.

The bus driver sighed and turned off the engine.

The *Trümmerfrauen* heaved the window frame into a trash wagon and picked up brooms. Charlie watched, her fingers tapping impatiently on the borrowed tape recorder in her lap. She was going to be even later than she thought.

\#   \#   \#

Charlie met Sophie on the afternoon she decided to stay in Munich.

She had come to Marienplatz, the old town square where Münchners have shopped and gossiped since the city's founding in 1157, hoping to find a room to rent. Munich, however, was still paying for the "honor" of being the spiritual home to Hitler's Nazi Party; in the closing days of the war, Allied carpeting-bombing left much of the city in ruins, and eleven years later, housing remained in short supply.

As she looked for signs reading *raum zu vermieten*—room to rent—Charlie stopped to scan the faded messages left on notice boards around Marienplatz, left for family members or friends gone missing in Europe's post-war resettlement chaos. *Albert Hiller, I have taken the girls to Aunt Hilda's,* read one. *Jan Schmidt, we are with your mother in Stuttgart, come soon!* read another. *Rolf Braun, we are emigrating to America, your brother knows how to reach us,* read a third. Charlie added a posting of her own, written in English and German. *Did you know Captain A. J. (Adolf Joseph) Atkins? Killed in action, spring, 1945, details unknown. Please leave word for Charlie Atkins here.*

Discouraged as the afternoon waned—there was not a single "room to let" sign to be seen—Charlie stopped in the *Viktualienmarkt,* Munich's open-air fresh market, for the makings of a cheap evening meal: an apple, the last wedge of cheese from a shop owner eager to close up for the day, and a day-old *Baguette-Brötchen* that still smelled fresh. She tucked it all in her canvas bag, and then watched the square's mechanical *Glockenspiel* come to life so that its carved-wood Bavarian duke might once again marry his bride.

Then: the slightest of tugs.

Charlie wheeled around just in time to see a boy running away, her bread—her dinner—in one of his hands.

"Hey, that's mine," Charlie shouted, outraged, and she chased after him, down a wide cobblestoned street lined by fine old Munich houses, some undamaged by the war, others mere ruins. The boy slipped through an old rusty iron fence. Charlie followed—or tried. Her white cotton blouse snagged on one of the bars. She tugged so hard to free herself that she slipped, landing hard on her tailbone on the cobblestones.

The boy was gone.

Charlie sat where she fell, tired, sweaty, and defeated.

A sudden, merry peal of laughter sounded. "He's a fast one, that one," an amused voice said in German. "Your bread is gone."

Charlie looked up. The voice belonged to a woman with short, dark curls pulled back behind a kerchief. She was older than Charlie, thirty at least, and pleasingly soft and round in all the places Charlie was not. She stood in front of a limestone façade embellished with carved bas-relief tendrils and leaves. It looked sturdy enough, but the house behind it did not. One wall had buckled in on itself, and much of the black slate roof was missing. A small cast-iron sign hung from a bracket near the front door, a threaded needle and thimble painted on it in gold gilt. *Sophie Müller, Näherin*, it read. *A seamstress*, Charlie thought.

"Nothing funny about it," Charlie said stiffly in her grandfather's German. Her tailbone hurt, and her shirt was ripped clean across the left side. "That bread was my dinner."

Sophie raised an eyebrow. "You're not German."

"No. American."

"You are lost?"

"No." Charlie stood gingerly. "I'm looking for a room to rent."

Sophie looked puzzled. "You Americans have special places to live in Munich. You have your own schools, your own gas stations, your own markets. Everything you need is in one place, just for you. Why would you want to live here? Our houses are barely standing."

"Those compounds are for military families," Charlie said, brushing herself off. "Besides, if I wanted to live with other Americans, I would have stayed home."

Sophie eyed Charlie critically, taking in her torn shirt and her canvas bag of groceries. "You can afford to pay rent?" she said. "In American dollars?"

"Yes."

"Perhaps I know someone." Sophie stepped to the side of her doorway. "Come in. While I think about it, I can fix that tear for you. It won't be perfect, but it'll be good enough to get you home. No charge."

Charlie looked at the sign with its needle and thread and then down at her shirt. Mending wasn't her strong point. "It's a deal," she said, and she followed Sophie into the half-ruined house.

#   #   #

Inside Sophie's house, a once-grand foyer with high, white-plastered walls had been transformed into a makeshift living space. One wall held the bones of a kitchen: a salvaged wood countertop with a white porcelain wash basin and a shelf that held a few dinner plates and a pitcher for milk. A huge, open hearth took up the facing wall; next to it was a horde of precious fuel for the fireplace—thin tree branches, bits of scrap wood, old newspaper and cardboard, dried pine cones, dead leaves, and long grasses the color of straw. A narrow bed was tucked into an alcove—formerly a closet, Charlie guessed—below a wide stone staircase that led to the house's second story. That upstairs area, along with the first-floor doorway into the rest of the house, was closed off, tacked over with layers of newsprint and old blankets that provided insulation from the cold and protection from the dust of the damaged house.

But the main feature of the room was fabric, a staggering, dizzying array of it, in every color and condition. Dozens of winter coats, yards of drawing room curtains, men's trousers and boys' short pants, water-stained damask tablecloths, cotton day dresses a decade out of fashion, and more filled nearly every available space, piled on the floor and all the way up the steps to the closed-off second floor. Still more items hung from wooden pegs or the staircase's wrought iron railing, some drying after a wash, others waiting to be pressed. On shelves— old boards supported on bricks—sat jars of buttons sorted by size and color and baskets of zippers and collar trimmings. In the middle was the room's only table, and on it was a Pfaff sewing machine so well-used that its black paint was flaking off. Two mismatched straight-backed chairs flanked the table.

Charlie's mouth hung open in astonishment. She turned in a tight circle, gaping in delight at the kaleidoscope of textures and colors.

Sophie stepped briskly to a neat stack of folded clothing and deftly extracted a single item, a baby blue bed jacket, the neat patch on its left sleeve nearly invisible. She handed it to Charlie. "You may put this on while I mend your shirt."

Charlie slipped off her torn blouse and handed it to Sophie. The bed jacket was too big, but it was soft and satiny to her touch. As she wrapped it around herself, Charlie caught sight of a black lace evening gown hanging from a peg, its neckline more daring than anything she had ever worn. She leaned close: Its bodice had been expertly mended with stitches so tiny and precise that Charlie nearly missed them.

"What is this place?" Charlie said, fingering the dress' sleeve. "And where did all of this stuff come from?"

Sophie held Charlie's shirt up to the light and inspected the tear across the left side of the chest. She ran her fingers over it, smoothing the frayed edges flat as if already seeing how the threads would come together again, with a patch deftly sewn in from underneath the tear. "This is—was—my parent's home," she said. "I live in this room because it is the only part of the house that is habitable, even if I had the money to furnish it. And this 'stuff' as you call is *Lumpenkleider*. Rags. It is how I make my living. I repair what I can or make new things from whatever the *Trümmerfrauen* find in the buildings they clear out and bring to me."

Satisfied, Sophie threaded her sewing machine. "This room you want to rent is for you and your husband?"

"I'm not married. I need a room just for me."

Sophie glanced at Charlie. "That dress would look nice on you. I can take it in to fit you. Buy it, and perhaps you will catch the eye of a nice American boy."

Charlie dropped the sleeve. "No, thanks. I have no intention of getting married anytime soon."

"Why not?"

"I have things I want to do. If I have a husband, I have to consider what he thinks and wants too, and that isn't for me. Not now, anyway." Charlie leaned in and looked closely at a faded picture propped up against the fireplace's stone mantel. It was Sophie in a simple calf-length chiffon dress, its lacy *dirndl* waistline cinched and fitted to Sophie's slender figure. She held a delicate bouquet of early spring snowdrops. "That's you, isn't it, on your wedding day? You look beautiful. Did you make your dress?"

"I did." Sophie clipped a thread and held Charlie's blouse up and inspected her handiwork: The tear was barely visible. "Here. Almost as good as new."

She handed it to Charlie. "There is no room for you here, but the woman who lives next door may rent to you. Tell her I sent you—and that you can pay in U.S. dollars."

"She won't mind an American tenant?"

Sophie raised an eyebrow. "Did you not hear? We are all friends now. Besides, I happen to know that she needs groceries."

Sophie's recommendation worked. Charlie moved in next door, and Sophie became her first and best friend in Munich.

Now Charlie watched from her seat on the bus as the *Trümmerfrauen* finished sweeping up the broken glass. The driver restarted the engine. With a groan, the bus jerked forward, and Charlie was finally back on her way for her interview with Sophie.

#   #   #

Charlie laid the pictures of Grace Kelly in her wedding dress on Sophie's small table. As Sophie studied the pictures, Charlie set up the tape recorder she'd brought, laying it flat and removing its protective cover. She plugged in the microphone, put it on its stand, and adjusted it so that it pointed toward Sophie.

"What do you think?" she asked eagerly. "Is this a dress for a princess?"

Sophie's eyes were distant. A single muscle in one cheek twitched. "This," she said finally, tapping one of the pictures with her finger. "This is the life that was stolen from me. *Herr* Hitler promised us a thousand years of peace and prosperity, ruled by right-minded Germans. Instead, he brought us nothing but shame."

For the next hour, Charlie listened in stunned silence as Sophie, usually so quick with a laugh, spoke, hot tears sliding down her face. Sophie had survived the war, but her story was far more painful than Charlie had known. Her worry about the lateness of the day vanished. When Sophie fell silent at last, Charlie quietly packed up the tape recorder and reached for the pictures. Sophie laid one hand on them. Charlie left the pictures where they lay, her thoughts already spinning with the story she would write.

#   #   #

Outside, the midafternoon April sun felt warm on Charlie's face. Her bus waited at the curb, but she didn't run to catch it. Instead, she stopped and studied the impassive faces of the *Trümmerfrauen*, working in silence as they added to the mounds of scavenged materials already at the curb: iron pipes, wash basins, porcelain tiles, individual bricks, long runs of wood flooring, old damask drapes. As he'd done to Sophie, Hitler had taken much from these women, too. Charlie boarded her bus, still thinking about loss and the cost of war as she headed back to Radio Free Europe to write her story.

5
STOLEN LIVES

By the time Charlie sat down at her typewriter, she knew exactly how her story would go. She had already replayed the interview tape, moving back and forth to find the exact quotes from Sophie that she wanted to use in her story. She noted each one's timestamp, length, and exact wording. Then she fed a clean white sheet of paper into her typewriter and began to write her story in Radio Free Europe's radio script-formatted style.

STORY TITLE	STOLEN LIVES
TOTAL RUNTIME	[05:51]
BYLINE	CHARLIE ATKINS
DATELINE	MUNICH, WEST GERMANY--APRIL 19
NEWS READER [DURATION: 00:23]	AMERICAN ACTRESS GRACE KELLY HAS MARRIED HER PRINCE, RAINIER III OF MONACO, IN A HOLLYWOOD FAIRY TALE WEDDING COME TRUE. BUT IT IS MISS KELLY'S STUNNING GOWN WITH ITS 25 YARDS OF <u>PEAU DE SOIE</u> SILK,

	THOUSANDS OF HAND-SEWN SEED PEARLS, AND ONE HUNDRED-TWENTY-FIVE-YEAR-OLD BELGIAN ROSE POINT LACE THAT BRINGS MUNICH SEAMSTRESS SOPHIE MÜLLER TO TEARS.
VOICE OVER GERMAN LANGUAGE QUOTE [DURATION: 00:07]	"THIS IS THE LIFE THAT ADOLF HITLER STOLE FROM ME. FROM ALL OF US WHO SURVIVED THE WAR."
NEWS READER [DURATION: 01:20]	SOPHIE WAS BORN IN 1923 INTO A WELL-TO-DO FAMILY OF WOOL MERCHANTS. AN ONLY CHILD, SOPHIE WAS DOTED ON BY HER PARENTS AND RAISED TO RUN A PROPER GERMAN HOUSEHOLD. AT SEVENTEEN, SHE BECAME ENGAGED TO OSKAR MÜLLER AND SEWED HER OWN WEDDING DRESS WITH CHIFFON AND LACE HER MOTHER HAD PUT AWAY BEFORE WAR RATIONING MADE SUCH AQUISITIONS PROHIBITIVE. BUT SOPHIE AND OSKAR OPENLY OPPOSED HITLER AND THE NAZI REGIME. ON THE MORNING OF THEIR WEDDING, THE SAME DAY THAT NAZI SECOND-IN-COMMAND HERMANN GÖRING ORDERED THE MELTING OF GERMANY'S CHURCH BELLS TO PROVIDE BRASS FOR GUN CARTRIDGES AND TIN FOR THE PLANES FLOWN BY THE LUFTWAFFE, SOPHIE AND OSKAR WERE ARRESTED AS POLITICAL DISSIDENTS.

	OSKAR WAS SENT TO THE FRONT LINES, WHERE HE DIED IN THE GERMAN INVASION OF BELGIUM. SOPHIE WAS ORDERED ONTO TO A TRAIN THAT VERY DAY AND SENT TO RAVENSBRÜCK, A CONCENTRATION CAMP FOR WOMEN SURROUNDED BY PINE TREES AND BARBED WIRE FIFTY MILES NORTH OF BERLIN. SHE WASN'T EVEN PERMITTED TO CHANGE OUT OF HER WEDDING DRESS. SOPHIE'S VOICE SHAKES AS SHE REMEMBERS ARRIVING AT RAVENSBRÜCK.
VOICE OVER GERMAN LANGUAGE QUOTE [DURATION: 00:30]	"THERE WERE SO MANY OF US—JEWS, GYPSIES, AND GERMAN WOMEN LIKE ME, WHO WERE THERE BECAUSE WE DID NOT LIKE HERR HITLER. WE GOT OFF THE TRAIN, AND WE WERE MARCHED TO A LARGE EMPTY ROOM, LIKE A SCHOOL GYMNASIUM. THEY TOLD US, LEAVE EVERYTHING HERE BUT REMEMBER WHERE YOU PUT YOUR THINGS SO YOU CAN FIND THEM AFTER YOUR SHOWER. TIE YOUR SHOES TOGETHER, SO YOU DO NOT LOSE ONE. OF COURSE IT WAS A TRICK SO THAT WE WOULD DO AS WE WERE TOLD—TO WALK LIKE SHEEP INTO THE NEXT ROOM. THE GAS CHAMBER."
NEWS READER [DURATION: 01:05]	BUT FOR SOPHIE, FATE INTERVENED. ONE OF THE AUFSEHERINNEN, RAVENSBRÜCK'S NOTORIOUSLY CRUEL FEMALE GUARDS, WAS ENGAGED TO BE MARRIED AND SPOTTED SOPHIE, STILL IN HER WEDDING DRESS. WHEN SHE LEARNED THAT SOPHIE MADE HER OWN DRESS, THE GUARD ORDERED SOPHIE TO LEAVE THE ROOM IMMEDIATELY. SOPHIE HAD NO CHOICE BUT TO OBEY.

	AT RAVENSBRÜCK, EVERYONE SERVED HITLER'S REICH. SOME JOBS WERE GRIMMER THAN OTHERS. MANY WOMEN WORKED AS UNPAID LABORERS IN FACTORIES, BUILDING ROCKETS OR TANKS OR MUNITIONS. OTHERS WERE FORCED INTO THE BROTHELS THAT SERVICED GERMAN SOLDIERS OR WERE USED AS TEST SUBJECTS FOR GRUESOME MEDICAL EXPERIMENTS. SOPHIE'S JOB WAS AT ONCE A TERRIBLE AND INTIMATE TASK. IMPRESSED WITH SOPHIE'S SKILL WITH A NEEDLE, THE AUFSEHERIN ASSIGNED SOPHIE TO GATHER AND SORT THROUGH THE CLOTHING OTHER, LESS FORTUNATE WOMEN LEFT IN THE GYMNASIUM, NEVER TO RETURN. SOPHIE'S ORDERS WERE TO SELECT THE BEST ITEMS AND TAILOR THEM TO FIT THE AUFSEHERINNEN. WEDDING DRESSES WERE IN PARTICULAR DEMAND.
VOICE OVER GERMAN LANGUAGE QUOTE [DURATION: 00:14]	"I WAS TOLD TO MAKE SURE NOTHING LOOKED TOO JEWISH. IT WAS SICKENING. THE GUARDS THOUGHT NOTHING OF WEARING THE CLOTHES OF WOMEN THEY MURDERED. MANY DAYS, I SEWED UNTIL MY FINGERS BLED. BUT I SURVIVED."
NEWS READER [DURATION: 01:40]	IN THE NUMB DAYS, WEEKS, AND MONTHS AFTER GERMANY'S SURRENDER, SOPHIE RETURNED TO MUNICH, ONLY TO FIND HER PARENTS DEAD AND THEIR ONCE ELEGANT HOME BADLY DAMAGED. AMID THE RUBBLE, SHE FOUND HER MOTHER'S SEWING MACHINE AND TOOK IT AS A SIGN THAT SHE MUST CONTINUE TO SEW TO SURVIVE.

THESE DAYS, SOPHIE'S MATERIALS STILL
COME FROM THE RUINS OF WAR. SHE BUYS
SCRAPS—CLOTHING, DRAPES, BEDCLOTHES—
SCAVENGED BY MUNICH'S TRÜMMERFRAUEN,
WHO, FOR SEVENTY PFENNIGS A DAY AND
AN EXTRA RATION OF BREAD, WORK SUN UP
TO SUN DOWN CLEARING OUT BUILDINGS
DESTROYED DURING THE WAR. SOPHIE TURNS
THESE SCRAPS INTO LUMPENKLEIDER, RAG
DRESSES, THAT SHE BARTERS FOR POTATOES
OR FLOUR OR COFFEE. SHE SEWS WHATEVER
HER CUSTOMERS CAN AFFORD TO BUY.

ANYTHING EXCEPT WEDDING DRESSES.

SOPHIE'S BLONDE HAIR IS NOW SILVERED
BY GREY, AND AT THIRTY-THREE, HER
FACE IS SOFTLY LINED. SHE STUDIES THE
WEDDING PICTURES OF MISS KELLY, NOW
KNOWN AS PRINCESS GRACE. SOPHIE'S KEEN
EYE NOTES THE DRESS'S MILLINERY FINE
POINTS—ITS HIGH, ROUNDED COLLAR AND
LACE BODICE, THE SOFT FRONT PLACKET
OF BUTTONS, AND THE MATCHING JULIET
CAP STUDDED WITH TINY SEED PEARLS AND
DELICATE PAPER ORANGE BLOSSOMS. EVEN
THE AMERICAN COPPER PENNY, RUMORED TO
BE SEWN INSIDE PRINCESS GRACE'S RIGHT
SHOE FOR GOOD LUCK, DOESN'T ESCAPE
SOPHIE'S ATTENTION. SHE CARRIES HER
OWN GOOD LUCK COIN, A SINGLE SILVER
REICHSMARK COIN SHE FOUND IN THE RUINS
OF HER PARENTS' HOME. SHE KEEPS IT AS
A REMINDER OF BETTER TIMES BEFORE THE
NAZIS CAME TO POWER.

SOPHIE SAYS SHE WILL NEVER MARRY
AGAIN.

VOICE OVER GERMAN LANGUAGE QUOTE [DURATION: 00:18]	"OUR MEN ARE TOO YOUNG, TOO OLD, OR TOO BROKEN BY WAR. FOR ME, FOR MANY WOMEN LIKE ME, OUR TIME IS PAST. THE NAZIS TOOK THAT FROM US. BUT FOR OTHERS, I THINK IT IS NOT TOO LATE. WE MUST LIVE OUR LIVES AND LEARN AGAIN TO ENJOY BEAUTIFUL THINGS."
NEWS READER [DURATION: 00:14]	EVEN WEDDING DRESSES? SHE IS ASKED. SOPHIE SMILES WISTFULLY AS SHE STUDIES THE PICTURES OF PRINCESS GRACE. YES, SHE SAYS, PERHAPS NOW, EVEN WEDDING DRESSES. # # #

Charlie pulled the script from her typewriter, exhausted but elated. Her story was as good as she could make it. She stacked the pages neatly and left the script with the tape on Owens's desk, right where he would see it first thing Friday morning. Then she turned to her day's work, sorting mail, slotting copy to the right editors, and washing the coffee cups left for her in the breakroom sink. When she finished, it was nearly midnight. She waved goodnight to the late-shift desk editor and left the newsroom quietly. All she could do now was wait for Owens's verdict in the morning.

6
IMPASSE

By one o'clock the following afternoon, Charlie couldn't wait another minute. She tapped on the door to Owens's office. He was at his desk, reading the Paris *Herald Tribune* as he finished his lunch. He didn't glance up. "Yes?"

"I left my story on your desk. As promised."

"I saw it." He took another bite of his sandwich and kept reading.

"And?"

Owens leaned back and looked at her, his jaw moving in a round *O* as he chewed and then swallowed. "Anyone help you? Any of the guys on the night shift?"

"No. You can ask them yourself. They barely noticed I was here."

"This lady, this Sophie, this is a real person? Or did you make her up?"

"She's real. She lives next door to me. We're friends."

His square leather chair squeaked under the weight of his ample frame.

"Well?" Charlie said finally.

"It is a decent story. Better than I expected, frankly." Owens's tone was brisk. "I sent it on to the individual radio services. They can decide whether to run it or not."

Charlie's heart leapt. "Does that mean I get the job?"

"I told you, I don't hire women for the news staff." His voice sounded like a door slamming shut. He pushed his plate away and reached across his desk and selected a cigar from the humidor on his desk.

Charlie's jaw dropped. "But you promised to consider me."

Owens clipped the end of his cigar and picked up a silver lighter from his desk. He lit the cigar and then pulled on it until the ash glowed red. "I did say that, and I have considered you." He tossed the lighter back on the desk. "The answer is still no."

"But you liked my story. You sent it on to the radio services."

"Two things can be true at once, Atkins." Blue smoke curled around him. "You did a good job, I will give you that. But hiring you as a reporter would be a waste of time and money. No source will ever take a girl like you seriously. You can't go to the places where men go when they need to have a candid conversation. And frankly, you would be taking a good-paying job away from a family man. If it were up to me, no females would be anywhere near this newsroom. But unfortunately we need secretaries and clerks." He turned his attention back to his newspaper. "Do the job I hired you to do or clean out your desk. I can replace you before the end of the day."

Charlie didn't move. "At least I'll get a byline, right? And paid the freelance story rate?"

Owens didn't bother to look up. "Bylines and freelancer's fees are for real journalists, not news clerks. I am doing you a favor. Don't push it."

Stunned, Charlie slunk out of Mr. Owens's office and returned to her small desk, her cheeks crimson. Automatically, she picked up the latest batch of mail waiting for her attention. *Mr. Owens lied*, she thought, her hands shaking as she sorted the envelopes into their proper slots. *He didn't really consider me at all. He didn't think I could do it.*

But she refused to give up.

She watched the daily program lineups for each of the radio services, which listed the name and runtime for every minute of the broadcast day. To her satisfaction, all five language services chose to translate and run her story.

Encouraged and determined, she kept writing stories throughout Munich's hot, muggy summer. Owens hadn't said she couldn't write stories—just that she was banned from applying for a job on the news staff. So, she made the most of her opportunities. A routine press release about food giant Swanson's new TV dinners turned into an essay about American innovation. First Lady Mamie Eisenhower's Millionaire Fudge recipe and its four-and-a-half-cups of white sugar became a meditation on soft power and the wide variety of inexpensive goods available to all in American supermarkets.

"This is how revolutions start," Charlie's story read in part, "when people are hungry for more than what they are being fed by their government. Especially sugar."

Throughout those months, Charlie worked hard, learning to write for listeners rather than readers. Unlike newspaper or magazine stories, which could be reread, radio offered one shot to get the clarity and flow right. She wrote simple, concise sentences and added vivid descriptions of the places and people she was writing about. She incorporated music and sound effects, and she learned to write tight lead-ins to her sound bites. She read every story aloud, varying her tone and pace: intimate and conversational for human interest stories, brisk and objective for stories with a harder edge. Only then did she leave her story on Owens's desk after he left for the day.

Owens never said a word.

But Charlie kept track. So far, all of her stories had been translated and broadcast on Radio Free Europe's airwaves. As long as she didn't talk to Owens directly about story ideas—or apply again for a reporter's job—he had yet to act on his threat to fire her.

Like Owens said, two things can be true at once.

Charlie's focus was interrupted only once, with the arrival in August of a thin envelope addressed to her at Radio Free Europe. Father Popov's name and return address were neatly written in the upper left-hand corner.

> *Dear Miss Atkins,* Father Popov's letter began in slanted, exacting handwriting.
>
> *As we discussed, I passed along your father's name to a former colleague of mine in Washington, D.C. He tells me that war department records indeed list a Captain Adolf Joseph (A. J.) Atkins. Your father was drafted into the Army Air Corps at the start of the war and sent to basic training and flight school in San Antonio, Texas.*

Charlie paused. A. J. was *drafted.* He did not volunteer to leave her or the Double Aught ranch. Even after all this time, this singular detail felt immensely comforting. A. J. had not left her on purpose.

After flight school, Father Popov's letter continued, *your father was assigned to an unusual military unit based at Ladd Army Airfield in Fairbanks, Alaska. It was a new outfit, created for the specific purpose of transferring all those fighter jets, bombers, and transport planes we provided to the Soviets when the Lend–Lease Act took effect in 1941. Nearly 8,000 American-built planes in all, which had to be transported across the U.S. and western Canada all the way up north to Fairbanks. Once in Fairbanks, American pilots like your father trained their Soviet counterparts so that they could fly the planes 6,000 miles away into Russian territory to the Krasnoyarsk Airfield in Siberia. Sometimes, American pilots even delivered the planes all the way to Siberia themselves. They flew what was called the ALSIB, the Alaska-Siberia Air Route. It was not the best or even the most direct route, but I'm told it was the only flight path Roosevelt and Stalin could agree on that offered the least potential exposure to the Nazi* Luftwaffe. *Once the planes made it to Siberia, Russian combat pilots took over. They flew those American-made planes all over the Eastern Front—from the Baltic Sea in the west and Byelorussia in the east to Leningrad in the north and the Black Sea in the south. No doubt those planes helped win the war.*

In Fairbanks, American and Russian pilots lived on the same base (in separate barracks, of course). Your father must have been a crackerjack pilot, Miss Atkins, to be assigned to such a unit. That goes without saying. Even so, it must have taken a certain kind of fortitude to live *cheek-by-jowl with—well, how can I put this? 'An ally of <u>necessity</u>'"—Father Popov underlined the word—"rather than one with a shared worldview. Difficult duty, I would say. I imagine there must have been some interesting interactions between the Americans and their Soviet guests, especially during those long, cold, winter months when there wasn't much flying to be done and more time was spent indoors in classroom learning or in flight hangers, developing their understanding of the mechanics of the planes.*

As to your father's unusual watch, perhaps it was a gift from a Soviet pilot. Maybe he won it in a poker game. Maybe he traded something of value for it—his own American-made watch perhaps. An intriguing mystery, to be sure.

Your father's service records end there—incomplete or perhaps classified. I have taken the liberty of writing to your father's commanding officer, Col. J. Allen Donovan, now retired, on the chance that he might recall when or if your father left Fairbanks and what happened next.

This is not a great deal more information, but it still is something, and I thought it was worth passing along. I daresay your father was witness to an all too rare moment in history, when great powers were able to set aside their differences for a common goal, the defeat of Nazi Germany. An excellent reason to study history and the fortitude of human nature, Miss Atkins, if you do not mind me saying so. Men like your father demonstrate that—given proper motivation—it is possible to coexist with others not of our own tribe.

Sincerely yours, Fr. Popov.

Charlie put Father Popov's letter down, her hands trembling. Her last memory of A. J. was the night before he left. The two of them sat for hours in his old Curtiss Jenny until A. J. rolled it into the barn to await his return. Then he carried her into the house and sat with her until she fell asleep. In the morning, he was gone.

She opened an atlas. She found Fairbanks, Alaska, and traced with her finger a route south to California's San Joaquin Valley. Thirty-six hundred miles, give or take. All that time, A. J. had been closer than she could possibly have imagined.

She wrote back by return mail.

Dear Father Popov, her letter began, *my father was indeed a fine pilot, at least as much as eight-year-old me could judge these sorts of things. I can only tell you that A. J. loved flying more than anything. Soaring across the sky felt like riding on God's wings, he said.*

Charlie paused. She slipped off her watch and rubbed the crystal clean with a corner of her shirt. Then she turned the watch over and ran her thumb lightly over the back.

When you looked at my watch, she wrote, *I did not think to show you the back where my father's initials—A. J. A.—are inscribed. For that reason, I believe this watch was meant specifically for him. There are two numbers, 1.1., also engraved on the back, but I don't know what the significance of these numbers are. If you learn anything more about where my father went or what happened to him, I would be most grateful.*

Yours truly, Charlie Atkins.

She mailed her letter to Father Popov that same afternoon. She still didn't know what had happened to her father but knowing that he spent the war teaching pilots in Alaska felt strangely comforting. A. J. had been a patient instructor when he taught her the flight mechanics of the Curtiss Jenny. She hoped his Soviet students had been just as appreciative.

#   #   #

Munich's muggy August heat continued into September and then gave way to an unusually cool October. Oktoberfest— beers, brats, and oom-pah-pah bands—came and went. The New York Yankees took the World Series in seven games over the defending Brooklyn Dodgers, helped by pitcher Don Larsen's first-ever World Series perfect game. The run-up to the November presidential election looked like a landslide for Republican incumbent Dwight D. Eisenhower over Democrat Adlai Ewing Stevenson II.

At Radio Free Europe, the biggest news was happening in Poland. In the nineteen months since Stalin's death, demonstrations against low wages, poor working conditions, and Soviet control grew bigger and louder. Polish security forces intervened, leaving scores of arrests, dozens of deaths, and hundreds wounded, and Soviet troops stationed in Poland

and near the border began moving toward Warsaw. Instead of frightening the Poles into submission, the protests intensified. Finally, on October 21, Khrushchev bowed to the inevitable and granted significant concessions to the Poles, including the return of party leader Władysław Gomułka, a popular reformer who had been purged from the party in the late 1940s.

Electrified, the staff of Radio Free Europe's Polish desk spoke of nothing else. They celebrated the remarkable changes unfolding in Warsaw with Polish vodka and predicted that Poland would lead the rest of Eastern Europe out from under Moscow's thumb.

#   #   #

As October waned, Charlie continued to leave stories on Owens's desk. He still said nothing to her, but he continued to forward them on to all of the radio services. Progress of a sort, Charlie knew, but it brought her no closer to her goal, a reporter's job on the news staff. When the editor of the Hungarian radio service got sick, Owens was tapped to fill in, to help keep the Voice of Free Hungary running. With Owens suddenly doing two jobs, Charlie saw less of him than ever, and her latest stories remained untouched on his desk.

Then, once again, war changed everything for Charlie.

7
OCTOBER SURPRISE

U ntil the wire service machines rang all at once at midafternoon—*Big news! Big news! Big news!*—Tuesday, October 23, was like any other work day.

Charlie arrived early enough to greet the departing overnight shift. She made coffee—Owens liked it hot and ready to drink as he swung by on his way to the Hungarian radio service's newsroom. Then she scanned the editorial rundown the night editor left scrawled on the chalkboard: in the US, sixty-five-year-old President Eisenhower, leading in the polls, made good on his campaign promise to get a complete physical before the election, results to be publicly released next Monday; in Pakistan, an industrial accident's death toll was nearing fifty; in southern Australia, Britain conducted its fourth nuclear test at Maralinga; in Hungary, the Petőfi Circle—an influential writers forum—published a daring call for greater autonomy from the Soviet Union. That last item on the board had a hastily scribbled addendum below it: *Hungarian students plan a march through Budapest tomorrow, inspired by the concessions granted to Poland.*

By the time the wire alerts sounded mid-afternoon, the Hungarian marchers were 20,000 strong. The students carried placards that read *Poland Shows Us the Way* and *We Support the Youth of Poland!* and they were armed with the Sixteen Points, a document that echoed the Petőfi Circle's letter a day earlier but went even further, calling for full Hungarian autonomy— the immediate withdrawal of all Soviet troops, the right to multi-party elections, economic and land reform, freedom of expression, religion, and the press, the release of political prisoners, and more. Word of the march spread like wildfire; thousands of ordinary Hungarians—bus drivers, shop girls, tram conductors, factory workers, teachers—spontaneously joined the student protesters. *Big news is right*, Charlie thought, her pulse quickening. If Hungary, like Poland, managed to pull back from the Kremlin, it would mark the biggest shift in power since the end of the war.

Charlie ripped all of the incoming stories about Hungary off the wires. The last one, a news alert from a local Munich wire service, brought her up short. The West German Red Cross was calling for blood donors, the alert read, to treat Hungary's wounded. Charlie frowned. There were no reports of shots fired, so asking for contributions now meant that the Red Cross expected casualties. A sobering thought, but Charlie's mind raced. German-Hungarian relations were deep, complex, and at times bloody. West Germans donating blood in support of Hungarians fighting Soviet oppression sounded like her kind of war story, one layered with history, memory, and—if her hunch was right—the possibility of redemption.

Impulsively, Charlie slipped the news alert into her pocket. If the situation in Hungary got hot—if shots were fired, if the

Hungarians really did suffer casualties—she would follow up. Right now, she had wire copy to deliver. She hurried down the hallway toward the Hungarian newsroom.

#   #   #

By the time Charlie reached the Hungarian newsroom, Mária was already there. Headset askew, the cuffs of her late husband's sweater shoved up out of the way, Mária, surrounded by a sea of stunned faces, was nearly breathless. "I am picking up reports that every moment the crowds grow larger. They say more than two hundred thousand are now marching through Budapest alone."

Viktor was already on his feet, his blue eyes electric. "Can this be true?"

"I think it must be. I am picking up similar reports from all over Hungary. In Budapest, the marchers are carrying Hungarian flags and singing *Nemzeti dal*." Mária caught sight of Charlie. "*Nemzeti dal* is our national song, which is banned by the Russians," she explained.

Mária sang softly in English. "'Arise Hungarians, your country calls you, meet this hour, whate'er befalls you. Shall we be free men be or slaves? Chose the lot your spirit craves.'"

Then she stopped, one hand over her mouth, as if overcome by the moment.

"Here's the latest." Charlie held up a handful of wire stories.

Béla Toth, the grizzled, dour-faced deputy editor of the Hungarian desk, snatched the wire copy out of Charlie's hands and skimmed through the stack quickly. "People are calling for the government to go. They want Imre Nagy to be reinstated as prime minister."

"That is good news," Viktor said, his voice cautious but optimistic. "People like Nagy. He thinks for himself. He's a reformer—when he was in power before, he gave land to back to the farmers, he released political prisoners, and he made sure there were goods in the shops for Hungarians to buy."

"Nagy is a Moscow-trained communist," Béla snapped back. "Hungary needs a moral leader—like Cardinal Józef Mindszenty. He has opposed the Communist regime from the start. He'll unify the country, and he'll never bend to Moscow."

"Cardinal Mindszenty?" Viktor nearly laughed. "Moscow would never hand over power to a communist-hating priest."

"Either way, we must go on the air immediately," Béla said. "Viktor, you must write something bold and stirring. We must encourage all Hungarians to get out and march! Show the Russians we won't back down."

Charlie hung on every word, her excitement rising. A moment like this was exactly why Radio Free Europe existed: to support resistance to Soviet rule and to stoke the flames of democracy. Thanks to Radio Free Europe, the Hungarians had received real, truthful information about the concessions the Poles extracted from the Kremlin days earlier. Now they were standing up and demanding their own freedom, too. Charlie could hardly believe her luck. Hungary was breaking free in real time, and she had a front row seat.

"Wait just a minute." Owens hoisted his bulk up onto a chair so that he could be seen by everyone in the newsroom. "Everybody, calm down. First things first. Before anyone writes anything, we need information, as much as we can get about what is really happening in Budapest. We also need guidance from New York on what we can say on the air."

"Wait?" Béla said, his voice incredulous. "No! We cannot wait. Look at the Poles. They fought back, and now they have a leader they trust in Gomulka, and the Russians have been forced into promising real reforms. We Hungarians, too, must seize this moment."

"Béla, we can't get too far ahead of ourselves," Owens said. His white cotton shirt was stretched taut over his round belly, and his black tie hung loose at his neck. "Suppose everybody marches today and then they all go home and that's the end of it? What then? We would look like we don't know what is going on in our own backyard. Our job now is to do what we do best. Check and double check the facts to make sure we have a clear picture of what is happening."

Owens nodded to Mária. "Back to your desk. Keep bringing us anything you think we ought to be hearing. Béla, you and your editors start working the phones. Call anyone and everyone you know in Budapest. Get facts and eyewitness accounts. I'll get on the horn to New York and see if they know anything."

The room exploded into noisy action, chairs, table and feet scraping the floor. Viktor was already reaching for the telephone as Béla gathered a group around his desk to divide up work. As Owens stepped down from the chair he was standing on, Charlie spoke up. This moment was too exciting to let pass. "Mr. Owens, how can I help?"

Owens spoke over his shoulder without a backward glance. "Atkins, you keep the coffee hot and the wire copy coming."

Deflated, Charlie watched him disappear into his office. She trudged to the kitchenette as around her the newsroom hummed. She rinsed the percolator and refilled it with fresh water. *What will it take for Mr. Owens to see me as anything more than a news clerk?* she wondered as she plugged the coffee pot into the wall socket. *Somehow, some way, someday, I've got to get through to him.*

#   #   #

By nightfall, the protests spread across Hungary. Spontaneous, and with no clear leader in charge, little Hungary, a small, landlocked nation of ten million, was standing up to the mighty Russian bear. Hungary teetered on the brink of a *forradalom*—a full-blown revolution—and if it succeeded, the Russians' grasp on Eastern Europe would be severely weakened.

Charlie kept busy, running wire copy and hauling trays of sandwiches up from the cafeteria. No one on the news staff noticed her: Their heads were down, working the phones, reading wire copy, or banging out the latest update. Charlie eyed them hungrily, wishing she were working alongside them.

Mária returned to the newsroom at midnight, her eyes wide with fear. The AVO—the Államvédelmi Hatóság, Hungary's secret police—had just fired the revolution's first shots into a crowd of peaceful protesters, she said, her voice shaking. "The students wanted their sixteen points to be read on Radio Budapest so that all of Hungary would know what they were asking for. Instead, the AVO threw tear gas at them and fired into the crowd."

"Dead and wounded?" Béla barked.

"Not clear. At least sixteen dead, people say, not confirmed, and many more injured."

Béla swung around to Charlie. "Anything from Moscow?"

Charlie shook her head. "Nothing on the wires yet."

At three A.M., Mária was back, shock written across her face. "Soviet tanks are rolling through Budapest," she gasped. "The rumor is that the government asked for them to come."

#   #   #

For days, no one left the newsroom; no one wanted to miss a thing. No one slept either, unless it was a few stolen moments, head down, on a desk. News and rumors poured in, chaotic and contradictory. The revolution was on.

Across Hungary, the fighting continued, and the casualties mounted. Citizens-turned-freedom fighters fought back, arming themselves with whatever they could: tommy guns and pistols, iron pipes and pick axes, kitchen knives or pavers pulled up from the street. They tore Soviet red stars from buildings and ripped the same red star out of the center of Hungarian flags and then hung them from nearly every window. Teenagers armed with homemade Molotov cocktails—a bottle of gasoline and a rag for a wick—harassed Soviets tanks firing on office buildings and apartment blocks. Hungarian army soldiers refused to fight their countrymen; instead, they opened their armories and gave the freedom fighters machine guns, rifles, and grenades. Even some Soviet soldiers joined the freedom fighters, flying the Hungarian tricolor flag from the turrets of their tanks.

Around the world, Radio Free Europe reported, supporters gathered in London, Paris, Washington, D.C., and elsewhere to cheer the freedom fighters on.

In Budapest, Prime Minister Nagy struggled to set up his new government, desperate to show Moscow that he could restore calm across the city. But no matter how quickly he announced reforms—an end to Soviet occupation, multi-party elections, the dissolution of Hungary's hated and feared secret police, the AVO, the release of Hungary's spiritual leader, Cardinal Mindszenty, from prison—the voices from the streets grew louder and more strident. The youngest freedom fighters were especially impatient, urging Nagy to make immediate, sweeping changes whether Moscow approved or not, and they refused to lay down their arms until Nagy met their demands.

Radio Free Europe's Hungarian exhausted but exhilarated staff listened in shock as one stunning announcement after another came. Trains loaded with Russians on their way back to Moscow were cheered in Budapest. Local workers' councils sprang up across the country to address low wages and harsh working conditions, and farmers in the countryside began reclaiming land that had been confiscated and collectivized. Nagy withdrew Hungary from the Warsaw Pact, the Eastern Bloc's answer to NATO, and declared the country's neutrality.

And yet, though Soviet troops disappeared across Hungary—sent home or confined to their barracks—there was no official response to the Hungarian riots from the Kremlin. Moscow remained strangely quiet, leaving a single unanswered question hanging in the air: When the Kremlin *did* respond, what would that response be?

Nor did the United Nation's Security Council, charged with maintaining the international order post-World War II, seemed poised to act. Though the United States called for Hungary to be discussed, any action—including even adding Hungary as an official meeting agenda item—required the approval of the council's five permanent members, which in addition to the United States, included China, France, the United Kingdom, and the Soviet Union. So far, the Russians had declined to discuss anything related to Hungary.

In Munich, Charlie slipped away from the newsroom long enough to ring the Munich office of the Red Cross. They were swamped with people wanting to donate blood to help the Hungarians, a tired voice told her on the phone. Charlie's hunch was right. It was a good story.

Inside Radio Free Europe, Owens, Béla, and Viktor argued over how much to encourage the Hungarians to keep fighting.

Béla pushed for the hardest line possible. "We cannot compromise on regaining full autonomy," he said. "Hungary must shed all its Soviet past—and that includes Prime Minister Nagy. There is no other way forward."

Viktor argued for supporting Nagy, to see if he could chart a way forward to an independent Hungary without angering Moscow.

Owens argued for going slow. "We're not even sure who is in charge. Until the UN acts or we get direct guidance from New York, we are going to err on the side of caution. Besides, Ike is in the middle of campaigning, and no one wants to see this situation blow up right before the election."

Hungary wasn't the only hotspot making headlines, either. On October 29, three months after Egyptian President Gamal Abdel Nasser nationalized the Suez Canal and six days after the start of the Hungarian revolution, Israel, Britian, and France invaded the Sinai Peninsula in a bid to keep the canal open for shipping oil to Europe. The issue immediately came to the Security Council, with the United States leading the discussion by presenting a proposal for a peacekeeping force.

Stunned, Béla watched the West's response to the Suez crisis unfold in mere days, lightning speed compared to the glacial pace around Hungary.

"The world's diplomats are too busy voting to send troops to the Suez Canal to even discuss the uprising," he said, his voice bitter. "A pity Hungary has no oil."

#   #   #

Mária was the first one in the newsroom to ask Owens about going home to Hungary. "My father is very ill," she said, refolding the too-long sleeves of her late husband's sweater. "If there is any chance to see him before he dies—."

Her voice trailed off.

The room fell silent. Every face turned toward Owens, including Charlie's, a tray of *Brötchen*—small crusty bread rolls accompanied by butter and jam—in her hands.

Owens's expression turned somber. He raised his voice to make sure everyone in the newsroom heard him. "Let me be clear," he said. "It's too early to talk about going into Hungary. I know other news organizations are already there. We're different. Our work puts us in direct opposition with the Soviet Union in a way that other journalists do not face. So we are going to be a little slower going in until the situation in Budapest stabilizes. That means no one on this news staff—I repeat, no one—is going anywhere near Hungary or Budapest until I say it's safe."

Owens's edict was followed quickly by the reports that a Kremlin delegation was in Budapest at that very moment negotiating the withdrawal of all Russians and Soviet troops.

"Celebrations can wait," Owens told the Hungarian staff even though Charlie thought he looked pretty excited, too. "Our jobs right now are to keep reporting what we know."

Béla nodded, but his face was gray, his eyes weary. "The waiting. It is impossible. We are out of ideas. We cannot tell them to keep fighting, and I for one cannot in good conscience tell them to stop. What do we do? How do we fill our airwaves?"

Owens, as exhausted as everyone else, nodded. "Ideas, anyone?"

Viktor shrugged and looked away.

No one spoke. Charlie's fingers touched the news alert in her pocket. Did she dare pitch it to Owens, in front of the whole staff? She took a deep breath. Now was as good a time as any to try and break through her impasse with Mr. Owens.

"I have one."

Every head turned toward Charlie.

"The West German Red Cross needs blood donors." Charlie held up the news alert.

"Of course they do—that's their job." Owens said dismissively. "Anyone else?"

"No, just think about it, Mr. Owens." Charlie gathered her courage and kept going. "During the war, the Nazis deported half a million Hungarian Jews to the death camps or to work as slave laborers. Now West German blood donated right here in Munich is going to help save Hungarian lives. This is what learning to live in peace with our neighbors is all about—helping each other in times of need. I've already talked to Andy Reynolds, the press officer at the Red Cross. He says the line to donate is out the door. I can interview Münchners about why they are donating blood to a former adversary and talk to some Red Cross workers about how the blood will be processed and transferred to Hungary—"

Viktor was already shaking his head. "You see?" he said, looking at Owens, his tired voice laced with contempt. "This is why Miss Atkins does not belong in this newsroom. She understands nothing about war."

"What do you mean?" The blood in Charlie's cheeks rose. Every eye in the newsroom seemed to be fixed on her. "This story is all about war, how ordinary people in the Free West are standing up to support the freedom fighters—"

Viktor cut Charlie off before she could finish her sentence. "*That* is the language of war," he said. He thrust a finger toward a wall speaker where his own recorded voice spilled out in fast, furious Hungarian. He translated the words of his own commentary into English for Charlie's benefit. "Hungarians, do not lose faith. We have the most powerful friend in the world, the United States of America, on our side. President Eisenhower himself tells us that America stands beside us, beside all of the captive peoples of Eastern Europe. If we, the Hungarian people, are strong enough and brave enough, America and all freedom-loving nations of the world will have no choice but to recognize us as a free and independent state."

Viktor jabbed his finger at Charlie now. "*That* is all my people need to know. Hard facts. America stands with us. Help will come in our time of need—real help. Tanks. Bombers. Infantry. That's the only thing that matters to Hungarians right now. Not rubbish written by a coffee girl."

"That's enough, you two. No one is sending bombers or tanks anywhere, at least not until the United Nations or Eisenhower says so." Owens plucked the wire story from Charlie's hand. He wadded it up and tossed it into the trash. "Atkins, go home and get some sleep."

"Go home? But you said you needed everyone here." Charlie's cheeks flushed a second time.

"'Everyone' does not include you." Owens's voice was cold. "We can do without a news clerk until Monday."

"But—"

"Go home, or you're fired. Fresh pot of coffee, stat, before you go."

Charlie walked across the newsroom to the kitchenette, her cheeks burning. She dumped the old grounds and rinsed out the percolator, staring at the swirling water. *Hungarians are fighting for democracy, and the Red Cross needs blood,* she thought as she scooped new coffee into the basket. *Not everyone who fights is a soldier—ordinary people can fight, too. It's a good story, no matter what they think.*

Mechanically, she plugged in the coffee, the way she had done many times a day since starting at Radio Free Europe. As the pot burbled, she washed the dirty cups in the sink and swept the counter clean of crumbs, her frustration growing. When the coffee was ready, she poured a fresh cup and added cream. She carried it out to the newsroom and set it down next to Owens. Then, head held high, she fished the crumpled story out of the trash, not caring who in the newsroom saw her. Owens refused to hire her as a reporter, yet so far, every story she had written was good enough to be broadcast on Radio Free Europe's airwaves. That meant something.

She picked up her coat. So what if Owens sent her home? Her time was her own. She planned to make it count.

8

BLOOD

S till smarting from Owens's comments, Charlie didn't go home. Instead, she went directly to the steel-and-glass Rotkreuzklinikum München, the Red Cross Hospital of Munich on *Nymphenburger Straße*. Her contact, Andy Reynolds, hadn't been exaggerating: hundreds of West Germans waited to donate blood in a line that stretched out the door and around the block.

"It's really like this all over Europe?" she asked.

Andy nodded, his fatigue showing in the heaviness under his eyes. He was older than Charlie by ten years at least, and lean and rangy like her father, with short, blond hair the color of pale winter wheat.

"We can barely keep up," he said. "People want to support the Hungarians, and rolling up their sleeves is a surefire way to help."

Charlie surveyed the room. It was as big and open as a college gymnasium and was filled with dozens of individual stations, each set up with a cot, a chair, a table with empty collection vials, and a screen for privacy. Every station was full.

Andy pointed to an open station. "You game?" he asked. "You can be my last donor for the day."

"Sure but I thought you were in public relations."

Andy patted the cot. "Have a seat. At times like this, we all pitch in. I was a medic during the war, so relax. I have done this before, many times."

He selected an empty vial and wrote Charlie's name and the date on it. "Roll up your sleeve."

Charlie tucked the sleeve of her white cotton shirt up out of the way. "What's that like? Being a combat medic?"

"Pretty boring until things get hot. Then it can get pretty rough out there." He tapped the bend in Charlie's arm until he found a vein. He moved deliberately, each step precise and careful, reminding her of the farm boys she grew up with in the San Joaquin Valley, used to delivering calves in the middle of the night or mending fences til dark. Whatever needed to be done, no matter the time.

"Medics are often the first friendly face a wounded soldier sees," Andy continued. "Our job is triage and basic first aid—do what we can in the field, and then get men moved on, quick as we can to a field hospital."

A prick, and then Charlie's blood began to fill the vial. She flicked her eyes away; she didn't want to watch.

"Fighting in a city like Budapest—that is altogether different. When cities go to war, everyone gets hurt. Bullets and shrapnel don't discriminate. Kids are always the hardest ones to treat. They don't understand what is happening, and they're scared."

Charlie listened, rapt.

"Supplies are a problem, too. People have to make do with whatever they can find. They set up an aid station somewhere safe, like a church. They don't have sterile instruments or morphine or clean bandages, so all they can do is basic stuff. If the wounded are lucky, there might be a real doctor available, who is probably exhausted because there is never a shortage of people who need help." Andy met Charlie's eyes and grinned. "So, you see drawing blood from a pretty girl is a piece of cake by comparison."

Charlie blushed. "What happens once the blood is collected?"

Andy removed the needle from Charlie's arm and then pressed a cotton ball onto her arm to make sure the tiny puncture where the needle had been clotted properly and stayed clean. "We spin the blood to separate it into plasma and then dry it. Once it's packed with distilled water and some tubing, it's battlefield ready."

He taped the cotton ball into place. "I'm driving a truckful of plasma to Budapest tonight. How about dinner the day after tomorrow? I can fill you in on what it's like."

"You're going to Budapest?" Charlie sat up abruptly and then reeled backward, suddenly dizzy.

Andy caught her with one arm. "Lie flat until the lightheadedness goes away." He waited until Charlie laid back down. "It'll be a fast trip. I'll leave around midnight. Six hours to the Austrian border where I'll pick up one of our local people who will translate for me. Another two or three hours to Budapest depending on how open the roads are. I'll deliver the plasma, find out what else they need, and then come right back home." Andy handed the vials of Charlie's blood to a passing nurse. "When you can get up without fainting, you can find me in my office."

Charlie watched Andy disappear into the crowd. The line of Münchners waiting to roll up their sleeves was longer than ever. The room pulsed with constant motion: up, down, in, out, fresh vials, *bitte*.

She turned her face to the ceiling. Her interviews with people waiting to donate blood were done, and Andy had given her the facts and figures she needed from the Red Cross—how much blood they were taking in and how much more they thought would be needed. A solid story. Too bad she was missing its emotional payoff: interviews in Budapest with the doctors who used the plasma and the patients who received it. Instead, she was stuck here in Munich, making coffee. *Martha Gellhorn couldn't get press credentials to cover the D-Day landings at Normandy, but she snuck aboard a hospital ship and went anyway,* Charlie thought. *That's what a real war correspondent would do. If only I were that brave.*

She rolled back over on to her side and then sat up carefully. Her dizziness was gone. Even if Budapest was safe to visit, Owens would never say yes to her, not in ten million "you're-only-a-news-clerk-who-really-should-be-home-looking-for-a-husband" years.

But what if she did go? What if she caught a ride with Andy? Charlie sucked in her breath, dazed by her own audacity. Did she really dare to go into a war zone?

#   #   #

Charlie found Andy in his office as promised, head back, eyes half-closed, nearly asleep in his desk chair. He opened his eyes, snagged his overcoat off a peg, and shrugged himself into it. "I'm going home for a couple of hours of shut-eye. I'll walk you out."

"You think you can actually get to Budapest?" Charlie said as they wound their way out through the loading bay door past crates of supplies being loaded onto waiting trucks.

"We know the main road, Route 1 to Budapest, is open, and that is the road that counts. As for how safe it is, that really depends on whether the Soviets are telling the truth about leaving, and whether the Hungarians believe them." Andy pointed at one of the trucks. "See that red cross painted on the sides of our trucks? Thanks to the Geneva Conventions, those crosses identify people like us delivering humanitarian supplies in a war zone, and most of the time, we're left alone. So yes, I'm confident I'll get there and back. If you say yes to dinner, I can tell you all about it."

"Sorry, Andy, I can't date a story source," Charlie said quickly, glad to have a good reason to say no. Andy seemed nice enough, but dating wasn't on her radar. "But I'll take a ride with you to Budapest." She kept her voice light, as if asking for a ride to a war zone was a routine request for her.

"Gee, I don't know—" Andy started.

Charlie kept talking. "I want to describe firsthand to our listeners how plasma donated in Munich is saving lives in Budapest. If you wouldn't mind letting me borrow your translator for a few minutes, I'd like to talk to the doctors and some of their patients."

"Yeah, sure, but this is pretty dangerous territory—"

"You said it yourself, Andy—a Red Cross truck is about as safe as it gets. Besides," she added pointedly, "it's not every day you get to see a new democracy being born. So, how about it?"

Andy hesitated. "Why not?" he said finally. "Just don't be late. Be here by midnight, or I'll leave without you."

#   #   #

Charlie arrived back at the Red Cross building with minutes to spare in time to find Andy ready to go in a truck loaded with plasma and other medical supplies. She had stopped by to tell Sophie her news—she was going to Budapest—and then dressed herself warmly: dark wool slacks, a fresh white cotton blouse and thick wool sweater to go under her one good winter coat, and sensible flat shoes. She packed her canvas bag with everything she thought a real war correspondent might need: a German language map of Budapest that Sophie tore from an old atlas for her, her reporter's notebook, her American passport and her Radio Free Europe credentials, plus two of her favorite Hershey milk chocolate candy bars, a splurge a day earlier from the Munich PX. No change of clothes; she would be home in Munich in less than a day.

As Andy waved her up into the cab, Charlie didn't hesitate. She had a plan, and it was as airtight as she could make it. They were driving east toward Nickelsdorf, the last Austrian village before the border, too small and too isolated to show up even as a dot on her map. Once Andy checked in with local Red Cross officials and picked up his translator, they would drive on to Budapest. They would be back in Munich in less than twenty-four hours. Her story would be on Owens's desk first thing Monday morning, alongside a hot cup of fresh coffee. Then the chips would fall where they may. If all went well, Owens might finally make her part of the news staff at last.

And if he fired her? There were other jobs, weren't there?

Somewhere outside Munich, Charlie closed her eyes. She had seized her chance. Martha Gellhorn—she hoped—would be proud. She slept but did not dream.

9

RUBICON

C harlie awoke and gasped.

It was dawn. Andy—nowhere to be seen—had parked just yards short of no man's land, where neutral Austria ceded to communist Hungary. A single bare Hungarian oak tree loomed over the truck. So did a guard tower, as real as a nightmare.

Charlie wasn't alone either.

Hundreds, maybe thousands, of people moved past her, flowing around the truck the way a river parts around an island. Most came from the Hungarian side of the border, and most didn't look much older than Charlie: couples carrying a child or two and maybe a small suitcase, or young men in their late teens or early twenties, traveling in packs of three or four or five. Some rode motorbikes, others pushed bicycles, and still more came in anything that rolled, from delivery vans to ox carts to commandeered city buses. They flooded toward Austria, moving as fast as they dared through no man's land with its twin rows of lacy, looping barbed wire flanking each side of a deep mud-and-rock trench. Some fell to their knees to kiss Austrian soil or just in sheer exhaustion.

Waiting to greet them were volunteers, pointing these new refugees toward hot sandwiches, warm blankets, and medical tents as news cameramen captured those first raw moments of freedom on film.

Charlie had never seen anything like it.

She wedged open the truck's door and stood on the cab's frame, her head above the surging crowd. This close, the guard tower didn't look like much—a crude, utilitarian shack on a raised platform. No windows. No doors. No guards. No dogs either, the ones specially bred by the KGB for their speed, power, and instinct to leap for the soft part of the throat.

Humble, yes. Grotesque and terrifying, also yes. If the Hungarians really did carry the day and push the Soviets out, guard towers like this one would be relics that were bound to disappear forever. *I might not get another chance to look inside one*, she thought.

Charlie looped her bag over her shoulder and jumped down from the truck. She worked her way against the flowing crowd toward no man's land, stepping carefully around the downed barbed wire and picking her way over rime-slicked rocks. It was slow going, and twice she nearly slipped and fell. *Imagine trying to get all the way across this trench while running away from guard dogs*, she thought.

At the center of the trench—more or less the official border, Charlie figured—she paused. Another step, and she would be officially in Iron Curtain territory. A tingle ran up her spine. *No going back now*, she thought and kept going.

When she reached the tower, she circled it first, once and then again. A metal ladder led up to the platform. She put one foot on the bottom rung, testing it with the heft of her foot. *Seems sturdy enough*. She looked up; the platform was twenty feet up at most. She began to climb, hand-over-hand, one rung at a time.

#   #   #

She reached the top of the watch tower's ladder and pulled herself inside. It was disappointingly empty, nothing but a bare wood floor and u-shaped bolts that once held machine guns or searchlights. The sides of the tower were open, and the air felt raw and bitter.

Charlie shivered.

From up here, one side of the Austrian-Hungarian border looked a lot like the other. The same bare trees stood amid the same ruined heaps of last summer's tall grass. The same dull-grey clouds covered the sun and pulled the winter sky down, oppressive, low, and close. The same black crows freewheeled overhead, swooping down for any soft tissue they could find—grubs, worms, field mice. The same, except for the thick, ugly scar of no man's land stretching in both directions as far as Charlie could see. All of it designed and built to keep people in and ideas—about freedom, democracy, and even Elvis—out.

Two miles to the east was Hegyeshalom, Charlie knew from her map, the first village on the Hungarian side of the border. After Germany's surrender to the Allies, Hegyeshalom had had the bad geographical luck to fall into the Soviet sphere of influence. Did it look much different than Nickelsdorf? Charlie suspected not.

She crossed to the other side of the tower. She followed the grooves worn in the wood floor by the guards—soldiers from the Hungarian home army, who manned this post—as they kept watch for anyone brave or foolish enough to attempt an escape. Once spotted, the guards had a clean shot: lift the rifle, fix on the target—don't think of it as human—and shoot. Ready. Aim. Fire. Even if the target was another Hungarian, desperate for a better life.

Andy's truck, with its bright Red Cross, stood out, a beacon amid the sea of moving bodies.

Charlie crossed her arms. Even her winter coat wasn't enough to keep her warm.

How had things gotten this bad, she wondered, with victorious allies now such bitter post-war enemies? The short answer was that the surrender of the Axis powers—Nazi Germany, Imperial Japan, Fascist Italy—left the United States and the Soviet Union as two superpowers with opposing ideas about what the postwar world should look like, American capitalism versus Soviet communism. The much longer answer was a complicated mix of extended memories, old grudges, political and economic rivalries, deep suspicion, and plain old fear. Would things have turned out differently had Roosevelt—who built a pragmatic working relationship with Stalin by providing the airplanes, tanks, and food Russia needed to defend its long Eastern Front from Nazi Germany—survived until the end of the war? *Maybe*, Charlie thought. *Maybe not*.

She heard a horn, loud and persistent. From the Red Cross truck, Andy waved at her as he honked. She waved back and then backed down the ladder, still shivering when her feet touched the ground.

10
YOU DON'T BELONG HERE

Charlie navigated her way through the crowd toward the large red cross painted on the side of Andy's truck. She was nearly there when *ooof!* Charlie hit the frozen ground, landing hard on her backside next to the woman who had slammed into her. The contents of Charlie's bag spilled, sliding and scattering on frost-slick dirt.

"*Bocsánat, pardon,*" the woman mumbled. She was hollow-cheeked and bone-thin, and as she pulled herself back up, her eyes riveted on the border yards away. Charlie's eyes followed her as the woman hurtled herself forward toward Austria.

"Miss Atkins?" a surprised voice asked. "What are you doing here?"

Charlie flinched. She knew that voice only too well. She looked up.

Viktor stood over Charlie, scowling, his voice disapproving as he put out his hand to help her up. "Mr. Owens was very clear. You were sent home. You must return to Munich at once."

"Nice to see you too, Viktor." She ignored his offered hand. "And no, I am not going back to Munich. Not until I finish what I came to do."

"And what is it you have come to do?"

Charlie took her time getting up. She brushed the frost and mud from the back of her coat and then picked up her notebook, map, and the candy bars that had spilled out of her bag. "I am going to report my story. It is a good, newsworthy story. Regardless of what you or Mr. Owens think."

"What story? This nonsense about what—donating blood?"

Charlie straightened up. She was close enough to see the freckles sprinkled across the bridge of Viktor's nose and the small precise stitches of his mended shirt collar. His wool coat ballooned around him, too big for his slight build. "That's right. What about it?"

"War is not for the reckless, Miss Atkins. You do not belong here."

"And you do?" Her eyes flicked up, past Viktor's broken teeth, and met his eyes. Her voice was hard. "Mr. Owens said that Hungary is off limits for all Radio Free Europe news staff. That doesn't include me, which you are only too happy to point out every chance you get. But it does include you. So, Viktor, what exactly are you doing here?"

Viktor flushed, a deep angry red.

Charlie and Viktor had been at war from the moment they met, their sorties often bruising. At an after-hours gathering at a Munich beer hall the day after Charlie's story about Sophie and Grace Kelly's wedding dress aired, yet another shot. That night, the group around the long wooden tables at the *Staatliches Hofbräuhaus*—where Adolf Hitler unveiled the Nazi Party's first political platform in 1920—included Americans, like Charlie and Owens, and Eastern Europeans, like Viktor. Others were French, including photographer Jerome Berger of *Agence France-Presse*, dark-haired and lean and usually in need of a shave or a cigarette, or British, like McAllister Hill—Hilly, to his friends—of *The Sunday Times*. Hilly, who wore tailored Saville Row suits even in battle zones, was accompanied as usual by Ian Haversham, a slight, rheumy-eyed Man Friday who Hilly kept on retainer for errands and the odd fact-checking assignment.

"I see our wedding dress correspondent has arrived." Viktor's lip curled over his broken teeth, and his voice, deep and resonant, carried. "What important fashion news will you bring us next, Miss Atkins? What Mrs. Eisenhower wears to tea, perhaps? And our listeners who struggle to find enough to eat or keep warm should care because—?"

Stunned, Charlie's cheeks burned. She opened her mouth, but no words came out.

"You see? Even she doesn't know." Viktor's sneer turned into an ugly smile. "A few words of advice for you, Miss Atkins. You will never be a real journalist, because a real journalist would understand everything about the stories they write—why the story must be told, and to whom it makes a difference."

He turned his back then, leaving Charlie open-mouthed and red-faced.

She vowed then that she would show Viktor how wrong he was about her.

Now Charlie answered her own question. "I know what you're doing here. You are going to Budapest." She considered her next words. "So am I."

"For what possible reason?" Viktor demanded. His voice dripped with scorn. "You know nothing of our history or our politics. You don't know our leaders or who can be trusted. You do not speak or understand our language. You will fail."

Charlie smiled. "As it happens, I have a ride to and from Budapest, and I even have a Hungarian translator. So you don't need to worry about me. I will manage just fine."

"Well, while you 'manage,' I will be watching and listening at the Hungarian Parliament building as our new prime minister and his cabinet begin the real work—creating a new Hungary." Viktor wheeled around and stalked off, disappearing into the crowd.

Charlie watched him melt into the surging tide of people. She didn't need a lecture from Viktor—or his help. Officially or not, she was determined to cross the border, no matter what Victor—or anyone else—thought. She turned and headed on toward Andy and the Red Cross truck that would take her on to Budapest.

#   #   #

She was still fuming about Viktor by the time she caught up with Andy. He waited under the oak's bare branches, its thick, rough bark faded to a pale brown. The Red Cross truck was now empty of its cargo.

"There's still fighting in Budapest." Andy spoke as soon as he saw Charlie, his words coming in a rush. "They need more blood. I'm sorry, but I have new instructions. I am to return to Munich for another load of plasma." He opened the passenger door for Charlie. "We need to leave at once."

Charlie's heart sank. Turn back? Instinctively, she shook her head. "Andy, you go on and do what you need to do. I'll find another ride to Budapest."

"Didn't you hear me? It's a war zone." He barely stopped to catch his breath. "There are bound to be armed patrols on the roads, and you won't be in a Red Cross truck—"

"I'll be fine." She laid a reassuring hand on his arm. "I'll be in and out in a couple of hours. We'll meet up tonight right back here next to this oak tree"—Charlie patted its gnarled, scaly trunk—"when you bring the next load of plasma. You did promise me a ride back to Munich."

"I can't leave you here."

"Andy, that's not your decision. You have a job to do. So do I."

Andy looked away, his expression unhappy. "Okay," he muttered at last. He pointed over Charlie's shoulder. "The plasma we brought is loaded in the ambulance behind you. I told the driver you might want to interview him. His name is Péter. His English is excellent. Maybe you can catch a ride with him to Budapest."

Andy opened the cab door and swung himself up into the driver's seat. "I'll be looking for you tonight. Right back here, by this tree."

Charlie nodded and then waved as Andy pulled away, back in the direction of Munich. She was on her own, a terrifying—and exhilarating—thought. *First things first. An interview with the ambulance driver and then find a ride to Budapest.*

11
PÉTER

Charlie turned around toward the ambulance behind her. Péter, its driver, was striding toward her, his arm already outstretched. He was dazzling: tall with clean, crisp features, cheeks rosy from the cold, a thick mop of lazy black curls falling almost to his white shirt's collar. An unbuttoned overcoat hung easily on his slim frame. He wore the symbol of the revolution, too, the tricolor armband with the green, white, and red colors of the Hungarian flag. He clasped Charlie's hand in both of his; his hands and his broad smile were warm.

"Hello, little *Amerikai*," he said, looking down at Charlie. "You are not much of an army."

Charlie couldn't help grinning back. "Sorry, but there is no army. Not yet, anyway. Just me."

"Well, tell your American troops that if they are coming to help us, they must hurry. Otherwise, we Hungarians will have won our freedom without them. How would that look?" His blue eyes, magnified behind the round *O* of his glasses, twinkled. "So, Radio Free Europe, what do you want to know?"

As Charlie opened her mouth to reply, her eyes flicked up over Péter's shoulder. Ten yards away, Viktor, seated in the cab of a snub-nosed truck, watched her, a faint sneer on his face. Amid the noise and crush of the people around them, their eyes locked. Charlie pulled her eyes away first. She turned her back on Viktor and fished her reporter's notebook out of her bag.

"Let's get started," she said to Péter, determined to ignore Viktor. "What is your full name, how old are you, and where are you from?"

"My name?" Péter blinked in surprise. "That could be very bad news for me if there are men from the AVO, our secret police, listening. But all right, you are from Radio Free Europe. I believe it will be okay. I am Péter Eszes. I am twenty-eight years old. I am from Szeged, in the southwest part of Hungary, but these days I am studying in Budapest." Péter stretched his hands out in front of him; they were scrubbed clean and pink with blunt-cut fingernails. "One day soon, I will be a surgeon."

A medical student and handsome as a movie star. Charlie could hardly believe her good luck. Too bad she didn't have a camera. "You left your studies to join the fighting?"

"How could I not?" Péter's voice swelled with pride. "We students were the first to take to the streets. Now more people from all over Hungary are joining us every day. We are united against the Russians. Even a famous war hero has joined our side—Pál Maléter resigned from the Hungarian People's Army to fight with us, and now Prime Minister Nagy has named him our Minister of Defense."

The jostling and noise around them grew. Charlie stepped closer to Péter to make sure she could hear his voice. "What are people saying in the streets of Budapest?"

"They are saying that they are not afraid." Péter's voice rose. "Everyone is finding ways to help. Our *nagymamáks*—our grandmothers—watch the rooftops for snipers while our brothers and sisters make firebombs with old bottles, gasoline and rags."

"They are making Molotov cocktails?" Charlie scribbled notes furiously.

"That's right—using cheap Russian vodka, too." He smiled with delight. "They throw them at the weak point in the tanks: the air vents. Even the *Pesti srácok*—the children of Pest—are fighting. They pull up the limestone blocks from our streets and pile them up to be thrown at soldiers or tanks. I am very proud to see us working together against the Russians."

"What about your family?"

Péter pulled a picture from his breast coat pocket and showed it to Charlie. In it, Péter beamed toward the camera, his arm around a petite, dark-haired woman. She, too, smiled at the camera—amused or shy, Charlie couldn't tell—with a boy, all long limbs and big ears, on her lap. Though the photograph appeared recent, it was already dogeared around the edges.

"This is my wife, Heléna, and my son, Lukács. Today, he is seven years old. Lukács is why I fight. Why all of us fight. We want our children to live in freedom."

Charlie studied Péter's face. "You could come to the West." She gestured at the sea of bodies surging around them. "That's the choice many of your countrymen are making."

Péter tucked the photo back into his pocket. "Why not help my country? That, for me, is the best thing. Hungary, run by Hungarians for the good of the Hungarian people. We do not need the Russians telling us what to do."

"If the revolution succeeds, what do you think will be different?"

"Everything, of course," Péter said, his voice filled with enthusiasm. "We'll vote for the leader we want and speak freely if we disagree with them. There won't be arrests in the middle of night, with people disappearing for months or years for no reason. We'll go to church again, and my son will learn about great Hungarian heroes, not Soviet ones. No one will be forced to speak Russian. Our workers will be paid enough to live, and the money from selling our uranium on the open market will benefit Hungarians, not Russians. Then Hungary will be a very nice place to live."

Charlie nodded toward the ambulance behind Péter. It was old—most of the chrome on the front fender was missing, leaving a wide swath of rust, and the driver's side door was badly dented. "That plasma in your ambulance—that's the story I'm following. People all over Europe are standing in line for hours to donate that blood. They want to help save the lives of your freedom fighters. What do you think about that?"

"That is good, yes. But blood is very democratic. It will save any life—blood doesn't care about politics. You see?" Péter paused, as if making sure Charlie understood his point. "We all share the same warm blood under the skin. That is the world I am fighting for—where we Hungarians are equal to all."

His eyes twinkled again, and he leaned forward to whisper loudly to her. "Equal even to Russians."

Perfect, Charlie thought. "I want to see how the plasma is put to use. Mind if I catch a ride to Budapest with you?"

Péter's face fell as he gestured toward the ambulance. "I am sorry, Radio Free Europe, but as you can see there is no room."

Charlie looked. Péter was right. Every inch of space save for the driver's seat was packed full of plasma kits.

"And now, I must go. As you say, there are lives to be saved."

"Wait." Charlie pulled the map of Budapest from her bag and spread it out on the hood of the ambulance. "Show me where you are taking the plasma. As soon as I can find a ride, I'll meet you there."

Péter hesitated. "You are sure? Where I am going, it is not an easy place to see. We are not a proper hospital. We have set up inside a school. There are many wounded and many more who are waiting to be buried. The sights and—" Péter touched his nose—"the smells are not good."

"I'm sure." Charlie smiled at Péter with as much confidence as she could muster. "I won't be there long, I promise. Just long enough to see that you have put the plasma to good use."

"Very well." Péter leaned over the map, turning it around to get his bearings. He traced an imaginary line across one of the seven bridges spanning the faint blue line of the Danube River that separated the city into its two halves, Buda and Pest. He tapped a spot on the map. "Here is the Corvin Cinema, in Pest. It is in District VIII. This is where many of the freedom fighters are positioned—more than 4,000 fighters in all, I think. The fighting is very bad. You must be careful. It is dangerous."

He moved his finger slightly and touched the map again. "The school is not far, just here. It is the Budapest Academy for Boys. This is where your plasma will save many lives."

Charlie watched him mark her map with her pen. She might not have a ride to Budapest—yet—but at least she had a destination. "One more thing," she said as she tucked the map back into her bag. "Okay if I carry one of those kits with me? I want to track them, so that I can report for sure that blood donated by West Germans was really used to save lives in Budapest."

Péter handed her one of the kits—it was lighter than she expected and about the size of an extra-wide shoebox. Then Péter folded himself into the ambulance's driver's seat. "Be careful, Radio Free Europe. Enough blood has been spilled."

He waved goodbye and then tapped the horn lightly in an effort to clear enough space to nose the battered old ambulance forward.

Charlie waved back and then, unwillingly, turned to glance back toward where she had seen Viktor. The truck was still there, but Viktor's face was turned away from her as he waited for a chance to maneuver through the crush of moving bodies and onto the one main road heading east to Budapest.

Darn it, Charlie thought. *Viktor is the last person I want to ask for a ride. Not that he would say yes anyway.*

Then she narrowed her eyes. His truck looked oddly familiar. Although its military markings were painted over, Viktor's ride was definitely US Army-surplus, a snout-nosed, squat World War II-era Signal Corps truck with faded olive-green paint and rear double doors. No locks on the doors either. *Not exactly first class*, she thought, *but it would do.*

She stepped back, out of Viktor's line of sight, her eyes fixed on the back of the signal truck. She waited until it slowly crept forward and then quickstepped after it as it picked up speed. Then she stepped lightly on the rear bumper, opened one rear door, and slipped herself inside, quiet as a cat.

Viktor would never even know she was there.

#   #   #

Inside, the signal truck was crammed full of supplies.

With food: tinned milk, coffee and black tea, fresh Bavarian cheese, onions, winter greens, apples, potatoes, and *Schwarzbrot*—good Austrian black bread.

With warm clothing: dozens of pairs of boots, lashed together by their laces, and boxes overflowing with overcoats, sweaters, and gloves.

With blankets: army-issue wool coverlets piled in stacks or draped like ghosts over piles of unseen supplies.

With toys: a jointed teddy bear sat merrily atop a box of children's playthings.

With gasoline—for the trip home, Charlie figured: its sweet, pungent odor prickled her nose.

With cigarettes: Lucky Strikes and Pall Malls.

With the truck so full, there wasn't enough room for Charlie to sit down, even with her small frame. She would have to stand all the way to Budapest—a couple of hours east along the one main road that stretched from the Austrian border to the Hungarian capital. She didn't mind. She wedged herself in as best as she could amid the boxes and baskets, her feet on the plasma kit. *Better than walking*, she decided. Then she flipped up her coat collar and thrust her hands deep into her pockets to keep them warm and settled in for the ride.

12
ANDRÁSSY STREET

nside a squat building slammed down on the corner of Budapest's Andrássy Street like a concrete fist, András Kovács couldn't help shouting.

"My men are swinging from lampposts. Strung up and gutted like pigs!" The fluent Russian that Kovács—fifty-eight, with ramrod straight posture except for the soft fleshy paunch around his belly—worked so hard to master during his years in Moscow tumbled out, one furious word after another. He had not been home in days. His loden wool uniform—its blue epaulets signified his top rank within the AVO, Hungary's secret police—smelled like two-week-old sweat.

Instead, Kovács remained hunkered down in his spartan, top-floor office at the AVO's headquarters, fielding the rapid-fire reports coming at him from his men on the street. None of the news they brought him was good. Those miserable students—*huligánoks*, hooligans, in his judgment—went from marching through Budapest to congregating at Bem Square, where, like frenzied lunatics, the rioters managed to blowtorch and then topple a magnificent, eighty-foot-tall bronze statue of

Stalin from its limestone plinth, leaving only his boots. From there, the chaos and lawlessness exploded across Hungary. *Every shop girl and bus driver suddenly feels entitled to have a say in how this country runs,* Kovács thought. *As if they have any idea what that means.*

Those wretched troublemakers nearly got to him as well. A mob had ransacked this very building's first floor, dumping years' worth of dossiers on anyone who dared to question the status quo into the courtyard and setting them on fire. Not that it mattered. Whoever came out on top after this mess—the Russians probably, the Americans, perish the thought, or even the Hungarians themselves—would create new files. That's just how power and control worked.

Worse, his AVO men were a particular target. One young officer, a favorite protégé of his, was stripped and beaten to death with a shovel by these so-called peaceful protesters. What remained of his naked body was left lying in the street like yesterday's garbage. Kovács directed his men to retrieve the body in the dead of night and bury it. He sent a personal condolence note to the officer's parents.

And what to tell Moscow? That the entire country had gone mad on his watch? Not that Kovács was surprised, of course. He sensed for months that trouble was coming, and although he warned Hungary's deeply loathed General Secretary Mátyás Rákosi directly, no one wanted to hear that unrest was brewing. Rákosi's replacement, Ernő Gerő, didn't listen to Kovács's warnings, either.

Instead, the pressure kept building, thanks to Khrushchev, Radio Free Europe, and that speech.

That damn speech.

What had Khrushchev been thinking?

Khrushchev had denounced Stalin's brutality and his cult of personality in a closed session during the 20th Congress of the Communist Party of the Soviet Union in February 1956. A crude attempt by Khrushchev to position himself as a great reformer, Kovács believed, and the kind of backroom politicking he expected from the men in the Kremlin. But then Radio Free Europe had got its hands on a copy of Khrushchev's remarks and had rebroadcast it across all of its radio services. Nonstop. For three days straight. That stunt sparked calls across the Soviet republics for change—starting with Poland. Khrushchev had gone soft there, too, in Kovács's opinion, granting wage concessions to striking factory workers and then allowing a known reformer back into power. Gomulka's thaw, people called it. Not exactly a win for Khrushchev.

Khrushchev's speech and his concessions to Poland only added to Kovács's headaches. Both of these emboldened the Petőfi Circle, a salon of sorts for a few reckless individuals on the dangerous fringe of society—writers, artists, intellectuals, and others unable or unwilling to be productive members of the state. None of their complaints—low wages, no say in government affairs, Hungarians should run their own affairs—was going to change anything, so he had allowed a few public meetings to be held, to let them blow off a little steam, yes, but also to make the ringleaders easy to identify and arrest.

Or so Kovács thought.

This time turned out to be different.

The Petőfi Circle grew only more daring, egged on by Radio Free Europe's constant stream of democratic nonsense. Suddenly, their meetings were attracting hundreds then thousands of attendees. A meeting discussing what a free press might mean for Hungary drew 6,000, most of whom listened over loudspeakers in the street. *I should have shot the trouble makers behind that damned Petőfi Circle months ago when I had the chance*, Kovács thought bitterly.

When one of his men brought him a copy of the protesting students' Sixteen Points manifesto, Kovács skimmed it and tossed it aside. It, too, sounded like it had been ripped from the airwaves of Radio Free Europe. Whether the stories about how much better life was in the West were true or not, he didn't care. His lot was cast firmly with the powers-that-be in Moscow, and his longevity was assured only as long as he kept a tight lid on any and all dissent in Hungary.

So far, Moscow had done nothing to help him manage the situation in Budapest. Kovács was left with no choice but to hold his nerve and wait for orders that had yet to arrive and to watch the crowds on the street grow bolder and more reckless. He didn't think that clarity from Moscow was too much to ask.

"Tell me, just what the hell am I supposed to do?" he demanded over the telephone line.

"You would be wise to watch your tone." The voice of Vasily Nikolaevich Zhirov, a trusted member of the Kremlin's inner circle, sounded stone-cold even all the way from Moscow. "I can assure you, Comrade Khrushchev is fully aware of all aspects of the situation."

"He has sent negotiators to talk to the protesters, for fuck's sake," Kovács snapped. "They are drawing up a timetable for the withdrawal of Soviet troops. What do you think is going to happen to the men I have left?" *Or to me*, Kovács thought.

That was the problem with being a small nation indentured to a big one. The Soviets expected the AVO to do its dirty work, propped up by a Hungarian home army that might or might not fight its countrymen, and a Red Army force made up of conscripts from its member states, many of whom had little understanding of the issues and even less interest in the outcome. So far, the home army was siding with the protesters, ripping the red stars off their own uniforms and handing their weapons over to anyone who asked. Even the Soviet troops had left or retreated to their barracks to wait for orders from Moscow. That left dutiful AVO foot soldiers like himself alone to face the mob.

"We will discuss these matters when I arrive," Zhirov said.

Despite the warmth of his office, Kovács felt a sudden chill. Something had changed. Zhirov, his mentor, his protector, and his benefactor inside the Kremlin had hardened toward him, he was sure of it. He could hear it, a certain tone, a new coldness, in Zhirov's voice.

Kovács fought to soften the sound of his words. "Of course, comrade, a great benefit for you to evaluate the situation for yourself. I will await you and your guidance."

Kovács replaced the receiver in its cradle. He needed to focus. Not on this mess in the streets—no, clearly the matter was out of his hands, or about to be—because Zhirov wasn't coming to counsel him but to replace him. Zhirov might even arrest him; after all, someone must be blamed for the rioters in the streets.

If only Khrushchev had been tougher and made an example of what happens to anyone who dares to oppose Moscow, none of us would be in this mess, Kovács thought. Now Budapest was a battleground, and it was not just the future of Hungary at stake. If Moscow continued to hedge, vacillate, and stall over whether or how much to loosen its grip, the rest of the satellite states were sure to fall like dominos—only this time, Kovács was convinced, they would fall the wrong way. They would fall toward the West.

By now, Kovács had learned to count on no one's judgment but his own. No matter where he was, he made sure he knew where the exit was; it was the only way he felt safe in unfamiliar circumstances. He had survived this long only because he was careful and disciplined and because he had learned to adapt to whatever the situation required.

Just like Budapest, city of his birth.

An old city, Budapest had been occupied and reoccupied since it was forged from three ancient settlements—Buda, seat of kings, Pest, home to merchants, and Óbuda, the oldest part of the city, established before Rome. Beyond the city, wide fertile steppes and the lack of defensive borders had for centuries made the region a constant target for invaders—the Mongols, the Ottomans, the Habsburgs, the Nazis, the Russians. Despite the turmoil, the city survived and thrived, even rivaling Vienna's cultural, political, and economic dominance during the late nineteenth and early twentieth century Austrian-Hungarian empire.

Kovács had survived as well.

He was born in a hovel on the edge of the city just after the turn of the century, growing up as Budapest transformed itself from a provincial agricultural backwater into the so-called brilliant butterfly of Eastern Europe, known for its art nouveau architecture and cafés filled with dissident writers, untrustworthy gossip, and clouds of smoke from the cigars Kovács could not afford.

Instead, Kovács—young, poor, and pragmatic—saw his future with the Russians long before Soviet troops arrived in the waning days of World War II to occupy his homeland.

Soon after Lenin's death in 1924, Stalin consolidated his power and put out the call for the best and brightest across Eastern Europe to make their futures in Moscow. Kovács, who had no other prospects, answered—better, he believed, to ally himself with Hungary's bigger, domineering neighbor even if it meant turning his back on his own country. He won a place in a party-sponsored school, applied himself, and married well, to the daughter of a minor Communist Party functionary. Better yet, he managed to attach himself as a trusted aide to Zhirov, no older than himself but already powerful, thanks to his own family's influential connections inside the Kremlin.

As Zhirov's star rose, so did Kovács's.

In 1945, after the Russians waited out the German Army in a brutal winter siege before seizing Budapest, it was Zhirov who arranged for Kovács's return to his hometown as a fast-rising and reliable lieutenant in Hungary's new internal security force. Not that Kovács was welcomed home as a prodigal son—Hungarians who worked in high-ranking security and intelligence roles for the Soviets were especially loathed as traitors by their countrymen. Kovács didn't care. His job was to ensure his countrymen's unquestioned submission to the Soviet Union through the accountable-only-to-the-Kremlin apparatus of the AVO. Kovács did his work with unsparing efficiency, punishing anyone who dared to speak out by arresting their friends or wives or children for long, tortuous detentions in Budapest's hellish Vác prison. University students who thought too much of their own ideas were a particular target.

Kovács's position came with the trappings of status, including his pick of one of the many mansions in the low Buda hills on the western side of the Danube River. Instead, Kovács chose an elegant, secluded home on the Pest side of the Danube, a short walk south from the headquarters of the AVO on Andrássy Street. He invited himself to tea with its owners, members of the *bourgeoisie* who hosted him graciously despite, he was sure, knowing precisely why he had come: Later that day and with a stroke of Kovács's pen, the house and everything in it, down to the fine French bed linens and kitchen cutlery, became his property. Its former owners were banished to a workers' collective in the countryside.

This life had been good to him. Now staying meant losing everything regardless of whoever came next to power. Kovács was too well known. Too feared. Too convenient to blame for doing his job or not doing it well enough. He knew he would die a hard, brutal death if the mob in the streets outside caught him. Should the Kremlin fail to consider his many years of loyal service, he might find himself shipped off to Lubyanka prison, courtesy of the Soviet state. Or worse. To leave it all behind was a pity, but there was not much he could do about that now. If he had to go, he would go, but not without taking what was his.

His exit strategy was already in motion. He had put plenty of money aside for just such an occasion as this one. Men he trusted—and paid well—were at his home right this very moment with a moving van that, once loaded, would make its way south to a secluded estate on the Black Sea where Kovács planned to disappear quietly and permanently. A driver, also well paid, would arrive later that evening to drive him under the cover of night on a discrete route to his new home. But there was one small item he needed to retrieve personally, precious to no one but himself. Driving the short distance to the house would be suicide—his black Zil limousine was too easy a target. He would have to walk, quickly and in disguise.

Given the quiet and the early hour, it was a risk Kovács was willing to take.

"Fekete," he shouted, summoning his aide, "time to go."

As he left the AVO headquarters building for the last time, Kovács didn't look back. Too many years taking Zhirov's scraps had left him cold inside. Warmth and sunshine on the Baltic coast would do nicely. Very nicely indeed.

13
THE PRICE OF BREAD

O nce outside the AVO's headquarters, Kovács walked
along Andrássy Street toward the Danube River, Sándor
Fekete at his side. Grimly, he surveyed the damage done
to the city over the last eleven days. Tram cars lay on their
sides, pushed like tin toys from their tracks and into the streets
to keep tanks from moving across Pest. Whole city blocks
were reduced to rubble. Some buildings looked untouched
while others burst inside out, the lives—and possessions—of
those who lived there exposed for all to see. Missing limestone
pavers, pulled up from the street to be used as weapons during
the fighting, left yawning gaps in the road like missing teeth.
And the bodies—radicals, AVO, Hungarian regular army, and
anyone else unlucky enough to be caught in the crossfire—lay
where they had fallen to await burial, their corpses dusted by
quicklime and snow.

Kovács swore under his breath, all but his eyes hidden
by the working man's cap and heavy scarf Fekete found for
each of them to disguise themselves. It wasn't the dead that
bothered him; it was the living, the ungrateful citizens of
Budapest, congregating in the streets, waving Hungarian

flags—all, he noted angrily, suddenly missing their center red Soviet star—and smiling or weeping with joy in the cold winter sunshine.

"Is it true? The Americans are coming?" A girl, maybe fourteen, looked up as Kovács and Fekete walked past her. She wore a freedom fighter's tricolor tied around her coat sleeve like a badge of honor. On another day, Kovács would have had her arrested for daring to ask such a question. Not now.

"I heard it on the radio," she continued, her voice excited. "Surely that means it must be so."

Kovács didn't stop to answer her. He strode purposefully forward, his hand tightening around the Walther P38 pistol he carried in the pocket of his oversized civilian coat.

"Stupid pig," he murmured once she was out of earshot, careful to keep his voice low so that only Fekete could hear him. "After all we have done to bring law and order and provide stability for these wretched people."

Fekete grunted. At twenty-one, he was thick and barrel-chested, with a badly healed scar along his hairline. He was also the son of a reliable party man who did what was asked of him without comment. Like father, like son. Fekete was an unimaginative sort. Kovács found him useful.

"We should keep moving." Fekete said, his voice low. "There are too many people on the street."

Fekete is right, Kovács thought. Amid the wreckage, Pest was coming back to life, and Kovács could feel it. Up and down Andrássy Street, shopkeepers busied themselves with getting back to business. A tall, thin man, a loose winter coat flapping about his body, swept up brick dust and broken glass under a sign that read *Vegyész*—chemist. Next door, a butcher, stout and thick-armed in his rust-stained apron, finished wiping down his shop's front door and then disappeared inside. New placards hung everywhere, announcing the formation of new political parties, side by side with the names and pictures of the missing and the dead. There was plenty of fresh graffiti as well—*Freedom or death* and *No more AVO*. All of it left Kovács cold. Things had worked well for him the way they were. There would be no place in this new Hungary for him.

There was something else in the air, and it filled Kovács's senses without warning: the bursting, yeasty perfume of fresh-baked bread.

Suddenly, he realized he was hungry. No, ravenous. He couldn't remember the last time he had eaten, and the bread's mouth-watering aroma wrapped around him.

He stopped abruptly in front of a small storefront bakery, one he had never bothered with before. It didn't look too damaged—just a long, spiderwebbing crack in the glass of its front window. Inside the shop, a shallow vat filled with gently sizzling rounds of *langos*—fried bread—sputtered in hot oil. A boy, thin as a puff of smoke, transferred neat loaves of *krumplis kenyér*—crusty, soft potato bread—three at a time onto a long-handled wooden paddle held by an older man, the baker and, by the looks of him, the boy's father. The baker slid the loaves into one of three narrow rectangular ovens cut into the back wall, sliding them off his paddle with a quick jerk of his wrist. The boy and his father worked in practiced unison, dough-slide-dough, wasting no time or effort. Wood for the ovens was stacked neatly to one side, next to piled bags of flour. Racks of freshly baked bread cooled nearby.

Kovács stared at the still-steaming loaves greedily and inhaled the aroma of the potato bread. His mouth watered.

"No stops." Fekete's voice was in Kovács's ear, his hand pressing against Kovács's back to keep him moving. "Too dangerous."

Kovács ignored him and stepped into the bakery. "How much for the bread?" he asked the baker, careful to keep his face hidden.

"Today, we celebrate—no charge," said the baker, barely pausing his work, his smiling face rosy from the oven's heat. "Tomorrow, the real work begins. Tomorrow, we start to build a new, free Hungary."

"Yes, I suppose so." *How pathetically naïve,* Kovács thought. It took guns and armies and, yes, useful men like himself and Fekete to build a stable system, one that endured. Free Hungary? Tiny, landlocked Hungary had fallen to one invading army after another, century after century, its flat rich farmland too tempting a target for its greedy neighbors. An independent Hungary would never last.

"Still," Kovács said, "you must admit that small countries need the friendship of larger ones."

"You are right, my friend," the baker said, "but now we Hungarians can choose who our friends will be."

With his paddle, he scooped up a fresh batch of *langos* and shook them off his paddle into the pan of oil. The baker gestured toward the racks of still-warm bread. "Please, help yourself."

Eagerly, Kovács seized a loaf of potato bread, savoring its steamy heft between his fingers. He tore into it hungrily. The crisp snap of crust yielded to the slightly sweet flesh of the inside. Delicious. He nodded his thanks to the baker. "May we choose our friends wisely."

Fekete, at Kovács's side, said nothing and left the loaves of bread untouched.

"To freedom," the baker said, and then he stopped.

Kovács followed the baker's eyes staring down at the toes of Kovács's fine leather boots, peeking out from the hems of the working man's trousers he wore. The baker looked up at Kovács, his eyes hard and suspicious. With the narrow handle of his bread paddle, he pushed aside the scarf over Kovács's face, and his expression shifted from cheerful to fearful to angry.

Kovács bit off another chunk of bread and sneered, enjoying the baker's discomfort. In a few hours, he would be gone for good. No reason he couldn't exact a little retribution at the baker's expense. *Compensation*, Kovács thought, *for the lack of appreciation for men like himself.*

"I know who you are," the baker hissed. He knocked the bread from Kovács's hands with his paddle. "You're AVO! You deserve nothing from us."

The boy, holding three unbaked loaves ready for the oven, froze. He watched his father, his eyes huge.

The baker jabbed the long end of his paddle at Kovács. "Get out of my bakery!"

Kovács tugged at his pocket for his Walther. It caught on the folds of his overcoat. His boots scraped and slid, and he fell, landing on one knee.

Fekete held the baker, close and tight, like a hug. The baker tried but couldn't move. With one meaty hand, Fekete squeezed the man's wrist until he dropped his bread paddle. It clattered to the ground.

Kovács got to his feet. He brushed himself off. A pity about the bread, but he was no longer hungry. He took his time freeing his pistol from his pocket. He checked it to make sure there was a bullet in the chamber.

No one spoke. The oil sizzled. Two of the three bread ovens, narrow slits built into the bakery's wall, hung open, roaring and white-hot.

Kovács walked over to the boy. He knelt, eye level with him, and studied the child's face. He wasn't more than ten or eleven years old and pale, with boney arms that stuck out from his too-short sleeves.

"And you," Kovács said to the boy. "What do you think? Do you think I deserve to eat a loaf of your father's bread?"

The boy's hands gripped his tray of bread, tight enough to turn his knuckles white. He glanced toward his father before answering. "I think the bread must go into the oven, or it won't get baked."

Kovács threw back his head and laughed. "You are right, my little friend. Let me help you."

He took the loaves from the boy, and slung them into the oven, not caring how they landed. He slammed the oven shut.

"Good, no?" he said to the boy. He jerked his head in the direction of the door. "Go."

The boy didn't move. "Not without my father." His voice, thin and high, quavered.

The baker spoke, his voice rough. "Your mother needs you, Zoli. Tell her I'll be along shortly."

Zoli didn't move.

"Now, Zoli," the baker said, and this time, Kovács could hear the fear in his voice.

Zoli heard it as well. He looked at his father and then sidled in small reluctant steps to the door. "What time will you be home?" he asked.

"Soon. Now go."

"You promise?"

The baker's face softened. "I promise."

Zoli glanced at Kovács and then folded himself around the front entrance and out of sight.

Kovács turned to the baker. "What? No thank you?"

"For doing the decent thing for a child? Never!"

"I did you a favor. Your son will remember this moment for the rest of his life." Kovács leaned in, close enough to smell the baker's sweat. "He'll ask himself over and over again, 'Could I have saved my father?' The answer will gnaw away at him for years until he realizes he's a coward like the rest of you. Brave only when you think you can get away with it."

"You AVO think you are gods. You're evil—"

Kovács raised his hand. He had heard it all before. He watched as Fekete angled the baker's chin up toward the ceiling and twisted it hard. *Crack!* Quick and quiet but for the snapping of bones. A thump as Fekete let the baker's body drop.

Kovács sniffed—the bread he threw in the oven was turning to char. *Good*, he thought. *Let it burn. Let it all burn.* Moscow no longer needed or appreciated his services, and his fellow citizens would never accept him as one of them. It didn't matter. He no longer cared who won or lost. He just wanted out.

He jerked a nod to Fekete.

Fekete was already busy, scooping up armfuls of kindling and shoving it into the open maws of the three wall ovens; the wood cracked and popped as it caught fire. Then Fekete hoisted a bag of flour and swung it hard against the oven wall. The bag burst, showering the bakery with fine white dust. A second bag and then a third smacked hard against the same wall with its roaring open ovens. Cheap flour—the only kind allotted to a little bakery like this one—was particularly flammable.

The ovens thrummed.

Fekete picked up a jug of water from the counter and threw it into the sizzling *langos*. White-hot flame shot up from the pan, a whoosh of steam and sparks. With the baker's paddle, Fekete tipped the oil over. Flames rippled across the wooden counter, ravenously devouring the thin sheets of newsprint used to wrap bread and the dry willow baskets that held unbaked dough. The bakery stank with the hard-edged stench of smoking oil and burning bread. Fekete wiped his hands on a towel and then dangled it over the flames until it caught fire. He threw the burning towel on what was left of the stacked kindling.

A powder keg, ready to blow.

Kovács grunted his approval.

Fekete checked his Walther, making sure it also was loaded.

"Time to go," he said, and he stepped to the front entrance. Kovács stepped over the baker's body and followed, his gun at the ready. Behind him, the flames snapped and spread.

14
PAYBACK

O utside the bakery, Kovács never saw what hit him.
Fekete disappeared first, grabbed by thick, muscular arms, and then something jagged ripped across Kovács's face, right temple to left jowl. He howled and staggered back, white light and blood filling one eye. Instinctively, he jerked his gun up, firing two quick shots—one up, where a head should be, another straight ahead toward the torso.

Nothing. Only echoes.

He swung around. His face burned. His eye stung, blurred by blood and tears. Out of his good eye, he saw Zoli, the little shit, still holding the sharp, rusty iron pipe he'd whipped across Kovács's face. Zoli had brought reinforcements too: the chemist, armed with his broom, and the butcher, stout and stony-eyed, sticky bits of rabbit fur still clinging to the blade of his wide, flat cleaver.

The cleaver the butcher held at Fekete's neck.

Fekete did not—could not—move. He was pinned in a headlock, hands up, his gun pointing skyward.

"Pápa, Pápa!" Zoli pushed past Kovács. He ran into his father's bakery—or tried to. Kovács caught the boy with one swooping arm.

"Your father is dead," Kovács said and nearly groaned aloud. *Fuck! It hurt to talk.* He tightened his grip on Zoli, so much so that the boy gasped and dropped the pipe.

Good, Kovács thought grimly. *Make the goddamn brat pay.*

He shoved his gun up into the soft part of Zoli's cheek, his good eye locked on the butcher. "A pity to lose a son and a husband on the same day," Kovács said, not bothering to disguise the menace in his voice.

Smoke—roiling grey, white, and black—billowed out of the bakery. The fire hissed and popped. Kovács's nose twitched at the stink of burnt sugar and dough. His good eye watered.

Fekete's eyes stayed locked on Kovács's.

The chemist glanced at the butcher and then at Kovács. "Let Zoli go," he said, his voice an insignificant man's bluster. "He is a child."

Kovács ignored him. The butcher was the dangerous one, armed with a sharp knife honed by use to feel like an extension of his hand. "You should have stayed in your shops. This is not your business."

"It is my business when an AVO pig kills my friend," the butcher's voice rasped like a knife against a whet stone. His apron was patched and stained sepia, the color of dried blood.

"Your friend made unwise choices. As did his son."

"The days of the AVO are over. Every one of you will stand trial and be held accountable." The butcher flicked his cleaver; Fekete winced. Blood oozed from the soft wattle under Fekete's chin. "Assuming you and your Russian masters live that long."

"Come now, comrade, we are reasonable men." Thick smoke burned Kovács's eyes and filled his lungs. He coughed. That hurt just as much as talking did. "Surely you understand that the Russians are here as our friends."

The butcher snorted. "Yes, imagine how much worse our lives would be if they came as our enemies."

"A trade then," the chemist said. "Zoli for your man."

Heat seared Kovács's back. And then, the slightest of sounds, a crack then a pop. Kovács knew exactly what it meant: cheap flour dust and flaming oil about to blow. He needed to move fast. The only way forward was through the butcher.

"All right. The boy for my man. Let him go."

"Zoli first," the butcher said. "No AVO can be trusted."

Boom! The bakery exploded then, showering the street with brick grit and glass. In that same instant, Kovács lunged out of the way, shoving Zoli hard as he could toward the butcher.

The butcher lowered the cleaver, to block the flying glass or catch Zoli—

—Fekete ducked—

—and Kovács fired.

Two shots. The butcher first, then the chemist.

He aimed at Zoli, but the boy was too quick, running, zigging and zagging, and then disappearing out of sight.

The chemist lay where he fell, still holding his broom.

The butcher moaned.

Kovács stood over him. "You should have minded your own business," he said and fired the Walther one last time.

Kovács turned to Fekete, staring at him with his good eye. "And you. This is your fault, comrade. You should have been better prepared."

Fekete's eyes looked over Kovács's shoulder and widened. "Run."

Kovács twisted around. Zoli again, this time with a crowd.

Kovács and Fekete ran.

15
FIRST DRAFT

In the back of the signal truck, Charlie pulled one of the blankets around her for warmth and to help cushion the bumpiness of the ride. She dug in her bag for her reporter's notebook—at least she could get a head start on her story.

Péter was going to be the star—that much she already knew. A young medical student, risking his life to make a better future for his family and his county, and drop-dead gorgeous to boot—this story was going to practically write itself. All Charlie needed now was to see Péter in action. As her body swayed with the rhythm of the truck, she closed her eyes and began to draft her story, picturing it formatted like a radio script.

STORY TITLE	BLOOD KNOWS NO BORDERS
BYLINE	CHARLIE ATKINS
DATELINE	BUDAPEST, HUNGARY—NOV 3
NEWS READER	PÉTER ESZES, A HANDSOME YOUNG MEDICAL STUDENT, SHOULD BE STUDYING FOR FINAL EXAMS.

INSTEAD, THIS TWENTY-EIGHT-YEAR-OLD
HUNGARIAN IS TODAY A FREEDOM FIGHTER,
A HERO, SAVING LIVES ON THE FRONT
LINES OF HUNGARY'S DESPERATE FIGHT TO
FREE ITSELF FROM THE IRON GRIP OF ITS
SOVIET-IMPOSED REGIME.

WE MEET EARLY IN THE MORNING IN
THE SMALL AUSTRIAN BORDER TOWN OF
NICKELSDORF, THE LAST STOP BEFORE
ARRIVING AT NO MAN'S LAND AND THE
EDGE OF THE FREE WORLD. ON ANY OTHER
SATURDAY MORNING, THIS TINY VILLAGE
WOULD BE QUIET EXCEPT PERHAPS FOR
THOSE WALKING TO MASS. NOT TODAY.
TODAY, NICKELSDORF IS FILLED TO
BURSTING WITH THOUSANDS OF HUNGARIANS
CROSSING NO MAN'S LAND TO MAKE NEW
LIVES IN THE WEST. THESE NEW REFUGEES
ARE MET BY VOLUNTEERS OFFERING HOT
COFFEE, SANDWICHES, AND DIRECTIONS TO
THE TRANSPORT THAT WILL CARRY THEM
FARTHER INTO AUSTRIA, TO REST, FIND
SHELTER, AND BEGIN NEW LIVES.

BUT PÉTER—MATINEE-IDOL HANDSOME WITH
THICK, UNRULY CURLS AND TWINKLING
BLUE EYES—IS AMONG THE HUNGARIANS
WHO HOPE TO BUILD A NEW HUNGARY, ONE
GOVERNED BY AND FOR THE GOOD OF THE
HUNGARIAN PEOPLE. FOR ELEVEN DAYS
STRAIGHT, HE HAS EXTRACTED SHRAPNEL
AND STITCHED UP GUNSHOT WOUNDS IN A
MAKESHIFT HOSPITAL NEAR BUDAPEST'S
CORVIN CINEMA, WHERE THE FIGHTING
REMAINS FIERCEST. "I DO THIS WORK,"
PÉTER TELLS THIS REPORTER, "SO THAT
MY SON WILL GROW UP IN A FREE AND
DEMOCRATIC HUNGARY."

HE HAS DRIVEN THROUGH THE NIGHT TO
NICKELSDORF ON THE CHANCE HE MIGHT
FIND FRESH MEDICAL SUPPLIES—STERILE
BANDAGES, CLEAN SURGICAL TOOLS, WARM
BLANKETS—HERE AT THE AUSTRIAN BORDER.
HE FOUND THE MOST PRECIOUS COMMODITY
OF ALL, BLOOD PLASMA DONATED BY
ORDINARY WEST GERMANS THAT WILL SAVE
THE LIVES OF CRITICALLY INJURED
FREEDOM FIGHTERS AND CIVILIANS.

"TO THE GENEROUS PEOPLE OF MUNICH AND
THE WEST, I SAY THANK YOU. THIS BLOOD
IS A GIFT OF LIFE. IT TELLS US WE ARE
NOT ALONE IN OUR FIGHT, THAT WE ARE
NOT FORGOTTEN."

PÉTER SPEAKS, ONE HAND ON HIS HEART,
HIS EYES MOIST WITH EMOTION.

AS HE EMBARKS ON THE ONE HUNDRED-
TEN-MILE TRIP BACK TO THE HUNGARIAN
CAPITAL, EVERY INCH OF HIS BATTERED
OLD AMBULANCE IS FILLED WITH PLASMA.
HE IS, HE TELLS THIS REPORTER, FILLED
WITH HOPE: IN HIS COUNTRY'S DARKEST
HOUR, BLOOD KNOWS NO BORDERS.

PÉTER'S DESTINATION IS THE BUDAPEST
ACADEMY FOR BOYS—

Charlie stopped there. She couldn't write the rest of the story until she finished her reporting in Budapest. As the signal truck bumped along the road, she grinned. *Not bad*, she told herself.

Hungry, she fished out an apple from one of the baskets—it smelled sweet, like a late summer rose—and bit into it. She pulled out her map of Budapest and studied it with its long, tongue-twistingly named streets spiderwebbing out from both sides of the Danube River. She found the Hungarian Parliament without much trouble and circled it; it occupied a large swath of land overlooking the Danube on the Pest side of the river. She traced a path south to the circles Péter drew marking the Corvin Cinema and two blocks away the Budapest Academy for Boys. The cinema and the school were two miles or so from Parliament, Viktor's destination. A reasonable walk under ordinary circumstances, but not if there was active fighting. She needed to proceed carefully so that she could slip out of the back of the signal truck as close as she could get to the school without being seen by Viktor or anyone else.

Then, once her reporting was done, she would find a ride back to the border—there were bound to be plenty of ambulances like Péter's going west for supplies. She would meet Andy tonight by the oak tree and head home to Munich with him. Then for better or worse, her story would be on Owens's desk first thing Monday morning. Was she ready to face what came next? *I'm as ready as I'll ever be*, she thought as she finished her apple. *Maybe I can be as brave as Martha Gellhorn after all.*

16
SECRETS

nside the back of the signal truck, Charlie checked her watch. Its arrow-shaped art deco minute and hour hands formed a hard right angle above the single bright red star, fashioned from matching bits of ruby red glass. Nine A.M. How did her father, a farm boy from the dusty flats of the San Joaquin Valley, come to own such a watch? Charlie could only guess. Her grandparents, if they knew, never said.

The watch was her father's secret.

István Kovács, a gifted young Hungarian classical pianist, was hers. Their brief encounter haunted Charlie even now, four months later. She had told no one about it. Not even Sophie.

Charlie and István's paths crossed in Vienna, Austria's capital city, known for the music of Mozart and Bach, sweet, flaky *Apfelstrudel*, and the country's pledge to remain permanently neutral between East and West. Charlie had gone to Vienna on her own, chasing a potential story: an international piano competition pitting the best young classical performers from Russia and Eastern Europe against their Western counterparts. It was an irresistible matchup, especially given that for the first time an American was heavily favored to win. Charlie hoped to land an exclusive interview.

Instead, the prize went to a seventeen-year-old Hungarian unknown in the West. István dazzled the judges and the audience with a stunning performance of Beethoven's Sonata No. 29, the *Große Sonate für das Hammerklavier,* a piece so notoriously difficult that even the great Hungarian composer Franz Liszt, the first to play the piece in public, waited to do so only after Beethoven's death.

István played for almost forty minutes, entirely from memory, his long fingers flying over the keyboard, from the passionate arc of the opening *allegro* to the furious intensity of the final massive fugue. When he crashed to a thundering, magnificent close, sweating and exhausted, he rested his hands on his lap, barely acknowledging the ecstatic *bravos* from the audience. Even his American competitor, the one tipped to win the competition, applauded wildly in the wings before leaving the performance hall in tears without speaking to anyone, including Charlie. István disappeared, too, whisked offstage by a short man in a dark suit before the cheering stopped.

Charlie, disappointed to go home without a story, arrived early at the train station the next morning. *It's going to be a long ride back to Munich,* she thought, even as she marveled at the station's main hall. It was wide and spacious with a grand, bifurcated staircase leading up to a second-floor Italianate colonnade and lit by high clerestory windows and cast-iron lamps, their glass globes glowing, round and clear, like bubbles.

Her train was not due for another thirty minutes, so she sat down on a hard, high-backed wood chair, one of a dozen in a row. Across from her sat István, last night's white tie and tuxedo replaced by an expensive-looking suit perfectly tailored to fit his long, lean frame. He held a book, but he wasn't reading. His eyes—Charlie was close enough to see they were a deep ethereal blue—swept the station hall as if absorbing its every detail. Charlie recognized the man next to him who had so quickly ushered István offstage. His head swiveled constantly as he surveilled the waiting area.

I might as well be gracious, she thought. She didn't speak Hungarian or Russian, the lingua franca of Eastern Europe, so pantomime would have to do.

"*Bravo.*" Charlie smiled at István as she mimicked playing a piano. "You played beautifully."

István's eyes snapped to her and then flicked away. The man with István—short and stocky with a cinder-block build—looked at her, too. He stared hard and unblinking, his eyes black as bullet holes. He clamped one arm down on István's sleeve as if trapping him in place. Not a word was spoken, but Charlie got the message loud and clear: *Leave us alone.*

Geez, so much for diplomacy, she thought. She picked up her canvas bag and walked to a news kiosk for something to read, settling on the week's edition of *Der Spiegel* and a two-day-old copy of the Paris *Herald Tribune*. She headed out to the platform, to await the boarding announcement.

#   #   #

Aboard her train, she found her window seat. She tucked her canvas bag under her seat, her *Herald Tribune* within easy reach, and then settled back for the ride. She was alone; the carriage was empty but for the conductor shuffling down the narrow aisle toward her.

"Ticket, please," the conductor said. As he punched her ticket, Charlie silently counted the twin rows of brass buttons on his dark wool suit. There were sixteen buttons in all. Coarse silver hair poked out from under his railroad man's cap; his eyes, a pale, watery blue, looked tired. *Zugführer*— train conductor—Geisel, his name badge read. Geisel handed Charlie her ticket, and then he shuffled on to the next car.

A hiss, a grind, and the train began to move.

She looked out her window. István stood on the opposite platform, waiting to board a Budapest-bound train, along with his—what? Associate? Colleague? Certainly not a friend. *An odd pair of ducks*, she thought.

As she watched, István wheeled around and bolted. He ran, his long legs leaping in great bursting strides, his eyes on the nearest moving train. Charlie's train.

István's companion pivoted, too. He grabbed for István's coat but missed. He jogged after István with short, scampering steps.

István was younger and faster.

The young man ran alongside Charlie's train. His eyes locked on hers for an instant. She stared back. *Are you mad*, she wanted to scream. Her words stuck in her throat.

István's eyes flew to the train carriage door. He lunged—

—Charlie rose to her feet—

—István landed with a *slap! bang!* on the carriage door's bottom step. He hooked his arm around the brass door handle and pounded on the carriage door to force it open.

She pushed the door open from the inside, and István flung himself inside the train.

"What are you doing?" she asked, astonished.

"Escaping, of course," he said in crisp, accented English. His face glowed; he was breathing hard. He twisted around to look out through the window for the second man, but he was not in sight.

"By leaping onto a moving train?"

"It worked, didn't it?" István grinned at Charlie. "Please, *Fräulein*, sit down. I didn't mean to be rude in the station, but my minder doesn't allow me to speak to foreigners."

He waited until Charlie perched herself on the edge of a seat before dropping himself down opposite her, his long legs splayed out in front of him.

"Your minder?" Charlie was still processing István's risky leap onto the train. Up close, he looked like a schoolboy, his pale skin smooth and unwhiskered, and his sandy blond hair blunt-cut short. "That's the man who was with you?"

"Tibor, yes. My father sends him with me everywhere I go. Bloody awful man." István put a hand on his chest as though his heart might be beating too fast. "But now I can speak to anyone. Who are you? You are British?"

"American. I'm Charlie Atkins from Radio Free Europe."

István's eyebrows shot up in surprise. "Are you? How exciting to meet you! We are forbidden to listen to your radio but of course we all do."

He barely paused, his words tumbling out one after another, like a dam burst open. "Jazz is forbidden, too. Too subversive, but my friends and I listen every chance we get. Duke Ellington, Charlie Mingus, Miles Davis, Charlie Parker, I have all of their recordings. Black market, of course."

His eyes shone. He fished a book out of his pocket and held it up—it was a well-thumbed guide to New York City. "When I get to New York, the first thing I'm going to do is go to every jazz club I can."

Charlie couldn't help smiling; István's excitement was catching. "Not classical music?"

István waved breezily, as if still catching his breath. "That, too. But jazz—that's the thing." His eyes flicked up over Charlie's shoulder.

Then his face paled. He shrank back against his seat.

Tibor—breathing hard and his eyes burning—grabbed István by the collar.

The young man held tight to his seat, his book forgotten on the seat beside him.

Tibor pried István's left hand loose and leaned menacingly into his face, the muscles under the minder's skin rippling with rage. He gripped István's fingers vise-like and squeezed, the jaws of a fox about to snap the bones of a dove.

István cried out in soft, agonizing pain.

Charlie grabbed Tibor's arm. "Hey, you can't do that—"

Tibor swept the back of one hand against the side of her head. *Whack*! She slammed back against her seat. Her head banged on the seat, making her see stars. Her cheek burned.

Tibor used István's trapped hand to pull him to his feet. The minder reached for the train's brake chain and yanked it once. The train jerked hard to a stop.

István's eyes were wet. "Help me. Don't let him take me back."

Charlie, stunned, didn't—couldn't—move.

Tibor shoved István down the carriage steps, off the train. He let go of the young man's hand but kept a firm grip on his collar.

István, hunched over, didn't resist.

Conductor Geisel appeared in the aisle, his face red. "Who pulled the brake?"

Charlie, her head buzzing, pointed out the open door toward Tibor, struggling to focus and form words. "The short man. He made the other man get off the train."

The conductor leaned out of the open door to look. He frowned. "They did not have tickets."

"You must do something." Charlie pulled herself up unsteadily and sank into her seat. The back of her head felt tender and bruised. István's abandoned guide to New York lay on the opposite seat. "He forgot his book."

Geisel barely glanced at it. "What? What must I do? They are not on the train. They are not my problem."

"Sit down," he snapped as he headed up the aisle to the next car. "We are already late."

With a jolt, the train started again. Charlie picked up István's book and then pressed up against the window. Outside, István and Tibor receded into the distance toward the train to Budapest and whatever punishment awaited István there. Tucked inside the guidebook was István's blue Hungarian passport. She opened it—István's black-and-white photograph stared stoically back, above his home address written in exacting, slanting handwriting. *His hands*, she thought. *He went back rather than allow his hands to be damaged. What an awful choice.*

She slipped István's guidebook and passport into her canvas bag. Then she closed her eyes and tried not to think. István had been snatched off a train in Austria in broad daylight. No one helped him. Least of all her.

#   #   #

She considered—briefly—writing a story about István but quickly reconsidered. Doing so might make things worse for him. She searched Radio Free Europe's archives and found a short profile on István written six months earlier. Mária translated it for her. István was spotted young, taught by Hungary's finest, and musically, was expected to achieve greatness.

Mária paused at the mention of István's father, András Kovács.

"He is the head of the AVO," Mária said darkly, "and the most hated man in Hungary."

Still, when Charlie found István's debut classical recording in a stall in Munich's black market, she dipped into her precious savings and bought it. For weeks, she listened to it over and over on a phonograph borrowed from her landlady. If she ever got the chance, she promised herself that she would do her best to find István. She wanted—needed—to know he was okay and to tell him how sorry she was she hadn't been able to help him.

#   #   #

Now, hidden in the back of Viktor's signal truck, Charlie wondered if she might have a chance to make good on that promise. She studied her map with István's passport in hand, searching until she found the name of the street where he lived. She circled it and then tucked the passport and the map back into her bag.

Suddenly, the truck stopped. Outside, she heard rough, hard shouts and a sharp *rat-a-tat-tat* on the cab door. Somebody wanted something. *Now.* And whoever it was didn't sound friendly.

The cab door scraped open; the weight of the truck shifted. Viktor was already speaking in that deep, persuasive cadence so familiar to regular Radio Free Europe listeners. *Victor Farkas, a Szabad Magyarország hangja, a Rádió Szabad Európa*, he was saying. Viktor Farkas, Voice of Free Hungary, Radio Free Europe. At once, everything changed. The voices turned welcoming. The roadblock belonged to Hungarian freedom fighters.

Viktor's voice sounded dangerously close.

She needed to hide.

She lifted one of the draped blankets. Underneath was a shortwave radio set, complete down to its transmitter, receiver, and push-to-talk microphone. It was fixed to a narrow metal table bolted to the side of the truck. There was no place to hide underneath the table either—that space was taken up by a sizeable bench nearly as big as the table and filled with coiled antenna wire, replacement components, and tools—wire cutters, a hammer, three screwdrivers, a soldering iron plus the shortwave's operator's manual, printed in English.

Viktor had a secret, too, it seemed.

The doors opened, and light flooded into the back of the truck. Viktor, silhouetted against the dull winter sky, stared at Charlie, the blanket still in her hand, at first in shock and then in fear. He shook his head as if to warn her: *Stay quiet!*

Charlie didn't move.

Viktor snatched up an armload of bread and cigarettes and slammed the doors shut again. Outside the truck, Charlie heard sounds of appreciation.

The weight of the truck shifted again. Viktor started the engine. The truck jerked forward. He was clearly in a hurry.

17
BARGAIN

A mile down the road, the truck wrenched to a stop again. Charlie was already moving. She hopped out of the back of the truck, her bag over her shoulder. She hurried forward, past an ancient tractor chugging westward and pulling an oxcart filled with anxious faces. The sensible, thin-soled flat loafers that had seemed so practical when she'd put them on the night before crunched on the slick, icy road.

The truck lurched alongside her.

"Are you mad?" Viktor hissed from the driver's seat. "Get in. There could be patrols anywhere."

"So you can dump me back at the border?" Only a hundred yards so far, and Charlie's feet were already freezing. "No thanks."

The truck jerked forward ahead of her. Viktor hard-reversed to keep pace. "It's too dangerous for you to be here. Do you know what I learned from the men at that roadblock? Three days ago, more than fifty peaceful protesters were massacred in the village of Mosonmagyaróvár, not more than five kilometers from here. Women and children are among the dead. The AVO do not discriminate."

Charlie sucked in her breath. Fifty dead, in one small town? No family would be left untouched.

"I'm sorry, Viktor," she said. "That's terrible news. But if it is too dangerous for me to be here, then it is dangerous for you, too, and I don't see you turning back."

"I am different," he snapped. He revved the truck too far forward again and jammed on the brakes to slow it down. "I have work to do."

"So do I."

"What? What work do you have to do that can be so important?" The truck crawled along beside her. "This nonsense story of yours is worth nothing."

"Given your country's history with the Nazis, you of all people should understand why it matters. West Germans donating blood to support Hungarian freedom fighters shows that people and countries can change for the better. You said it yourself. I won't be a real journalist unless the stories I write matter. Well, this one *does*." Charlie stepped over a child's mitten frozen to the rimy ground. "What's with the stuff in the back of the truck?"

"Humanitarian supplies. For Hungarians in need."

"Since when is shortwave gear considered a humanitarian need?"

Viktor shifted the truck's gears. The engine groaned. "You must not ask such questions. You are not authorized to know these things."

"Out here, I'd say that hardly matters." Charlie's breath puffed out in front of her like cold smoke. The hard winter sun hurt her eyes, and her feet felt numb. "Budapest is off limits to anyone on the news staff, so the shortwave gear isn't from Mr. Owens. That means your 'work,' whatever it is, is not for Radio

Free Europe. And a shortwave set like that one must cost a fortune, even assuming you could find it on the black market."

"This is not your concern." Viktor's voice held a new note: the sound of caution.

"Maybe you're a spy." Charlie tried to clench her teeth to keep them from chattering. "Are you a sp-sp-sp-spy, Viktor?"

"Do not be foolish. You are cold. Get in." Viktor backed up again—or at least he tried. The engine sputtered, whined, and then died. Viktor turned the key. Nothing.

Charlie kept walking.

Viktor turned the key again. The ignition clicked, but the engine did not start. He tried again. Still nothing.

Charlie turned around. Viktor sat in the cab of the truck, frowning at the dashboard. "The engine is flooded," she said.

"I see." Viktor didn't move.

"Well?"

"Well what?"

"Aren't you going to do anything?"

"What would you suggest? I am not a mechanic."

"Pop the hood."

Viktor's frown deepened. "I do not know how."

Charlie walked back to the truck. She opened the cab door and pointed. "Pull that lever."

Viktor did. The truck's front hood popped open.

Charlie stepped up on the front bumper and propped the hood up, grateful for the engine's warmth. She sniffed. Gasoline. "Find me a rag, will you?"

Viktor brought a scrap of cloth from the back of the truck and watched Charlie unscrew and remove the air filter. She peered down into the carburetor and then wiped the rim clean with the rag.

"You are certain you know what you are doing?" Viktor asked, his voice hesitant.

"When you grow up on a farm like I did, you learn to fix pretty much anything." Charlie eyed the rest of the engine. Everything else looked fine; the truck was just old, probably fresh out of long-term storage somewhere, and jerking the truck back and forth had flooded the carburetor. As soon as the extra fuel evaporated, the engine would fire right up. Not that Viktor needed to know that all he needed to do was wait it out. "I can get the truck going but in return I want a ride to Budapest in the front seat—and the real scoop on what you're doing here. Otherwise, we can both freeze to death walking to Budapest."

Viktor opened his mouth and then closed it.

Beep-beep-beep! An Army Jeep swung around the corner, horn blaring, and came into view. Hilly from the *Sunday Times* sat in the passenger's seat, dapper in a fine wool coat and a cashmere scarf. Haversham, Hilly's ever-present shadow, sat in the back, behind the driver.

Charlie smiled and waved. "Hey, b-b-b-boys, over here!"

Viktor's tone suddenly changed. "Please, you must say nothing of this matter to them."

"Do we have a deal?" Charlie kept smiling despite her chattering teeth.

"If you can get the truck going, then yes, yes, you have my word," Viktor said hurriedly. He disappeared around the side of the vehicle.

Hilly's Jeep pulled up. Charlie, still balanced on the truck's front bumper, could barely feel her toes.

"Charlie? What the devil are you doing here?" Hilly peered at her over the rims of his horn-rimmed glasses. "Has Owens lost his mind, sending you out here? This is no place for a girl."

"Going to Budapest. You, too?"

"We've just been—heading back to Munich."

"The revolution isn't over, is it?"

"The Hungarian people think they have carried the day—they are practically dancing in the streets. Too soon really, to say how this business will all turn out. Khrushchev is an unpredictable sort, wouldn't you say, Haversham?"

"Quite right, quite right." Haversham's head bobbled up and down.

"Viktor, is that you?" Hilly said as Viktor reappeared, carrying thick wool socks and a pair of plain black boots. "What the devil do you mean, bringing Charlie out here?"

"I wish you luck trying to say no to Miss Atkins," Viktor said. He handed the socks and boots to Charlie. "Put these on."

Charlie jumped down and sat on the bumper. She pulled one wool sock on, and then the other one. *Ah, warmth,* she thought gratefully, and she wiggled her toes to get her circulation going again.

"Hungary is old news, Charlie—the story is practically over," Hilly said. "The Suez Canal is under attack. War in the Middle East over who controls the world's supply of oil—now *that* is front-page stuff. The world has moved on." Hilly jerked a nod toward the Jeep's backseat. "Come back to Munich with us—we have plenty of room, haven't we, Haversham? I'll have a word with Owens on your behalf. Straighten things right out for you."

Haversham was already nodding. "Plenty of room," he said, and patted the seat next to him. "Come along then, that's a good little girl."

Charlie took her time slipping on the boots. They were a little too big but an improvement over her thin loafers. Then she looked up, wearing her best over-my-dead-body smile, the one with no shred of humor or warmth. "Thanks, boys, but I can take care of myself. And no need to talk to Mr. Owens. We have an understanding. I can write any story I want, as long as it is on my own time. So, no, I am not going back to Munich with you."

"Viktor," Hilly demanded, "are you going to allow this?"

"Miss Atkins appears quite capable of making up her own mind," Viktor said. He climbed back into the truck cab. "Regardless of what you or I may think."

"See you back in Munich, boys," Charlie said. She waggled her fingers at them and watched as Hilly and Haversham drove off. Then she hopped back up on the bumper. She checked the engine: the smell of gasoline was gone. She dropped the hood back into place.

"Put the truck in neutral and then pump the engine," she said. Then she climbed up in the cab and slammed the door shut.

Viktor didn't move. He stared at her, his eyes narrowed. "This 'understanding' you have with Mr. Owens. Does he have any idea where you are at this moment?"

On the other side of the road, a car filled with young men and women drove into view. They were singing and waving Hungarian flags, and as they rolled past the truck, they waved and shouted: "*Üdvözöljük a Szabad Magyarországban! Welcome to Free Hungary!*"

Charlie waved back. "Look at them. Aren't they the reason we are both here? To tell the world that Hungarians are brave enough to fight for their freedom?"

She tucked her feet up, cross-legged on the seat, one arm propped on the transfusion kit Péter had given her that morning. "As for Mr. Owens, I agreed only that I would not apply again for the news staff. In the meantime, I write the stories I want and leave them on his desk. So far, every single one has wound up on the air. So yes, I say we understand each other just fine."

"And?"

"And what? Does he know where I am? No, but you already know that. Mr. Owens sent me home. As long as I show up on time to make coffee first thing Monday, what I do on my own time is none of Mr. Owens's business. Or yours." She looked straight ahead, her jaw firm. "I kept my word. You should keep yours. Shall we go?"

Viktor still did not move. "That watch of yours. With the red star. It is Russian, is it not? I find it repugnant."

"This watch belonged to my father. Or at least, it was sent home with his personal belongings. And before you ask, no, I don't know why he had it. But it was his, and I wear to remember him."

Viktor said nothing. He twisted a silver ring he wore on one finger and stared out the window at the barren landscape—low shrubs and bare trees, frosted by light snow. Finally, he pumped the engine, and turned the key, his face tight. The truck's engine roared back to life. He pulled back out onto the road, past a bleary-eyed woman carrying a toddler on her back as she trudged west, too exhausted to notice Charlie and Viktor.

Charlie kept her eyes facing forward toward Budapest. In her new boots, her feet felt warm. Hilly might think the story in Budapest was over, and Viktor might be right—she didn't know what to expect in a war zone. But she was not about to turn back to Munich either. If the Hungarian people indeed carried the day, a new democracy was about to be born. *War stories*, Charlie thought, *don't get much better than this one.*

18
ROUTE 1 TO BUDAPEST

C harlie sat cross-legged on the front seat and listened as
Viktor spoke, her eyes narrowed. They were on Route
1, the main road connecting Nickelsdorf to Budapest, a
hundred and ten miles of red-roofed villages, fallow wheat,
corn and sunflower fields, and the occasional town of size such
as Győr, twenty miles ahead. Viktor had promised to tell her
the truth. So far, Charlie wasn't sure she believed him.

"Three days ago, a man came to see me in Munich," Viktor
said. His hands rested on the steering wheel, where his silver
signet ring caught the light. "He said Mr. Owens gave him my
name, and he asked if I would be willing to help the American
government understand the Hungarian situation."

"Did he give you his name?"

"Cordell Tanner. I am sure I have seen him before, at the
American Consulate in Munich." Viktor glanced at Charlie.
"Perhaps you have seen him, too. You would remember his
eyes. One is blue, the other is brown."

Charlie shook her head. "Sorry. I'd remember, but no."

"Mr. Tanner told me that there are important people
in America who want to help us, but they need accurate

intelligence from someone on the ground in Budapest. Who's in charge in Budapest? Who's leading the revolution? Is Nagy too close to Moscow? Who speaks for the people? Who can be trusted?"

"Someone like you."

"Of course, someone like me. Who better? I understand Hungarian politics intimately. My listeners trust me completely. Why shouldn't your government?"

"Why didn't this Tanner work through our embassy?"

"There is no American embassy in Budapest, only a legation. A legation is much smaller and much less consequential. And your legation has been without an ambassador for many months. Your new consul arrived in Budapest only one day ago. There is no one else there on official American business except a low-ranking *chargé d'affaires*." Viktor's voice was stern. "If you want to be taken seriously as a journalist, Miss Atkins, you must know these things."

Charlie ignored Viktor's scolding—Budapest and her first byline from a cold war hot zone were too close. She could see his breath as he spoke, small puffs of warm air through his broken teeth. His sentences were complete, but his words seemed carefully chosen, as if to keep himself from saying too much.

"The Security Council hasn't even discussed Hungary yet—the Russians won't allow it," Charlie said. "But you said yes to this Tanner anyway."

"Of course. There is nothing I would not do for my country. It is Mr. Tanner who arranged for this truck to be left for me at the border."

"And the shortwave gear?"

"Yes, that also." Viktor kept his eyes on the road ahead. "As soon as we arrive in Budapest, I am to send word to Mr. Tanner and provide to him my initial impression of the situation."

"Which is?"

"That Hungarians have had enough. You cannot understand what life is like for us under the Communists. They are spiders that crawl into every corner of our lives. They take over everything—the banks, the police, the newspapers, the schools, the way we farm, the way we think, what we are free to say to one another. In Moscow, they draw up plans— three-year plans, five-year plans—and force our farmers onto state farms to grow wheat or sunflowers or apples for Russian tables while we cannot feed ourselves. We freeze in the winter because there is no coal for heat, yet we are told day after day how much better life is under communism. Our children must learn Russian and are rewarded for turning in their parents or anyone else who dares to disagree. Even our priests must take an oath of loyalty to the state or risk arrest. The head of our church, Cardinal Mindszenty, was tortured and sent to prison for life because he fought back. He is free right now, today, in Budapest, only because we, the Hungarian people, have had enough."

"And you believe Nagy will be a better leader for Hungary?" Charlie asked.

"I do. You can see already that important change is happening and why this moment of our history is so delicate. Nagy is making good decisions—but will the Kremlin accept them? If Poland and Hungary can break free, why can't Czechoslovakia? Or Romania? That is why this hour of our history is so important. We are close to taking back our country.

With Mr. Tanner's help and with American tanks and troops, we will send the Russians back to Moscow for good."

"What about Radio Free Europe?"

"I have resigned from Radio Free Europe," Viktor said. "I cannot risk being associated with the radio, and the radio cannot risk being associated with me. I must be seen to have returned to Hungary of my own free will. I can tell you only that whatever happens, I will remain in Budapest. I will not leave my country again."

The Hungarian radio service without Viktor? *His listeners might miss him*, Charlie thought, *but I most decidedly will not.*

"Is it true you spent time in prison?" she asked.

Viktor paused. "You are too direct, Miss Atkins," he said finally. "There are some questions you should not ask."

Charlie turned and looked out of the window. Thatched-roofed cottages and flat farmland were giving way to the outskirts of Győr, an old city founded in the fifth century BC at the confluence of the Rába, Rábca, and Danube Rivers. During the war, Győr's factories churned out tank engines, airplanes, even wool for the uniforms of Soviet armored troops until Allied bombers came through. They were driving past what was left of those factories, a wasteland of skeletal brickwork raw from exposure and abandoned machinery too damaged even for scrap.

Viktor changed the subject. "Tell me where it is in Budapest you wish to go."

Charlie pulled out her map. She tapped the spot Péter had circled only hours earlier. "There is a makeshift hospital here, near the Corvin Cinema. That is where the fighting is supposed to be at its heaviest."

Viktor glanced down at her map. "And the other circle? What is that?"

She hesitated. How much should she say? "Someone I came in contact with lives there. Not someone I actually really know, but if Hungary is truly free, I would like to know that he is okay."

"That is District V. Belváros-Lipótváros. I know this part of Budapest very well. Perhaps I know this person."

Charlie paused. "His name is István Kovács. He is—"

"Yes, yes, I know—the classical pianist," Viktor said impatiently. "You cannot be alive in Hungary and not know István Kovács. He is young and gifted. He also has a very dangerous father. A Hungarian, who prefers to serve the Soviets by torturing and murdering his countrymen. You came into contact with István? How? Where was this?"

"I didn't meet him, not really." She spoke slowly as she thought back to that June evening in Vienna. "I saw him perform at an international competition in Vienna. An American was favored to take first prize. I thought it was a good story—East versus West. Instead, István won—he was absolutely brilliant."

Viktor listened intently.

"I saw István again the following morning at the train station," Charlie continued. "There was a man with him, like a guard. His name was Tibor. István called him his minder. As they waited for their train to Budapest, István ran away from Tibor and got on my train, which was already moving. He was trying to escape, but his minder caught up with him."

Charlie swallowed hard, remembering the terror in István's blue eyes when he realized he had no choice but to return to

Hungary with Tibor. "Tibor forced István to change his mind by crushing the bones in his hands. For someone like István, with so much talent, that must have been frightening."

She cleared her throat. "István had no choice but to get off the train with Tibor. That was the last I saw of him." She showed Viktor István's passport. "He left this behind on the train. That is how I know where he lives."

Viktor's expression shifted. "You are certain of all of this? That he wished to defect? Why did he not go to the border like so many others are doing?"

"This happened four months ago—before the revolution when the border was still sealed." Her stomach churned at the memory of Tibor pushing István off the train. "He said his minder went everywhere with him. István begged not to be returned to Hungary. He said he was afraid of being punished by his father."

"Who else knows about this?"

"No one. I was afraid if I said something, I might make matters worse for István."

For a long moment, Viktor was silent. Around them, the ruined factories gave way to winding cobbled streets that led into Győr's downtown.

"István benefits from our rotten system," he said at last. His voice sounded bitter. "Yes, he is talented, but his father is also powerful. As long as he plays for the glory of the Soviet state, he has access to anything he wants or needs—the best teachers, the best instruments. Time and money to study. Permission to travel. Leaving all of that behind would be a great deal to give up."

"Yet many people do. Including you."

"It is not at all the same." He shot a quick glance at Charlie, his blue eyes bright. "What you do not understand, what you can never understand, is that I left Hungary not to live in comfort somewhere else. I left to fight so that all Hungarians can live like free men. Every day, I live two lives—one in Munich, doing what I can to keep my countrymen strong, and the other in the Budapest of my memories, the proud, beautiful city she once was. Now my parents are dead. There is no one else left in my family line."

Viktor held out his hand to Charlie. His silver ring, Charlie saw now, was forged in the shape of a wolf's head, its etched expression at once wise and wary. "You have your father's watch. I have my father's ring. 'Farkas,' my family name, is Hungarian for *wolf*. This ring is all I have left. The Russians took everything else. That is why I fight and why I will never leave Hungary again."

"What happens if the Russians don't leave? Or if you are arrested?"

"I am on my own. Mr. Tanner will not help me. Radio Free Europe will not help me. The Americans will not help me. That is why you cannot remain with me."

"Don't worry," she said. "Once we're in Budapest, you go your way, and I'll go mine."

"Yes, yes, I look forward to that as well. But it is not so simple. You will need my help."

Charlie opened her mouth, but Viktor continued to speak. "No, not with this foolish story you insist must be written. But you don't speak Hungarian, you don't know the city, you don't know who to trust. I will take you to your hospital. I will contact Mr. Tanner while you report your story. You will remain with me until you have a safe way to return home.

Then—" Viktor gestured—"go. I will remain in Budapest, awaiting the arrival of your American troops."

"Assuming they come. You heard Mr. Owens. No one wants to risk nuclear world war with the Reds over Hungary."

"Every day, Radio Free Europe tells my people that the West stands with us," Viktor snapped. "All we must do is be brave enough to stand up and show we are willing to fight for our freedom. Now we have done it."

Viktor rounded a curve, and suddenly, the landscape changed. Gracious old mansions painted red or yellow or green lined cobblestoned streets. Freshly printed posters hung everywhere, advertising new political parties. Hungarian national flags, the red Soviet stars ripped from the center of every single one, fluttered from nearly every window. Trams and buses were running. As they neared the main square, Charlie spotted a familiar face from Munich: Jerome, from *Agence France-Presse*, three Leica cameras hanging around his neck. She rolled down her window. The air smelled sweet, perfumed by the sweet buttery char of roasted chestnuts.

The people looked different too. *There is only one word to describe it*, Charlie thought.

Hopeful.

Hopeful that after eleven years, Soviet rule was over. Győr was celebrating. Hungary was nearly free.

19
WELCOME TO FREE GYŐR

Viktor held up a pile of newspapers to Charlie and Jerome, who stood with them in the cold morning light.

"Look at these," he said. Viktor's face glowed, his jagged teeth bared in a rare smile. "For years, our newspapers have all printed the same communist propaganda. These papers are all different. There are many points of view—socialist, labor, communist, peasant. Real news—new political parties forming, workers negotiating for better wages, many ideas about reshaping our economy to benefit us instead of the Russians. This is what Free Hungary looks like."

For most of an hour, Charlie, Viktor, and Jerome—chain smoking and in need of a shave—had walked around Széchenyi Square, Győr's eighteenth-century town center, a grassy plaza nestled amid honey-colored baroque houses and sinewy, winding waterways. They shared a bag of roasted chestnuts. Viktor stopped frequently to read freshly hung posters. Trailing them everywhere they went, Charlie noticed, was an old man accompanied by a small girl.

The old man watched as Charlie nodded at the front page of the newspaper Viktor held. She recognized Nagy, plump and bespectacled, but not the much taller man, grinning proudly alongside the prime minister. "Who is that with Nagy?"

"That is Pal Maléter. Colonel Maléter. He is a war hero, and now he has joined our fight. Nagy has named him our new minister of defense."

"*Bocsáss meg.*" The old man stepped forward, the girl's hand in his. His white hair was combed straight back from his wide forehead, and he stood tall, his posture erect. He shared the same dark, deep-set eyes and strong jawline with the girl; both wore tricolor armbands tied around their coat sleeves. "*Nem tudtam nem hallani a hangodat,*" he said. "*Ön a Szabad Európa Rádiótól származik?*"

Viktor smiled. "My voice has been recognized," he said happily. To the old man, he replied, "*Igen, Viktor Farkas, a Szabad Európa Rádió.*"

The old man's face lit up. He embraced Viktor—a kiss on each cheek, then a two-handed shake.

"This is Ferenc Varga, but he says everyone calls him Zacis, for Uncle. A term of respect—many years ago he was the mayor of Győr," Viktor translated for Charlie and Jerome. "And this is his granddaughter, Zuzu."

Viktor spoke with Uncle in rapid, tumbling Hungarian.

Zuzu eyed Charlie from the safety of behind her grandfather's legs. Charlie waved and fished one of her chocolate bars out of her bag. She broke off a piece and offered it to Zuzu, who stayed firmly put behind her grandfather. She peeked out at Charlie. Charlie popped the chocolate in her mouth. She broke off another piece and tried again, holding it out to Zuzu. This time, Zuzu tugged on her grandfather's sleeve until he nodded—*yes, okay.* Zuzu took the chocolate, tasted it cautiously, and then smiled.

Charlie smiled back at Zuzu. "What is Uncle saying?" she asked Viktor.

"He says there are many rumors," Viktor said. "Prime Minister Nagy seems hopeful about the talks with the Soviets—they have promised to withdraw all of their troops. But there are also rumors of troops and tanks gathering at the Czech border, and no one knows why they are there. Our new minister of defense is leading another round of negotiations tonight."

Charlie broke off another piece of candy for Zuzu. This time, the girl took the chocolate quickly, her big eyes never leaving Charlie's face.

"You have made a friend," Jerome said as he took a picture. He switched cameras for a second shot.

"What's with all the different cameras?" Charlie asked.

"So I can get different shots—near, far—and so I don't have to reload film under pressure. See if she will sit on your lap."

Charlie patted her lap, and Zuzu sidled up next to her.

"Nice," Jerome said, his cigarette in the corner of his mouth, as he took Charlie's picture. "Very maternal. *Une mère naturelle*."

"Uncle says the citizens have taken control of the city government from the communists," Viktor said. "The farmers are already talking amongst themselves about what they want to grow next year. No more taking orders from central planners in Moscow."

Charlie gave the last bit of candy to Zuzu. Then she folded the candy bar's smooth white glassine wrapper against her knee, fashioning it into a simple paper airplane. She tossed it into the air. It looped once and fell to earth. Zuzu laughed as she picked it up and brought it back to Charlie.

"You like that, do you?" Charlie said, and she tossed the airplane again. This time, something caught her eye. A tiny dot in the sky. She squinted. It was a plane, and it was moving fast.

Suddenly Viktor burst out laughing.

"What's so funny?" she asked, her eyes on the plane.

"Uncle says the Russians are demanding a parade to see them off, with full military honors." Viktor grinned, delighted. "I can guarantee their request will be granted. We cannot see the back of them too soon."

Jerome grinned, too. "Your whole country will turn out to see that."

"Ma halottainkat gyászoljuk." Uncle shook his head, a sour expression on his face. *"Hamarosan meglátjuk, hogy ezek a szemétládák hagyják-e felépíteni saját országunkat."*

"He says, 'Today, we mourn our dead,'" Viktor translated. "'Soon we will see if those bastards will let us build our own country.'"

"He doesn't sound optimistic," Charlie said, her eyes still on the plane. Its nose was down. So was the landing gear.

"He says he has lived too long to be optimistic."

"Hey, Viktor, ask Uncle if there is an airport near here."

"There is—Tököl Military Base, on Csepel Island, in the middle of the Danube," Viktor said. "Maybe a hundred kilometers from here. Why?"

She nodded at the sky. "See that plane?" Its wings dipped and quivered, as if the pilot were struggling to keep the plane level. "I don't hear engine noise. I think it's in trouble."

Viktor's eyes followed the plane's trajectory. Jerome and Uncle watched as well.

Charlie squinted. The plane was close now, close enough to see the single red star. "Holy smokes, is that—"

"A MiG—*oui, oui*, it is," Jerome finished her sentence.

The plane sped past them and then disappeared below the sightline of the buildings lining the square.

Viktor and Charlie scrambled into the truck. Jerome hopped up on one running board, his arm over his cameras to keep them safe. Without asking, Uncle scooped up Zuzu and stepped on the other one.

"If there are MiGs here, it means bombers are coming, too." Viktor's face was white as he shoved the truck into gear. "It means that the Russians have no intention of keeping their word. They do not intend to leave Hungary. They intend to kill us."

20
HUNGARIAN BLOOD RUNS COLD, MISS ATKINS. AS IT SHOULD.

Viktor rolled the truck to a stop.

The MiG had landed outside the city proper, on a long, rime-slicked field fallow for the winter. A single five-pointed star winked out from the hull like a blood-red evil eye. Its identification number was painted near the tail in large bold red letters.

Jerome was already running toward the plane, one hand against his chest to hold his cameras in place. Charlie, Viktor, and Uncle, holding Zuzu, followed.

Ten yards from the plane, everyone stopped.

The MiG's exterior navigation and landing lights blinked off. Then: *click! whir! whoosh!* Its electrical systems shut down next.

Silence followed, except for the faint hum of traffic behind them from Győr.

A *clank*. A *creak*. The hatch popped open just wide enough for an arm to appear. It slowly waved a white cloth the size of a man's pocket handkerchief.

A moment later, the hatch opened all the way. A man stood in the cockpit. He waved his handkerchief again, back and forth. Then he looped his legs over the edge of the cockpit and dropped seven feet to the ground. He faced Jerome, Charlie, Viktor, Uncle, and Zuzu, and waved his handkerchief again—big, wide gestures as if to make sure he was seen. Then the man turned back to the plane, hands up toward the cockpit.

A second, much smaller head popped up next.

"*Mon Dieu*," Jerome muttered as he raised his camera. "A child."

Mon Dieu is right, Charlie thought. *And what a story.*

The child—a boy in short pants—lowered himself over the edge of the cockpit, dangling for a moment, then dropped into the man's arms. Together they faced the gathering. Zuzu peeked out from behind her grandfather's legs.

The man and the boy dropped to their knees in front of the MiG. The man still held the handkerchief, but now his other arm rested on the boy's shoulder. They were both wiry and compact, whippet-thin mirror images of each other. The boy wore a knit vest over a plain white button-up shirt, long socks, and scuffed, sturdy-looking shoes, as if heading off to school. The man wore old, greased-stained clothes, with a name patch that read *H. Horst*.

Jerome knelt and switched cameras to take a wide-angle shot, capturing the man, the child, and behind them, the MiG.

"Please do not shoot. We wish to defect," the man called out in German. "We are not Russian. We are *Ost Deutsch*. East German. I am Hans Horst. I am not a pilot, I am a mechanic. This is my son, Walter."

"*Amerikanisch*," Charlie shouted back, grateful that she had worked on her German. "Where did you come from?

"Tököl Air Base."

"What happened to your plane?"

"Not enough fuel." The man licked his lips nervously as his eyes flicked over their shoulders.

Charlie turned. A small crowd from Győr was gathering, their faces and their voices angry. *Just like the day Annie left on that bus to the internment camp*, Charlie thought, *only this time, the crowd is armed.* One man wore a tommy gun strapped across his chest while another one carried a length of thick rope. A third man, a farmer, jabbed the air with a pitchfork.

"What are they saying?" Charlie asked.

"They are arguing over what with to do with him," Viktor translated. "Kill him right now, put him on trial, or keep him as a hostage in hopes that the Soviets pay to have him back."

"We can't let them do that."

"This man is the enemy, Miss Atkins. He knew the risks the moment he got in that plane. We do not have to stay and watch what happens, but Mr. Tanner must know about this at once. This is very bad news. If there are MiGs, there will be bombers, too."

"We can't leave him here. He is asking for our help—and I bet he has information that can help you and your Mr. Tanner, if you take the time to talk to him," Charlie said. "Remember that North Korean pilot a couple of years ago? He flew his MiG right into Kimpo Airbase in South Korea. We got a real good look at a MiG, and that pilot is now an American citizen." She nodded toward the crowd. "Talk to them. Make them understand that he is surrendering."

Uncle watched Charlie and Viktor, a slight frown on his face. Jerome took pictures: the crowd, Horst and his son on their knees, Charlie, arguing with Viktor.

"And if they let the pilot go, then what?" Viktor snapped. "Tell him to walk to Austria? He will never make it." Suddenly his eyes narrowed. "I see. This is a story to you."

"Of course it's a story! A Red Army pilot defects? Sure, that's front-page news. But it's not my story to tell—it's his, and right now all I care about is two lives." Charlie thought fast. "Look, Viktor, we don't know when—or if—American troops will come. As soon as I finish my story, I'll leave for Munich—in this truck. If Horst wants to come with me, I will take him. And yes, if he agrees, I'll interview him. But first, I'd like to save his life. Both their lives."

"You cannot trust this man. He is a stranger to you. You do not know what he is capable of doing. And if you are stopped—do you have any idea how much trouble you will be in if you are found with a defecting Soviet pilot?" Viktor demanded.

"*If* I am stopped. Besides, I don't need your permission. Just the signal truck. Which, may I remind you, is technically the property of the US government."

"And what do these people tell the Russians when they come looking for their pilot and his plane? Because the Russians *will* come looking, I am certain of it, and they will make life a living hell for these people if they do not find him."

"Why not ask them? Or is the chance to make a new life in the West a privilege reserved only for Hungarians?"

Viktor flushed. "You do not understand what you are asking. When it comes to Russians, Hungarian blood runs cold, Miss Atkins. As it should."

Charlie took a deep breath. "Maybe you are right. Maybe I don't understand fully what I am asking you to do. But I do know that in a free country, even the worst of us is entitled to a trial. If we leave him here, we are sentencing this man—this father—to certain death."

She paused to consider, and then with a softer voice, she said, "Ask them if they are willing to kill a man who wants the same thing as they do, for himself and his child. A better life. Please, Viktor. They will listen to you."

The muscles in Viktor's cheeks, red from the cold, twitched.

"I do this against my better judgment," he said finally.

He turned to the crowd and began to speak. As he finished, Uncle stared at him amid the fury of raised voices and clenched fists. Then Uncle put his hands up, quieting them, until the crowd let him speak. Viktor translated.

"He says he has listened to me on the radio, and he believes he knows my heart—that I only want what is best for Hungary. And if I say these lives are worth saving, then so be it. But he asks us to remember that at this moment it is the Hungarians who are showing compassion and mercy."

Charlie's heart rose. "Tell them thank you, and that one act of kindness deserves another. You said the food and the blankets in back were for Hungarians in need. How about these Hungarians?"

Viktor hesitated and then relented. "I do not think this is what Mr. Tanner had in mind—but why not?"

Charlie opened the back of the signal truck. She handed down cabbages, apples and bread, tins of milk, packets of coffee, sugar, cigarettes, blankets, toys—everything she could give except the gasoline for the trip home, a small basket of food, and some blankets.

She set the teddy bear aside, too. When she was done, she carried it to Zuzu and crouched down to the girl's level. She waved one of the bear's jointed arms, as if to say hello.

Zuzu's eyes grew huge. She tugged urgently at her grandfather's sleeve until he nodded. Then she opened her arms and took the bear, clasping it to her chest, her eyes shining.

Viktor watched without comment. To Uncle, he said, "You must be ready. You know the Russians will come looking for their plane."

Uncle drew himself up. He leaned forward and whispered to Viktor. When he was finished, he winked conspiratorially, patted Viktor's shoulder, and turned to go.

"What did he say?" Charlie asked.

Viktor smiled. "He said that once, Győr built the finest Turán tanks and fighters—Messerschmitt 109s. Those factories are ruined now, but there are still many places in Győr where even a MiG will never be found."

Charlie put a hand out to Horst's son and helped him to his feet. "We haven't been properly introduced," she said in German with a smile. "My name is Charlie."

Jerome's shutter clicked.

The boy glanced at his father, who nodded. "I am Walter," he said shyly as he shook her hand.

"How old are you?"

"Seven."

"Well, nice to meet you, Walter. What do you like studying in school?"

Walter's face lit up. "I like machines."

"I like machines, too," Charlie said. Then she looked at Horst, her face serious. "You have a choice to make. You and Walter can find your own way to the border if you prefer. It's about thirty-five miles west of here, and you will have to walk or find a ride. Viktor and I are going to Budapest. I am here to report a story for Radio Free Europe. Viktor will stay in Budapest, but as soon as I am finished, I'm going to drive this truck to Austria. You and Walter are welcome to come with me."

Horst glanced from Charlie to Viktor, his son's hand tight in his own. He licked his lips and then nodded. "We will come with you to Budapest, and then to Austria. And thank you."

Viktor turned to Charlie. "You should leave now. We do not know exactly what the Russians intend to do, but now that there are MiGs involved, whatever it is will not be good. The story of Horst and his son is enough, don't you think?"

Charlie looked away. Viktor wasn't wrong: that would be the safe choice.

"We're too close to Budapest," she said, turning back to him. "I'm willing to take the risk. I will be in and out as fast as I can."

Viktor held Charlie's eyes a moment longer. "Very well," he said, his lips pressed into a thin line. He pointed Horst and his son toward the signal truck's rear doors. "You two can ride in back."

As Charlie turned to climb up into the cab, she caught sight of two antiquated tractors. They were rolling steadily toward the MiG to tow it away to a quiet resting place, never to be found. Jerome followed the tractors on foot, capturing it all on film.

Charlie settled into the cab, quietly exhilarated. She had helped save two lives. Her first war story byline was within reach. And now Horst, about to escape—if he agreed, that was another great story. *Not a bad day's work*, she thought. *It sure beats making coffee.*

21
GAUNTLET

From outside the bakery, Kovács and Fekete ran south toward the Danube, pursued by Zoli and his *huligánok*, relentless as a pack of wolves. The mob followed, banging on shop doors and chanting: "AVO! AVO! We are coming for you!"

Kovács, pressed flat against an alley wall, swore under his breath. Zoli's voice, singsong high and enraged, was loudest of all. *I should have shot that little shit when I had the chance*, Kovács thought. His face throbbed like a sonofabitch. Running made it worse.

Across the alley, Fekete beckoned from a back stoop next to an open door. He gestured: *Come!* Kovács snuck a peek toward the street. He saw no one. He sprinted across the alley and through the door.

#   #   #

Inside, Kovács and Fekete recoiled.

They had stumbled into a kitchen, deserted mid-shift by its staff. A half-gutted fish rotted on a counter. Raw game hens, trussed and ready for the oven, crawled with maggots. Trifles and torts on a dessert cart under glass had exploded with soft grey fuzzy mold. Kovács gagged and pulled his coat over his nose. *If I were still in charge, I'd make the goddamned cooks eat every bite of what's left. Join the mob on the street, suffer the consequences.*

"AVO! We are coming for you!" The *huligánok* were in the front lobby.

Shit. Zoli again.

Fekete checked the rear kitchen door. Outside, two men upturned the ash cans, hunting for them.

Kovács checked in the pantry. Plenty of food—kilos of sugar, flour, coffee, and salt, racks of fresh eggs, wheels of good cheese, and baskets of pears, clementines, and apples—but no place to hide.

They were trapped.

Doors banged. Voices shouted. Feet stomped.

Then Fekete pointed down. Next to the dessert cart, a dull brass handle was set flush into the floor. A trapdoor to the wine cellar. Fekete opened it quickly, checked inside, and then beckoned to Kovács.

Kovács shrank back.

Not from the dank musty air wafting upward or the skitter of cockroaches and silverfish. Not from the dark either. Kovács hated being confined anywhere where there was no clear escape route. But right now, they were out of options. He forced himself down the makeshift plank steps, one hand on the rough rock wall. As soon as his feet hit the cellar floor, Fekete tugged the dessert cart forward to cover the trapdoor and then carefully eased the door shut into total darkness.

Kovács clamped his lips tight to keep himself from crying out.

# # #

The wine cellar was cramped, overflowing with wine racks and dusty with cobwebs and fine grit. There was barely room for both Kovács and Fekete; they sat side-by-side on upturned wine boxes. The cool, humid air was so stifling that Kovács thought he might choke. His heart pounded. But he—they—were safe, at least for the moment. Kovács forced himself to concentrate on his breathing, to slow down his racing heart.

In the kitchen above them, Kovács could hear the sound of racing feet.

Breathe in, breathe out. Breathe in, breathe out.

The feet slowed. Kovács heard muffled shouts. Banging noises. The crash of dishes. *For fuck's sake, what are they doing up there?* He gritted his teeth, but there was nothing to do but wait them out. *Breathe in, breathe out. Breathe in, breathe out.*

A faint twitch along the edge of the slash across his face. A loose cobweb, perhaps. Kovács brushed it away and then touched the edges of the cut. His fingers came away wet and stinking of pus.

Breathe, Kovács told himself, trying to ignore the voices overhead. *Just breathe.*

Another twinge. Kovács slapped his own face, knocking away something warm. A rat, attracted by the smell of blood. He lashed out, hitting a rack of wine bottles.

Fekete grabbed the rattling bottles of wine and eased the rack back into place.

"They are too busy eating to hear us," Fekete whispered.

Kovács nodded, even though he knew Fekete couldn't see him. He felt a scurrying over his boots. More rats. He kicked them away, his soles scraping against the cellar's dirt floor. He pulled his feet up. Miserably, he covered his head and his face with his arms. Shielding himself as best as he could.

There was nothing for him to do but wait.

#   #   #

When the kitchen above them finally fell silent, Fekete reached up to quietly nudge the dessert cart out of the way. Kovács didn't wait for Fekete to ease up the trapdoor—he burst past Fekete, shoving the trapdoor up and out of the way. He gratefully sucked in the air, not even caring about the stink of rotting food.

Fekete checked the exits for a way out—through the front lobby or maybe out the rear kitchen door. Kovács looked around. The kitchen and pantry had been stripped clean. Every gleaming copper pan, every sharp knife, every egg, gone.

Fekete, by the kitchen's back door, waved him forward. The door was open.

They crept out into the alley. They were nearly to the street when a shout rang out. Zoli again.

"There they are," he shouted, his high-pitched voice echoing in the empty alley. "AVO! AVO!"

Kovács and Fekete ran the only way they could—straight ahead, away from Zoli and the mob.

22
WORDS OF WAR

Behind his desk at Radio Free Europe's Munich office, the knot in Ernie Owens's stomach tightened. He stared at the pages in front of him, direct quotes from stories and commentaries that had run on the Hungarian radio service since the start of the uprising. Mária translated and typed up the passages for him.

Now she sat on a chair across from Owens's desk, waiting as he read. Behind her, Béla leaned against the back wall of Owens's office, scowling in silence. Neither spoke as Owens worked through the pages for a second time, blue cigar smoke curling upward between his knuckles in flat, lazy circles.

"If the Hungarians hold out for three or four days, then the pressure upon the government of the U.S. to send military help to the freedom fighters, will become irresistible...," Owens read.

"The American Congress cannot vote for war, as long as the presidential elections have not been held...

"Do not give up your weapons as a guarantee of the freedoms and independence has been won...

"Residents and local authorities must provide food, supplies, and arms to the freedom fighters, and hide any fighter who becomes separated from his units…

"If the Hungarians can continue to fight until next Wednesday after the American election, we shall be closer to a world war than at any time since 1939."

Owens pulled on his cigar. *Hell's bells*, he thought. *If New York sees this stuff, they'll blow a gasket.* Each quote came from a different story, suggesting a pattern of stories that violated Radio Free Europe's editorial standards. Conjecture rather than fact. Emotion rather than cool-headed analysis. Worse, the Hungarian radio service was rebroadcasting "news" picked up from shortwave transmissions inside Hungary without independent verification.

"All one needs against a Soviet T-34 tank is a wine bottle filled with a liter of petrol and a lit rag for a fuse…

"Hungarians must continue to fight vigorously to influence action by the Security Council…

"Keep your weapons to guarantee freedom and independence…

"The West will not let the revolution fail…

"Military aid is sure to be forthcoming if the Hungarians establish a central military command…

"We await official word of action by the United Nation at any moment."

Owens pushed his thick black glasses back into place, his dread growing. No one had seen the Hungarian revolution coming, least of all him. And nothing in the half-dozen years Owens had spent working his way up the ranks at Radio Free Europe prepared him for a moment like this one, when the decisions he made in his Munich newsroom might impact whether his listeners lived or died.

He had come to Europe eager to see action as a soldier but—because he knew how to type—found himself instead assigned to a desk job in Munich, preparing army administrative papers—transfers, discharges, requisition orders. Once discharged, he had stayed in Munich. He had learned German well enough to pick up odd jobs for American news men passing through, serving as part-fixer, part-guide, and part-translator. When Radio Free Europe opened up its European headquarters in 1950, he hired on, thrilled to be part of something bigger than himself at last. There was a nobility to his job, he believed. Where else would the captive peoples of Europe hear the truth, if not for Radio Free Europe? Owens liked that.

When he was asked to fill in on the Hungarian desk, he figured it would be a cheap way to earn extra credit with the brass in New York.

"Why not?" Owens had told his boss over the phone line, even though it meant doing two jobs at once. "The Hungarian desk is usually pretty quiet. I can keep an eye on things."

Two weeks later, Hungarians took to the streets, and suddenly Owens was in the hot seat.

Owens's bosses in Radio Free Europe's New York offices were no help. They were too far away to understand the kind of pressure he was under or how much was on the line for people like Béla, Mária, and the rest of the Hungarian staff—the lives of their family and friends, the fate of their nation, even their faith in the United States' promise to stand with them in their hour of need. Instead, New York hounded him for updates—what was he hearing about Khrushchev's long game, did the revolution have a leader, was Prime Minister Nagy serious about free and fair elections? New York also telexed a constantly changing stream of editorial direction. One day, New York's directives said Nagy was too close to the Kremlin and to make sure the Hungarian service's commentaries pushed hard for real, democratic concessions from Moscow. A day later came new orders: Hold back judgment on Nagy; maybe he is the one person who can successfully lead this revolution.

Owens reached for his coffee cup, but it was empty. No one thought to make him another pot. Sending Charlie home yesterday may not have been his best idea. Caught between New York and the Hungarian staff, for whom the stakes could not be higher, Owens fought the urge to panic. How far could he let the staff—Hungarian émigrés who knew firsthand the brutality of life under Soviet rule—go in encouraging their compatriots to keep fighting? A step too far, and even more people might die. Not far enough, and the moment for Hungarians to wrest their country away from Moscow's control might be lost.

He looked up from the pages on his desk, his voice incredulous.

"We actually told the Hungarians their freedom fighters were stronger than the Soviet Army?" He stubbed his cigar into the overflowing ashtray on his desk. "These quotes never should have been on our airwaves. They violate the letter and spirit of every editorial policy we have."

"We should tell people to sit at home and do nothing?" Béla's expression was a thundercloud about to burst. He spoke the way he wrote his Radio Free Europe commentaries: urgent, principled, scolding. "We must tell them to fight with everything they can—there is no other way."

"You're not the one listening to their voices," Mária shot back, her voice raw with fear. "At first, all the news was good. People were happy to be in the streets, they were protesting peacefully, and Prime Minister Nagy was talking about the things people cared about. Higher wages, an end to the AVO, freeing political prisoners, the right to form new political parties. Then the AVO and the Soviet soldiers started killing people—children, old women, the Russians do not care. Now all I hear is the panic in their voices. People don't know what to do, what is true and what is a lie. The telephone and telegraph lines are not working. No one knows what is happening."

Mária's voice cracked. "People are frightened and desperate." Her eyes were red and heavy from lack of sleep. "They are begging for help, for guns, for tanks, for bombers. The more we encourage them to keep fighting until American troops come, the more danger they are in."

She stared hard at Béla. "You of all people should understand this."

"I do understand," Béla snapped. "But Hungarians are looking to us for guidance. We must tell them to keep fighting."

"It's not our job to tell the Hungarians what to do." Owens rose to emphasize his point. He prided himself on running a tight ship—no editorializing unless the copy was clearly identified as an opinion piece and passed Owens's journalistic bar of *who* says *what* to *whom, how, why,* and with *what effect*. But tempers and emotions were running high, especially now. The fact that he didn't speak or read Hungarian didn't make his job any easier. "Our job is to be objective and dispassionate, to tell people what we know and can verify, and then let them decide what to do. Guidance from New York says—and I quote—'not one word in these statements on liberation can be used to encourage militant anti-Communists to go over from passive to active resistance in the expectation that such resistance will be supported by Western elements'—end quote."

"That's not possible, not now!" Béla smacked his hand against the wall. His jawline, stubbled gray, twitched with fury. "You ask how we know we make a difference to our listeners. *This. This* is our impact. At last, Hungarians have stood up and said, 'No more.' No, we are too close to victory. We cannot, we must not, tell the freedom fighters to stop. Every demand of the Hungarian people must be met. Every. Single. One. Our people are in the streets, and for the first time, we have the upper hand on the Soviets. We must force our government into taking a firm stand. We cannot compromise one inch."

"Oh, c'mon, Béla, even if the Security Council passes a resolution recognizing Hungary's independence right this very minute, it won't mean a thing if the Russians don't play fair." Owens, hands on his hips, was as close to shouting as he ever came. "Yes, we can and should encourage the Hungarian people to use every legitimate means to fight back against the Reds, but Radio Free Europe's official position is to encourage reform, not to promise liberation by sending in troops. No one—not us, not the Brits, not the French—is going to march into Hungary, guns blazing. No one wants another world war. Especially now that we know the Reds have the bomb. That is just the way it is, whether we like it or not."

"That's it? You stand by while my people die because they believed America meant what it said: 'If you rise up, we'll stand by you.' Is it all just a lie?"

"Of course not. We stand with the Hungarians. Hell's bells, we stand with *all* the captive peoples of Eastern Europe,"

Owens said. He took a deep breath and tried to soften his voice. "But there is a limit to what we in the West can do. You know that. You have to be realistic."

Realistic. The word hung in the air, like the stink of bad news. Béla shook his head as if he did not quite believe what he was hearing. "That is the trouble with people like you. You come to Europe, you go to parties at your consulate, you spend your weekends in Paris or London or Rome. You think you are seeing the world when really you see nothing."

Béla pushed himself away from the wall and yanked open the door to Owens's office. He paused and looked back at Owens, the bitterness in his voice rising. "You arrive here knowing nothing about us, and you leave knowing even less. Someday, you will go home to America, and we Europeans will have to live in whatever misery is left behind for us. Forgive me, but it is not us who needs a lesson in being 'realistic.'"

He slammed the door behind him as he left.

Owens stared after him. He didn't like conflict in his newsroom, especially when he wasn't sure he was on the right end of it. Not that he blamed Béla. Béla's extended family and many friends lived in Hungary, and even under the best of circumstances—if Hungary really did free itself from Moscow's grip—these were dangerous, unsettled times.

Mária stood, her sweater wrapped tight around her. "I will be at my desk if you need me," she said quietly.

"Thank you for bringing these quotes to my attention. I'm glad you did," Owens said. "You should go home. Get some sleep."

"My parents are in Budapest," Mária said. "They are too old and too sick to leave. If I cannot help them, I can at least be here."

She closed the door to Owens's office softly as she left.

Alone in his office, Owens, smarting from Béla's words, reached for his hat and overcoat. He needed fresh air, and his favorite bar was a short walk away. When he returned to the office, he would read through the material from Mária one more time and decide what to do. That was good; it would give Béla time to calm down too. Owens's pace quickened as he slipped out the door.

23
NO JOKE

O wens stared down into his scotch. Most days he didn't touch the sauce until cocktail hour, when the usual crowd began gathering for another long boozy evening. But right now, the mahogany-and-crushed velvet quiet of his favorite bar was just what he needed to take the sting off Béla's parting shot.

Trouble was, Béla was right, Owens brooded, swirling his drink in small, rhythmic circles. Americans like himself lived well in Europe, like a benign conquering army whose sacrifices and resources saved the continent from the Nazis and their Thousand-Year Reich. Only instead of guns, our stock-in-trade is the certainty that old problems—no matter how rooted in history or habit or hatred—could be solved by American-style democracy. Like what to do about Hungary—a small, fiercely proud nation, and a prisoner of its own geography, the one thing that would never, could never, change. The Reds saw Hungary as resources—wheat, timber, uranium, pork, manpower to build tanks and airplanes—ripe for the picking and, like the rest of the satellite states, a natural geographic buffer zone against the armies and ideas of the Free West. Meanwhile, to the West, Hungary's fight for freedom was a symbol of the potency of democratic ideals and a talking point for sober-minded diplomats. It just wasn't a country anyone, most of all the United States, thought worthy of risking a third world war over.

Owens caught the bartender's eye. He tapped the bar. Another, *bitte*.

He was easing into that second drink, his scrap with Béla dulled by the scotch, when a hand clapped him on his shoulder.

"I say, Owens," said Hilly. The Englishman slid onto the stool next to Owens and nodded to the bartender. "Gutsy move that, letting a girl do a man's job."

"Anything for a fresh angle," Haversham said, appearing next to Hilly, his head bobbing up and down. "With a war zone under her belt, next thing you know, Hilly, Owens here will have Charlie covering the United Nations. Or Parliament, God forbid."

Owens smiled, waiting for the joke to play out. But neither Hilly nor Haversham were laughing.

"Let Charlie go to a war zone?" Owens said finally. Even as he spoke, the knot in his stomach wrenched back to life. "I did no such thing."

Haversham blinked. "Sure you did. We saw her, clear as day. Isn't that right, Hilly?"

"Yes, yes, quite right," Hilly said. "On her way to Budapest with that funny little Hungarian fellow of yours, the one with the deep voice." Hilly lowered his voice. "'I am the Voice of Free Hungary.'"

"You saw Charlie. In Hungary. On her way to Budapest." Owens spoke slowly, not sure he had heard Hilly right. "With Viktor Farkas."

"We did," Hilly said. "We told her to come back to Munich with us, but she couldn't be bothered, isn't that right, Haversham? Said she had an understanding with you about writing stories. Going on to Budapest to see what's what. Mind of her own, that one."

"Quite right, quite right."

Owens stood. His pleasant buzz was now a sudden, throbbing headache. He gulped down the last of his drink and then threw a handful of Deutsch marks on the table, not bothering to count them. Viktor's presence in Budapest was easy to explain—after all, he gave Tanner Viktor's name. Besides, Viktor was a patriot, volunteering to do a man's job for his country. Plus, Viktor's resignation, effective yesterday, also meant that no fingers could be pointed at Radio Free Europe.

Charlie was an entirely different matter.

Hilly was right: he did have an understanding—of sorts—with Charlie. Her stories showed up on his desk, and if they were any good, he passed them along to the language desk editors. No skin off his nose, the price—free—was right, and so far, all of her stories had been as good as anything else on the radio. He was doing Charlie a favor. Would she really pull a stunt like this, after all he had done for her? The situation was too hot, too volatile, too fraught for someone as young and inexperienced as Charlie. If things went sideways, if Charlie so much as scraped her knee, he was sure to be blamed. A girl reporter, arrested or injured, even if it wasn't his fault? He would be fired for sure and would never find another job in journalism—ever. *Hell's bells, Charlie*, he thought angrily. *What were you thinking?*

Owens burst out through the bar's walnut-and-polished-brass doors and into the rain—big, sloppy drops that promised wet snow by nightfall. In the rain, Munich looked as grey and bleak as he felt. He barely paused. He hurried to the corner, turned left past storefronts shuttered for the weekend, and stepped out onto the main street. He flagged down a taxi and headed toward the old part of the city, where he knew Charlie rented a room. Maybe she was home—sick or sleeping in. Maybe she had crossed the border but had changed her mind and had the good sense to come home. Maybe, but before things got out of hand he had to know for sure.

The closer the cab got to Charlie's address, the worse he felt. His head hurt, and his stomach did, too. Despite the rain, he was sweating. Charlie wouldn't do this to him, would she? He dreaded what he already suspected the answer would be.

24
SCHNEEGLÖCKCHENGASSE 22

O wens maneuvered his bulk out of the cab in front of the address where Charlie rented a room. He mopped his face with his handkerchief and then stuffed it back into his pocket. "*Warten sie hier, bitte,*" he told the cab driver. *Wait here, please.*

The house sat back from the street. It had been a beauty once; now it was a shadow of its former self, a dowager faded to the color of old lace. The front portico sagged, its missing balustrade had been torn away—scavenged for firewood, perhaps—and the white-sashed windows had lost most of their wrought-iron fretwork. Ivy spiderwebbed unchecked across the house's grand, stuccoed façade. Yet, unlike most of its neighbors, the house had survived the war intact.

Owens pushed his way through what was left of the front gate. At the door, he lifted the door knocker, a heavy iron ring looped through a lion's bared teeth, and let it fall. *Boom!* The sound echoed into nothing until finally a key turned slowly inside the lock. The door opened just enough for one old milky blue eye to peer out.

"*Ja?*" a woman's voice snapped.

"*Fräulein* Atkins?" Owens asked.

"*Nein.*" The door slammed shut.

Owens knocked again. He kept knocking—*boom! boom! boom!*—until finally the door opened again, this time all the way.

A tiny woman glared at him. She wore a man's heavy winter coat buckled tight around her thin, bent frame. Her white hair was braided and pinned away from her face. She stared at Owens, her blue eyes sullen.

"*Was möchten sie?*" she said, her voice sharp.

"I want some information, that is all," Owens replied in German. He reached for his wallet and showed her his Radio Free Europe identification card. "*Radio Frei Europa.* Okay?" He pointed toward the house. "*Fräulein* Atkins?"

The woman barely glanced at Owens's press card or the Deutsche marks sticking out of his wallet. Instead, she fixated on the US greenbacks Owens kept for spending at the PX or trips to the New York office. She looked at Owens, rubbed her fingers together, and held out one hand. If he wanted information, he was going to have to pay for it.

He handed her his cash. All of it, even the Deutsche marks, leaving himself only enough money for the waiting cab.

"*Nein Fräulein,*" the woman said, loud and emphatic to make sure he heard, and then she slammed the door shut.

He didn't bother to knock again. Message received. Charlie wasn't there.

As he waddled back toward his taxi, something else caught his eye. A subtle sign, black and painted with a needle and thread, hung from a bracket on the house next door. *Sophie Müller, Näherin,* it read.

That's right, Owens thought, staring at the sign. *The woman from Charlie's story lived next door. Charlie called her a friend. Maybe she knows where Charlie is.*

Owens told the cab to wait a little longer. He wiped his face with his handkerchief as he knocked on the seamstress' door.

A dark-haired woman, pleasingly round and pleasantly smiling, answered. Her mouth was full of straight pins, and she wore a well-washed white smock with deep front pockets. In one hand she held a pair of long-bladed dressmaker's scissors, as if interrupted mid-cut.

Owens stared at her. "You are Sophie Müller," he blurted out in German.

Sophie arched an eyebrow as she removed the pins from her mouth. She pinned them to her shoulder strap, one by one. "Do I know you, *Herr*—" Her voice hung in the air with a question mark.

"*Herr* Owens. I am looking for Charlie. You are her friend."

"I am." Sophie's expression tightened, like an open window pulled shut.

"I am her boss. She didn't come in to work today."

Sophie's eyes narrowed. "You already know why she is not at work. You sent her home."

Owens nodded eagerly. "That's right," he said, stuffing his handkerchief back into his pocket. "I did send her home. I want to check on her, and make sure she is all right."

"Of course she is all right. Why wouldn't she be? Now you must excuse me, I am busy." Sophie started to close her front door.

Owens put his hand on the door to hold it open. "Wait. She's here?"

"Did I say where she was?" Sophie said. Her voice turned hard. "I did not. I do not share other people's business."

Cold rain slid down Owens's neck, and he shivered despite himself. "Please, *Frau Müller*. I'm sorry for bothering you, but I must know. Do you know where Charlie is?"

"Why? Why must you know?"

Owens took a deep breath. "Charlie may have done something foolish and very, very dangerous. She may have crossed into Iron Curtain territory. If this is true, Charlie needs to know that the situation is changing fast. We're picking up eyewitness reports that there are tanks massing at the Czech border, waiting to cross into Hungary. If the Reds really do roll into Budapest, things are gonna get hot pretty quick. Charlie needs to get out, quick as she can, and she might need help. Help from me."

Sophie scowled. She crossed her arms and leaned against the door jamb. "Even if it is true, you don't seem to be in the business of helping Charlie."

Owens tried not to raise his voice. "Well, I am now. If the Reds catch her, she'll be arrested. She could get hurt or killed." He pushed his thick black glasses back into place. "Charlie isn't the only one who might suffer, either. If anything happens to her, it could cost me my job."

"How sad for you." Sophie's voice held no note of sympathy.

Owens gritted his teeth. "Look, Charlie is not at work—we both know why. That is my doing. Her landlady next door says she is not home, and I am guessing she isn't here, either. That means that there is a damn good chance that Charlie really is on her way to Budapest." He paused, trying to soften his tone. "All I'm asking is whether Charlie is here, right now, or if you have seen her today. You don't have to tell me anything else. And yes, I would also like to keep my job."

Sophie considered Owens's words. "How do I know you are telling me the truth?"

"You don't," he said. "But since you already know I'm not in the habit of helping Charlie, you must also know I would not be here otherwise."

She stared past him at his cab waiting at the curb and then at the ruined houses that lined her street. "Charlie is not here," she said finally. "She left last night, about midnight. She said she had a ride to and from Budapest with a man from the Red Cross. Andy. I do not know his full name. She also said they will be home tonight."

Hope and relief flooded Owens's brain. Charlie had a plan to come back tonight? Thank God. He knew where the Red Cross Office was. He would go there now and find out when Andy—and Charlie—were expected. Maybe he would even wait there until he was sure she made it home, safe and sound.

"Thank you," he said. "If you see Charlie before I do, please ask her to get in touch with me. She can call anytime—night or day. She knows how to reach me."

As Sophie's door closed, a nearby clock tower chimed. It was twelve-thirty, which meant New York was still asleep. *Too early to call on a Sunday,* Owens thought as he cut across the street toward the waiting cab. *Maybe Charlie and Andy are already on the way back to Munich. Maybe New York will never even need to know what Charlie did.*

He settled back in the cab, blinking through his rain-streaked glasses. Next stop: the Munich Red Cross. For the first time since seeing Hilly and Haversham, Owens's heart felt a little lighter.

25

ROTKREUZKLINIKUM MÜNCHEN

The cab dropped Owens at the Red Cross building on *Nymphenburger Straße*. This time, Owens didn't bother to ask the cab to wait. He was in too good a mood, his stress fading to a memory. *Charlie was right*, he thought generously, noting the long line of Münchners waiting in the rain to donate blood for the Hungarian freedom fighters. *All these West Germans donating blood is a good story*. If this story was as good as the rest of the ones she wrote, Owens would send it on to the language desks. Should he let her keep her job? She did have a knack for the unexpected story and turn of phrase. A pity, but a girl news clerk with ambition was the last thing he needed.

He snaked through the Red Cross building until he found his way to the loading dock where crates of supplies—bandages, blankets, and boxed kits of blood plasma—were being hustled onto trucks bound for Hungary.

"Andy?" said a West German man with an official-looking clipboard. He pointed Owens toward one of the trucks. "Over there."

Great news. If Andy is back, so is Charlie, Owens thought.

Inside the truck, Owens found a man, eyes closed as he catnapped under a wool blanket. Owens rapped smartly on the cab's door to wake him. "You Andy? Where's Charlie?"

"Charlie? I left her at the border." Andy straightened up, blinking and running his fingers through his hair. His eyes looked red and heavy from too little sleep, and he needed a shave.

Owens's optimistic mood crashed. "You left her where?" The knot in his stomach wrenched, red-hot and tight. "Hell's bells, don't you know how dangerous a place like that could be for a kid like her?"

"Yes, sir, ex-field medic here. We're pretty good at assessing danger. The border area is okay, but she was determined to go to Budapest."

Owens swore under his breath. "Did you actually see her cross into Hungary?"

Andy reached for his coffee cup on the dashboard. He took a sip, made a face, but downed the cup anyway. "Sort of. She crossed no man's land and climbed up into one of the guard towers."

Owens gripped the edge of the cab's window. "She did what?"

"Don't worry—it was empty, not a guard in sight. I guess she wanted to look around. She came down and crossed back into Austria."

"Was that the last time you saw her?"

Andy nodded. "By that time, my truck was empty, and I was due back in Munich. When I left, she was interviewing a doctor from Budapest who spoke English."

"Was anyone with her?"

Andy rubbed a hand over the stubble on his chin and shook his head. "Not that I saw. I think she was going to try to catch a ride to Budapest with the doctor. That's something, isn't it? Radio Free Europe, sending a girl reporter like Charlie into a war zone."

Owens banged his hand down on the cab door's frame. "Damn it, Charlie works for me, and I assure you, I did no such thing."

"You mean she went on her own?" Andy's eyes widened, and he whistled, low and slow. "That takes some nerve."

"Stupidity, that's what it takes."

"Tell you what, as soon as this truck is packed up, I'm going back to the border. Charlie said she'd be in and out in a couple of hours. We're supposed to meet right where I left her—by the oak tree closest to the border crossing. If she's there, I'll bring her back."

"You do that." Owens handed Andy his business card. "You call me the minute she shows up."

He made his way back out to the street, his foul mood restored. He wished he had not dismissed the cab. Hilly was right; Charlie did have a goddamn mind of her own. And Viktor—where did he fit into this story? Charlie and Viktor loathed each other, far as he knew.

At the curb outside the Red Cross building, he hesitated. At least he knew Hilly and Haversham were correct: Charlie *did* cross the border. Now what?

Tanner, that's what. Or rather, who.

Tanner sent Viktor to Budapest. Surely he must have a way to reach Viktor. If he did, and if Charlie was with Viktor, Owens could order her home. *Now.* Before she got hurt. Or arrested. Or killed. Before New York found out what Charlie had done. Before he got fired.

First, of course, he needed to find Tanner. He turned west toward the only place he thought he might find him: at the American Consulate on *Ludwigstraße*.

26
HOME

K ovács burst through his own front door, his blood pumping, Fekete a step behind him. They had finally managed to lose Zoli and his *huligánok* by hiding inside a clothing wardrobe in the ruins of a bombed-out apartment. What should have been a short ten-minute walk from the AVO headquarters building had taken hours.

He touched his cheek gingerly. The slash was deeper than he'd realized and was turning an ugly purple and yellow along its edges. "Marta!" he called. His housekeeper would know what to do until he managed to see a doctor. "Quickly, please."

"Marta's gone."

Kovács followed his son's voice into the house's front room. Fekete, the dried blood from the butcher's cleaver still visible, was already positioned at his usual post near the front door. Tibor sat on the couch, his stocky legs splayed out in front of him. He scrambled to his feet as Kovács stepped through the doorway.

"Gone?" Kovács asked, his voice sharp. "Gone where?"

István stared at his father. "Your face—"

"Yes, I am aware," Kovács snapped. "Where's Marta?"

István averted his eyes. "She hasn't been here in days."

He sat in front of a deep ebony Red October concert grand piano, made to István's exacting specifications at the Leningrad Musical Instrument Factory on Vasilyevsky Island. Beyond him, through the house's front windows was a mesmerizing view of the steel blue waters of the Danube and, on the river's opposite bank, the low Buda hills. "She said she was joining the people's revolution. You would know this if you had been home."

Kovács scowled. By now, this room should have been empty, its thick Persian carpets and mahogany furniture long since transferred to the moving van—all but István's piano and bench. He was in no mood to fight with his son, certainly not in front of Tibor. Kovács jerked a thumb at Tibor. "You. Make yourself useful. Go outside and help the movers. I want everything loaded within the hour."

István's eyes followed Tibor as he left the room. "I would have gone to the revolution myself but for your ape." His fingers rippled over the piano keys, a terse, bitter arpeggio.

"All the more reason he stays here to protect you from your unwise ideas." *So very like his late mother*, Kovács thought. István inherited not just her high cheek bones and immense blue eyes but also her staggering inability to see the world as anything other than revolving around her. Fitting, perhaps, in István's case, Kovács had to admit: István's talent was beyond question.

His son had been spotted early for his uncanny ear and for his gift for playing long, exquisite passages of music with flawless precision despite hearing them only once. As István grew, his hands grew, too, giving him more than an octave's reach and an impossibly fluid, nimble style of playing. By the time István was accepted early into Budapest's finest musical school, the Franz Liszt Academy of Music, his concert portfolio included an astonishing repertoire: Chopin, Rachmaninoff, Beethoven, Mozart, Bartok, and of course, Liszt.

Despite István's disturbingly naive attitude about politics—one his son regrettably shared with so many other young Hungarians—Kovács sought and received permission for his son's early admittance to the *Magyar Dolgozók Pártja*, the Hungarian Working People's Party, two full years ahead of István's eighteenth birthday. Party membership allowed István to tour. He dazzled audiences with his emotional range and technical ability, playing to packed, rapturous crowds in Riga, Sofia, Bucharest, Leningrad, Beijing, and—just four months ago—Vienna.

But did István appreciate all that his father had done for him? Clearly not, not after that business on the train. Foolish and very, very unwise. Fortunately, Tibor's silence came at a relatively cheap price. In the four months since, Kovács focused on keeping his son occupied, most recently trying to install István as a professor at the Liszt Academy. Even at seventeen, István outplayed his own instructors. Days ago, such a task required nothing more than a discreet word to the minister of culture, followed by a more specific hint if needed. Now, with the academy closed by the street riots and the minister missing from his post and whispered to have gone west, even such a trivial thing was impossible.

"Protect me? From what? The rest of the country has the same unwise ideas, in case you haven't noticed, and no one, not even you, can stop it."

"Of course, I can stop it. Regrettably, Moscow can't seem to make up its mind how to respond. Until it does, my hands are tied," Kovács growled. His cheek ached, and conversations like this one with István left him irritated. The boy simply had no sense of how the world worked.

"You seem to have had no trouble deciding what you would do. Tell me, were you going to let me know that you were leaving Budapest, or was it your plan that I should wake up to find the house empty?"

"My apologies for the short notice. I have been busy."

"Does Comrade Zhirov know that you are leaving?"

"Comrade Zhirov knows all he needs to know. There is nothing he can do for me now." *Or won't*, Kovács thought. He had survived this long by keeping his eye on the exit—whether from across a room or from the life he'd made for himself. Now he knew exactly what he had to do next: leave, and the sooner the better. In case the radicals won. Or the Americans came. Or, perhaps worst of all for him, the Russians decided to stay. Kovács no longer cared who prevailed. By the time Zhirov showed up to arrest him, he would be gone. "Comrade Zhirov will take charge of all matters once he arrives."

Fekete, standing quietly by the door, stirred. "You are really leaving, comrade? For good?"

"There is nothing left for me here," Kovács said. "This foolishness in the streets won't last. Comrade Zhirov will be here to make sure order is restored."

"That is good, isn't it?"

"Yes, of course. But Comrade Zhirov will want a new man in place." Kovács smiled at Fekete with as much cheer as he could muster. "I do him a favor by making it easy for him."

Fekete frowned. "I see."

Kovács clapped his hand on Fekete's shoulder, surprised at the sudden welling of emotion in his throat. He hadn't considered Fekete's loyalty even for a moment. "You can accompany me if you wish. I can use a good man like you."

Fekete shook his head. "My mother and father, comrade, they are old. I cannot leave them alone in Budapest. There is no one but me to take care of them."

Kovács nodded. He understood. But he was also tired and starting over while he still could held a certain appeal. He had considered and then decided against going to Warsaw; it was too cold, and with Gomulka's return to power, too uncertain. Berlin was too close to the Americans for his taste. No, once he crossed south into Yugoslavia, he would head east through Bulgaria and then quietly disappear inconspicuously along a sunny stretch of the Black Sea coast. He owned a house purchased for just such a moment as this one, plus he had plenty of cash and multiple sets of travel papers. His Russian was good enough that no one would dare to question him. Regrettably, the men who transported himself and his belongings would not survive the return trip; Kovács would be sure to reload his sidearm before his car arrived. He was taking no chances; he planned to disappear for good. "Then I thank you for everything you have done for me."

Kovács cleared his throat. "I ask one last thing of you. Meet Comrade Zhirov's plane at Tököl Air Base, please, and see personally to his safety." He hesitated briefly: what he was about to ask Fekete next was delicate, the razor's edge between appearing to fulfill his duties to the Kremlin no matter what personal price he paid and committing treason. "Comrade Zhirov will want to go right to Andrássy Street, to my office, to assume command. You must assist him in every way possible. But you must take him the long way around the city. That will be the safest for him. The safest for you too."

It was also the route that would give Kovács enough time to tidy up his affairs. "Can you do that for me?"

Fekete nodded. He stepped to the door and then turned back. "You are sure?"

"Quite." Kovács watched as Fekete closed the front door softly behind him.

Behind him, István's hands rippled lightly over his piano keys. "A pity your son is not a loyal lapdog, too."

Kovács turned and looked at his son, appraising István as he considered his answer. "I plan for every eventuality. It is the only reason I am still alive. Besides, after your half-assed attempt to defect in Vienna, I have done you a favor. You should thank me."

"Thank you?" István's voice was incredulous. "For what? Keeping me a prisoner? With your thug threatening to break my hands?"

"Your hands have fully recovered, your physician assured me of this fact himself. In the meantime, I bought you time and maybe your future. I kept you here until you were old enough to understand the real cost of leaving. Your place at the Liszt Academy, your concert schedule, your fine clothing, your private car—all of that disappears the moment you leave. You will have nothing."

"You think I do not understand this?"

"At seventeen? No, I do not believe you do." Kovács touched his cheek gingerly; talking this much hurt like hell. "I am leaving because I must. Zhirov is on his way to Budapest to arrest me or to escort me to Moscow. Either way, I will not survive. I am to be blamed for this nonsense in the streets. And yes, I said nothing of my plans to you because it was safer for you not to know until I was gone. To protect both of us."

"How very noble of you. How very convenient."

Kovács kept talking. "You now have a choice to make. You can stay here. You are favorably viewed in Moscow. They understand you are gifted, and talent is useful to the powerful. Tell Zhirov you tried to stop me if it helps you and swear allegiance to whoever comes along next. That, and your abilities are enough to save you."

"I will never swear allegiance to Moscow. Ever."

"Then come with me. You are welcome. But if you leave Budapest with me, know that you will have to disappear with me. I do not intend to be found—ever. Just say the word, and my men will load your piano at once."

"There is a third choice," István said. "Call off Tibor and let me go. Now, while the border is still open."

Kovács studied his son's face. "If you go west, you will never play anywhere in Eastern Europe or Russia again. You will be branded a traitor, and even those who taught and admired you will erase you as a coward. You will never see Budapest again. Is that what you want?"

"With all my heart."

Kovács sighed. There was no point arguing any further. "Very well, make your own way then. I have arranged for a car to pick me up this evening. I can take you as far as Belgrade or Sofia. Or you may make your own way from here. I suggest you wait until dark—there is less chance you will be seen. I will take care of Tibor, so there will be no one to ask questions."

He took a good hard look at his son. He would miss him. "I have always wanted only the best for you," he said, his voice civil and formal. "I will watch for your performances in the West. If and when it is safe to do so, I will be in touch."

István nodded; the fight had gone out of him, too.

Kovács cleared his throat and loosened the top button of his uniform. "And now you must excuse me. I have work to do before I leave. Please, play the *Hammerklavier* for me one last time since it may be some time before I hear you play it again. From the beginning."

István's hands twitched. "I don't know. I have not attempted it…since Vienna."

"Try. For me. I will feel better, knowing that you are playing like your old self again."

István's hands moved to his keyboard. He played a few tentative notes and then began the quick, commanding notes of opening *allegro* to the *Hammerklavier*.

Kovács listened for a moment and then turned toward his private quarters. A few moments at his desk, and then he would wash away the sweat and stink of the last ten days. He touched his cheek again. The blood along the edge of the cut was finally drying.

It feels good to be looking forward, Kovács thought. He was sorry to part ways with István, but perhaps it was for the best, at least for a while. Keeping his son in line was exhausting, even for him, head of the AVO. Let him make his own way—perhaps then István might come to appreciate all that had been done for him. For himself, leaving Budapest could not come soon enough. He would be done—forever—with Zhirov. Kovács couldn't wait.

27
TREASURE

Ⅰn his study, Kovács moved quickly. He needed to be efficient, to finish before his car arrived. Or before Zhirov came looking for him—as Kovács knew he would. His instruction to Fekete to take Zhirov to the office first merely delayed the inevitable. He left the study's door ajar; he never tired of hearing the *Hammerklavier*.

Kovács left instructions that his desk and chair were the last items to be loaded onto the moving van. His personal files were his first order of business—no point in leaving them to be found by whoever came next—and he worked through them quickly. He burned the least important files—notes on low-ranking party members too insignificant to be of future use to him—in the fireplace, making sure nothing was left but ash. The next set of files—those on Zhirov and other bureaucrats, the people who actually got things done inside the Kremlin—he set aside to carry with him as insurance. He intended to remain hidden for good, but it never hurt to have a little leverage, just in case.

Through the open door, the sound of István's playing paused for a moment. Then, the rapid, rippling opening of the second movement of the *Hammerklavier*. István hit every note perfectly, just as he always had. Tibor had done no lasting damage. Would István's talent be enough to keep him safe in these new, uncertain times? *Perhaps in the West*, Kovács thought, *assuming he makes it.*

Next—and because he was a creature of habit—Kovács turned to the day's cables from Moscow waiting on his desk. *A thinner pile than usual*, he thought. Another sign that his tenure was growing short. Still, Kovács worked his way through them systematically, scanning each one for clues to what Moscow's plans might be for Hungary. More reports of Soviet troops at the Czech border even though—he noted, annoyed—there had been no word to him regarding Khrushchev's intention to send troops into Hungary. A good thing he had spies of his own. Another cable concerned Pál Maléter, now passing himself off as Prime Minister Nagy's minister of defense. A priority arrest, Moscow stressed. The final cable in the stack amounted to little more than juicy gossip: A MiG-15 had gone missing this morning from Tököl Air Base, along with an East German mechanic named Hans Horst. There was no radar data available; everyone else on the base, including all of the superior officers and the flight tower crew, claimed to have been asleep. Horst was another priority arrest and also no longer his problem. Let the Russians deal with Maléter and their missing mechanic. Both cables went into the fire along with the last of his files.

Kovács turned next to the large iron safe behind his desk. Inside was a brown leather attaché case. Methodically, he checked its contents: it held his various sets of new identity cards and thick bundles of cash—Hungarian forints, Russian rubles, American dollars. He counted out a stack of cash for

István—it was the least he could do—and tucked the bills in his pocket to give to his son. Next, he pulled out a handful of personal documents—some forged, others authentic—that he might or might not ever need again. Everything looked in order.

Finally, from the bottom of the case he brought out a knotted bundle of cheap cloth still smelling faintly of lye and smoke. He untied it with care. Inside lay his mother's plain black wooden rosary beads and cross. He kissed it by habit. Not that he had any interest in religion—the Communist party was right about that nonsense. But these beads were the last things his mother touched, and they were all he had left of her. They were dear to him, too precious to leave behind. He fingered the beads one by one, just as his mother had done, her lips moving in silent supplication as she prayed for luck or money or maybe just something to eat. Prayers that went unanswered. Then he rewrapped them carefully. Instead of putting them back into his attaché case, he slipped them into his pocket. He would carry them with him into his new life, a small gesture in memory of his mother.

He checked his watch. Nearly two P.M. The car and driver he paid for—unofficially and with plenty of cash—wouldn't arrive for another two hours, when the short days of winter turned to dusk early and there was less chance of being spotted or stopped under the cover of night. Given Zhirov's arrival, the timing would be tight, but by then, the moving van would be loaded with as much as could be taken and sent on ahead to await his arrival while he followed discreetly by private car. Now that the time had come to go, Kovács was ready.

The unrelenting adrenaline that had sustained him for the last two weeks was fading. He welcomed the idea of deep, luxurious, and uninterrupted sleep. He longed for a bed, but his bedroom was already empty. He leaned back in his chair and let the slow, sorrowful notes of the third movement, the *adagio sostenuto*, wash over him. A few more hours, and this life would be behind him for good. His eyes closed. Kovács let himself drift just for a moment. He fell asleep to the sound of István's piano.

28

BETWEEN ALWAYS AND NEVER

Outside Győr, Route 1 stretched east toward Budapest past barren fields. Only Viktor, Charlie, Horst, and Walter drove toward Budapest. Every other vehicle on the road was heading west toward the Austrian border, back the way they had come.

"You are sure?" Viktor asked, his voice laced with dread. His hands gripped the steering wheel so tightly that Charlie saw the veins on the back of his hands pulse. "Fifteen bomber squadrons?"

"I am sure." Horst sat on the edge of the bench in the back and leaned through the rear cab window. "The planes are to take off at first light."

Charlie turned to look at Horst. Behind him, she could see Walter seated in front of the shortwave, studying the pictures in the manual and then finding the corresponding part on the set in front of him.

"We pay a terrible price for daring to want to run our own country." Viktor's voice was grim.

"It will get worse," Horst said. "*Русский поцелуй*. It is called a Russian kiss, and the target is the city of Budapest.

Kill anything and anyone that moves. Those are the orders to the pilots for tomorrow."

"The attack is coming from Tököl?"

Horst nodded. "The bombers are to destroy anything that moves. Bridges, armories, Parliament if necessary. Civilians are not to be spared."

"Civilians?" Charlie said, dismayed. "But that is specifically outlawed by the Geneva Conventions."

"The Russians have never agreed to the Geneva Conventions," Viktor said, his voice cold with anger. "I see now that the Russians never intended to withdraw. They have been buying time while they gathered their forces. Tomorrow, they intend to destroy Budapest."

"They intend to make an example of you Hungarians. In case anyone else gets ideas."

"The ideas are already there, I assure you," Viktor snapped. "Every single one of the satellite states wishes for the same thing—to be independent."

"It is true. Our officers tell us we are liberators, that the Hungarian people are asking for our help against fascists and Nazis. It's garbage. We know why you are fighting. We're not that stupid." Horst rubbed one hand over the greying stubble on his chin. "But you will never beat the Soviet Army. There are too many of them. You Hungarians are screwed, just like the rest of us. *Zwischen immer und nie.* Between always and never. This is the world Russia curses us with. We are always afraid, we are never safe."

Charlie's brow furrowed. "My grandfather used to say the same thing—*zwischen immer und nie.* He left Prussia when he was young. That was after the Great War. There were no jobs, no food, no prospects for a poor boy like him. He walked all the way to Hamburg, hired on as a cabin boy on a cargo ship, and eventually made his way to the United States. He never looked back."

"Nothing has changed," Horst said. "There are still no jobs except the collective farms, the factories, or the army. And no matter where they put you to work, you are barely paid enough to eat. It is a shit life."

"But why did you choose to attempt an escape now?" Charlie asked. "Were you inspired by the Hungarians?"

"Perhaps we should not know so much about each other." Viktor's expression looked somber. "In case we are stopped by Russians."

"If we are stopped by Russians, it will not matter. The truth is always whatever they want it to be." A shadow passed over Horst's face, and his lips tightened. "Was I inspired by the Hungarians? Yes and no. Even before Walter was born, my wife and I discussed what to do. We did not want to bring our child up under communism. My wife died seven years ago, the day Walter was born, and ever since then, my desire to leave with Walter became even stronger. I had hope but not an opportunity." He put his hand on his son's back, gently rubbing it. Walter glanced up from his reading and leaned closer to his father.

"So, my mother looked after Walter for a time, but she died, too, last winter," Horst continued. "Influenza. Then, a week ago, I was ordered to report immediately for duty at Tököl—the Russians needed people like me to look after their planes. But there was no one to look after Walter. My superior officer told me to put him in a *Jugenderziehungstalt*, a home for children to be raised by the state, and be done with it. Those are terrible places." Horst pulled Walter closer to him. "I could not let my son be raised by strangers. I decided I would make this the chance I was hoping for. And so we are here."

Viktor, listening as he drove, flushed.

"You're really a mechanic?" Charlie asked. "A mechanic who can fly MiGs?"

Horst sighed. "It is complicated. During the war, yes, I was a pilot in the *Luftwaffe*. I flew mostly Heinkels or Dorniers. Bombing infrastructures or factories during war time is a soldier's job, but killing civilians, bombing their houses and villages, destroying their fields—tell me, what purpose does that serve? That is not why I learned to fly. After the war, I knew I could never do such things again—especially not for Moscow's benefit. The Russians told me I was too stupid to be a pilot anyway, and they assigned me to fix their planes instead."

"But you are smart enough to steal a MiG?"

Horst almost smiled. "Only an old one. One that would not be noticed missing right away."

"No one tried to stop you?"

"They could not. They were asleep. I put sleeping draughts in the morning coffee." Horst patted his pocket and pulled out a small bottle. "Chloral hydrate. Very effective."

Charlie's fingers brushed against her watch. A. J. had disappeared from her life when she wasn't much older than Walter. "My father was a pilot. He flew an old Curtiss Jenny biplane, and sometimes he took me flying with him. He let me work the controls and taught me how to glide the Curtiss Jenny to a smooth landing."

Horst listened intently. "So, now you are here with your husband?"

"We are not married." Charlie and Viktor spoke in unison.

"We are—we were—colleagues at Radio Free Europe," Charlie said. "Viktor worked for the Hungarian radio service as a commentator until a few days ago. He is going home to help Hungary build a new future."

"Yes, and Miss Atkins is a news clerk and wedding dress correspondent, who believes she now is qualified to write about a revolution from the front lines."

Horst raised his eyebrows as his eyes flicked from Viktor to Charlie.

"Ha ha. Very funny," Charlie said, unamused. "Viktor is right. I am a clerk, but he's wrong about everything else. I did write about a wedding dress, but Viktor missed the point. It wasn't about the dress but about a woman named Sophie, who was raised to be a good German wife and mother and to run her own household. But Sophie and her fiancé were arrested on their wedding day for daring to speak out against Hitler and the Nazis. He died in Belgium, and she was sent to Ravensbrück. She survived, but like so many others, she lost everything, including the one thing that mattered most to her—her chance to marry and raise a family. You are East German, she is West German, but your stories are not so different. War does terrible things to people, and then they have to spend the rest of their lives making sense of it."

"You cannot write about such things in Munich?"

"I can, but the best reporters are the ones who go where history is happening. That's our job—to be witnesses to what is really happening, not just what a government wants you to believe. Our friend Viktor here can tell you why something matters in the long sweep of Hungarian history, but I aim to tell you how it feels to the individuals who live through it and survive. Do Viktor's stories change the way people think or feel? I don't know, but I sure hope mine do."

Charlie pulled up the plasma kit onto her lap and showed it to Horst. "This is the story I am working on now."

She slid back the kit's lid. Inside, the freeze-dried plasma powder filled a thick, square-shouldered glass bottle alongside a second bottle of sterile, distilled water and nine inches of thin, flexible tubing to be used with a needle as an intravenous line. "This is a transfusion kit—a doctor or medic mixes the plasma and water together and three minutes later, it is ready to be used."

Charlie tapped the bottle with one finger. "But here is why this particular plasma kit matters to me. The blood for this plasma was donated by West Germans, the same people who looked the other way when Hitler deported their friends and neighbors to the death camps or into forced labor. Now they are standing in line to support Hungarians, who are trying to free themselves from the same kind of evil. The West Germans I interviewed in Munich want to help save lives, but they also hope to reclaim what's good and decent about themselves—that Germans are more than Nazis. I am going to Budapest so I can tell the rest of the story—what this plasma means to the doctors and patients who receive it."

"I cannot get away from war fast enough," Horst said. "I want only to live a quiet life and raise my son. I would like to work with my hands—to build things, not destroy them. That is enough. Perhaps one day, you will write about me. If my story can help someone else, I would like that."

Charlie smiled, delighted. "I'd like that too," she said, and she shook Horst's hand just to make it official.

She looked up through the windshield. The road ahead looked clear. Not just the road to Budapest—her road. Her future, the one where she was a real reporter. A war correspondent, even.

But first things first. Right now, her job was to find Péter in Budapest and finish her reporting. Then she would leave her story on Owens's desk first thing Monday morning, along with a proposal for an exclusive interview with Horst, who—almost—managed to fly a MiG to the Free West. If Owens didn't take her seriously after that—well, that was on him. *There are other jobs*, Charlie thought. *Whatever happens now, I'm on my way.*

29
PATRIOT NEEDED

The trouble was, Owens thought, as he hurried toward the American Consulate on *Ludwigstraße*, he didn't know Cordell Tanner all that well. The man had a knack for appearing—or disappearing—when least expected. Come to think of it, Owens didn't remember where or when he had met Tanner for the first time. Tanner had simply always been around.

The last time Owens saw Tanner had been three days ago. Owens had been on the phone receiving yet another round of confusing direction about whether or not Radio Free Europe should support Imre Nagy from the brass in New York when Tanner materialized unannounced in his office. Without asking, Tanner closed the door to Owens's office, selected a fresh cigar from the humidor on Owens's desk, and lit it with Owens's favorite silver lighter. Then he folded himself into one of the chairs across from Owens and lit up, waiting for Owens to finish his call.

"I'm looking for a name," Tanner said through the yellow-blue gauzy haze of cigar smoke as soon as Owens's call ended.

Tanner's suit—Owens couldn't tell whether the fabric was black or a particularly deep shade of navy blue—white shirt, and narrow tie were as unremarkable as Tanner's features: thin lips pressed into a perpetual near smile and a face with enough mileage that, Owens guessed, put Tanner closer to forty-five than forty years old. Tanner had no discernible accent, as if he had been plucked from central casting to play a man least likely to be noticed by anyone. Except for his eyes—one blue, one brown.

"A name of a Hungarian patriot who loves his country," Tanner continued. "Someone willing to go back home as soon as it can be arranged. Quietly, of course."

Owens replaced the telephone earpiece in its receiver, at once annoyed and flattered. Annoyed that Tanner so casually made himself at home; flattered because Tanner wouldn't have come unless he needed something from Owens. "This official business?"

Tanner shrugged and considered his cigar, rolling it between his fingers before putting it back between his lips.

Hell's bells, Owens thought. He reached over and took his time selecting a cigar for himself. He wanted more information before giving up a name. Both of them could play this waiting game.

"Truth is, we've been caught napping," Tanner said finally. "We don't know the players in Budapest, who to back, or how to help."

"Interview the refugees at the border. They have the latest information."

Tanner was already shaking his head. "We have that covered. This is something different. My chain of command needs someone who can put us close to the government and the people in charge of this business. We need to know whether there is a horse in this race we can and should back. That means boots on the ground. In Budapest. As soon as humanly possible."

"What about the new guy? The new American ambassador to Hungary. What's his name? Wailes. Ed Wailes." Owens lit his cigar and then tossed his lighter back on the desk. "Can't he help?"

"He's been in country less than forty-eight hours. He's about as well-connected as a dead battery. Besides, he's been told by Washington to sit on the bench until we know what we're dealing with. Or whom. Ike doesn't know Nagy, the new prime minister, or how cozy he may be with Moscow."

Owens forgot his annoyance. He didn't get tidbits like this from the top very often. "That so?"

Tanner nodded. "I need a local man. Someone discreet, who can get the inside scoop. Someone reliable."

"An advance team?"

"Whoever goes in goes in alone." Tanner hesitated. "If you ask our president, that's one man too many. Containment, not confrontation, when it comes to the Reds. But my brass says we need to give the president options whether he wants them or not. Exploratory work. In case the president decides to make a move."

Owens pulled on his cigar as he digested this information. Should he give Tanner a name? If he did, was he stepping over the line of what constituted good, ethical journalism? Were journalistic standards different during times of war? Did it matter who was doing the asking, in this case an officially unofficial official for his own government? Did a cold war count, same as a hot war? *I guess a name won't hurt as long as the man has the right to say no*, Owens thought. Not that the man he had in mind would say no.

"Viktor Farkas," Owens said finally as he exhaled a cloud of smoke. "Smart. Articulate. Knows Nagy and the rest of them. He will give you straight information." He nodded out toward the newsroom. "He's on the floor now. Third desk on the right."

Without another word, Tanner nodded his thanks, stubbed out his cigar, and disappeared through Owens's office door.

Owens had forgotten about his conversation with Tanner until this morning, when he found Viktor's resignation letter on his desk. Now he knew why: Viktor was on his way to Budapest for Tanner.

He rounded the corner and turned onto *Ludwigstraße*. The American Consulate, a long, low, and unremarkable-looking grey box of a building, was on the far corner. If Tanner had a way to reach Viktor, and if Viktor and Charlie were still together, then maybe Owens could get a message to Charlie.

Too many ifs for Owens's liking, but finding Tanner was the best—and only—shot he had.

30
THE CONSULATE

Owens sat in a windowless room off the consulate's voluminous lobby, furnished with only the bare necessities—an old table and hard wooden chairs. It was cold; like many Munich buildings, the heat was turned off on the weekends.

"Cord Tanner?" Harold—Schmitty—Schmidt, the consulate's duty officer, faced Owens across the table. Tufts of gray hair stuck out on both sides of his bald head, like the whiskered bristles of a stiff brush. "Boy, you got as much chance finding him as you do the Easter Bunny."

"But you know him?" Owens asked eagerly. He had liked Schmitty as soon as he said hello—one word, and Owens knew he was talking to another Bronx transplant. "You can find him?"

"You been around a place like this as long as I have, you know everybody," Schmitty said. He wore a thick wool cardigan buttoned all the way up to the top over a white shirt and navy-blue tie. He drummed his fingers lightly on the table. "He's a slippery one, all right, but yeah, sure, I can find him. Give me a day or two."

Owens's face fell. His conversation with Schmitty had started off cautiously, Owens hopeful that he wouldn't have to share all of the details about why he was so desperate to find Tanner. He didn't want word of what Charlie had done getting back to New York, especially not through informal channels. If there was bad news to be delivered, he wanted to do it himself.

"I don't have that kind of time," he admitted.

"Yeah? What's the fire?"

Reluctantly, Owens filled Schmitty in, outlining the situation only in broadest of strokes. Tanner had recruited one of Radio Free Europe's most recognizable commentators to return to Hungary—yes, in the middle of a revolution—and he, Owens, needed to reach him right away.

"I need to speak to Viktor as soon as possible. It's a matter of life or death—" Owens pushed the point hard—"or else I wouldn't be sitting here."

Schmitty whistled. "Your man's got some nerve, going back to Budapest now. Those Russians, they make up their mind to do something, they don't kid around. If the word on the street is true—and we think it is—the Reds are already on their way back to Budapest, and they ain't asking for permission, if you know what I mean. It's gonna get hot pretty fast, and it's gonna get ugly."

Owens nodded, his face grim. "We hear the same thing. There isn't much time."

"I gotta think a minute," Schmitty said. He threw back his head and looked up at the ceiling, as if it might hold answers for him. "Here in Munich, everyone at the consulate has been told to sit tight and stay quiet. No statements official or otherwise, so it doesn't look like we're taking sides. We don't want Moscow saying that we are the ones stirring up trouble."

"What about your people in Budapest?"

Schmitty snorted. "We got one part-time guy there who keeps things running for us. He does the small stuff—visa letters, meeting visitors, official contacts, help for tourists. Not a guy in the know, if you follow me."

"I thought you people were paid to keep your eyes open for stuff like this."

"We are, and we do, but you gotta remember that things are moving pretty fast in Budapest, faster than anybody knew," Schmitty said. "I gotta think Tanner knows what he is doing, sending someone in—we all need information since we sure as hell can't read Khruschev's mind. But now that your guy is in, I am thinking there is not much we can do to help him."

"But we—Tanner—asked Viktor to go."

Schmitty scratched his chin. "Yeah, but if your guy went back, he did it on his own say so. People like your guy—what is his name, Viktor?—people like Viktor, who have lived under the Russian thumb, they know the score better than anyone. Even if I can find Tanner, I'm not sure there is anything he can do. Fact is, we could just make things worse. We risk tipping off the Reds that your man is in Budapest. They might find him first, and that won't do anybody any good."

Owens shifted uncomfortably on the hard narrow chair and grimaced. "I am afraid there is more," he said, and he laid out the rest of the problem for Schmitty—that the youngest and greenest news clerk in his organization was apparently on the way to Budapest with her Radio Free Europe credentials in hand. An organization the Russians hated. Against his direct orders. And one who happened to be female.

Schmitty listened, his expression unreadable. "Dumb kid," he said when Owens finished. "If the Reds find her, she will be in a world of hurt. They will put her on trial just for show. She won't have a chance."

Owens finished Schmitty's thought. "They look like they are playing by our rules—a free, fair, and open trial. Meanwhile, we look bad for sending a girl to do a man's job in a war zone. A girl they will claim is a spy for the West. Which we didn't. And she isn't."

Owens paused. "So now you know why I need to find Tanner, and the sooner the better. If Charlie is still with Viktor—and I hope to hell she is—I need to tell her to come home."

Schmitty tapped the table again. "Lemme pull out all the stops and see what I can do. Best I got right now. Tanner knows how to reach you?"

"My office at Radio Free Europe." *Assuming I haven't been fired*, Owens thought. He stood, shook Schmitty's hand, and headed back out into the rain.

#　　#　　#

Outside the consulate, the afternoon's showers were now a cold, joyless rain. Thick drops pooled on his hat brim and then ran in rivulets inside his collar and down his back. The wet gloom only added to his misery. Even if Schmitty managed to find Tanner quickly, it might not be soon enough to reach Charlie and tell her to get the hell out.

Owens shivered—at the rain, maybe, or more likely, at the prospect of what was to come: a tough phone call to the brass in New York and the consequences of what might happen. The Soviets loathed Radio Free Europe and claimed its only goal was to destabilize their control of the Eastern Bloc. If Charlie did get arrested, Schmitty was right: she would be put on trial and her sentence—years in prison—would be a foregone conclusion. Even if Radio Free Europe tried to negotiate for Charlie's freedom, the price would be unthinkable; the Reds were sure to demand that Radio Free Europe turn off its transmitters for good. And meanwhile, Charlie would be rotting away in a Soviet prison. Could she survive that? Owens didn't want to even think about it.

For a few minutes, he waited in vain for a taxi. Then by habit—and because he was out of ideas on all fronts—he turned south away from the consulate and toward *Englischer Garten*, Munich's grand old central park. Radio Free Europe's offices were on the far side of the garden, and the sodden walk through the park's winding pathways matched his foul mood.

All I can do now is sit tight and hope for good news, he thought. Otherwise, an hour from now, he would be on the phone to New York to tell them the bad news: his most junior news clerk—a girl—was unreachable in an Iron Curtain war zone with the Red Army poised to attack.

31
THE SPOILS OF WAR

Viktor, wary of Soviet tanks and troops, kept to Pest's side roads.

They had driven up from the south of Budapest, dropping down from Route 1 to skirt the outer rim of Buda, crossing the restless waters of the Danube on the northern end of Csepel Island, and then finally entering Pest.

It was slow going.

Many roads were blocked by concrete, brick or glass rubble, or with barricades hastily shoved together to slow down tanks rolling toward the Danube and its bridges. Street meridian strips—where spring grass usually grew—were filled with fresh, shallow graves marked with stick crosses and names written on cloth. No late afternoon sun broke through the thick, blue-gray clouds, either; the air felt heavy, as if already weighted down by the coming storm.

Viktor turned onto a side street.

A burned-out tank blocked the street but not before it had damaged most of the surrounding apartment buildings. Viktor cursed under his breath, reversed the truck, and slowly began to maneuver the truck backward.

In back, Horst and Walter bent over Viktor's shortwave set. Horst was explaining in a soft voice to his son how radio communications worked. Charlie watched them together for a moment, Horst's arm around his son. She caught a few words of Horst's patient explanation—how the amplifier boosted the strength of the radio transmissions, how the push-to-talk microphone worked, how shortwave radio connected people who would never meet in person. *We did the right thing, saving Horst and Walter*, she thought.

Outside her window, two men emerged from one of the ruined buildings. The older of the two was short and sturdy-looking with bushy grey eyebrows and half-a-dozen wrist watches strapped over one coat sleeve. He carried an overflowing pillowcase to the curb, where he dumped it out unceremoniously alongside a jumbled accumulation of radio sets, cameras, clothing, household linens, a small armchair, and a heavy electric floor lamp. His companion, younger by a dozen years at least, was lean and muscular. His head—hair shaved close to his skull—leaned back as he chugged from a bottle of cheap Fóti vodka. He wiped his mouth on his sleeve and then caught Charlie's eyes.

The red stars on their uniforms and their Mosin rifles gave them away.

Red Army soldiers.

Russians.

Looters.

Charlie opened her mouth—

Too late.

"*Ubiraysya.*" The younger soldier wrenched open the door and grabbed Charlie, vise-like, around her arm, and pulled her out of the truck. The other soldier banged on Viktor's door with the buttstock of his rifle. Up close, his face was broad and flat, and his eyes were dull brown like muddy water.

Viktor, hands raised, got out. His eyes were locked on Charlie. "They want the truck," he translated for Charlie's benefit.

"*Menya zovut Boris, a eto moy drug Ivan,*" the young man said, grinning as he looked Charlie up and down. "*Kak vas zovut?*"

"He says his name is Boris, and this is his friend Ivan," Viktor said, his voice level. "He wants to know your name."

Charlie wriggled, trying to pull herself free. Boris smelled of sweat and stale beer. "Tell him to let me go, and I'll tell him."

Viktor translated.

Boris just laughed.

"*Proverte szady.*" Boris pointed Ivan toward the back of the truck. He kept his rifle leveled at Viktor and his grip on Charlie.

Ivan returned a moment later, pushing Horst and Walter in front of him, their hands over their heads. "*Privet, Boris. Ya nashel etikh dvoih v kuzove gruzovika s korotkovolnovym radio.*"

"*Khorosho. Bolshe deneg dlya nas. Pust' rabotayut, zagruzhayut gruzovik.*"

"They say they will sell the shortwave. We are to load these things they are stealing into the back of the truck."

Ivan rubbed the sleeve of Horst's coat, feeling the fabric between his dirty fingers, and gestured to Horst: take it off. "*Mne nravitsya tvoye pal'to.*"

Horst stepped in front of his son, as if shielding him from Ivan and the business end of his Mosin rifle. Then slowly, carefully, he slipped out of his coat, careful to keep at least one hand up over his head. He held the coat out to Ivan with one hand, but Ivan was squinting at Horst's name patch. Ivan frowned, and then his eyes widened in surprise.

"*Ey, Boris,*" Ivan said. *"Eto tot chelovek, kotorogo my ishchem. My poluchim nagradu.*"

"*Aga?*" Boris took another swig from his bottle and then offered it to Charlie. She shook her head. He leaned in close to her, rubbing his stubbled face against hers, trying to catch her lips with his. His breath stank.

Charlie turned her head away, her fear rising. Viktor, Horst, and Walter stared at her, dread written across their faces.

"They were told to look for Horst—there is a reward,'" Viktor translated.

"*Moya nagrada nachinayetsya pryamo zdes'.*" Boris's words slurred. He grabbed Charlie's ass and lifted her up to him, forcing her legs to wrap around his waist.

"He says—"

Charlie didn't wait for Viktor's translation. She head-butted Boris as hard as she could as she wrenched her body, trying to free herself.

Boris's eyes lit up, mean and angry. He shoved her against back the truck, one hand around her throat. Charlie pulled at his hand and kicked—at least, she tried to kick. He pinned her against the cold, hard metal with his body, her legs dangling. He tugged at her coat, yanking it open and pushing his tongue into her mouth. His hands were on her sweater, then up inside. Between her legs. Charlie fought the urge to panic.

A flash—

—Horst pushed Walter back and then threw his coat over Ivan, catching him off guard—

—Ivan struggled under the coat as Horst grabbed his rifle by its steel barrel—

—Horst swung it around hard, like a baseball bat—

—The rifle's steel buttstock struck Boris in the head—

—He fell sideways, hitting the curb—

—Charlie fell, too, scraping down the side of the truck onto the hard, cold street.

Horst flipped the rifle around. He whipped the coat off Ivan and fired at point blank range. Ivan dropped.

Viktor seized the floor lamp. He smashed its base down on Boris's head. Again. Again. Again.

Horst put one hand on Viktor's arm.

Viktor stopped. He was sweating, his face full of rage. He glanced at Horst and then dropped the lamp. He knelt next to Charlie. "Miss Atkins—"

"I'm fine." Charlie cut Viktor off. She stood, shaking. Her skin crawled, as if she could cast off the rough, grasping feel of Boris's hands on her. She wiped her face—her mouth—on her sleeve, but his smell, his taste, remained.

No one spoke. Charlie pulled her coat around her. Horst hugged Walter and then bent down and picked up both rifles. He lifted each one's bolt handle, checked inside the chambers for ammunition, and then closed each one. "We should take these with us. Just in case."

"Leave their bodies where they fell." Viktor's voice was hard. "Let everyone see them for what they were—thieves."

Charlie forced herself to move toward the truck. She didn't look back.

#   #   #

Under other circumstances, Charlie might have found Budapest breathtaking. On the west bank of the Danube River stood the stone parapets of the thirteenth-century Buda Castle and the soaring, one-hundred-and-thirty-foot tall bronze Liberty Statue of a woman built to commemorate the Soviet liberation of Hungary during World War II. On the Pest side of the river, the three domed towers of St. Stephen's Basilica stood tall, not far from the red roof and white spires of the Hungarian Parliament building on the eastern shore of the river. In between, five bridges spanned the Danube—a sixth, the Elizabeth Bridge, awaited reconstruction—connecting Buda and Pest.

Charlie didn't speak again until they neared the school, a low, two-story brick building. Lettering chiseled over its heavy wooden entry doors read *Budapesti Fiúakadémia*, the Budapest Academy for Boys. It was close enough to Budapest's grand, ornate Corvin Cinema, the freedom fighter's headquarters and where the fiercest battles raged on such that Charlie could smell smoke and gunpowder. Péter's ambulance—unmistakable with its missing front fender and dented driver's side door—was up on the curb in front of the school, every one of its doors flung open like the wings of a startled bird in flight.

"That's it," she said, her voice low.

Viktor pulled alongside the school where the truck would be shielded from the road by trees. He turned off the engine.

"I will contact Mr. Tanner," he said, without looking at Charlie. "When I am done, I will find you inside and translate for you."

"No need—Péter speaks excellent English," Charlie said stiffly. She looped her bag over one shoulder and hefted the plasma kit. "How do you say, 'ambulance driver' in Hungarian?"

"Mentőautó vezető," Viktor said.

"Mentőautó vezető," Charlie repeated, letting the strange syllables settle on her tongue. She repeated them like a mantra. An hour, maybe two, and she would have her story reported. Then home to Munich, with her first cold war hot zone byline. But passing Péter's ambulance, she still tasted Boris's boozy stink.

32
BLOOD IS NOT ENOUGH

The smell inside the Budapest School for Boys hit Charlie first: shit, vomit, and ether.

The dank, sweaty air hit her next and then came the sight of casualties, too many for her to count. The injured lay on stretchers on the floor or leaned against walls, blood seeping through rag bandages or drying in a scaly patchwork on exposed skin. No one was spared: teenage fighters sat alongside white-faced grannies and whimpering children too young to understand what had happened to them. Volunteers moved among the chaos, doing what they could by offering fresh water and quick prayers.

Charlie shivered and tried not to gag. On a distant radio, Radio Free Europe's distinctive, top-of-the-hour four-bell chime rang over the slam and bang of stretchers and the moans and cries of the wounded. *No one wants to miss any bit of news,* she thought. She covered her nose and mouth with her scarf. *Just find Péter. Mentőautó vezető.*

Her story, once she found Péter, wouldn't take long to report. But where to start?

She tapped the arm of one of the volunteers, a short, stooped-shoulder man barking terse instructions in Hungarian. He wore a blood-spattered apron over a tweed suit, his face haggard, his eyes exhausted.

"Excuse me," Charlie said. "*Mentőautó vezető?*"

The man looked sharply at her. "You are not Hungarian. British? American? You bring troops?"

"American, yes. No troops. You speak English."

"I am László Dobos, director of this school. Yes, I speak English. Between the wars, I studied in London. Who are you? But your troops are coming, yes? I am sure I heard it on Radio Free Europe."

Had something changed since last night? Charlie was sure Owens would not allow such a definitive statement about the United States' intentions to be broadcast unless it were true. "Could it have been another station? I am from Radio Free Europe. We wouldn't say American troops are coming unless the Security Council says so. And as far as I know, that hasn't happened."

Dobos grabbed Charlie by the shoulders, his face inches from hers. His fingers dug into her shoulders, like claws. "This war. The wounded. The dead. This is all your fault. Your radio told us we must fight for freedom, that we cannot—should not—give up even when it is clear we can never win. Have you seen what is happening in the streets? Our fighters are armed with shovels or pickaxes or old guns from the Great War. Our wives are making bombs out of wine bottles and gasoline. Even our children fight because Radio Free Europe tells us to hold out hope. Meanwhile, our prime minister is making promises the Soviets will never let him keep, our government is paralyzed, and the Russians are at our borders. Where is the help you promised us?"

"I-I-I-don't know," Charlie stammered.

Dobos shook her, spitting ferocity and rage. "Do you understand? We are dying. Your soldiers must come."

Charlie tried to pull herself away from Dobos, but he held her fast. She said, "Our presidential election is in three days—maybe after that President Eisenhower will send troops—"

"We cannot wait that long. We need guns and soldiers and tanks. We need doctors and nurses, too, and we need morphine, sterile tools, more blood for transfusions—"

"Plasma, yes, did it come this morning?" Charlie finally wrenched herself free. "I am looking for Péter, the doctor who brought it from the border this morning." She held out the plasma kit. "This one I carried myself. Have you seen him?"

Dobos stopped. He stared at the plasma kit and then took it from her hands. "Yes. I have seen him. He is here. Come with me. Perhaps then you will understand."

"Understand what?" Charlie asked, but it was too late. Dobos strode across the hall into a large, cold room with high ceilings and windows. *The school's gymnasium*, Charlie thought, as she followed Dobos around a set of parallel bars and two pommel horses shoved together near the door.

Dobos stopped. Péter lay on the floor. He might have been sleeping but for his blue eyes. They stared out through round glasses, past the point of caring. His shirt was torn open and so was his chest where a doctor had tried to will him back to life.

Charlie sucked in her breath, hard as a cold slap. She sank down next to him, unable to tear her eyes away from Péter's face. She understood death; on a farm, death was part of life. But not this death. Not Péter. Péter was supposed to save lives.

"How—what happened?"

"A sniper, maybe two blocks from here, he told us. He barely made it here."

"But he brought plasma—lots of it. Couldn't you save him?"

"Blood alone cannot save a life, let alone a country," Dobos said, his voice bitter. "We need doctors and nurses and a thousand more things to save our wounded. But most of all we need the army that was promised to us, if only we are brave enough to stand up and fight back. You tell your President Eisenhower that we have done all that was asked of us and more, and we are paying the price in blood. Go home and tell your president you must keep your word."

Dobos turned, a curt dismissal, and left Charlie alone on her knees.

But she wasn't alone.

Nearby, a woman cried and murmured to her dead daughter, a teenager who still wore a tricolor armband around one sleeve. One among many—the gymnasium, Charlie saw now, was a morgue with bodies laid out in rows, their faces, like Péter's, left uncovered for more efficient identification.

She turned back to Péter. The photograph of Lukács, the one he'd showed her hours earlier, was still tucked in his shirt pocket. She eased it out gently and held it. It was spattered dull brown and reeked with the coppery tang of dried blood.

Charlie stood, her body shaking, the picture still in her hand. She hurried out of the gymnasium, away from Péter's body, her bag banging against her side. She stumbled over a man lying on a stretcher but kept going, a wave of bile building up. She pushed inside a bathroom just as she vomited.

She squeezed her eyes tight. *A real war correspondent wouldn't cry*, she told herself fiercely, but the more she tried to hold it in, the worse it got, until she couldn't hold it in any longer. She stayed there, arms wrapped around herself, until her sobbing stopped. *Péter wasn't supposed to die. This isn't how his story was supposed to end.*

She didn't move for a long time.

At last, she stood and washed her face, her hands trembling. In the mirror, a strange, sad version of herself looked back. She barely recognized her own face. She blew her nose and wiped her eyes. Her mind was clearer now. She had a plan. She would tell Viktor that he was right: she didn't belong in a war zone. Indiscriminate deaths like Péter's were too much for her to bear. She would go back to what felt safe and familiar in Munich. Maybe she would even go all the way home to California. She did the math in her head—she had enough money saved for her last month's rent and a flight home.

But before she left Munich, she promised herself she would write her story. Only in this version, she stayed at the border, and Péter drove away in the morning sunlight, optimistic about Hungary's future and still very much alive.

33
AN AUDIENCE OF ONE

Charlie found Viktor hunched over the shortwave transmitter as he sent his first report back to Tanner.

"Again, I must stress to you that the news here is desperate," Viktor said. He spoke rapid, urgent English into the microphone. It was gray with a rounded head and a black push-to-talk button on the handle. He glanced at Charlie and held up one finger to keep her from speaking.

Walter sat next to him, watching with rapt attention, even though he didn't understand a word of Viktor's English. Horst, sitting back against the other side of the truck, looked better, too. His face was clean, and the color had returned to his cheeks.

"Negotiations for a complete Soviet withdrawal are continuing, but Prime Minister Nagy is far too trusting of the conventions of war," Viktor continued. "The Russians are not negotiating in good faith. They have no intention of leaving Hungary. Before the Russians cut telephone and telegraph lines, eyewitnesses reported several tank divisions crossing into Hungary. If they are not stopped, the tanks will reach

Budapest within hours. The Russians are taking over the train stations as well—no one can get in or out."

Viktor's ring winked in the low light. "Finally, I tell you again I have firsthand testimony that a full-scale bombing attack against Budapest will begin tomorrow at dawn. The MiGs are already at Tököl air base, and their orders are to kill anything that moves. You must hurry, or Budapest will be lost. We must have heavy guns and bombers. Our fighters will hold out as long as they can, but they cannot withstand bombing. My next report will come from the Parliament building. That is where Nagy and his cabinet are, and I will report the latest from there."

Viktor stood and turned to her. "The situation is dangerous, Miss Atkins. You must file your story quickly and go."

"There is no story." Charlie's voice was short. "Péter's dead. Shot by a sniper."

"So?"

"Péter was supposed to save lives with the plasma from the West." Charlie forced herself to keep her voice even. "That was the whole point. Without him there is no story."

"Write a different story."

"There is no other story. All the plasma in the world won't make a difference. I was wrong. Your people don't need hope— they need heavy artillery and soldiers and field hospitals and doctors and a whole lot else, too." She could not keep her voice from hardening. "You were right. I had no idea what I was getting into by coming here. Happy now?"

"Of course there is another story," Viktor snapped. "Write about what happened, not what you wanted to happen. Happy endings don't change minds. The truth does."

He turned his back to Charlie and picked up his microphone. "This Péter sacrificed himself for what he believed in. That is what a patriot does. A real war correspondent would make his death mean something. If you cannot do this, then, yes, go back to Munich. Write more stories about wedding dresses and leave them on Mr. Owens's desk when he is not there. The sooner you go, the better."

Charlie stared at Viktor's back. Her cheeks burned. Make sense of Péter's death, give it meaning? How? From a safe distance—like the Free West—the sacrifices made in war sounded noble, even honorable. But right now and this close, Charlie saw nothing but grievous loss in Péter's death.

Horst cleared his throat. "The truck is ready. Shall we go?"

Walter stood. Next to his father, the two of them looked so much the same: the same light blond hair, the same lean bone structure, the same clear blue eyes. Horst was risking everything to give his son a chance to grow up in freedom. Péter had done the same thing. Only Péter would never get the chance to see his son grow up.

Viktor was right. There was a story here after all—about fathers and sons, the lucky ones, and the ones who will never come home. She could tell Péter's story and Horst's too.

"Give me thirty minutes," Charlie said.

#   #   #

Charlie sat cross-legged on the truck's front seat, strangely grateful for the deep, familiar rumble of Viktor's voice emanating from the back as she worked. She promised herself she would mourn Péter—but not now. Now her job was to make sense of the senseless.

She worked quickly, ignoring the draft she had written earlier in the day and starting again with a new idea, scribbling in her reporter's notebook as fast as she could. Blood plasma from the West would not save Hungary—but something else might: the strength of blood ties, father to son, bonds that didn't break no matter what. She wrote fast and from the heart.

By the time she looked up, she felt calm and clearheaded, as if writing what actually happened, as ugly as it was, had changed her, too. She couldn't bring Péter back, but Viktor was right—she could make his death mean something.

Viktor glanced up but said nothing when he saw her. He found the right frequency for her, one that Radio Free Europe's transcribers regularly monitored, and then moved out of her way.

Charlie didn't hesitate. She sat down and picked up the microphone; it was still warm from Viktor's hand. Owens was about to find out where she was, but right now that hardly mattered. What mattered were the words she'd written. She cleared her throat and began to speak.

34
COLD COFFEE, HOT NEWS

O wens stood in the newsroom's kitchenette and frowned. His walk across wet, gray *Englischer Garten* did nothing to improve his mood. Now he found nothing but cold dregs left in the communal coffee pot. Didn't anyone besides Charlie pay attention to how he liked his coffee—hot and fresh? Grumpily, he poured what was left in the percolator into a cup, tasted it, and made a face. It was cold and bitter, and the pitcher of cream Charlie kept full was empty. He stared at his cup sourly but carried it with him into the newsroom. Charlie made better coffee. *Makes*, he corrected himself, the knot in his stomach tightening. *You don't know yet that anything has happened to her.*

With phone lines down across Hungary, not much news was getting through. Mária kept bringing in the latest transcripts she picked up, but at the moment the newsroom was mostly quiet—a couple of editors worked the phones, their voices low, as several others caught a few minutes of rest, heads down on their desks. Owens made a small loop of the room—anything to avoid going back to his office or, more accurately, the telephone on his desk. He dreaded calling New York.

Béla, watching the wire machines, shook his head. "Still nothing from the Security Council," he said as Owens passed. Béla's eyes were red from lack of sleep. Owens just nodded. They were all tired.

He glanced at the newsroom clock—in Munich, it was nearly dinner time—and considered his options. If he called New York too soon, he would look like he had lost control of his newsroom. If he waited too long, he would look like he was hiding bad news. Not that it was his fault that Charlie was in the middle of a war zone, but regardless, he was about out of time, excuses, and ideas. No point in putting the call off any longer.

He carried his coffee into his office and sat down behind his desk. He contemplated the phone and made a few notes about what he needed New York to know—that Charlie had disobeyed his direct orders and that he was doing everything he could to find her.

"Here goes nothing," he muttered and rang Radio Free Europe's switchboard.

"Get me a line to New York," he said, and gave the operator the number to call.

He put the receiver down. Now there was nothing to do except wait; transatlantic calls could take minutes or hours. One never quite knew. He turned his chair around to the windows overlooking *Englischer Garten*. He liked this view; if Charlie's stunt got him fired, he would miss it. At fifty-three, he was comfortable and hoped to ride this job out to retirement—assuming he got the chance.

"Hey, how ya doin'?"

Owens turned around. Schmitty was in his doorway, raindrops still glistening on his coat and fedora, a wet umbrella tucked under his arm. "I think I got something for you."

"You found Tanner?" In his relief, Owens nearly knocked over his coffee. "Thank God."

"No, no, not exactly, but after you left, I got to thinking about where I outta look for him, and it came to me all of a sudden. C'mere."

Schmitty stepped up to the map of Europe on Owens's wall. "Munich is, what, 300 miles from the Austrian border?" He pointed at it with the handle of his umbrella. "Not a bad drive if you've got diplomatic plates. Not a bad place to be either, especially if you are waiting for shortwave messages from Budapest."

Owens stared at the map.

"If I was Tanner, this is where I'd be." Schmitty tapped the spot where neutral Austria met communist Hungary. "Right there. There is a tiny village there, Nickelsdorf, the last stop before no man's land. It's about as close to the action as you can get without stepping on the wrong toes."

Schmitty's right, Owens thought. *That's where I'd be.*

"I asked around," Schmitty went on. "Karl Koch is Tanner's usual driver. I tried to find Karl, but it turns out he left Munich early this morning with Tanner and one of the shortwave radio operators. They didn't say a word to anyone, so nobody knows anything. That Tanner is a pretty smart cookie—but I think we got him. I'll bet you dollars to doughnuts he is at the border."

He let his words sink in and then added, "I gotta a car and driver out front. You in?"

Owens hesitated. He picked up his coffee and swirled the cold dregs around in his cup. "I don't know if that is a good idea. Andy, Charlie's contact from the Red Cross, said he'd look for her when he gets back to the border. And besides, I really ought to let New York know what's going on."

"Suit yourself," Schmitty said, "but how is sitting around here gonna make that call any easier?"

Before Owens could answer, a shout came from the newsroom. "Come quick, everyone. To the transcription room." Mária looked frantic. "It's our Charlie. She's on shortwave."

Owens bolted up from his desk, slamming his cup down so hard that a brown slurry of coffee slopped over the edge onto to his desk. He didn't stop to mop it up.

Owens, Schmitty, and the rest of the Hungarian staff hurried after Mária.

"Wait—you must see this," Béla said as Owens passed him on the way to the transcription room. Béla pointed at the black-and-white image materializing on the photographic paper wrapped around the wirephoto machine's synchronized rotating drum.

"Bring it," Owens said tersely, not bothering to stop. Charlie had surfaced, and that trumped everything else.

35
BYLINE BUDAPEST

With a click, Mária turned on the reel-to-reel tape recorder as Owens, Schmitty, and the rest of the newsroom staff crowded around her transcription machine, filling the small room to overflowing. "This just came across one of the frequencies from Budapest that we regularly monitor."

Despite the static, Charlie's voice was unmistakable. "Slugline: Blood Knows No Borders," she began. "November third—"

Owens felt the knot in his stomach clench tight. The good news: Charlie was alive. The bad news: She really was in Budapest.

"This is the story of two fathers and two sons," Charlie's disembodied voice continued. "I identify them here by their first names only to avoid putting them or their families in danger.

"This first story is for Lukács in Szeged, who turns seven years old today, a birthday that comes amid a desperate battle between lightly armed civilians and the mighty Soviet Army. It is a fight for Hungary's soul and its future.

"On any other day, Lukács, your father, Péter, would be studying for his medical school exams and looking forward to coming home to wish you a happy birthday.

"Instead, ten days ago, peaceful protesters asking for change were shot dead by the Hungarian secret police. Your father, a few months shy of realizing his dream to become a surgeon, volunteered to help the wounded at a makeshift hospital set up in the basement of a Budapest school gymnasium.

"I met your father just this morning, at the edge of the Free World, and here is what I can tell you. He was exhausted after spending a long night teasing shrapnel out of human flesh and sewing open wounds closed. But he was exhilarated, too. He believed he was helping to make a better, brighter future for you and thousands of other young Hungarians.

"By two A.M. this morning, the aid station was out of everything—ether, clean blankets, adhesive tape, tourniquets, gloves, surgical thread, and most of all, blood—but the wounded kept coming. Your father volunteered to make the three-hour drive to Nickelsdorf, a small border town where fresh supplies were rumored to be waiting. There, he filled his ambulance with boxes of bandages, sterile tools, and plasma, donated by ordinary West Germans who, like your father, believe that freedom is worth fighting for.

"'Why take such a risk?' I asked him.

"'Because my son must live like a free man,' your father told me as we stood together in the cold morning air. He showed me a picture of the two of you, together with your mother. You are tall for your age, Lukács, your father told me proudly, and an excellent student."

Hell's bells, Owens thought, his head down and his eyes closed as he listened to the cadence of Charlie's voice.

"Sometimes war stories have happy endings," Charlie continued. "A just cause—in this case, Hungary's right to set its own course—prevails. The world becomes a better, fairer place. Fathers come home from the war and grow old, watching their children marry and have children of their own in a world where they can speak, worship, and vote freely. Unfortunately, Lukács, this story isn't one of them.

"Your father made sure his precious cargo of plasma and medical supplies arrived safely at their destination. But somewhere along the way, probably just blocks from the aid station, a Russian sniper fired a fatal shot. It pierced the windshield of the ambulance and then your father's body. Your father kept driving. As a doctor, he must have understood the cost of this decision. Stop, treat his own wound, and risk his ambulance full of supplies. Or keep going so that others might live. Sacrifice and freedom are sacred ideas to men like your father, Lukács.

"A short time ago, Lukács, your father's fight came to an end, in that same building where he worked tirelessly to save the lives of others. By the time he was rushed onto a makeshift operating table, he was weak and pale. Not even blood carried all the way from the Free West could save his life.

"But even in the darkest of times, hope can remain alive, an idea that hardens around itself waiting, like a seed, until its moment comes.

"Just such a hope remained alive for an East German father named Hans in the long, bleak years after the war. A widower, Hans struggled to make a life for himself and his son, seven-year-old Walter. Life was hard, but his son gave Hans's life meaning and purpose.

"Then came his orders: as a Soviet Army conscript, he was assigned to report with his company to Tököl Airfield in Budapest. With no one to look after Walter, Hans was told to put his son in a state-run institution for children without parents. His job—to help keep Soviet planes flying, their pilots ordered to shoot anything or anyone who moved—mattered more.

"Hans couldn't stomach the thought of leaving his son to be raised by others or the work he was being ordered to do to punish the Hungarians for daring to fight back against the Soviets. Nor could he shake the thought—the hope—of a better life for them both. He reported as ordered to Tököl Airfield, but he smuggled Walter onto the base with him. Then, Hans, a former *Luftwaffe* pilot, and Walter made their break for freedom in a stolen MiG that ran out of fuel thirty-five miles from the Austrian border. Tonight, they hope to complete their journey to freedom.

"Hope feeds and nurtures fathers like Péter and Hans, even if their stories end differently. Péter did not live to see his son grow up as a free man, but Hans—if he makes it across the border—will. Someday, Lukács, perhaps you and Walter and I will meet in person. If and when we do, may it be as fellow citizens of the Free World.

"This is Charlie Atkins for Radio Free Europe, Byline Budapest."

Charlie's voice stopped. The tape hissed into silence. Mária paused the recorder with a single loud click.

Owens raised his head and opened his eyes.

Every face in the room stared back at him, shocked. Charlie, a news clerk, just filed a story from Budapest while they were explicitly forbidden to go anywhere near Hungary.

Schmitty pursed his lips and shook his head. "Stupid kid," he muttered.

Owens cleared his throat. "Any chance we can reach Charlie on that frequency?"

Mária shook her head. "No. Now the signal is being jammed. But there is more you need to hear. We are picking up shortwave messages from all over Hungary."

She turned the tape recorder back on.

"Urgent! Urgent. Calling Radio Free Europe," a voice said, in thick, accented English. "This is Budapest calling. Hundreds of Soviet tanks are crossing the Czech border into Hungarian territory. Please send help, we are in immediate danger. Radio Free Europe, please acknowledge."

Another voice spoke: "This is Radio Free Vác," it said. "Attention, Radio Free Europe, attention. We request immediate information. Is help coming from the West?"

Another: "This is Radio Free Dunapentele. We ask the United Nations to send immediate help. We ask for parachute troops to be dropped over our cities immediately. It is possible that our broadcasts will soon stop, and you will hear us no more. We will only be silent when they have killed us.... We don't know when we shall be massacred."

Another: "Our railway stations and airports are surrounded. Our telegraph and telephone lines are down. All communications with the outside world save shortwave is cut off. I don't know how much longer I'll be able to keep broadcasting—tanks are rolling toward Budapest. We are in urgent need."

Another: "This is the Union of Hungarian Writers. To every writer in the world, to all scientists, to all writers' federations, to all science academies and associations, to the intelligentsia of the world, there is little time. You know the facts. There is no need to give you a special report. *Help Hungary*. Help the Hungarian writers, scientists, workers, peasants, and our intelligentsia. Help. Help. *Help*."

Mária turned the tape recorder off and wrapped her sweater tight around her. "There are many more like these if you wish to hear them," she said, her voice low. "Every message says the same thing. The Russians are coming. The freedom fighters cannot hold out much longer. They need help from the West."

"And then there is this." Béla pushed his way forward and handed Owens a photo fresh from the wirephoto machine. It was Charlie. The caption read: *Győr, Hungary—Nov 3— Charlie Atkins from Radio Free Europe negotiates for the freedom of a captured Soviet pilot and his son. Photo by Jerome Berger, Agence France-Presse.*

Owens's heart sank. Charlie's picture—*Christ, with a goddamn MiG, no less*—soon would be on front pages around the world. There was no hiding what she had done now. Worse yet, the Russians would know as well and would have a picture of exactly who they were looking for.

"You knew about this." An accusation, not a question, from Béla.

"No. Yes. I found out a couple of hours ago." Owens had no choice but to confess. "Hilly and Haversham said they saw Charlie on their way back to Budapest. I've been trying to confirm whether or not this is true. Clearly it is."

The knot in his stomach wrenched tighter. "Unfortunately, any minute now the Reds are going to know that someone associated with Radio Free Europe is in Budapest. Even if that someone is a goddamn news clerk."

He smacked the picture of Charlie angrily.

"Let me be clear," he continued, his voice picking up strength. "Charlie has no business being in Budapest. I sent her home on Friday to cool off. Whatever it is she thinks she is doing there, she has done it on her own. Without permission, from me or from anyone else at Radio Free Europe. Everybody clear on that?"

A few heads nodded.

Owens pushed his glasses back up his nose. "As for Viktor, you all might as well know that he resigned, effective yesterday. He is in Budapest, too, but he is there for his own reasons. Somehow—and no, I don't know how or why—Charlie and Viktor may be traveling together. That's all I know right now. In the meantime, I am doing everything I can to reach Charlie and get her the hell out. It's dangerous for her, especially if the Russians find her, and something like this could be fatal for Radio Free Europe."

Owens looked around the room at the silent faces staring back at him. "Anyone else has any ideas about going, I'll fire you first."

No one spoke.

Owens stood there a moment longer, breathing hard but at a loss for words. That damn picture would change everything. New York would know as soon as they woke up. If he was going to show New York he was on top of things, now was the time.

Schmitty is right, he thought. Waiting around for a call from Andy or for Tanner to show up in Munich is wasting time. The sooner he found Tanner, the better his chances were of reaching Charlie. And if he didn't find her, at least he could tell the brass in good conscience that he'd tried.

"Béla, I put in for a call to New York. Cancel that for me, will you?" Owens turned to Schmitty. "That offer of a car still good?"

He didn't wait for the answer. He headed for the newsroom door with Schmitty one step behind him.

36
GOODBYE AND GOOD LUCK

I n the back of the signal truck, Charlie lifted her thumb from the push-to-talk button. Done. Her first story filed from a front-line war zone, making her at least technically a bona fide war correspondent. But instead of feeling victorious, she felt hollow, empty of everything but deep, shattering sadness. For Péter, for Lukács, for the mother in the gymnasium weeping over her daughter's body, and for the two dead Russian soldiers. Even for Horst and Walter, whose story wasn't yet over. *War doesn't discriminate*, she thought. *It is equally merciless to all.*

"Well done, Miss Atkins." Viktor spoke in English. His voice held none of his usual contempt.

"No insults about wedding dresses or the uselessness of hope? I hardly know what to say."

"I was wrong to say those things." Viktor's voice was thick, as if his words nearly caught in his throat. "I was impolite. And unfair."

Charlie twisted around to look at him. In the low light, Viktor's face was somber, almost sad. His ragged teeth no longer scared her; they were a part of him, like an old scar faded into skin.

"From the moment we met, you've made it clear you hate me," she said. "Now that we'll probably never see each other again, at least tell me why. What did I ever do to you?"

"I do not hate you, Miss Atkins. I hate what you represent. Someone who does not have to spend every day hungry for freedom, as though it is some exotic food reserved for a fortunate few."

Charlie gathered up the pages of her story. "Great. You hate me because I was born an American, and you were not."

"It is not that. Not precisely. But you Americans have such confidence that you can do things, if only you put a shoulder against it. We Europeans cannot help but to see things through the lens of our long history of wars and petty grievances. You Americans seem so unencumbered, so free to do as you please." He smiled faintly. "You in particular. You do not belong here, in a war zone. And yet here you are. I find that unsettling."

"Yeah, well, if I had waited for permission from the likes of you or Mr. Owens, I'd be waiting a long time."

Viktor flushed and looked away. "For that, I am sorry too. May I be frank?"

"You mean you haven't been all this time? Please, by all means."

"I did not like seeing that soldier—"

Charlie cut him off, her voice sharp. "What did you think happened in war? Isn't that what you said? Lesson learned."

"Please, Miss Atkins, let me finish. What he did, or tried to do—I did not like it because I did not wish to see you hurt. If our circumstances had been different—" his voice softened— "perhaps you and I might have been friends. Perhaps more."

Charlie reached for her canvas bag. This admission from Viktor was unexpected. "You sure have a funny way of showing it."

"You are not the only one who has lost those you care for most, Miss Atkins. Grief is an unpredictable teacher."

Charlie took her time slipping her notes inside her bag. "You should come back with us to Munich," she said finally. "It's dangerous here for you, too."

"I left Budapest once before. This time, my place is here. Whatever happens. Good luck to you, Miss Atkins. I will miss your company."

"You really ought to call me Charlie. All of my friends do."

Viktor held her eyes and then cleared his throat.

"And now you all must go," he said, switching to German so that Horst and Walter understood him. "The real battle for Budapest may not start until tomorrow, but the Russians will try to cut off the city before morning. Give me your map."

Viktor laid the map out on the bench, and then as Charlie, Horst, and Walter watched, he traced a route out of Budapest with Charlie's pen.

"Here is the Danube. When the road turns to the west, here—" Viktor tapped the map—"follow it. It will take you back to Route 1, the main road back to Austria. Stay on that road. Drive as fast as you can. The Russians will consider it a priority to close the border to prevent American troops from using it to reach Budapest. Do not stop for any reason. Not even a roadblock if you can possibly avoid it. You understand?"

Charlie and Horst nodded. Walter's eyes were huge.

Viktor's finger moved across the map to the circle Charlie had drawn around the Parliament building on the Pest bank of the Danube. "I will come with you but only as far as the

Parliament. When the Russians come, this is where our prime minister will be. So, this is where I must be, too, standing with my country and with my government at the hour of its deepest need."

Viktor looked at Horst. "We know the Russians are looking for you. You and Walter must remain hidden until you cross the border. Inside here, maybe." He tapped the shortwave bench. "It will be tight, but there is room enough for two."

"We will pretend it is a cockpit," Horst said. He removed the bench's lid and rummaged inside it among the antenna wire, pliers and spare parts until he pulled out a hammer and screwdriver. "A cockpit with holes for air so that we may breathe."

Viktor nodded. "Good." He slid his finger to Charlie's last small circle, halfway between the Budapest Boys Academy and Parliament. "István lives here."

"This is the address I found in his passport, yes," Charlie said.

Viktor stared at the circle on the map for a long moment. "The house is on the way to Parliament. I would like to see it again."

"Again?" Charlie said, surprised. "You know the house?"

"I know it well." Viktor paused as if weighing his next words carefully. "I have many reasons to hate István's father. This house is one of them. It belonged to my parents. When I was arrested, Kovács took it and everything in it. My parents were already under suspicion—they were too *bourgeoise* for the Communists. Kovács sent them to a collective farm in the countryside. My mother picked field crops, and my father shoveled pig sties. Every night was spent in mandatory reeducation sessions. Even their excrement was monitored, collected, and reused for fertilizer because in our perfect communist system, nothing goes to waste. Of course, they did not survive."

Charlie sucked in her breath. "I'm sorry about your parents, Viktor."

Viktor tilted his chin to one side. "If we see István…if he is alone and unguarded…perhaps we can even help him escape."

"Help István escape? If Kovács is as dangerous as you say—"

"He is far worse, let me assure you, Miss Atkins."

"Charlie."

"Charlie." Viktor spoke her name, its syllables soft on his tongue.

"If Kovács is as dangerous as you say," she repeated, "why would you go anywhere near him? Even driving by the house is risky."

"What better indictment of the Soviet system than the defection of one of its most privileged sons? It is proof that even those who benefit the most know our system is rotten. If I can exact even a small bit of revenge by helping his son escape, then yes, it is worth the risk." Viktor folded the map and handed it back to Charlie. His cheeks were flushed, his eyes unreadable. "You may have a most unusual return to Munich. A defecting mechanic who can fly a MiG and the talented son of Hungary's most hated man."

He smiled faintly. "Perhaps Mr. Owens will not fire you after all."

#   #   #

Charlie hopped down from the back of the signal truck. The cold air felt clean on her face, but she was tired, weary all the way down to her bones. The long drive back to Munich would give her too much time to think. István, if they found him, would be a welcome distraction.

Her eyes caught Péter's ambulance. Light snow had fallen, and the vehicle was dusted with fine white powder.

"Just a minute," she said. She laid her palm against the ambulance's hood, as if she might find warmth or a heartbeat. Instead, the metal was cold and hoary to her touch. She shut each of the ambulance's open doors one by one, gently, as if closing the eyes of the dead. *Maybe something good will come from Péter's death*, she thought, trying not to look at the dark stains on the front seat, though right now, she didn't know what that could possibly be.

Viktor opened the passenger door for her, his silver ring glinting on the handle. He didn't look at her.

"Budapest is a beautiful city," he said as she climbed inside. "Perhaps when we are truly a free country you will return, and I will show you how lovely it is. Assuming there is anything left of Budapest after this war."

"I would like that," she answered, and to her surprise, she meant it.

37
YOU CAN'T GO HOME AGAIN

From the front seat of the signal truck, Charlie saw that Pest was blacked out. No light shone anywhere save for their headlights and the bright moon glittering off the restless, lapping waters of the Danube. Hours earlier, she had imagined what Budapest would be like as Hungarians celebrated their newly won freedom. Now she was driving through a silent city holding its breath.

Viktor drove slowly, avoiding the potholes left in the street by missing pavers. Horst and Walter were hidden inside the shortwave bench; the air holes Horst made formed neat patterns on all four sides.

As they neared István's address, Viktor looked from side to side as if hoping to glimpse familiar shapes and faces along the quiet road. It was night now, and most of the houses were hidden behind tall walls and iron gates. No one was out on the cobblestoned street.

They rounded a curve, and Viktor turned off the truck's headlights and its engine. He coasted down a long road until they came to a stop across the street from a high hedge. The wrought-iron front gate, adorned with twin medallions in the shape of a wolf's head, was open.

Beyond the gates was an immense, cream-colored house. Wide steps swept up to an elegant, stuccoed façade carved with bas-relief flowers and graced by huge, arched windows covered with delicate, twining ironwork. The roof line was steeply pitched and marked by dormer windows. Every available light blazed brightly. A driveway ran alongside the house, occupied by a boxy, unmarked moving van. Piled around it were things waiting to be loaded into the van—a large bed frame and mattress, a heavy safe, a huge carved wood dining table, and many messily packed boxes of household goods holding dishes, pots, and wadded-up drapes.

Charlie had never seen a house this grand, much less knew anyone who lived in one.

"It looks like a castle," she whispered.

"I always thought so as well." Viktor's voice was so low that only Charlie could hear him. He stared at the house, seeming to drink in every detail: the way it nestled against the old sycamore trees that surrounded the house on three sides and glowed in the dusky light. "Kovács must be leaving—he's emptying the house out."

Charlie cocked her head. She heard something. A piano? She cracked her window and strained to listen. "Do you hear anything?"

The front door opened, and suddenly the commanding, demanding notes of the *Hammerklavier* broke the night's stillness. Charlie's heart leapt.

"That's István. It has to be," she breathed.

A tall, brawny man in workman's overalls backed out of the front door, carrying the heavier end of an étagère with elegant, sinuous lines. The other end was held by a second man with a stocky, cinderblock build. With a jolt, Charlie recognized his cheap suit and then his face. It was Tibor.

Tibor's attention locked immediately on the signal truck. He dropped his end of the étagère, jerked a nod to the other man, and with short, scampering steps, ran straight at the signal truck.

"Go," Charlie cried. "That's the man who pulled István off the train."

Too late, Viktor reached for the ignition.

Both cab doors wrenched open. Tibor jerked Viktor from the signal truck and held him, one thick hand clamped around his arm. Viktor tried to pull himself free, but Tibor held him tight. An instant later, the tall man grabbed Charlie, grazing her head against the truck's frame as he pulled her from the cab. He scooped her up under one arm and carried her around the truck to Tibor. He set her down, but he didn't let her go.

Tibor peered at Charlie in the low light, frowning as his eyes searched her face. Charlie turned away—his breath stank like sour cabbage and gristle.

"*Ismerlek,*" he said slowly. Charlie didn't need to understand Hungarian to figure out what he was saying; she could hear it in his voice. Tibor recognized her.

Charlie tried to pull her arm away but couldn't. Her stomach clenched. Even if she managed to break free, Viktor was trapped, and Horst and Walter were still hidden inside the signal truck.

"Stop it," she cried in German, hoping Horst would hear her. She kicked and twisted even though she knew it was useless. "You're hurting me."

Tibor slapped her and then shook his finger in her face.

"Csend legyen!" He put a finger to his lips and then mimicked hitting her again to make sure she got his point. *Be quiet!* He grabbed her canvas bag from the signal truck's front seat and then pulled the keys from the ignition. Charlie's heart sank. Horst and Walter needed those keys to get away.

Tibor jerked a nod to the tall man, and together Charlie and Viktor were pushed toward the house, up its wide steps, and finally inside. Charlie's feet moved unwillingly, her mind spinning. What just happened? How could they get away? What would happen to them if they couldn't? Inside the house, the *Hammerklavier* crashed and pounded, dense, furious runs of notes, building to its crescendo. Tibor locked the front door behind them. They were trapped.

38
THE AUTOBAHN

O wens squirmed, his frustration growing.

At first, the three hundred miles between Munich and the small Austrian border town of Nickelsdorf flew by. Since the border between Austria and Hungary had closed, little commercial traffic traveled this far east, and there wasn't much out here save for tiny, white-washed villages already tucked in for the night. The highway was so empty that the diplomatic plates on the black sedan Schmitty borrowed from the consulate hardly seemed necessary.

Until now.

Ten miles from the border, the *Autobahn* was jammed with traffic in both directions. Red taillights stretched out ahead of them far as Owens could see, vehicles of all shapes and sizes filled to bursting with donated supplies for Hungary. For the last hour, the sedan had barely moved.

"No way to go around this traffic?" he asked. He already regretted this trip. He should have stayed in the office, made his call to New York, and faced the music. Then at least he could have gone home to a couple of scotches, his wife's

Schweinshaxe—slow-roasted pork knuckle over mashed potatoes—and his own bed.

Otto, Schmitty's taciturn, grey-haired driver, gestured toward the windshield. "Tell me, where am I to go?"

His pale milky-blue eyes met Owens' in the rearview mirror. "We are *stecken fest*."

Otto was right. They were stuck. Owens groaned and pushed his black glasses back up his nose. "Hell's bells," he muttered.

"At least the roads are good," Schmitty said cheerfully. He sat next to Owens in the sedan's roomy backseat. "You got Hitler to thank for that. Built the *Autobahn* straight into Austria. Easier to move tanks that way."

Owens glanced at the other side of the highway. A parallel line of vehicles streamed away from the border, he saw, crammed full of newly minted Hungarian refugees on their way to temporary resettlement somewhere else—Vienna, perhaps, or maybe Salzburg or Munich.

"Look at them," Owens said to Schmitty. "On their way to God knows where."

"Yeah? Wouldn't matter a bit to me." Schmitty stretched his arms. "If I had to choose between living under the thumb of the Reds or starting over somewhere, I'd be on my way outta town, quick as a bunny. You?"

"I've started from nothing before." A couple of times, in fact. But the thought of doing so again at his age felt terrifying and exhausting. He was too old, too comfortable, too lazy. If this situation with Charlie went sideways, God alone knew what would happen to him. He looked again at the picture lying on the seat of Charlie in front of the MiG. Every time he caught sight of it, the bile in the back of his throat rose. *Goddamn it, Charlie—this is all your fault. This is your mess, and I am the one stuck cleaning it up.*

He looked back at the red taillights in front of him. What was he thinking? Here he was, on borrowed time, stuck in a traffic jam, watching the minutes tick by until the Reds invaded Budapest, or the picture of Charlie hit the front pages, or all of the shit hit the fan at the same moment. His only out was if Tanner found Charlie, a needle in a haystack about to catch fire.

39
WELCOME HOME, COMRADE

K ovács slept in his chair, mouth open, head back, his legs splayed out on his desk.

Rat-a-tat, rat-a-tat. A sharp, insistent knock on his half-open door.

He opened his eyes, surprised to find that he had fallen asleep. He heard voices from the front of the house, but István's piano had gone silent. Perhaps his car was early.

His face throbbed.

"Comrade Kovács!" Tibor knocked again. "I must speak with you at once."

What the fuck did Tibor want? "Come," Kovács said wearily.

Tibor stepped into the room, his face eager as a puppy's.

"You will be most pleased, comrade." Tibor's voice filled with triumph. He held out a man's wallet and a strange, unfamiliar canvas bag to Kovács. "I have found a way to be useful."

\#   \#   \#

"But what are you doing here?" István's voice carried into the hallway as Kovács approached.

"A very good question," Kovács said, entering the front room. It was now empty of all its furnishings except István's piano and bench.

"My question is for her," István said, pointing to a young woman—a girl, really—standing next to his piano. She was small-boned and fair with the stunned look of a caught bird.

"Not now, István. I will get to you later," Kovács said, his voice sharp. He held the canvas bag Tibor brought him in one hand. He ignored the girl. He focused on Viktor, looking him up and down. Kovács's eyes gleamed. "Viktor Farkas, the Voice of Free Hungary. How delightfully unexpected. Missed us, did you? How nice to see you again."

Viktor eyed the gash on Kovács's face. "A taste of your own medicine? How fitting. This is Free Hungary now. You and the AVO are finished."

"Maybe your radio listeners are naïve enough to believe such fairy tales. But you, Viktor, you are a man of the world, are you not? Surely you know that won't happen." Kovács shook his head, almost amused. "Do you really think the AVO goes away just because the so-called prime minister Nagy wishes it so? Or that the Soviet Army can be defeated by a few pathetic rock throwers in the streets?"

"I do, because why we fight and what we fight for matters," Viktor snapped. "Do you even remember what that feels like? To love your country so much that you are willing to die to save it?"

"You mean do I remember being a small, weak country that is easy to invade or slice up and give away? That is the Hungary I remember. We are much better off with powerful friends. We do as we're told, and there is no trouble. A lesson you never learned. You should have stayed in Munich, like the coward you are."

"Where I am doesn't matter. I will never stop fighting until you and every other Russian is gone. And remember, we too, have powerful friends."

Kovács laughed, hard and cutting. "The Russians aren't going anywhere, and neither is the AVO. As for your American friends, even you can't possibly believe they will risk nuclear war with Moscow over little Hungary. I am right—you will see. The Kremlin will prevail. And you, little man, are going to help."

"I will never help you."

István's eyes flicked back and forth, a slight frown on his face.

The girl didn't move either. She watched, her eyes wary.

"But you already have—in more ways than you can imagine," Kovács said. "You have been on Radio Free Europe for years, calling for the overthrow of our freely elected government. I have heard you myself. Yes, that's right. We listen to your pathetic calls for revolution. And now here you are, in Budapest, in the middle of just such a riot. A coincidence? I think not. Did you come to lead the *huligánoks* through the streets? Were you homesick? Or did you come home to spy for the Americans?"

Kovács didn't wait for Viktor's answer. He looked at the girl. "And you? What's your story?"

The girl looked at Viktor.

"She doesn't understand Hungarian," Viktor said. "She is no one. She does not belong here."

Kovács considered Viktor's response for a moment. Then he whipped the back of his hand across Viktor's face, hard enough to almost knock Viktor backward. "I have her documents," he said, hold up the canvas bag. "She is from Radio Free Europe, just like you. Lie to me again," he said, switching to speak English to make sure the American understood him as well, "and I'll take the rest of your teeth."

Viktor didn't make a sound. A welt rose on his cheek, raw and blood-red.

The girl winced but didn't turn away.

Kovács jerked a nod to Tibor. "Put them in the library. Lock the door and bring me the key."

Kovács waited until he was alone with István. His brain was already working furiously. Viktor and the girl were valuable to him—but how best to use them to his advantage? First, there was another, more urgent matter to address with his son.

"There was a second passport in her bag. Yours." Kovács tossed it onto the piano. "You care to tell me how this American came to have it?"

István picked it up. "That is what I was trying to tell you. That girl was on the train in Vienna. I lost my passport that day. She must have picked it up."

"And yet here she is, in our living room. Why?"

"She said she was sorry she couldn't help me on the train. She was worried about what happened to me."

"Do you understand how serious this could have been for you if anyone other than me found it?" Kovács hissed. "Your passport, in the hands of Radio Free Europe. It would ruin you."

"It hardly matters now since I am leaving."

Kovács blinked. *Of course*, he thought. *Problem solved*. "Yes, you are right. It is dark enough outside. You should go now, the sooner the better."

Kovács tossed the packet of cash he had put aside for his son onto István's piano. "Here. Enough money to get you wherever you want to go."

"You asked me to play the *Hammerklavier* one last time. I am not yet finished with the third movement."

"I have heard enough." An idea was forming in Kovács's mind. Was he audacious enough to try to pull it off? "And now you must excuse me. I have new matters to attend to."

István didn't move. "What will happen to her? To them?"

"What difference does it make? They are nothing to you."

"I'd like to know."

"I will turn them over to Zhirov. The only question is how much he will pay for them."

István stared at his father. "You can't be serious."

"Of course I am serious," Kovács said. He felt energized. Sleep had helped, but now the prospect of these two prisoners changed everything. "Viktor is one of ours. Moscow will see to him. But do you have any idea how valuable the girl is? Or how much the Americans will pay to get her back? It's almost unimaginable."

"She came to see if I was all right. An act of kindness. Doesn't that mean anything to you?"

Kovács tried to contain his irritation; this wasn't how he wanted to part ways with his son. "Honestly, István, can you not see this from my perspective for once? They are whatever I say they are. I say they are spies, sent by Radio Free Europe, to stir up trouble in the streets. They are in our country illegally, and they must be punished."

"She isn't a spy—" István started, his voice indignant.

"No more discussion. Leave now, or I will change my mind and keep you here."

Istvan stood. He left the cash where it lay on his piano. He walked toward the hallway to the front door. On his way, he passed Tibor without a word.

#   #   #

By the time Tibor handed him the key to the library, Kovács had new instructions for him. "Bring their truck inside the gates," he told Tibor. "Guard it personally. And make sure István's piano is in the moving van before it leaves."

He had paid a fortune for it—he might as well take it with him.

Kovács didn't linger. He needed a bath and a shave. And he needed time to think about how to make the most of this unexpected windfall—two Radio Free Europe spies, caught red-handed in Budapest and now safely locked in his library. *A fine problem to contemplate*, he thought. Very fine indeed.

40

CALCULUS

Kovács left his soiled uniform in a heap on the bedroom floor. He bathed quickly, glad to wash the dirt and dust off, and promised himself a good long soak as soon as he reached his new home. He dried off and then looked at his face in the mirror. *Horrifying*, he thought, but there was nothing to be done about it now.

He filled the basin with warm water. He splashed his face, gasping at the shock and sting of the water on his wound. Then he lathered his face and started to shave the undamaged side of his face first.

He had expected to be on his way out of Budapest by now. But the chance arrival of Viktor and the American girl—and the opportunity they represented—changed that calculus for him. They were valuable; the only question was what he could get for them. Cash was always welcome, but there was something else that mattered more to him. Recognition. He wanted to see the look on Zhirov's face when he realized that he—Kovács—had something the Kremlin did not.

Proof.

Absolute, iron-clad, flesh-and-blood proof that the United States and the Free West were attempting to interfere with Moscow's business.

He tapped his razor on the edge of the basin then rinsed it in the sink. He continued shaving with quick, efficient strokes around his chin.

Of his two prisoners, Viktor was technically the prize; he was well known by the Kremlin for his incendiary broadcasts on Radio Free Europe. For years, Viktor had urged his countrymen to revolt against the Russians and people like Kovács who helped keep them in power. To find Viktor here in Budapest in the middle of this nonsense in the streets—*ach*, not such a surprise, was it?

Viktor had been in jail before but this time, he would not get off so easily. A loyal party man or two would be tasked with finding Viktor's breaking point—a threat to the girl perhaps. There would be a trial, of course, and Viktor's own broadcasts on Radio Free Europe would be used to convict him. If Viktor were lucky, there would be a single shot to the back of the neck once the trial was over. If he wasn't—well, that's what places like Vác and Lubyanka were for. Warehouses for the damned and the forgotten.

Kovács turned his other cheek to the mirror. He leaned in close to inspect the gash and then nudged his shaving blade against it, watching as sour-smelling yellow pus seeped out. He dabbed it clean, gritting his teeth to keep from crying out. *Miserable little shit.* Under normal circumstances, Kovács would have had Zoli hunted down, beaten to within an inch of his life, and then left to rot in a prison cell. *But these are not normal times*, he reminded himself. He raised his blade and began to carefully shave close, as close as he dared, to the gash.

The girl—a pretty one, at that—now she was an altogether different kind of opportunity. She was young and no doubt inexperienced. It wouldn't take much to extract information from her. Besides, the Americans would not have the stomach to let her linger in prison, especially with the drip-drip-drip of judiciously released information about her plight. She would be freed—eventually—in a magnanimous gesture by the Russians once they'd managed to extract as many concessions from the Americans as possible.

Kovács's hand slipped, and he nicked the edge of the cut. A thin drip of blood ran crimson against the white lather. He ignored it.

Could Zhirov simply seize his prisoners? He paused and stared at his own reflection. A risk, but one he thought he could manage. No one knew who his prisoners were or that they were here except István—now on his way to the Austrian border—and Tibor, whose silence could be bought or assured with a bullet if necessary.

Besides, he already had an angle in mind. Zhirov was as greedy as the rest of the Kremlin lot and always on the hunt for an advantage. Once Zhirov paid up, he could invent whatever story he wanted and claim all of the credit for capturing Viktor and Charlie himself. Kovács would throw in the signal truck—a prop Moscow was sure to appreciate—for free. A win for both of them.

If he were going to confront—*no, if I am going to extract what is due me from all these years of bowing to Zhirov*, Kovács corrected himself—he needed to look like he was still in control. Instead of disappearing quietly, disguised in old civilian clothes as planned, he would put his filthy uniform back on. By the time Fekete appeared with Zhirov, he would be back at his desk, demonstrating that he remained in control. This time, he would be driven to the office and shoot anyone who even dared to look in his direction.

He dressed quickly, ignoring the stink of ten days' worth of sweat on his AVO uniform. The car he had arranged would wait. Once his new business was concluded with Zhirov, he would disappear as planned and make his way south. He smiled at his reflection. The gash would heal, although there was sure to be a nasty scar. But beating Zhirov at his own game? That was a moment Kovács knew he would savor for the rest of his life.

41
THE LIBRARY

As soon as Tibor closed the library door, Charlie wheeled around to face Viktor, her hands on her hips, as angry as she was frightened. By now she should have been on her way to Munich with Horst and Walter; instead, she was in a locked room as the prisoner of Hungary's most hated man.

"What did Kovács mean, 'take the rest of your teeth?'" she said.

Her voice echoed in the empty, cavernous room. Overhead, a brilliant crystal chandelier lit the room with shimmering, rainbow-colored drops of light. Bare mahogany shelves flanked a massive fireplace, the ashes in its hearth cold and unswept. Shadows marked the parquet floor where a large carpet had been hours before.

"Isn't it obvious?" Viktor's voice was short. He was already halfway across the room, his shoes clicking on the wood floor as he hurried to a wall of floor-to-ceiling French doors. The glass-paned doors were covered by wrought-iron shutters. Viktor tugged on the scrolled handles of the first two doors. Neither door budged. "Kovács took them."

Charlie ran to the other end of the wall of French doors and did as Viktor did, pulling and jiggling to see if the doors might open. They didn't. "What do you mean, took them?"

"He snapped them off." Viktor stepped quickly to the next set of doors. He tried to rattle them open, jerking the handles up and down as if that might somehow jar them loose. "One tooth at a time when I didn't give him whatever answer it was he wanted from me. He said it gave him particular pleasure to use my father's tools."

Charlie winced; one hand flew to her mouth, an image of Viktor—strapped down, helpless, and in hideous, excruciating pain—flashing through her mind. "Why didn't you tell me?"

The last set of doors didn't open, either. Viktor slapped one door with his palm, frustrated. "So you could feel sorry for me? I, too, have my pride."

Charlie's eyes followed Viktor as he moved to the fireplace, her dread growing.

"What if there isn't a way out of here?" Her voice sounded small, even to her ears. "Will anyone ever know what happened to us?"

"I assure you, everyone will know exactly where we are." Viktor ducked inside the fireplace, ignoring the fine bits of pillowy ash in the firebox. His voice echoed from inside the chimney. "There will be a show trial, of course, but only so the Soviets can appear to be as fair and just as the West. There will be no witnesses for the defense and no testimony in support of the accused. Only a verdict, which is predetermined before the trial even starts."

He reappeared, his hands black with soot and creosote. He wiped them on his trousers. "We will be found guilty on made-up charges—for entering the country illegally to spy for the United States, maybe, or inciting a revolution. But because you are a woman and an American, the Russians will treat you with care. Someone, the Swiss perhaps, will suggest a quiet trade for something Moscow wants in exchange for your release."

Charlie's heart sank. "Shutting down Radio Free Europe's transmitters." Her voice was a whisper. "In exchange for us."

"Perhaps, yes, the transmitters for you. As for me, I am Hungarian. There will be no trade. Moscow will never let me go."

Charlie opened and then closed her mouth, too stunned to speak. She, an American and a woman, would be protected and eventually freed, potentially at great cost to her country. But Viktor—she closed her eyes as the weight of his words sunk in. Viktor would spend years—maybe the rest of his life—in jail.

Viktor broke into her thoughts, as if reading her mind. "You asked if it was true that I spent time in prison—yes, it is true."

In the bright overhead light, Viktor's face looked different to her, as if reshaped by the shock of coming face-to-face with Kovács, his torturer, again. "Imagine, if you can, spending weeks standing in freezing, waist-high water until your skin peels off, and you can barely stand. You're hungry all the time for food that is barely enough to keep you alive. You spend days, weeks, months in total isolation, no books, no paper, no daylight, no one to talk to, not even the guards. And the man responsible takes everything from you—years of your life and the lives of your parents." His face looked pained. "I can't go back to prison. I won't."

Charlie's eyes were fixed on him. "I'm sorry I told you about István. I never meant for this to happen."

"It is I who insisted we come." His voice sounded raw.

Charlie swallowed hard. "So, what do we do now?"

Defeated, Viktor shrugged. "We wait."

Click! The key turned in its lock. István opened the door, a finger to his lips. "Quiet. Come quickly. I took the key while my father was bathing. He intends to sell you to the Russians. I have a car in the back of the house, but we must hurry."

Charlie nearly cried out in relief. There was a way out after all. She started toward the door, Viktor one step behind her.

42
ZHIROV

A s it turned out, Kovács didn't need to worry about getting to AVO headquarters. Comrade Zhirov—stout, square-shouldered, greying at fifty-seven—simply appeared in Kovács's front room in full military dress. Instead of taking Zhirov the long way around, as Kovács had explicitly ordered, Fekete had brought Zhirov here to Kovács's home.

Well, well, Kovács thought as Fekete positioned himself silently in his usual spot near the front door. *Loyalties have changed.*

Not that he blamed Fekete—Kovács had made many of the same kinds of pragmatic decisions himself over his long career. It wasn't personal; it was just how the system worked. Leverage advantage whenever it came along, period.

No matter, Kovács thought. He needed to stay focused. This opportunity—two Radio Free Europe spies, caught red-handed right here in Budapest—was the chance of a lifetime.

Zhirov stared at Kovács's face. "You are getting soft if a child can inflict so much damage," he said, not bothering with hello. He glanced around the room, taking in its bare walls and floor. "We are going to Moscow. We leave immediately."

Kovács smiled, enjoying the moment. He felt refreshed, ready to take on anything or anyone. Even Zhirov. Especially since—for once—he had the upper hand. "Comrade Zhirov, how good to see you. But no, I won't be going to Moscow with you."

"It is not a request."

"Am I under arrest?"

Zhirov paused, his expression neutral. "You are ordered to come with me for questioning. It is not clear to us in Moscow who among the Hungarians can be trusted."

There it was. It wasn't his capability that was being questioned; it was his loyalty. The kiss of death. Any lingering thoughts that Moscow might still have a use for him were now answered. "I've done nothing but what's been asked of me, Vasily Nikolaevich. You know that. And when troubles come, suddenly I am not to be trusted?"

"This is not the time for such a discussion."

"Oh, but it is," Kovács said, enjoying himself. "Even though I've been left hanging for days, making it impossible for me to do my job, my loyalty has never wavered. In fact, I still wish to be useful."

"Make yourself clear."

"I want to slip away quietly. We're old friends. Surely, you can allow me that." Before Kovács put his cards on the table, he wanted—he deserved—the chance to push Zhirov. To let him know he, Kovács, was not so needy as to beg for his own life. Not after the sacrifices he had made, all to ensure Soviet authority remained unchallenged by his countrymen.

Zhirov grunted. "*Nyet*. That is not possible. Your presence is required in Moscow."

"And if I have something—or someone—of value to trade? What then? Will my presence still be required?"

Zhirov's eyes narrowed. "What are you offering me in exchange?"

Kovács hid his satisfaction. He was right. There was still an opening for him, however small.

"I believe these documents will be of great interest to you," Kovács said. He handed Zhirov Charlie's passport and press card. "A girl with Radio Free Europe credentials, apprehended personally by me, right here in Budapest. An *American* girl."

Zhirov studied the documents, flipping them over and over to examine each one. Finally he looked back at Kovács. "This proves nothing."

Kovács made a show of looking in Charlie's canvas bag. He pulled out the map of Budapest and handed it to Zhirov. "This bag belongs to her, as does this map. The main area of fighting, circled. This house, circled. Parliament, circled. Undeniable proof that these troubles were incited and encouraged in person by Radio Free Europe."

Kovács could not resist a note of pride in his voice. "A coincidence? I think not."

As Zhirov hesitated, Kovács unwrapped the candy bar he had found in Charlie's bag.

"Hershey's chocolate, made in Pennsylvania," he said, stumbling over the unfamiliar pronunciation. He broke off a piece of the candy and put it in his mouth. He offered the rest to Zhirov, enjoying the moment as he chewed. "Too much sugar for my taste. Wasteful. Would you not agree?"

Zhirov flicked his eyes down at the candy, but he did not take it. "Deliver this girl unharmed to me, and I will make your regrets known in Moscow."

Kovács smiled. He had Zhirov right where he wanted him. "I have your word? Safe passage?"

"*Da.*"

"Very good. Now, this girl did not come alone. For this second person of interest, I want cash."

"You want many things." Zhirov's response was curt.

Kovács offered up Viktor's identity card. "Viktor Farkas. Petőfi Circle, Radio Free Europe. A traitor by any measure. He has returned to Budapest in the company of this girl. In fact, I captured them together—driving a US military signal truck filled with shortwave equipment. I can show it to you, if you like. It is right outside."

He continued, his voice smooth and persuasive. "Imagine, two spies for the Americans, captured in Budapest in the middle of chaos on the streets. Absolute proof that the United States is interfering in Soviet affairs."

Kovács leaned forward, his voice conspiratorial. "Think of what this will do for you at the Kremlin. And all of the credit will go to you."

Zhirov thrust Charlie's documents back at Kovács. "I do not believe you. This cannot be true. The Americans are not that stupid. They would not send a girl to do the job of a man. And Viktor Farkas is not foolish enough to return to Budapest."

Kovács pursed his lips and nodded. "Very well. You know best. I will have my men dispose of them." He paused. "A pity about the woman. Pretty, if you like them young and thin."

Zhirov's expression shifted. He was thinking about it; Kovács saw it in his face. Finally, Zhirov grunted. "If they are truly spies, then I must notify Moscow immediately."

"We have an agreement then?" This was the delicate part, the part where Kovács's plan to disappear would be tolerated or seen as an act of treason by the Kremlin. "Safe passage in exchange for the girl. Gold, not rubles, for Viktor Farkas and his signal truck."

Zhirov's expression didn't change. "If all is as you say, you will have your reward. But I require indisputable proof before there is any more discussion of rewards."

"Of course. I expect nothing less." Kovács kept his voice smooth. "Right this way."

43

OUR SPECIAL GUEST

nside the empty library, relief flooded through Charlie as István beckoned from the doorway. There was a way out, after all. She started toward the door, Viktor right behind her, and then stopped.

Kovács, his mangled face furious, stood behind István. He snatched the key István still held and then elbowed his son aside to make room for two more men.

The first man—sturdy, with an old scar at his hairline and a fresh one scabbing at his neck—was clearly a guard. He stepped inside the library and stationed himself next to the door, eyes alert but distant, his hands crossed respectfully in front of him. *A good soldier, awaiting instructions*, Charlie thought.

The second man was something else entirely. He strode into the room, every step precise and intentional. He was heavyset with shrewd, stony features; hard, narrow eyes; an angular nose; and hair the color of slate. His Soviet Army officer's uniform boasted more medals than Charlie cared to count.

A man used to being obeyed, Charlie thought, *and feared*.

The fat Russian stared at Viktor, his eyes narrowed. "Viktor Farkas, you must be reminded not to take Russian friendship for granted."

He spoke English—for her benefit, Charlie figured—in a raspy voice that scraped like hardened steel on stone.

"I remember Russian friendship all too well." Viktor's face paled, but his voice stayed firm.

"Fekete, see to it," the fat Russian said to the man by the door. Have those two"—he nodded at István and his father— "wait in my car."

Kovács opened his mouth as if to speak and then closed it. He pushed István through the library door. Fekete gripped Viktor by the arm.

"This man is not your friend," Viktor said to Charlie before the door closed behind him.

The Russian turned to Charlie. His uniform's tight collar exaggerated the soft round flesh of his jowls. "Your friend Viktor is correct—I am not your friend. But it is not necessary that I am your enemy."

"You speak English." Charlie hoped she sounded braver than she felt.

"You Americans have short memories. We were allies during the war. I served in Washington, D.C. Speaking English was a requirement."

"Who are you?"

"I am Comrade Zhirov. Special assistant to Comrade Khrushchev. Who sent you here?"

"No one. I came on my own. What do you do at the Kremlin?"

"I do what I am told. A wise strategy—one you would be wise to follow." Zhirov clasped his hands behind his back and started to circle Charlie with slow, meticulous steps. "I don't believe you. Again, who sent you?"

Charlie weighed Viktor's parting words. What difference did it make what she said, as long as she told the truth? She hadn't done anything wrong. "I told you, I came on my own. Legally, since the border is open and unguarded."

"The border has been violated by hoodlums. You are in this country illegally." Zhirov continued his circle around her. "We know you are from Radio Free Europe. Tell me why you are here, and perhaps things will go easier for you."

"What things? I am a civilian and a journalist. I know my rights under the Geneva Conventions."

"The Geneva Conventions do not apply unless a police action is formally recognized and, even then, only under limited circumstances," Zhirov said. "Outside the door is a man. His name is Fekete. He is also not your friend. One word from me, and he will shoot István. In one hand. Maybe in both. Either way, he will never play the piano again. Or perhaps Fekete will aim for your friend Viktor. Accidents happen in war. No one will ever believe otherwise."

Charlie swallowed hard. "I told you. I came on my own. I came to report a story. About blood plasma donated in the Free West to save the lives of freedom fighters in Budapest."

"Such a story provokes a mob of rioters who are acting in violation of Hungarian law. You are in the company of Viktor Farkas, a well-known agitator who has returned to Hungary to incite violence. You have abetted Hans Horst, a thief who stole a Soviet plane." He glanced at her. "Yes, we know all about you."

"That's not right—" Charle started, her voice indignant.

"I do not require your agreement or your cooperation, although it will make things easier for you," Zhirov continued as if Charlie had not spoken. His voice was cool, almost bored. "I have your American passport, and I have your Radio Free Europe press card, both with your photographs, so there is no mistaken identity. I have also a photograph of you with our missing mechanic and aircraft. Do not worry—we will find him. I have the story you wrote and your notebook, which no doubt contains many more details about this Péter. Where he lives. The name of his wife. I am certain our monitors recorded it, which means your own words will be proof of your guilt."

Zhirov continued his slow circles around Charlie. "You should not have attempted to make a hero out of this Péter. If he kept to his studies, he would still be alive. That is why we do not like your radio. You encourage people to take sides."

Fear flooded through Charlie. Zhirov was twisting the truth. Yes, she was with Viktor, but he came to help the freedom fighters win Hungary's freedom. Yes, she worked for Radio Free Europe, but they didn't send her here—in fact, Owens would be furious when he found out. And as for Péter's family and the identifying details she'd written in her notes—Charlie didn't even want to think about the danger she had put them in.

"Journalists don't take sides—we tell people the truth."

"Of course you take sides. Your government pays you to broadcast nonsense about democracy and truth. Look what happens. People take to the streets. They get hurt, they get arrested, or they die."

"Our government doesn't pay for Radio Free Europe. It's paid for with truth dollars—"

Zhirov chuckled. "Just how many of those so-called truth dollars do you think it takes to buy one of your transmitters? They cost almost two million American dollars each, just for construction. And you have twenty-eight of these transmitters designed especially for Radio Free Europe! Believe me, we know. Very expensive. The truth is what the State needs it to be and what it pays for it to be. Even if it is paid for in secret. This is true in your country and in mine. You will learn this lesson soon enough."

Charlie's sweat turned clammy. "What do you mean?"

"You will spend a little time with us in Moscow as our special guest. If you are lucky, your government will reward us handsomely for taking such good care of you. Then we will send you home."

"You mean send *us* home."

"Viktor is Hungarian, and as such, he will remain under the care of the Soviet Union. Protected by us. Accountable to us. We have much to discuss with him."

"Hungary is a free country now. There are international rules about these things."

"Free Hungary does not exist," Zhirov said. "We will restore order, and the citizens of Budapest will go back to their lives and their jobs as productive members of the Soviet Union."

Charlie put her hands to her face. Everything had changed as if she had awoken into a nightmare. She was about to be sent to Moscow, only to be ransomed at great cost back to her home country and leaving Viktor behind.

Zhirov suddenly moved. He grabbed her wrist and wrenched her arm toward him. He stared at her watch with its ruby red star.

"Where did you get this?" he demanded.

Charlie tried to pull her wrist free, but Zhirov held her tight. He said, "This is a very special watch, only for very important party members."

His tone had changed. Suspicious. Accusatory. "Where did you get this?"

"It belonged to my father."

"Your father's name?"

"Why?"

"I ask the questions. You answer. If you answer with the truth, things will go better for you." As he spoke, Zhirov deftly unbuckled the watch from Charlie's wrist. "Your father's name?"

Charlie grabbed for her watch. "That's mine."

Zhirov pulled the watch out of reach and stuffed it into his pocket. "Do not be in such a hurry to get it back. How your father acquired this watch may decide your future. Did he do so honorably, or are you the daughter of a thief? Or worse."

His voice hardened. "Your father's name. Now."

"No."

Zhirov stared at her. In the silence, the French doors began to rattle, a low, chattering hum. He removed a fountain pen and a piece of paper from his coat's breast pocket and thrust them at her. "Your father's name. Write it down."

"Not until you give me back my watch."

"One word from me to Fekete and your friends die."

Charlie took up the pen and paper. Shaking, she wrote her father's name: *Captain Adolf Joseph (A. J.) Atkins.*

Zhirov shouted for Fekete. He gave the piece of paper to Fekete and barked out an order in terse Russian. Charlie caught only a couple of words—Moscow and Tököl, the name of the airfield south of Budapest. Fekete nodded and disappeared.

The rattle grew louder. A new sound began: grinding, clanking, clunking. The house shook.

"What is that?" She knew the answer even before he answered. Soviet tanks were crawling into Budapest.

"That is the sound of law and order. Budapest is surrounded. We leave for Moscow at once."

The roar of the tanks outside grew louder. The chemical tang of diesel fuel hung in the air. Fekete reappeared. He pulled Charlie away from the rattling French doors, following Zhirov out of the library.

#   #   #

Outside the house, the sky lit up, a blinding white-hot yellow, long enough for Charlie to see that both the moving van and Viktor's signal truck were gone. Tank fire struck a heartbeat later—buildings exploded nearby, vomiting a show of concrete and glass. The air stank of tank fire, smoke, and dust. As Fekete pushed her toward the long black Zil limousine waiting on the driveway, she covered her ears and tried not to gag on the greasy-tasting air stuck in her throat. Fekete shoved her into the car, one thick hand firmly against her back.

Inside, István, his blue eyes huge, was squeezed into the backseat next to his father; Kovács's expression was unreadable, his bright, piercing eyes made small by the slash across his face. Viktor lay across the rest of the seat. His face was swollen an angry red, and his arms were bent awkwardly against his bloodied shirt. His eyes were closed; he moaned as Charlie was crowded in next to him.

Zhirov settled himself into the front passenger's seat. Fekete closed Zhirov's door, rounded the car, and slid behind the wheel.

Boom! Boom! Boom! A nonstop barrage of shells illuminated the Zil's interior as Fekete pulled out into the street. István's lips were pressed tight together; his hands twitched nervously on his lap. Beside him, Kovács's face looked etched with cold fury. She could feel rather than see Viktor's breath. It came in shallow, jagged gasps.

Overwhelmed by both noise and fear, she could barely think. She had come to Budapest to prove herself but not like this, trapped in the back of a Russian Zil in the middle of a war zone and on her way to a one-way flight to Moscow.

44
RECALCULATION

Kovács sat behind Zhirov inside the Zil, his attaché case on his lap, and fumed.

Through the Zil's back window, he watched indifferently as streets he knew well disintegrated into ruins. Budapest was no longer his problem. The city was going to endure whatever the Soviets thought it deserved. He ignored his son, too: István should have left when he could. What happened to Viktor and the girl, however, was very much on Kovács's mind.

Boom! A shell detonated close to the car, showering its shiny black exterior with brick grit and glass. The noise made conversation impossible, which was just as well—Kovács needed time to consider his next move. Technically, he had struck a deal with Zhirov—safe passage and gold in exchange for his two prisoners. He didn't belong in this car unless Zhirov had changed his mind. If so, Moscow would be fatal for him.

Play it straight, Kovács decided. *Act as if nothing has changed.*

He held his tongue until Fekete turned down a quiet side road, a momentary respite from the shelling.

"I must know," he said, as if this particular ride were no different than any of the others he had taken with Zhirov over the years; he was annoyed to be addressing the back of Zhirov's head, like a supplicant. "What took Moscow so long? These street thugs could have been dealt with two weeks ago."

If only you had listened to me, he added silently.

"Comrade Khrushchev took the requisite time he needed to study all potential options." Zhirov's voice was brusque. He did not, Kovács noted sourly, bother to turn around to face him. "Comrade Tito of Yugoslavia was consulted, and he will not oppose us. Comrade Novotný stood aside as our tanks crossed Czechoslovakian territory. Comrade Mao urged Comrade Khrushchev to show strength. Wise counsel, in my judgment. We Russians are far too fond of your fat hogs and good brandy."

"And what is the plan of attack?" Kovács asked.

"We have split the city in two. We took control of all of the Danube bridges, the rail lines, and most of the communications before a single shot was fired. We control Tököl Airport, so there is no chance of any more rogue planes taking off. We are deploying seventeen divisions, 200,000 troops, and five thousand tanks. A reminder for our Hungarian friends why it is better to be our friends than our enemies."

The girl listened, frowning. *She'll learn Russian in Moscow whether she likes it or not*, Kovács thought. Beside her, Viktor didn't move.

"All T-34 tanks?" Kovács asked. The tanks must have come up from the south to Soroksári Road and down from the north to Váci Road, using the Danube to shield their flanks. *Good strategic choices*, he thought.

"Mostly. There are some T-54s also. We are testing the new models," Zhirov said. "They are smaller and designed to be easier to maneuver around street corners. We want to see how well they do in city fighting."

"Impressive." Kovács tried to keep the bitterness he felt out of his voice. No one in the Kremlin, least of all Zhirov, bothered to consult, let alone inform, him that Moscow planned to strike back hard. An unforgivable slight.

"You asked for decisiveness," Zhirov said. "There will be no Gomulka thaw here. We are clear on what it will take to prevail."

"You have air support?"

"Of course. At first light. The planes will be lifting off from Tököl soon."

Thud! A limestone paver hit the side of the truck and bounced away. Kovács did not flinch.

"We expect it will take only a few days' work to clean up your mess," Zhirov continued.

Kovács's sweat turned cold. He was right—he was to be blamed for this damn revolution. But there was nothing he could do about that now, not if the Kremlin's mind was made up. Very well. He needed to keep Zhirov focused on the deal they had struck. "You are taking quite the prizes to Moscow. You will be well rewarded."

Zhirov grunted. "I have not forgotten. You will be rewarded as well."

Fekete murmured softly to Zhirov.

Zhirov nodded.

Fekete pulled back out onto a main street, back into the thundering crash of live tank fire. He pulled quickly to the curb, letting the engine idle. Kovács looked out his window in disbelief. Fekete had stopped in front of the smoking rubble of the bakery they had visited only hours earlier. In front, a group of men stood guard behind a makeshift barricade lit by a bonfire. In its light, Kovács saw three shallow graves— *one each for the baker, the butcher, and the chemist*, he thought. Weapons—long-handled shovels, pickaxes, iron rods, sharp wooden sticks, more limestone pavers—were piled up for ready use.

Kovács's heart pounded. This could not be happening to him.

"You will get out of the car here," Zhirov shouted over the booming tank fire. He didn't bother to turn to face Kovács. "This is your safe passage."

Smack! Another paver hit the Zil. It struck the windshield, leaving a glassy, frozen spiderweb as it bounced away. Fekete, gun drawn, got out of the car. He walked purposefully around the Zil, his weapon at the ready, and opened the passenger back door for Kovács.

The men behind the barricade watched Fekete warily.

"Be quick," Zhirov said, his voice brusque, "before I change my mind. István as well."

"Vasily Nikolaevich, please." Kovács fought to keep his voice calm. "After all I have done for you. Not like this. I have a new life waiting for me—"

"You think I didn't notice? Budapest is in chaos while you fill your pockets and empty your house, so you can sneak away like a thief in the night. Only a traitor abandons his post. This cannot be tolerated. Your moving truck will accompany me to Moscow—it is now property of the state. Be grateful that I stuck my neck out this far for you. This is the best I can do for you."

Kovács gritted his teeth. *Goddamn Russians can't be trusted,* he thought. Zhirov was honoring the word but not the intent of their deal. *Well, fuck him.* Inside his attaché case was his Walther P38, extra ammunition, and plenty of cash. Enough to shoot or buy his own safe passage back to his house and the car that would be waiting for him there.

"Your attaché must remain with me," Zhirov said, as if reading Kovács's mind. "I cannot risk any sensitive information falling into the wrong hands."

Kovács's arm tightened around his attaché case. *Like hell.* He owed Zhirov nothing.

He swung his feet out of the car as Fekete reached in for the attaché case. Kovács didn't let go. A third paver hit, this one thrown from the barricade. It hit just above the passenger door. Kovács ducked; Fekete didn't. He pried the attaché case loose from Kovács, a triumphant gleam in his eye, and handed it to Zhirov in the Zil's front seat.

Kovács's panic rose. He struggled to keep his voice level. His AVO uniform would give him away instantly. "Give me back my gun then. At least give me a chance."

Zhirov looked inside Kovács's case. He hefted the Walther. "I like this gun. I will keep it. Besides, a friend of the Hungarian people should not need a gun."

Zhirov put the gun back into the attaché case. "István. Get out."

"At least spare István. He has a future. A gift. You know that."

"His commitment to appropriate musical themes has never been in question. His political choices are unwise, however. He has the same opportunity as you do to save himself. I can do nothing more."

István didn't wait for Fekete to open his door. He bolted from the other side of the car. Kovács's last glimpse of his son was as István ran for cover from the shells exploding overhead.

Fekete leaned in and strong-armed Kovács out of the car. He slammed the Zil's door shut and then leaned close so that only Kovács could hear him.

"This is your fault, comrade," Fekete said, echoing Kovács's own words spoken in this very spot only hours earlier. "You should have been prepared."

"Remember who you are speaking to," Kovács snapped, but it didn't matter. Fekete, if he heard, did not care. He whistled—one loud, sharp blast—to the men behind the barricade to get their attention. He jerked a thumb toward Kovács and then hurried back around to the driver's seat. A moment later, the Zil lurched away from the curb.

"AVO! AVO! AVO!" Kovács recognized Zoli's voice even before he saw him. In an instant, Kovács was surrounded by Zoli and the men from the barricade. They wielded iron bars and shovels; one man hefted a pickax.

Kovács stepped back, but there was nowhere to run. He felt naked—no gun to protect him, no money to buy his way out. He was trapped. He shoved one hand in his pocket. His fingers found his mother's rosary. He didn't bother to pray.

The last thing Kovács saw was Zoli, backlit by the bonfire and bright as an avenging angel. Then one man swung his shovel, fast and hard, and everything went black.

45
JUSTICE SERVED

Charlie didn't—couldn't—look away. She stared out the Zil's back window as István disappeared and Kovács fell to the cobblestones. Then the car swerved around a corner, and Kovács was out of sight. Fekete was driving as fast as he dared, maneuvering the Zil around huge chunks of concrete from collapsed buildings and cars flattened by tank treads.

"This is Russian justice?" Charlie turned around to Zhirov, fear rising in her voice. She shouted to make herself heard over bone-jarring bursts of shell fire outside the car. "Even Nazis got their day in court."

"Justice is best served at the hands of those wronged," Zhirov shouted back. He was busy looking through Kovács's attaché case. He tossed a thick packet of Hungarian forints on the Zil's dashboard with a nod and a grunt to Fekete. Charlie caught a flash of American dollars and Russian rubles—Zhirov stuffed those back into the attaché case. "The Hungarian people decided the outcome. A trial would change nothing. Same result. This way is much more efficient."

"It's more efficient to destroy Budapest rather than to let the Hungarians run their own country, isn't it?" Charlie said. "Is that Russian justice, too?"

"Nagy was too quick to respond to the demands of the mob. A little restraint and deference and our response might have been different."

"President Eisenhower—"

Zhirov cut her off. "President Eisenhower is busy protecting oil interests in the Middle East. No American troops are coming. The Hungarians must face what they have done and pay the price." With that, he slammed the partition between the front and back seats shut, as hard as a slap to the face.

Fire-lit columns of smoke whirled around the Zil; the sharp, acrid tang of burning metal hung in the air. Charlie slumped back against the seat. She fought her growing panic, trying to slow her breath and her pounding heartbeat. There was no escape. Even if she got a running start, there were tanks and soldiers everywhere. And if by some miracle she did make it out of the car, Viktor was in no shape to move. Just this morning, she wanted nothing more to do with him. Now she touched her fingertips to his. Viktor's fingers twitched slightly at her touch.

#   #   #

At last Fekete swerved onto a narrow rail-and-road bridge to an island in the Danube. The Zil's headlights caught a small sign that read *Csepel-sziget*—Csepel Island—home to Tököl Airbase. As they neared the air field, the lights in Csepel's iron works and aircraft production plants burned brightly. Hungarian flags—red stars torn from their centers—hung defiantly from nearly every window. Csepel looked ready for what was to come. Charlie, alone with her thoughts, hoped she was ready, too.

46
NICKELSDORF

"We are close," Otto announced finally as they inched toward Nickelsdorf and the Austrian border. "Maybe one kilometer."

"Well, why didn't you say so?" Owens jerked up the door handle and pushed open the sedan's door. "I'll walk the rest of the way."

"Hold your horses," Schmitty said. "Tanner isn't going to be standing around, waiting for you to find him. There are too many people here. Our best shot is finding Karl, Tanner's driver. If we find Karl, we got Tanner."

Schmitty was right. Reluctantly, Owens pulled the door shut again and slumped back in his seat.

"So how exactly are we going to find Karl?" he asked.

Schmitty turned to their driver. "Hey, Otto, you know Cord Tanner's driver, right? Karl, thin guy with the big glasses, no sense of humor."

"I know him. He will be driving a car like this one. Not marked. It will be parked somewhere quiet. But I will recognize it."

"Okay. You start keeping an eye out." Schmitty turned back to Owens. "What did I tell you? You find Karl, you find Tanner."

"I hope so," Owens said. "I don't like the options if we don't."

Schmitty raised his eyebrows. "You are not thinking about going in after her, are you? On account of that would be adding stupid to stupid."

Owens was already shaking his head as the knot in his stomach wrenched tighter. "I'm not cut out for that sort of thing. Besides, we have strict rules about travel in an Iron Curtain country. I'm in enough hot water as it is."

#   #   #

When the sedan finally pulled into Nickelsdorf, Owens saw Schmitty was right. On a summer afternoon, this pretty little village—population 2,225—was no doubt a charming little Austrian outpost surrounded by quiet forests and lush meadows.

Not tonight.

Nickelsdorf was overrun. People moved, sat, or stood everywhere Owens looked: sitting on park benches, lying on blankets spread out on the village green, huddled in the churchyard and its graveyard. Nearly all were refugees— hundreds, maybe thousands, of them. Weary-looking volunteers moved among the new arrivals, offering coffee, sandwiches, and blankets. Every available light seemed to be on. *Like a dreamscape*, Owens thought, *or a nightmare, depending on where your politics land.*

Otto parked on the far side of Nickelsdorf, close to no man's land.

Schmitty opened the trunk and pulled out a couple of flashlights.

"Okay, the good news is that wherever Tanner is, he is not gonna want to be seen. He has a radio guy with him, so he will need a quiet place to operate. That means we can skip any place that is too open, too public, or too loud. Otto, you look for Karl or his car. Start on the periphery of the square, one or two blocks away from the action."

Schmitty handed Otto a flashlight. Otto nodded and set off toward the far side of the village green.

"What's the bad news?" Owens asked as Schmitty handed him a flashlight.

"The bad news is that you and I are gonna be knocking on a whole lotta doors. Check hotels, inns, rooming houses, office buildings—whatever looks like a possibility."

"Assuming Tanner is here," Owens said.

"Assuming he is here," Schmitty agreed. "Maybe we guessed wrong. Either way, we're here, and we gotta give it a shot. Meet back here at the car in an hour, and we will compare notes."

Before Owens started for the nearest building, he looked out toward no man's land. In the artificial light, he spotted the old oak where Andy had said he planned to meet Charlie. It hung over the border crossing as still more Hungarians poured into Austria. There was no sign of Andy, his Red Cross truck, or Charlie. Owens commandeered a sandwich and a lukewarm cup of coffee—*nein* cream, he was told by a volunteer with a tired smile—and headed off to knock on doors.

#   #   #

By the time Owens got yet another *"nein"* from a harried innkeeper at his fifth stop, he was sure Tanner was nowhere to be found in Nickelsdorf. Owens's black wingtip shoes were soaking wet from the frost-covered grass, and he was cold down to his bones. Just beyond the inn's reception desk, he saw the bar and its bottles of scotch lined up, ready to be poured. *Maybe just a quick one*, he thought but then sighed regretfully. Instead, he helped himself to the tray of *Vanillekipferl*—vanilla crescent cookies—sitting on the counter and headed back out into the cold.

Schmitty caught up with him just outside, triumph written all over his face.

"You found Tanner?" Owens said, brushing cookie crumbs from his lips.

"Not yet—but we got his driver," Schmitty said.

"And to think I doubted you," Owens said, the weight in his chest lifting. Now all he needed was for Tanner to reach Charlie. New York would still have plenty of questions about the picture of Charlie and the MiG, but maybe all would be forgiven if he got her out alive and unhurt.

#   #   #

Karl, Tanner's driver, was parked two blocks off of Nickelsdorf's main square.

He sat in the front seat of his black sedan—a twin to the one Otto drove—drinking coffee from a Thermos and reading a folded newspaper with a flashlight through oversized glasses. Karl pointed Schmitty and Owens toward the Nickelsdorf Inn, tucked back from the street.

"*Herr* Tanner has a room on the top floor, last door on the left," Karl said. "You must be quick. I have orders to be ready to leave at any moment."

"Roger that," Schmitty said.

Owens was already heading up the inn's front steps past a young couple bundled up in Red Cross blankets. His steps felt light. Despite the odds, they had found Tanner. All Owens needed now was to find Charlie—alive—and get her home.

47
TANNER

T anner, a lit cigar in one hand, finally answered the door on Owens's third knock. His expression registered quick surprise and then immediate caution. He stepped out into the hallway to check up and down the dim, empty passage. "Come in, before you're seen."

Owens and Schmitty slipped past him.

Inside, Tanner's hotel room was dark and cramped. The curtains were drawn tight, and the room's only light came from a single bulb overhead. The room was narrow; if he stretched out his arms, Owens could have touched both walls at once. There were two hardback chairs, one already occupied by a man hunched over a shortwave radio at a tiny desk. He wore headphones, and his hand moved furiously as he made notes on a pad of paper.

Tanner looked at Schmitty. "We'll get to how you found me later. What are you doing here?"

"Official business." Schmitty pointed at Owens. "*His* official business."

"Your driver told us you were up here." Owens, out of breath from four flights of stairs, gasped. His heart pounded as he sank onto the bed.

"Viktor Farkas," he wheezed. "I need to reach him right away."

"What, he forgot to clock out or something?"

"Russians ... coming." Owens barely got his words out.

"We know. We're picking up their traffic. They are crawling all over Budapest. What about it?"

"There's someone with him," Owens wheezed. "Charlie Atkins. News clerk. Works for me."

Tanner looked confused. "You sent a news clerk to a war zone?"

Owens shook his head and gulped in air. "She went on her own."

"*She?*" Tanner's eyebrows went up. "What the hell did she think she was doing?"

Owens waved the question away. "Doesn't matter. She was seen earlier today on the way to Budapest with Viktor. I need you to get on the wire and tell her to get her fanny home."

Tanner reached one long arm over, tapped the radio man on the shoulder, and then handed him some crumpled Austrian schillings. "Willie, how about you and Schmitty rustle us up a pot of hot coffee?"

"And some sandwiches," Owens added. His heart rate was slowing. His breath was nearly back to normal.

Tanner tapped his cigar over an ashtray and then parked it there. He waited until the door closed behind the other two men.

"No one—repeat, no one—is ever authorized to interrupt me like this. *Capeesh?*"

Owens nodded. "This is an emergency. Sorry. I didn't have another option."

"I don't have a way to reach Viktor. He reported in a couple of hours ago, and none of it was good news. He said the Reds are coming in hot with tanks and bombers, and the best the Hungarians have are light arms. Viktor is on his way to Parliament—" Tanner looked hard at Owens—"and he made no mention of anyone else."

"Can't you ask him the next time you hear from him?"

"Sorry, but no can do."

"What do you mean, 'no can do'? Isn't that why you are here at the border instead of Munich?"

"To listen for Viktor's reports, yes. But his instructions are to transmit only. Quick reports, then move on to a new location so the Reds' signal hunters don't find him. He isn't listening for transmissions from me. Besides, if the Reds happen to hear it, too—and there is a damn good chance they would—we would be putting a target on his back."

"But don't you people use—" Owens waved his hands in frustration "—secret codes or something?"

"Usually we take security precautions, yes. But there wasn't enough time to train Viktor. Events simply moved too fast."

"What the hell can you do?"

"Me? Hard to see how this is my problem."

"Charlie is a member of my staff—and let me remind you, an American citizen." The room was cold, but Owens was sweating. "Viktor is the only way I know to reach her before all hell breaks loose."

"You don't think she's smart enough to figure this out on her own?"

"She's a kid, Tanner. Twenty-three and green as they come. So no, I don't think she's smart enough to know when to quit."

Tanner picked up his cigar, pulled on it, and exhaled hot, blue smoke. "Even if I could reach Viktor directly, it's too late. We're about to pull out."

"Out?" Owens's voice was sharp. "What do you mean 'out'?"

"Out, as in Willie and I are heading back to Munich. This mission was exploratory only, to provide options for the president should he want them. I have been informed that the president is not interested in intervening on behalf of the freedom fighters—we are officially hands off whatever happens in Hungary. My orders are to pack up and be in the office in time to wrap this up over lunch with the boss. Viktor is on his own."

"So much for Ike's promise to roll back the Iron Curtain." Owens didn't bother to disguise the bitterness he felt.

"What the president says in public and what he means by it in private are two very different things. You know that."

"When I passed along Viktor's name, I had no idea you could cut him off like that."

"Viktor knew. He knew this was off the books, in case things got messy. Which—" Tanner tipped his cigar toward Owens—"they have, thanks to your girl news clerk. No fault of mine, I'd like to add."

"Isn't there anything you can do?"

Tanner frowned, annoyed. "What does your brass in New York have to say about all this?"

Owens said nothing.

"They don't know." Tanner put his cigar back in his mouth. "Jesus H. Christ."

"I was hoping to have some progress to report before I have to make that call." Owens's voice sounded small, even to his own ears.

"You realize that the chance Viktor will actually hear a message is close to zero? And even if by some miracle he does, things may already be too hot for either of them to get out."

A faint glimmer of hope stirred.

"But you'll try?" Owens said. "If this gets out, or Charlie gets hurt, it's gonna look bad for all of us."

"Bad for you, you mean." With a sigh, Tanner handed Willie's pad of paper and pen to Owens. "I'm going against direct orders here, you understand. Write the message you want us to send. Keep it short. No specifics. Just enough that Viktor will understand it and pass it along to your girl."

Owens stared at the pad. Willie's notes were on the top sheet, written in quick, precise shorthand. He tore off a clean sheet of paper and licked his lips. What would get Viktor's attention and convey the urgency needed? *Tell Charlie*—Owens began and then stopped—*tell Charlie what exactly?*

The door opened. Schmitty and Willie returned bearing a tray with *Wurstsemmels*—sausage-filled rolls—and a pot of coffee. Owens sniffed. The coffee smelled burnt and stale. Charlie made better coffee—

That's it, Owens thought with a jolt, and he scribbled on the pad. *Red alert, Atkins!* he wrote. *Coffee, stat!*

He stared at the words he'd written and then made a quick edit. *Red alert, Atkins!* he wrote. *Oak tree, stat!*

Red alert so that she would know it was an emergency and the oak tree, her meeting place with Andy, so that they could find each other. Would that do it? He hoped so.

Tanner scanned the message without comment and then handed it to Willie. "Before we pack up, put this out quietly. All channels you can find. Send it in German, Hungarian, and English. Repeat for one hour."

Willie nodded and put his headset back on. He flicked a switch, leaned close, and began to murmur softly into the shortwave's microphone.

"Now what?" Owens said as Schmitty handed him a cup of coffee.

"Now we wait," Tanner said. He stubbed out his cigar and sat down in the unoccupied hardback chair, his legs stretched out in front of him. He leaned back, his odd-colored eyes staring up at the ceiling, like a long, lean snake going into hibernation.

Schmitty sat on the far end of the bed. He leaned back against the wall, arms crossed, and closed his eyes.

Owens helped himself to a sandwich. The sausage filling was thin, and there was none of the sweet-spicy mustard he liked. *An hour is better than nothing*, he thought. As he ate, Willie's voice droned softly in the background.

48
HUNGARIAN SOIL

At Tököl Airbase's main gate, Charlie watched miserably from the backseat as the Zil was waved right through. Once inside, Fekete pulled up short next to the airfield's headquarters, a half-round prefabricated steel Nissen hut white with frost. He left the motor running as he disappeared inside the hut.

After leaving Kovács and István to their individual fates, Fekete had gotten the four of them—himself, plus Charlie, Viktor, and Zhirov—out of Pest as quickly as he could. Now at Tököl, Charlie saw an airfield readying for war. It buzzed with furious energy in the dawn light, busy as a beehive kicked awake. Ground crewmen hustled across the tarmac, running ammo carts among the planes and shouting instructions to one another over whining jet engines. Fuel trucks swarmed along the edges of the tarmac near more Nissen huts—a mess hall, barracks, and a repair bay where mechanics hovered over the engine of a MiG. *A day ago, Horst would have been among them*, Charlie thought. She covered her ears; even inside the Zil, the air vibrated from the roaring howls of MiGs and bombers taxiing down the long central runway, ready to take off.

Tököl—its men, its machines, and its materiel—were at full throttle.

As the Zil idled, Charlie spotted a familiar shape a dozen yards away and flinched. It was Tibor. He was inching Viktor's signal truck up the rear cargo ramp of a pudgy, grey twin-turbo prop military cargo plane, a red star painted on the fuselage. The plane's crewmen watched, passing a Thermos of something steaming hot among them; they had been pressed into service, she saw, to help load the contents of the moving van onto the plane, including István's piano, propped up on one side, its legs removed. There would be other pianos for István, Charlie thought, but for Viktor, watching his family's belongings shipped off to Russia was going to be another cruel blow. She glanced at him. He hadn't moved at all. Helplessly, she slipped her hand into his and squeezed; this time, his fingers didn't move.

The Zil's door opened. Fekete maneuvered himself back into the driver's seat and handed Zhirov a military telex, one long rolled-up sheet of rough, cheap paper. Fekete leaned in close to speak to Zhirov, who looked surprised and then smiled.

He opened the partition between the seats. "Viktor, you will be interested in this." Zhirov spoke in English so that Charlie would understand him. "We have a very special guest here at Tököl. Your famous war hero. Your so-called minister of defense, Pál Maléter."

Viktor's eyes barely opened. "I do not believe you," he said, his voice a murmur.

"He was taken into custody earlier this evening and is now under arrest," Zhirov continued, his voice smug. "He should not have sided with the agitators. See for yourself. He is just there. He is being moved right now into a cell."

With effort, Viktor, wincing, raised his head high enough to look out the Zil's window.

Charlie looked, too.

It was true. Maléter's height gave him away first, then his long, thin face. He towered over the heavily armed Soviet soldiers marching him toward the Nissen hut that served as the base's guard house. Maléter's handcuffed hands were crossed in front of him. In the low light, his expression looked grim.

Charlie felt Viktor stiffen. He sucked in his breath, his head swiveling to follow Maléter as he was marched past the Zil.

Zhirov kept talking. "You see? Prime Minister Nagy will be next. This nonsense of yours is over. You and the rest of your so-called revolutionaries will be dealt with."

Viktor pulled himself all the way up. His eyes met Charlie's. He pressed his silver ring into her hand. "Do not forget me, Charlie."

Viktor jerked open the Zil's back door. In an instant, he was gone. Up and out of the car. Heaving himself forward with great effort. Gasping, limping, loping, half-bent, lurching like a man possessed toward Maléter. Waving his hands. Shouting Maléter's name.

Maléter turned.

Viktor staggered closer to him.

Crack! Crack! Crack! A quick volley of shots from Maléter's Soviet guards rang out.

Viktor jerked. His arms flailed. His knees folded.

Charlie's hand flew up as if to catch him.

Viktor fell backward onto the tarmac, still as a stopped clock.

Maléter's face registered shock and horror. He stared down as dark blood pooled around Viktor's body. Then his guards shoved him forward, away from Viktor and toward the guard house.

Zhirov hurtled himself out of the car, screaming in loud, angry Russian at Maléter's guards, spitting his words out. But Maléter's guards didn't stop; they kept going until they—and Maleter—were out of sight.

Stunned, Charlie started toward Viktor though the open car door, but—*oof!* Fekete grabbed her roughly from behind. He tossed her over his shoulder like a sack of flour. She bounced on his shoulder as he hustled her toward the cargo plane. As they hurried, she managed one last look at Viktor. His body lay face-up, his eyes wide open and staring into the sky.

#   #   #

Inside the cargo plane, Fekete slammed Charlie down into a metal seat bolted to the side of the fuselage, hard enough that Charlie's head banged back against the naked strut of the stripped-down cargo hold interior. He jabbed his finger in her face, spitting furious Hungarian at her.

Charlie shrank back from him. She got it: *Stay here, or else.* She waited until Fekete turned away to open her hand. Viktor's silver ring lay in her palm, warm and damp, its wolf's eyes wise but wary. She slipped it onto her finger. It felt heavy against her skin, like a new memory forming and hardening in place.

Around her, the plane's flight crew—the uniformed pilot, co-pilot, communications officer, and the navigator—continued to load the plane. They worked slowly and sloppily. An ancestral portrait—an elegant woman who shared Viktor's high cheekbones and piercing blue eyes—was left leaning against the signal truck's back wheel well. A canopy bed and mattress teetered kitty-corner atop a carved dining room table; the table's dozen matching chairs were piled hastily atop the bed. Two extra-long red silk settees were propped against the side of the fuselage, adrift amid boxes piled high with china dishes and silver serving pieces. Tools—rakes, hammers, boxes of nails, clipping shears, shovels—lay on the cargo hold floor where they'd been tossed.

Overhead, a rumbling, high-pitched whine split the air. The first MiGs were taking off, the deep, throaty roar of their turbojets screeching as they rose in the dawn light and banked toward Budapest. Charlie closed her eyes and covered her ears, trying to shut the crushing reality of this moment out. She was cold, hungry, and overwhelmed by the white-hot shock of Viktor's suicide-by-Soviet-soldier. She had come to Budapest to prove that she could file a story from a war zone; instead, she was on a one-way flight to Moscow to be put on trial with her story, her Radio Free Europe credentials, and Jerome's picture of her with Horst's MiG as evidence.

Budapest and its poorly-armed freedom fighters didn't stand a chance against the Soviets.

If Zhirov's ominous hints about her father and what his watch might mean proved true, neither did she.

49
JUST SHORT OF TREASON

"Shh. *Bitte.*" Inside Tanner's small hotel room, Willie removed his headphones and turned up the volume of the shortwave radio in front of him. It was nearly 5:30 in the morning. "You must hear this."

Tanner stopped speaking in midsentence. Owens, on his second sandwich, stopped chewing.

"This is Premier Imre Nagy speaking." Nagy's voice sounded calm as he spoke in deeply accented English. "Today at daybreak, Soviet troops attacked our capital with the obvious intent of overthrowing the legal democratic Hungarian government. Our troops are in combat. The government is at its post. I notify the people of our country and the entire world of this fate."

Owens, Tanner, and Schmitty stared at the radio. Willie took notes. Owens yawned to keep himself awake. It had been a long night.

Nagy's disembodied voice continued.

"This fight is the fight for freedom by the Hungarian people against the Russian intervention, and it is possible that I shall only be able to stay at my post for one or two hours. The whole world will see how the Russian armed forces, contrary to all treaties and conventions, are crushing the resistance of the Hungarian people. They will also see how they are kidnapping the prime minister of a country, which is a member of the United Nations, taking him from the capital, and therefore it cannot be doubted at all that this is the most brutal form of intervention."

Nagy's voice did not waver. "I should like in these last moments to ask the leaders of the revolution, if they can, to leave the country. I ask that all that I have said in my broadcast, and what we have agreed on with the revolutionary leaders during meetings in Parliament, should be put in a memorandum, and the leaders should turn to all the peoples of the world for help and explain that today it is Hungary and tomorrow, or the day after tomorrow, it will be the turn of other countries, because the imperialism of Moscow does not know borders and is only trying to play for time."

Nagy's voice stopped. When he began to speak again, he spoke in French.

"It's a repeat," Willie said. He turned the volume down. "He said the same thing in Hungarian and German."

"This is as close as Nagy dares to come to asking for direct help from the outside world," Tanner said. He drained his coffee cup and set it back in its saucer with a slight clink. "He knows the game is over. The revolution has failed." He nodded to Willie. "We are done here. Pack it up."

Willie pulled off his headphones with one hand, while clicking the shortwave off with his other hand.

"You can't stop—you said you would try for an hour." Outraged, Owens watched as Willie shut the shortwave case and latched it closed.

Tanner looked at his watch. "I gave you fifty-three minutes. Close enough. Budapest is crawling with tanks and troops by now."

"You can't leave her there." Blood rushed to Owens' face. His heart raced. "She's an American citizen."

Tanner took the cigar out of his mouth. "The hell I can't. Orders are orders. I stuck my neck out once already. Your girl got herself in there. She's on her own until we see how things shake out. Best-case scenario is that she gets herself to the border, and we pick her up there. If the Reds find her, they'll arrest her, but at least she'll be alive."

Owens sagged back on the bed. "I can't believe this. Charlie will never survive on her own. She's just a kid."

He looked up at Tanner, squinting unhappily. "What am I going to tell New York?"

"You tell them whatever you planned to tell them had you stayed in Munich." Tanner's voice sounded cutting. He picked up his hat and stepped next to Willie, already at the door, the case with the shortwave set in hand. "We're out of here. See you boys back in Munich."

Schmitty looked at Owens. "I guess that's it."

Owens stood, angry and unhappy. He grabbed the last two sausage rolls, wrapped them in a napkin for the ride home, and then followed Schmitty, Tanner, and Willie out the door and down the dimly lit hallway. He was going home empty-handed with nothing to tell New York other than he tried—and failed—to find Charlie and bring her home.

Damn kid didn't just put herself at risk, Owens thought angrily as he thumped down the stairs. *Radio Free Europe might have to pay the price—and so might I.*

50

TAKEOFF

With her eyes closed, Charlie sniffed. Coffee—delicious, earthy-smelling coffee. For a moment, she thought she was back in the small kitchenette adjacent to Radio Free Europe's Central Newsroom. She lifted her head and opened her eyes. Reality sank back in—she was still aboard a cargo plane, waiting to take off for Moscow.

She looked around for the source of the coffee. The flight crew was nowhere to be seen although their work seemed to be done. The cargo hold was stuffed to bursting with household items, packed every which way around the signal truck. István's piano, still legless and on its side, was close enough for Charlie to touch. Zhirov sat near the cockpit door, engrossed in his telex. Tibor sat a couple of seats away. Charlie's canvas bag and Kovács's attaché case rested on the seats in between them.

Charlie sniffed again. The wafting aroma of coffee emerged with the pilot through the cockpit's lightweight aluminum door. He held two cups and a crew Thermos; steam rose from the top of the Thermos in low, lazy circles. Charlie's mouth watered; she couldn't remember the last time she'd had something to eat or drink. The pilot offered the first cup to Zhirov, who drank it quickly, barely glancing up from his reading. Tibor gulped down the second cup greedily, smacking his lips.

There was no third cup of coffee for her.

Crushed, Charlie met the pilot's eyes.

It was Horst. He wore a pilot's uniform, and stared purposefully back at Charlie.

The last time she'd seen him, he was climbing into the bench seat inside the signal truck with Walter to hide for the ride back to the border. The same signal truck sitting in the plane's cargo hold. That moment seemed like it happened a lifetime ago—so much had changed. Now Horst patted a nonexistent pocket on his uniform's chest—where he'd kept the sleeping draughts he used to commandeer a MiG just hours earlier, she remembered—and then disappeared inside the cockpit.

She watched the aluminum cockpit door close, her mind spinning. Her head swiveled to Zhirov. He yawned loud and long, and then his eyes caught hers.

"Your father was well known to the Kremlin," he said, his voice cold.

"What do you mean?"

Zhirov's mouth contorted in a round O as he yawned again. "Now is not the time for such a discussion. You will be told what you need to know in Moscow at the proper time."

"At least give me back his watch," Charlie said. "Please."

He yawned again. "*Nyet*. I will keep it safe, in case it is needed as evidence."

"Evidence of what?"

Zhirov didn't answer. His head fell back and his eyes fluttered closed. The telex slid out of his fingers and onto the cargo hold floor. Charlie stared at it hungrily: it held information about her father, she was certain.

She glanced at Tibor. His head nodded, too. His eyes drooped, his short legs splayed out in front of him.

Horst put sleeping draughts in the coffee, she thought. Her heart hammered as if it might beat right through her chest.

The cargo plane came to life. Its twin turboprop engines rumbled with deep, throaty growls. The china dishes and silver pieces in the hold rattled as the vibrations from the engines built in intensity. The cargo plane slowly taxied down the runway, its propellers humming. It picked up speed, engines groaning, and then lifted off.

They were airborne, with Horst at the helm. *But to where, exactly?* she wondered. Had Horst been pressed back into service for the Soviets? Where was the flight crew? Could Horst be flying the plane solo? For the first time in hours, she allowed herself a cautious flicker of hope.

51
ONE HUNDRED MILES DUE WEST

With her heart pounding in her chest, Charlie waited until Zhirov's snores sounded deep and even. Tibor, also asleep, hadn't moved.

She stood tentatively, pretending to stretch. Neither man stirred. She put her hand on István's piano, using it to help her step around the piled crates; it wobbled at her touch. As she slipped past Zhirov, she edged the telex toward her with her foot. She picked it up—it was written in Russian—and carefully reached for her canvas bag. She slid the telex deep inside and then looped the strap over her shoulder, grateful for its familiar heft. She wished she could find her father's watch, but she didn't dare to hunt for it in case Zhirov woke up. She left Kovács's attaché case where it was; Zhirov's arm rested on it, securing it.

\#   \#   \#

Inside the cockpit, Horst, strapped into the pilot's seat, sat in front of a black, utilitarian-looking instrument panel filled with a bewildering array of dials, gauges, and switches. Only the control yoke, rudder pedals, and Horst's radio headset looked even remotely familiar to Charlie.

"Lock the cockpit door behind you," he shouted over the flat, droning whine of the turboprop's engines. "Our friends are asleep? I didn't have much of the sleeping draughts left."

"Yes, asleep. Both of them," she shouted back. "What are you doing here? Where's Walter?"

"Walter is in Viktor's truck, asleep. He's exhausted. We had no time to get away. When they drove the truck on board, I decided to improvise." Horst glanced at Charlie. "I saw what happened to Viktor. I am sorry."

"Viktor told me he would never leave Hungary again. He meant it." She shuddered and quickly changed the subject; she didn't want to think about Viktor and whether his body was still laying exposed and alone on the tarmac. "Where are we going?"

"Austrian airspace. One hundred miles due west. Nineteen minutes flight time. Then on to Vienna. It is the closest airport. It is another fifteen minutes farther."

Relief surged through Charlie like a burst of new energy. Nineteen minutes, and they would be safe in the West. *Thank God.* "Where's the flight crew?"

"Asleep and locked inside the moving truck." Horst allowed himself a small smile. "I am afraid the pilot will awaken and find he is missing his uniform."

He eased back on the control yoke, keeping the cargo plane level. "You must be my navigator. Look out the windshield and tell me what you see. If you see something, use a clock face to tell me where it is."

Charlie climbed onto the copilot's seat and stood on it. The cockpit was tight, even for her small frame. She pushed aside a fire extinguisher hanging from one of the bare struts so she could lean over the instrument panel to look out and down from the front windshield. The instrument panel felt warm on her hands; by contrast, the windshield was cold as the outside air whooshed past. "I see a wide river. Four o'clock."

"That is the Danube. Good."

The radio crackled. Horst put a hand up to his earpiece to listen and then responded in terse Russian. To Charlie, he said, "The control tower is asking for our flightpath. I told them we are flying farther out to avoid the MiGs and bombers over Budapest. They have many other planes to worry about today. They'll forget about us, I hope. Seventeen minutes."

Horst kept the radio pressed against his ear. "There is something else. Very faint. Shortwave, I think." He listened.

"Red alert, Atkins. Oak tree, stat," he repeated. "You are this Atkins? Does this mean anything to you?"

"It means my boss knows where I am." Was she glad? Afraid? Did it matter? Either way, she couldn't worry about Owens right now. She checked the ground again. "I see low hills and some villages along one main road, six o'clock. Route 1, maybe. And a good-sized city. Two o'clock."

"Győr maybe—" Horst stopped mid-sentence as he looked past her.

Charlie followed his stare.

A red star—red like the star on her father's watch—winked against a dull steel hull. A MiG flew alongside them, close enough that Charlie could hear its engine's grumbling roar. Close enough to see the pilot's face. Close enough to see the pilot point down, toward the ground.

"MiG, three o'clock."

"Noted," Horst said dryly. "Diverted from bombing Budapest to chase us. The control tower did not forget about us after all. A pity. Sixteen minutes."

The MiG pilot fired a single shot. A blip, bright and imprecise—it missed the cargo plane's nose by six inches.

"Is he trying to shoot us down?"

"No, not if he knows the fat Russian is on board. He is trying to force us to land."

"What do we do?" Charlie tried to keep her voice calm.

"We keep flying. Fifteen minutes, Charlie. That's all we need. Once we're in Austrian airspace, there is nothing he can do."

A thrust of engines and the MiG roared past the windshield, cutting right in front of the cargo plane's path.

Horst grimaced and pulled back. The MiG shot out ahead of them, banked, and turned straight back at them.

"Fourteen minutes." Horst's voice was as steady as a ticking clock.

The MiG, predatory as a hawk, pulled alongside them, hovering off their wingtip. Then it dropped back behind them, out of sight. Charlie heard its cannons fire again, this time, a precise, staccato volley.

Boom! Boom! Boom! A deep, thudding roar.

The cargo plane yawed, a hard violent jerk sideways. It shook and trembled, slamming Charlie against the side of the cockpit. Her head hit the fire extinguisher.

Horst worked the rudder pedals, easing them in the opposite direction as smoothly as he could, like turning a bicycle to keep it from falling.

"Port engine out," he said as he righted the plane.

"Out?" Charlie rubbed the back of her head where she'd bumped it.

"Dead. Not working."

The MiG dipped its wings, a sharp and pointed message: *Land or else.*

Jiggle-jiggle-jiggle! The cockpit's aluminum door suddenly rattled. A hand slapped against it.

"What is going on? Who is shooting at us?" Zhirov's voice sounded slurry at the edges, as if he'd drunk too much vodka. "Open this door immediately."

"Ignore him. Thirteen minutes."

Bam! Something heavy hit the door. It vibrated against its frame. *Bam!* Another blow. A deep divot appeared, denting the door's aluminum. *Bam!* The third time, a hammer's claw smashed all the way through, ripping a hole big enough for Tibor's hand to reach through and wrench the door open.

Zhirov held Kovács's Walther. His eyes looked heavy and red, as though he were struggling to keep them open. Tibor, beside him, held a hammer, ready to swing it again.

"What are you doing up here?" Zhirov shouted at Charlie. He gestured with the Walther at her. "Get back to your seat!"

Then his eyes locked on Horst, and his expression shifted. His eyes narrowed.

"You," he growled over the noise of the remaining engine. "You must be our missing mechanic."

"Twelve minutes. Hold on!" Horst jerked back hard on the control yoke. Charlie grabbed the back of her seat as the plane's nose popped up. The rest of the plane followed, slanting up, into a steep climb.

Crash! Behind Zhirov, the contents in the cargo hold slid toward the rear cargo ramp, one giant jumbled mess. Even the signal truck rocked, as if it, too, wanted to move. Crates spilled, cabinets toppled, dining room chairs tumbled onto the floor. Zhirov fell, his feet scraping the floor. He gripped the cockpit's doorframe, the Walther still in hand. Tibor clung to the door frame beside him. He flailed at Charlie with his hammer.

She shrank back. Her shoulder brushed against the fire extinguisher, and she quickly turned toward it, unhooking it. It felt heavy, like steel. She propped herself against the back of her seat and raised the fire extinguisher over her head. Her eyes met Tibor's.

"This is for István," she shouted and brought it down as hard as she could on Tibor's fingers.

He howled and let go of the doorframe, his face contorted with pain. Charlie's eyes followed him as he flew backward into the cargo hold. His head hit István's piano, and he slid down its polished edge, dazed. His eyes met Charlie's one more time, glazed and surprised.

Charlie raised the fire extinguisher again.

Bang! Bang! Bang! Zhirov fired the Walther three times before he let go of the door frame. He fell back against the piano as Tibor had, hitting the keyboard. The piano lurched and twisted with the force of the impact of Zhirov's bulk.

Enraged, he waved the Walther and shouted at Charlie, his words lost in the noise of the engine.

The plane's nose dropped.

Zhirov grabbed the edge of the keyboard to hoist himself up off the floor. The piano teetered. He pulled at it, trying to clamber to his feet, but the piano's cabinet, weighted by the cast-iron plate in its frame, tipped and fell forward. It landed squarely on Tibor, crushing all but his legs. The instrument's fall nearly missed Zhirov—it pinned his arm, the one with the Walther in hand, trapping him in place.

The nose dropped farther.

Charlie turned back to Horst and sucked her breath in.

Blood oozed across Horst's chest, soaking his uniform and the harness. His hands clutched the yoke as he worked to level the cargo plane. His eyes followed the MiG as it turned back toward them.

"You're hit." Charlie fumbled as she ripped open his uniform. Two of Zhirov's bullets had passed through Horst's shoulder. She didn't like the sight of her own blood, let alone that of anyone else. Still, she threw off her coat and tore a wide strip of cloth from her shirt.

"You must fly the plane now." Horst's voice sounded strangely calm. "Nine minutes."

"I can't—" Charlie wrapped the cloth as quickly as she could around his shoulder. She tied a tourniquet, tight between the wound and the heart. She propped up Horst's arm above his heart.

Outside the MiG flew closer.

"You must," Horst said. "He is coming for the other engine. We'll do it together. Eight minutes."

She put Horst's finger on the tourniquet. Her hands, wet and sticky, shook. "Press here, hard as you can. What do I need to do?"

Boom! Boom! Boom! Another volley ripped the sky. This time, the MiG shot from the front before zooming over them. The cargo plane shuddered, jerked and slowed like a huge, wounded bird. This time, Charlie didn't need to ask. Their starboard engine was gone.

"Sit on my lap so you can see. Buckle the harness around us both. Seven minutes."

"Seven minutes? Are you sure?" She fought her rising desperation as she wound the harness around the two of them. Horst's blood felt warm as it seeped through her shirt. "But we have no engines."

"Listen to my voice. Only me. Nothing else. You can do this." His voice was in her ear, soft and close. *Just like A. J.'s,* she thought with a pang. "Can you see the horizon? Six minutes. I keep the time in my head."

She looked out over the top of the instrument panel. "Yes. Straight ahead. Twelve o'clock."

"You take the yoke. No sudden movements. Keep us level. Flat, like a tabletop."

"I've never landed at an airport—what do I do when we get to Vienna?" Charlie tried to keep the fear out of our voice.

"Too late. Vienna too far. Five minutes." Horst used as few words as he could. "MiG wants to force us down before Austria. Not good. We…glide…down."

"Glide?" Charlie cried. "You mean crash land?"

"This plane…rugged. Need flat place to land. Field. No power lines. No water." Horst's voice sounded weaker. "Where…MiG?"

Charlie leaned as far forward as she could and looked. The MiG was circling back. She looked down. No man's land stretched out in front of her like a long, rocky runway. Open. Wide. And filled with people.

"MiG, twelve o'clock. No man's land, six o'clock. There are too many people."

"Ignore MiG. Nose up. Little bit. Fly past people then land. Three minutes."

"Where's the landing gear—?" Charlie cried.

"Too late. Belly landing."

"Brakes?" Charlie screamed. Her pulse pounded in her ears. The plane sank lower. She gripped the yoke, desperate to keep the plane steady.

"*Riasztás! Riasztás!*" screamed the altitude alarm. The plane was dropping fast.

Horst's voice stayed in her ear. "Belly first. Slow us down. Then brakes. Two minutes."

Above them, the MiG angled down. A flash, a burst of cannon fire. The windshield shattered, its flying glass sucked outward by the rushing wind. Freezing, howling air surged past her.

The ground rushed up toward her.

Pull up! Charlie's mind screamed. She fought back. With every ounce of energy, she focused on Horst's voice: *Stay level. Hold on. Steer straight.*

Every lurch slammed her against the harness; it dug into her flesh. She held onto to the yoke, her knuckles white. Her fingers dug into the wheel. Her arms ached. The ground rushed closer.

"One minute."

"Hang on, we're going to crash," Charlie shouted.

52
END GAME

Outside the Nickelsdorf Inn, Owens looked across the village green toward the border and its massive oak tree. Andy's truck stuck out, the red cross on its side bright as a beacon. It was parked right where Andy had told him it would be—the spot where he'd agreed to meet Charlie. From the truck cab, Andy met Owens's eyes and shook his head. No sign of Charlie yet.

Figures, Owens thought, his foul mood deepening.

Tanner offered his hand. "You fellows need a ride back to Munich?"

"We have a car," Owens said. He was in no hurry to leave; going back to Munich meant finally facing the music. By now, Charlie's picture was sure to be all over the news. His conversation with New York wasn't going to be pleasant. "Can I at least tell New York your boys are keeping an ear to the ground for anything you can pick up?"

"You bet. No hard feelings. Wish I could do more." Tanner nodded to Schmitty. "See you back at the ranch."

Owens looked past Tanner. No man's land swarmed with activity. The flood of Hungarian refugees had swelled, only now they were joined by Soviet and Hungarian troops, working fast to reharden the East-West border. Two heavy guns and a huge, round searchlight were being hoisted up into the guard tower to be reinstalled. Along the rock trench running down the center of no man's land, a dozen men were unspooling new barbed wire to replace what had been cut down. The soldiers ignored the refugees flooding past them— for now. Those hurrying across into Austria pulled down the new wire wherever they could to give those behind them a little more time.

"Look at those bastards," Owens said in disgust. "They aren't wasting any time."

Tanner turned to look. "I'd say the revolution is well and truly over. Sorry to see it." Then he frowned. "What the hell is that?"

Owens and Schmitty looked.

A thick bulky plane glided silently out of the clouds, its starboard engine in flames. Its wings trembled and seesawed up and down, as if whoever was flying the plane were struggling to keep it level. The plane skimmed the top of the trees on the Hungarian side of the border, shearing them flat. It kept dropping—five hundred feet, three hundred feet, a hundred feet—as it headed directly at the border crossing.

"*Vigyázz!*" someone shouted. *Look out!* On the ground, refugees sprinted over the border. Soldiers retreated to the safety of the trees.

The plane's nose lifted just enough to keep it aloft as it barreled over the border crossing. Owens, Schmitty, and Tanner followed the plane as it passed, the red Soviet star on the hull a blur. Its tires hit the ground, screeching and spewing dirt, and then entire aircraft bounced back up into the air.

"Jesus H. Christ—that's a Red plane," Tanner said. He followed it with his eyes. The plane hit the ground again, spewing dirt, trees, rocks, and barbed wire in its wake as it slid on the hard, frosty ground. Tanner was already running, his long legs moving fast. He kept well to the side of the plane, Owens could see, away from the flying debris. Former medic Andy was a few steps behind him. Schmitty, and then Owens, ran too.

53
HARD LANDING

The fuselage struck the ground, bounced up, and hit the ground again.

Everything shuddered.

Charlie, bone-jarred and white knuckled, fought to keep her hands on the yoke.

The plane's nose hit the ground for the last time. It plowed straight ahead, its metal frame screaming and screeching. Wind roared in through the broken windshield. The stench of burning rubber filled the cockpit.

Charlie pushed every thought out of her head except the sound of Horst's voice.

"Brake pedals. Easy, slow."

She worked those pedals at her feet until the plane finally slowed, slowed more, and then came to a stop, its nose buried in dirt.

Charlie didn't—couldn't—move. Every part of her hurt. Her eyes stung. Her throat was raw. Around her, wires snapped and sparked. The altitude alarm sounded: "*Riasztás! Riasztás!*" Steam hissed.

"Master switch. Overhead panel. Off." Horst's voice was a whisper.

She looked up. Overhead, the MiG banked slowly and then turned back toward Budapest. Her hands trembled as she found the switch and flipped it off. Every blinking light winked out.

"Two crash landings in one day," Horst murmured. "I am a lousy pilot."

Shaking, Charlie unbuckled the harness. She was soaked with sweat and blood—her own and Horst's. Her hands were numb and raw. Her legs trembled—she grabbed the back of the seat to hold herself up. Her canvas bag, still looped over her shoulder, banged against her leg. Then she put her arm around Horst. His weight sagged against her.

"Step," she croaked. "Door frame."

Together, they staggered out of the cockpit and into the cargo hold.

A tall man with different colored eyes—one blue, one brown—was already there. The force of the crash had shifted the piano, freeing Zhirov, and the man was helping him to his feet. Zhirov, his face covered with cuts, his uniform filthy, clutched an attaché case and cradled his crushed hand against his body.

"My watch." Charlie's voice was a whisper.

But Zhirov stepped over Tibor's feet and hurried out the port passenger door—and into Hungary, taking Charlie's watch with him. The tall man watched, but made no move to stop him.

Charlie and Horst stumbled out the starboard door. To Austria. To the Free West.

#   #   #

Outside the plane, Andy's face was the first one Charlie saw.

"He's bleeding," she managed, her tongue thick in her mouth, as Andy accepted Horst's weight from her. Lightheaded now, she thought she might faint. Then a pair of hands grabbed her.

"What the hell were you thinking?" said an angry voice. It was Owens, and then he fired her, right there on the spot.

Charlie sank down to the cold ground, grateful to find it underfoot. "You can't fire me." She spoke almost without thinking. "I quit."

To her surprise, she meant it.

#   #   #

In Munich, Charlie answered as many questions as she could from her hospital bed, asked by a steady stream of government men in dark suits and by Owens's bosses, who flew in from New York just to talk to her.

Owens came by to see her, too, hat in hand. He got right to the point. "I didn't mean what I said about firing you, and I'm sure you didn't mean what you said about quitting. I want you to come back to work as soon as you're ready. You can write about Horst first thing. A long profile about how he escaped."

Charlie wasn't sure she'd heard him correctly. "Are you offering me a job on the news staff?"

Owens blinked in surprise. "Well, no, you're a news clerk. You'll write stories on your own time, same as always."

Charlie was already shaking her head.

"No?" Owens looked confused. "But what about all stories I let you do?"

Charlie nearly laughed. "Let me do? Without bylines or pay? *Those* stories?"

"But now people know who you are. It'll look bad for us if you leave."

"Bad for you, you mean," Charlie said. "Sorry, Mr. Owens, but I am done making coffee."

Dutifully, she followed her doctors' orders to rest and lied to them about how much she still hurt. All she wanted was to leave the hospital, the sooner the better; Zhirov's telex, the one detail she had told no one about, remained shoved deep inside her canvas bag. More than anything else, she wanted to know what it said about her father.

#   #   #

When she was released from the hospital, she went straight home. Waiting for her was a box Mária had packed for her, her personal belongings from her desk at Radio Free Europe. On top was a stack of messages all marked urgent—*Collier's*, *Look*, and *Time* wanted to talk to her. *No wonder Mr. Owens offered me my old job back*, she thought, once again glad she had turned him down. There were half a dozen messages from Andy and a letter from Father Popov. She ignored all of it. She crawled into bed fully clothed and slept without dreaming. She'd figure out what to do next—starting with Zhirov's telex—but that would have to wait until tomorrow.

54

REWARD

The day after leaving the hospital, she awoke to a loud, persistent knock. She made her way gingerly to the door and opened it. It was Cordell Tanner, the tall man from the plane, with his mismatched eyes, one blue, one brown. Like snake eyes. She turned back into her room without a word.

Tanner followed her inside. He dropped his hat on her table and made himself at home in the only chair in the room. She let him wait in silence as she washed her face and made two cups of tea on her small hotplate. She set one cup on the table and held the other between her hands as she sat carefully on the bed, her back against the wall.

"Officially, this conversation didn't happen," Tanner said. "But I thought you deserved to hear the truth directly from me."

"Does the truth matter? Either way, Viktor is still dead."

"Viktor understood the risk. He made a choice. In the end, no one could have helped him. Not Radio Free Europe. Not the American government. Not even you."

"What was it even for, then? The UN did nothing. We never seriously considered sending troops or tanks." Charlie paused. "Did we?"

"We had to take a swing, Charlie. That's what people like me do. We lay out the options for the politicians, just in case. Viktor knew that. But without real, meaningful assets in place in Budapest—people we trust, weapons we can count on, a network of people who keep us informed—there's nothing to work off of. Where exactly do you intervene? Who do you trust when you don't know the players on the ground? How far do you go? At what cost in lives, especially when the bad guys are already deeply entrenched in power, and both sides have the bomb?" Tanner shifted in his chair. "But at the end of the day, no, we were never going to send troops in. No American president is going to risk nuclear war over a landlocked country with no strategic value."

"A landlocked country with no strategic value," Charlie repeated. "Tell that to the Hungarians."

"You should know that there were some people in my chain of command who *did* want to go in. People at the very top. We considered something like the Berlin airlift, dropping food and medical supplies over Budapest. Maybe weapons, too. But the final decision rests with the president, and whether you and I like it or not, this was the call he made."

Tanner considered the cup Charlie had placed in front of him, leaving it untouched. "The president's choice was to decide we couldn't risk the Soviets saying we intervened. But I'll tell you this: The fact that the Reds went into Budapest so hard only proves that we're on the right side of history. They know all too well that the Hungarians, the Poles, the Czechs, and the rest of the satellites don't want Moscow running things. But if things are going to change, *they* are the ones who are going to have to change things. In the meantime, no one was willing to risk a third world war over ten million Hungarians."

"So, we make promises we don't intend to keep," Charlie said, her voice bitter.

"People hear what they want to hear. The president never promised to send troops. Do I wish we had gone in? What I think doesn't matter. My job is to provide options."

Charlie wasn't finished with her questions. Something Zhirov said kept coming back to her, and she didn't like what it implied. "Truth dollars don't really pay for Radio Free Europe. Do they?"

Tanner shrugged. "Does who writes the checks make Radio Free Europe's work any less important?"

So it was true, Charlie thought. Father Popov was right—even telling the truth with a point of view could be considered propaganda. And Zhirov was right, too—classified government budgets, not truth dollars, funded the scale and breadth of Radio Free Europe's operations. She had liked working for Radio Free Europe. Did its secret funding by the American government taint her as a journalist? *Maybe*, she thought, staring at the bare linden tree outside her window. *It depends on who you ask—someone in the West with many choices for news, or someone trapped behind the Iron Curtain with nothing but what the state tells them is true.*

By habit, Charlie's fingers brushed her wrist where her father's watch should have been; she still wasn't used to its absence. "The Russian—Zhirov. You let him go. Why didn't you arrest him?"

Tanner paused as if contemplating his words carefully. "Zhirov and I crossed paths in Washington during the war. Under the circumstances, it seemed the best outcome for all."

He changed the subject. "You should know that István Kovács has surfaced in New York. He has been offered a full ride at Julliard while his passport issues are worked out."

Good, Charlie thought. "What about Horst? And Walter?"

"Horst has two cracked ribs in addition to the two bullets through his shoulder. He's weak, but he'll heal. He is still being debriefed. Turns out Horst is an excellent listener with a good analytic mind. He is providing us with excellent intelligence about Soviet military readiness. Walter is a little banged up, but he's already enrolled in school. That was a brave thing you did, saving their lives."

"What will happen to them?"

"I expect Horst and his son will be offered American citizenship if they want it. Or West German, if they stay here."

"Is there a reward?"

Tanner paused. "There could be."

Charlie raised her eyebrows.

"What do you want?"

Whatever happened next, Charlie knew she wouldn't be here. "I want whatever survived the plane crash. Kovács stole those things from Viktor and his family. Viktor's dead, and there is no one else left to claim what's left. I'd like whatever is still useable to go to Sophie Müller. She lives next door to me. Her house was bombed during the war, and all of her furnishings were destroyed. She'll put it to good use."

Tanner looked surprised. "Odd request."

"Viktor would understand, and I think he would appreciate it. Better it goes to her than to some Russian dacha." Charlie took a breath. "One more thing. I would like to ask that Horst and Walter to be the ones to bring these things to Sophie. Can you make sure that happens?"

Tanner cocked his head. "Matchmaking?"

"That's not up to me. But Horst and Sophie both lost everything in the war. If they can find a way to be happy again, why not? Do we have a deal?"

Tanner threw his head back and looked up at the ceiling, considering Charlie's request.

"I believe we do," he said looking back at Charlie. He picked up his hat, turning it between his fingers, but made no move to leave. "You're leaving Radio Free Europe."

It wasn't a question.

"That's right."

"You're famous, in case you haven't heard. I imagine you have a number of choices as to what you do next."

Charlie shook her head. "I want nothing right now. Just peace and quiet."

"I have a job coming up in Moscow. Easy, no risk. Babysitting really. A group of young Americans invited to a music festival. I need someone to keep an eye on them. All expenses paid plus a nice salary." He cocked his finger like a gun and pointed it at Charlie. "You could do that job for me."

"You mean spy on my fellow Americans? No thanks."

"No spying required. Everything's on the up and up."

"Unless you've forgotten, I entered Hungary without official permission and probably violated two or three dozen laws. The Russians won't let me anywhere near Moscow."

Tanner waved his hand. "You'll have full diplomatic immunity. Not a problem."

Charlie shook her head. "Sorry, Tanner. I've had enough. Viktor died for what he believed in. I don't know what I believe any more, and I need time to figure that out."

"Going to Moscow might give you a chance to learn more about your father."

Charlie's eyes narrowed. "What do you know about A. J.?"

Tanner pulled a piece of paper from his pocket. It was one of her posters, its edges curled and frayed. He laid it on the table. "I know that you've been looking for him. And I know that one Captain Adolf Joseph Atkins was last seen in Moscow, in April 1945. Come to work for me, and I promise you I'll do my best to dig up whatever information I can."

Charlie stared hungrily at the paper on the table. It seemed like a long time ago since she had posted it. Was the possibility of information about A. J. enough to make her feel better about working for Tanner? Slowly, she shook her head. "Sorry, Tanner, but the answer is still no."

Surprise registered on Tanner's face. He laid a business card with a handwritten telephone number on the table. "If you change your mind, call this number anytime in the next twenty-four hours. Give the operator your name. That's all you need to do. Exactly twenty-fours hours and one minute from now, no one will answer, and this line will be permanently out of order."

"Twenty-four hours? Really?"

"It keeps things simple. Either you're in or you're out." Tanner stood, put on his hat, and stepped to the door. "Good luck to you, Charlie. You've got guts. I like that."

After Tanner left, she opened the envelope from Father Popov. It contained another letter—unopened—and a brief note.

Dear Miss Atkins, it read.

Col. Donovan, your father's commanding officer, responded to my letter. I am forwarding it on to you to read as you see fit.

The note was signed F. Popov.

Charlie opened Colonel Donovan's letter with trembling fingers.

Dear Father Popov, it began.

Captain A. J. Atkins did indeed serve under me at Ladd Air Force Base (1942–1945). He was a fine officer, smart, capable, and well-liked by everyone, including myself and my senior staff. But even smart men do foolish things, especially when it comes to matters of the heart.

Charlie paused. Matters of the heart? A. J.'s last letter mentioned a friend. Was that friend female? Charlie had never considered such a possibility.

As you may know, Captain Atkins was responsible for the technical education of our Soviet guests. That meant not just flying time but often detailed, highly specialized classroom training. Although the Red pilots spoke some English, none of them were proficient. For that reason, they brought along a translator to make sure the men understood their instruction. The translator's name was Ilena Ivanova.

With a pang, Charlie wished yet again for her missing watch. Her father's initials were entwined with the numbers 1.1. on the back. *Those aren't numbers but initials—I. I., for Ilena Ivanova,* Charlie thought excitedly.

Officer Ivanova assisted in Captain Atkins's training courses. As sometimes happens, Captain Atkins and Officer Ivanova became fond of each other, and as the war was coming to an end, they came to me to state their wish to get married. I, of course, had no objection, but at that time, Russian citizens were forbidden from marrying foreigners without official permission. Because

Officer Ivanova was the daughter of a high-ranking Kremlin official—her father, Sergei Ivanov, was a member of the Council of Ministers, the folks who do much of the work of running the U.S.S.R.—she said she thought such permission might be possible. Failing that, Officer Ivanova stated that she planned to ask for asylum. No rings were exchanged as far as I know, just the watch your letter mentions, which was a gift to Captain Atkins from Officer Ivanova. I am glad to hear it made its way to Captain Atkins's family.

Unfortunately, Officer Ivanova confided her plan to marry Captain Atkins to one of her countrymen, Aviator Yuri Sokolov, a pilot and childhood friend who was also at Ladd for training. Aviator Sokolov alerted Officer Ivanova's superior officer. Before I could intervene, Officer Ivanova was arrested, accused of anti-Soviet activities, which carried the potential of severe penalties, and ordered home at once. She was put on the next plane out of Ladd, which took her to Krasnoyarsk Air Base in Siberia. I assume from there she was to be flown on to Moscow.

Charlie, rapt, kept reading.

As I said, love can make even the best of men do foolish things. Regrettably, Captain Atkins took matters into his own hands. He followed Officer Ivanova to Siberia on the next available flight on the pretext of conducting routine pilot training. For someone with Captain Atkins's standing, it was not an unusual request and no alarms were raised.

The Alaska–Siberia air route to Krasnoyarsk was long and complicated. During that flight, Captain Atkins had time to think and to plan. When he arrived, it is believed that he bribed one of the Russian guards to alert Officer Ivanova of his presence and to facilitate her escape.

Captain Atkins then boarded an American military transport plane, which routinely ferried our pilots back to Ladd. The plane was on the Krasnoyarsk tarmac ready to take off when permission to take off was suddenly denied. Soviet Komendatura—*military police—boarded the plane, searched it, and found Officer Ivanova hidden aboard. The flight was canceled, and the entire crew was detained. Captain Atkins took the blame, saying that no one else knew, and that he had kidnapped Officer Ivanova against her will. Eventually, the rest of the crew was released and permitted to return home.*

Charlie could barely breathe.

Unfortunately for Captain Atkins, this wasn't the first time American GIs were caught doing something they should not have been doing on Russian soil. His actions were considered especially egregious because he admitted to the attempted kidnapping of a Soviet citizen. I am told that Stalin personally demanded to Truman that he be disciplined.

Captain Atkins's case fell under the jurisdiction of the American Military Mission in Moscow. I offered to testify at Captain Atkins's hearing, but Captain Atkins declined. He took full responsibility. He was found guilty, of course, sentenced to time served in detention with his pay docked for six months, and told he would be deported back to the U.S.A. immediately. All by the book, and even Stalin appeared to be satisfied. At the conclusion of the hearing, Captain Atkins was escorted to a U.S. military vehicle to be driven directly to the Moscow airport. Only the car never arrived. To this day it is not clear what happened to Captain Atkins. His status remains listed as died in service, no remains recovered.

I hope you find this information useful. Captain Atkins was a good man, and I daresay Officer Ivanova was an excellent match for him. In more peaceful times, I can imagine they would have had a long and happy life together. Sadly, in these dark and frightening days, it was not to be.

Please extend my regards to Captain Atkins's daughter.

"Yours, Col. J. Allen Donovan, Rtd."

Charlie reread Col. Donovan's letter a second and then a third time. The War Department had given Charlie and her grandparents no information about A. J.'s death, other than that his body was not recoverable. No mention was made that A. J. fell in love, stood trial or went missing in Moscow. Charlie could scarcely breathe. Could it be…was it possible…that after all this time A. J. was alive?

Charlie dressed as quickly as her injuries allowed, pausing only to run her fingers through her short blonde hair. She slipped Colonel Donovan's letter into her bag along with Zhirov's telex. She checked the address on Father Popov's letter and left the house. What information did Zhirov's telex hold? If Father Popov could translate it, Charlie dared to hope that she might finally learn A. J.'s fate.

55
FINDING A. J.

Father Popov lived in a rectory behind one of Munich's oldest cathedrals, one of the few churches to survive the war. It sat amid old oak trees that were bare save for a few stubborn leaves that clung to the lowest branches. Charlie moved as fast as she could, trying not to wince at every step.

She found the priest in the library, reading the day's newspaper. She cringed; Jerome's photograph of her in front of Horst's MiG was on the front page, next to a second shot that showed her slowly making her way to a waiting car as she'd left the hospital the day before.

Father Popov rose as soon as he saw her, one hand on his cane. With his other hand, he pulled out a chair for her.

"You have had quite the adventure, Miss Atkins," he said, scrutinizing her face closely. "Are you sure you are well enough to be up and about?"

"I'm sure," Charlie said even though she knew it was going to be a long time before she felt anything approaching normal again. Her fractured rib would heal, and the black-and-blue bruises that covered her body would fade. The scars on her spirit, and her heart, would take much longer to mend. "Thank you for Colonel Donovan's letter. I brought it, in case you'd like to read it. I brought this telex, too. I think it has information about my father. Can you translate it for me?"

Father Popov read Colonel Donovan's letter first and then bent over the telex, keeping his place with his fingers as he read. Behind him, morning light poured into the library through high, clerestory windows and illuminated the room's mahogany reading tables and bookshelves with a soft, white glow. They were alone in the library, and without a fire, the room felt cold.

She waited, trying not to let her impatience get the better of her.

When Father Popov finished reading, he clasped his hands together. "There's no good way to say this, Miss Atkins. I'm sorry, but the telex says that the day after your father went missing, Aviator Sokolov was arrested and charged with your father's murder. Apparently he, too, wished to marry Officer Ivanova."

Charlie sagged back in her chair as if all her breath had been sucked away. She knew it was a long shot, but Colonel Donovan's letter had given her the tiniest bit of hope that A. J. might still be alive.

Father Popov leaned forward toward her, his bright eyes focused on hers. "The telex goes on to say that Aviator Sokolov was released from custody the same day, at the request of Officer Ivanova's father. I am aware of Minister Ivanov's reputation. He is ruthless and very, very powerful."

"Why didn't the War Department tell us?" Charlie asked, her voice small. "If A. J. was murdered, surely they must have found…" She didn't even want to say the words, "…a body."

Father Popov laid his hand on the telex. "The official records ends with Aviator Sokolov's release. If I were a betting man, I'd wager that the situation was messy for all concerned. You father's attempt to smuggle Officer Ivanova out of Siberia embarrassed the U.S. military. It probably embarrassed Minister Ivanov as well. Allowing his daughter to marry a foreigner would have been a disgrace. Perhaps he even encouraged Aviator Sokolov, since he took pains to make sure he was released. As for what happened to your father's body, or where he might have been buried—I'm afraid this telex doesn't say."

"Does the telex say what happened to her? To Ilena?"

"I am afraid not." Father Popov folded his hands. "There is one more thing. The telex goes on to say you were not to be harmed, but frankly it's clear that the Kremlin was not at all sure what to do with you. You were to be assigned a room at the Kremlin—doors to be locked from the outside, I imagine. Hardly Lubyanka Prison, and the Kremlin is a most intriguing place, but it would have been a prison for you, nonetheless. They were waiting to hear what Minister Ivanov had to say about you. Now, of course, we'll never know what his answer would have been."

#   #   #

Charlie left the rectory, her head spinning. Zhirov's telex had given her a few more pieces of the puzzle, and yet she still didn't definitively know what happened to A. J. Would going to Moscow help? Should she take Tanner up on his job offer? Full diplomatic immunity, he said, so no one—including Minister Ivanov—could touch her. Tanner gave her twenty-four hours to think it over; she still had time left to consider his proposal.

#   #   #

That night, Charlie packed her few belongings. There wasn't much—everything she cared about fit neatly into her canvas shoulder bag, including Father Popov's letters and Zhirov's telex. She left István's recording of the *Hammerklavier* next to the phonograph she had borrowed from her landlady, along with a month's rent and a note. She didn't have a plan right now other than to keep moving.

By early morning, she was ready to go. She wrote to her grandparents, telling them not to worry and promising to write again soon. She wrote to Andy care of the Munich Red Cross and thanked him for taking good care of her but made no mention of keeping in touch. She left a note for Sophie, too, explaining that Horst and Walter would be by to see her with belongings that had come from the Budapest home of her friend and colleague, Viktor Farkas.

Hans Horst is a decent man, Sophie, and a devoted father, she wrote, and she left it at that.

Her last letter was to Horst.

Good luck to you and Walter—we'll meet again, I hope. She signed it, and then added an afterthought. *Like you, Sophie lost everything in the war. She's been a good friend to me—perhaps she'll be a good friend to you and Walter, too.*

Then she picked up Tanner's business card, tucked it into her bag, and left.

#   #   #

At Munich's main train station, she avoided looking at the terminal's squat, boxy pay telephones, a ten *Pfennig* coin in her pocket. By habit, she checked the empty spot where her watch used to wrap around her wrist. She rubbed it, missing her watch, and instead seated herself in front of the station's clock, staring at it as the minutes ticked by.

Should she call?

She had eleven minutes left before Tanner said the number would be disabled for good. *It might be the only chance I get to find A. J.'s grave and say a proper good-bye*, she thought.

Nine minutes.

My savings won't last long—I'll have to find a job soon.

Eight minutes.

Working for Tanner is dangerous, dirty business.

Seven minutes.

It's too soon to make sense of how indiscriminately death comes for good people in war.

Five minutes.

I need to get used to this new version of A. J., so in love that he followed Ilena halfway around the world just to bring her home.

A minute to go.

She pulled out the ten *Pfennig* coin. Against her palm, it was nearly the same steel color as Viktor's silver ring. Her eyes flew back to the clock. She held her breath as the last few seconds ticked by. Tanner's deadline passed. Her breath slowed.

At five after, she dropped the coin in the phone box, dialed the number, and listened as the phone rang. No one picked up.

Charlie hung up and exhaled slowly. This part of her life was truly over. Someday, she'd find a way to get to Moscow—and maybe learn A. J.'s fate—but on her own terms. She picked up her bag and slung it over her shoulder. Time to start fresh. At the counter, she bought a ticket for the next train out of Munich. She wasn't particular about where the train went, only that it left Munich behind.

AFTERWORD

T he historical events in this book are real, as are some of the
personal details that inspired this story.

On November 4, 1956, the Security Council, frustrated by
the Soviet Union's unyielding veto on the matter of Hungary,
called an emergency session of the United Nations' General
Assembly. The General Assembly voted to condemn the
Soviet occupation of Hungary with fifty votes in favor, eight
against, and fifteen abstentions. The Security Council then
moved swiftly on to more pressing business: creating the first
multinational peacekeeping task force to protect commercial
shipping interests in the Suez Canal.

That same day and shortly after his last radio address to
the Hungarian people, Prime Minister Nagy was given refuge
in the Yugoslav embassy in Budapest. Hours later, János
Kádár, appointed by the Soviets to replace Nagy, gave a radio
address, declaring the illegitimacy of the Nagy government
and announcing the formation of a revolutionary workers'
and peasants' government, supported by the Kremlin. Most
of Nagy's reforms—including the withdrawal of Hungary
from the Warsaw Pact—were immediately discarded. The
hated AVO, however, was replaced by a new organization, the
Belügyminisztérium, or Ministry of Interior. Although the new

ministry tried to distance itself from the brutality of the AVO, it found little trust for its work among Hungarians.

On November 22, Nagy was promised safe conduct out of the Yugoslav embassy by Kádár and his government. Instead, he was arrested. He was tried in secret alongside Minister of Defense Pal Maléter, found guilty of treason, sedition, and colluding with foreign powers. Both men were executed by hanging on June 16, 1958. Exactly thirty-one years later, on June 16, 1989, Nagy and Maléter were reburied with honors, part of Hungary's political shift away from the authoritarian government that had ruled the country since the 1956 revolution and toward its own unique flavor of democracy.

President Eisenhower won reelection in November 1956 by a landslide. Stung by criticism that his government had done nothing to help the Hungarians' desperate fight for freedom, the president defended the American government's lack of action:

> *Our hearts have gone out to [the Hungarians] and we have done everything that is possible in the way of alleviating their suffering, but we must make things clear,* Eisenhower's statement read. *The US does not now and never has advocated open rebellion by an undefended populace against force over which it could not possibly prevail. We, on the contrary, have always urged that the spirit of freedom be kept alive; that people do not lose hope. But we have never, in all the years that I think we have been dealing with problems of this sort, urged or argued for any kind of armed revolt which could bring about disaster to our friends.*

By November 10, the Hungarian uprising was over. The last combatants, thirty or so young Hungarians, were shot as they surrendered on Csepel Island. In all, more than 2,500 Hungarians died during the uprising, most of them in Budapest and half of them under the age of thirty. Another 20,000 Hungarians were wounded. Thousands more were arrested in house-to-house searches and were imprisoned— the unluckiest among them shipped in sealed boxcars to prison camps in Siberia to serve out their sentences. And by the time the Soviet Army fully closed Hungary's borders to the West, more than 200,000 Hungarians had crossed no man's land to start new lives in the United States, Canada, or Western Europe.

Soviet losses consisted of more than 650 dead and some 1,250 wounded. Later, the Kremlin would blame the uprising on mistakes made by the previous government and on "fascist, Hitlerite, reactionary and counter-revolutionary hooligans financed by the imperialist West." Moscow's intervention, the Kremlin maintained, came only at the request of good honest Hungarian socialists who were duly installed as the country's new leaders.

The term "freedom fighter" came into widespread use in the early 20th century to describe the moral legitimacy of the anti-colonial and Nazi resistance movements of the 1940s and 1950s. During the Hungarian Uprising, Radio Free Europe and other Western media outlets used the term extensively to describe the Hungarian revolutionaries; in fact, *Time*'s 1956 Man of the Year was "the Hungarian Freedom Fighter," a symbol of the heroic struggle against communist oppression.

In January 1957, the United States Congress held hearings into Radio Free Europe's role in the Hungarian Uprising. The hearings found that Radio Free Europe's broadcasts played a significant part in encouraging and prolonging the revolution by providing Hungarians with information and moral support that implied that Western military support might be forthcoming. The result was tighter scrutiny over the policies, practices, and governance of Radio Free Europe and its sister organization, Radio Liberty, which aired similar pro-Western content to the U.S.S.R.

During the uprising, Frank Wisner, head of the Central Intelligence Agency's Directorate of Plans under Eisenhower, had argued passionately but without success for covert assistance for the Hungarians. Wisner reportedly never recovered from the "loss" of Hungary. He suffered a mental breakdown soon after the Soviets retook Budapest and committed suicide in 1965. Intriguingly, files later released by the C.I.A. listed a truck made available at the Austrian border for use by a lone, unnamed patriot to gather intelligence for the American government.

As for the personal details, my father, Walter Wagner, worked for Radio Free Europe in the early 1950s, believing fervently in the written word as an alternative to the death and destruction of conventional warfare. He left Radio Free Europe shortly before the Hungarian Uprising in the summer of 1956 with his pregnant wife, my mother, Maxine. They wanted their first child born on American soil in case it was a boy and he—as was the case in those days—wanted to grow up to be president of the United States.

And that mysterious phone number, good for twenty-four hours only?

As a young, unmarried woman, my blonde-haired, blue-eyed Miss-Illinois-second-runner-up mother was invited for an unsolicited, in-person interview for an unspecified job with the United States government. She remembered the experience as pleasant but unremarkable because there was no mention of the specific work she might be asked to do. She was told only that should she receive a job offer, she would need to decide within twenty-four hours whether or not to accept it.

Sure enough, she received a telegram almost immediately, asking her to "please call Delaware 7-5787 concerning employment with the United States Government." On the advice of family and friends, she hesitated to call. When she finally did call hours after the deadline had passed, Delaware 7-5787 was no longer in service.

That telegram hangs in my office to this day.

Thank you for reading my book.

The best way to help this work reach others
is to leave a short book review.

Please go to Amazon and leave a review here:
amazon.com/review/create-review/?&asin=B0FTZRYLCS

ACKNOWLEDGEMENTS

I t takes a village, right?

Mine grew out of a unique international community of colleagues at Microsoft, who taught me to see the world through a different lens: that we are at our best when we value what we share in common. Among them are Susanne Banks, Kate Conner, and Jeff Olund, readers extraordinaire, who graciously commented and greatly improved this manuscript, and the late James Douglas, who told me I had something worth writing.

Thank you to Steve Travis, who tutored me on how planes take off, fly, and in this case, crash land.

A particular thanks to Scott Driscoll, a fine editor who suggested I turn an unsold screenplay into the novel that became this book, and to Harlan Lebo, an accomplished author and my longest, dearest friend, who read multiple iterations with enthusiasm and encouragement. Charlie only exists, thanks to you both.

Finally, to Jeff Harbaugh, thank you for keeping the faith that there would actually be a manuscript at the end of this process. *Tetelesta.*

ABOUT THE AUTHOR

I n addition to *The Byline Series*, Diane Wagner is the author of *Corpus Delicti*, the true story of a notorious, precedent-setting 1956 Los Angeles murder that includes the killer's confession.

Diane's work has appeared in *The New York Times*, and she has written for film and children's television. She lives in Seattle with her family.

(DRAFT)
BYLINE MOSCOW
CALAIS, FRANCE - JULY 1957

1:
CONTACT

Charlie Atkins held the still-hot baguette between her fingers, careful not to burn herself, and eyed it critically. The crust looked good—her best yet. It was glossy and the color of honeyed amber, with one long pale streak running down the center of the loaf ridged by golden umber where the baguette's 'ear' rose during baking. Its underside thunked nicely when she tapped it, sounding just the way a perfectly baked baguette should. Charlie squeezed the crust. It yielded with a pleasing crunch to a soft, creamy interior that was—alas—no where near as airy and irregular as Michael's.

Charlie groaned. She studied the bread, trying to work out what might have gone wrong. Had she overworked the dough? Used too little water? Was the oven not yet hot? She took a bite. *Not terrible, but missing something … imperceptible.*

Like most mornings, Charlie, twenty-four, slim and small-boned, had arrived early at *La Boulangerie du Coin*—the Bakery on the Corner—which was located just off the main thoroughfare on the way to the Port of Calais. The port—Calais was the last French city before England's white Dover cliffs—was busy all day, which meant the bakery was too, with French- and English-speaking customers. It was a modest, unassuming place run by Michael—at thirty-five, he shaped bread faster and more efficiently than anyone Charlie had ever seen—and his wife, petite, chain-smoking, ten-years-younger Françoise, who managed the front counter and their four-month-old son, Nico, with equal ease.

Charlie hung her canvas bag on a peg by the back door. By habit, she laid one hand against the side of the oven's chamber, a narrow slit built a hundred years earlier into the bakery's rear wall. Its bricks remained warm from yesterday's bake, like a dozing creature waiting to be awakened. Technically, Charlie's shift didn't—couldn't—start until four A.M.: French law specified exactly the hour bakers were permitted to begin work. But when the faces of the dead didn't let her sleep, Charlie found comfort in the quiet repetitions of the bakery: filling the bins with fresh flour, cleaning the seams of the workbench with a stiff, wire brush, or writing out the day's offerings on the chalkboard in English and her rudimentary French.

At four A.M., Charlie opened the iron door to the firebox below the oven. She cleaned out yesterday's ashes, careful to push what embers remained into a pile. Gently, she blew on them until they glowed red, and then added handfuls of twigs until the fire caught; it burned high and hot, and then died down. When the tiles on the floor of the oven turned white, Michael had taught her, the oven was ready for baking.

Charlie scrubbed her hands clean with soap Francoise made from sheep's tallow and lye and then slipped on a clean apron. She hoisted the flat, wide bin of dough she left to rise overnight up onto the counter. She touched the dough lightly: it felt smooth and pillowy, and sprang back slowly from her touch, as if it too, knew that baguettes taste better with time.

Charlie turned the bin on its side and let gravity do the work of transferring the dough onto the work bench. She dusted it with quick tosses of flour and then cut the dough into equally sized pieces. By now, Charlie knew the right heft for each single loaf: 250 grams, about the same as a ripe apple. She shaped the dough into slender ovals and laid them side-by-side to rest in a linen *couche* until it was time to bake.

#   #   #

By six A.M., the narrow maw of the oven was once again filled with bread. Michael, bleary-eyed thanks to Nico's poor night's sleep, had joined Charlie at the bench. They worked side-by-side in companionable silence, shaping loaves of sturdy country bread and long batons studded with raisins and walnuts. After an hour, Michael turned to rolling crescent-shaped croissants, dotting custard tarts with fresh berries, and painting rich, buttery brioche with egg wash to make it shine. At mid-morning, Charlie started making sandwiches for the lunch crowd: *jambon-beurre*, ham and butter, and *croque-monsieur*, cheese and ham, on fresh baguettes.

As the afternoon wore on, Charlie prepped for the next day's bake, cleaning up and mixing dough. She checked the larder too, for whatever Françoise might need to order. She took pleasure in leaving everything spotless, and in knowing as one day ended how the next one would begin. It was hard, repetitive work but it kept her mind busy. Charlie didn't like having too much time to think. She had learned the hard way that sometimes things needed to burn to ash.

# # #

Eight months earlier, Charlie had left Munich, West Germany abruptly—no plan, no job, no forwarding address. Her attempt to establish herself as a war correspondent during the Hungarian Uprising had gone disastrously wrong, leaving her numb with grief and uncertain about everything including her future. She bought the cheapest train ticket out of Munich she could, with a vague idea of getting to London, and then finding her way home to California to rest, to hide, and to lick her wounds.

In Calais, hunger—and fate—intervened. On her way to buy a ferry ticket to England, she passed *La Boulangerie du Coin* and its window sign: *pain d'un jour*—day-old bread—it read, right above *English-speaking sales clerk wanted.* Charlie went in for a baguette and came out with a job.

She found the work suited her, and graduated quickly from counter clerk to apprentice baker. She loved repeating the same task over and over, making tiny adjustments, one at a time, to see what, if anything, changed. She learned to lift and fold the dough lightly, and how to rotate loaves inside the oven with a long-handled paddle so that each one browned consistently and evenly. She developed her own distinctive slash atop each unbaked loaf—such a cut allowed built-up carbon dioxide from the yeast to escape and because Michael taught her that each baker's slash was unique, like an artist's signature on canvas.

Charlie wrote home to her grandparents in California, telling them only that she was happy in Calais and promising to write more soon. She didn't tell them how close she'd come to arriving home in disgrace, or that the best thing about being a baker was that here her mistakes were edible.

#   #   #

Françoise called her name twice before Charlie looked up, so intent was she on the bin of ingredients in front of her. It was the end of the day, and the bakery was about to close. Charlie was finishing up the dough for tomorrow's baguettes, marveling at how such simple ingredients—flour, water, salt and yeast—morphed into something as magical and miraculous as *un baguette*.

"A customer is asking for you," Françoise said, balancing Nico on one hip. She lit the butt of a cigarette, inhaled deeply, and then stubbed it out, careful to blow the smoke away from the baby.

Charlie's flour-covered hands paused for the briefest of moments. "The customer must be mistaken," Charlie said, careful to keep her voice even. "I don't know anyone here but you."

Françoise frowned, confused. "But he asked for you by name. He is waiting for you at the counter."

"Please tell him to go away," Charlie said, but it was too late. Françoise had disappeared, trailed by a whiff of smoke.

Charlie stared down at the dough. She jiggled the bin but there was nothing more to be done. The dough was tight, and ready to rest until tomorrow. She brushed her hands against her apron. She started to take it off, and then stopped. She retied the string around her waist, making it snug. *This is my life now,* she thought. She would wear her apron proudly, like armor.

#   #   #

Cordell Tanner stood at the bakery counter, looking as unremarkable as the last time Charlie had seen him, in her small, rented room in Munich. Then, Tanner had come not in his official capacity as an agent of the Central Intelligence Agency and the American government but as a courtesy, to explain to Charlie what she had already figured out: that war really was hell, that what governments say and do are two very different things, and that for many, the price of freedom was grotesquely high.

Now, despite the heat of the June day, Tanner wore a dark suit. He held his hat in his hands as his odd-colored eyes—one blue, one brown—met hers.

"How did you find me?" Charlie skipped the formalities.

"Nice to see you too. Your grandparents were kind enough to share your address."

"What do you want?"

Françoise, cleaning the counter, watched, Nico on one hip.

Tanner gestured to the bakery counter with his hat. "Those baguettes look pretty good. I'll take the last two."

Charlie fished the loaves off the rack. She wrapped them quickly in cheap brown paper and held them out unsmiling. "These are on me. Now please leave."

"That job I mentioned is still open."

"Not interested. Good-bye. Enjoy your baguettes."

"At least hear me out."

"We're closed."

"Five minutes, Charlie. You can keep me company while I eat."

Charlie glanced at Françoise. She shifted Nico to her other hip and shrugged.

Reluctantly, Charlie led Tanner to the table closest to the door. "Two minutes, Tanner. Eat fast."

Tanner put the baguettes on the table. "I told you in Munich that I could use a girl like you."

"And I told you I wasn't interested in being a spy. I didn't call either."

"I noticed."

"Then why are we having this conversation?"

"I thought you might change your mind."

"I haven't. You have ninety-seven seconds left."

"C'mon, Charlie, this isn't the life for you—"

"Who do you think you are to tell me what's right for me?" Charlie hissed. "I happen to be a pretty darn good baker. And guess what? No body dies."

Over Tanner's shoulder, Françoise's eyes met Charlie's.

"It wasn't your fault, Charlie. You know that."

"Doesn't matter. *Tick-tick-tick,* Tanner. Let's get this over with."

A bead of sweat appeared on Tanner's lip. "Khrushchev's music festival—next month in Moscow? You know about it?"

"I read the news. What about it?"

"There are delegations going from all over the world, including one hundred and sixty Americans. I'd like you to be the one hundred and sixty-first."

"*What?*"

"Is everything all right?"

Françoise stood over the table, one arm around Nico. She was looking at Tanner but the question was really to Charlie. "I see you have not eaten your bread, *monsieur*. Perhaps you should try another bakery."

Tanner kept his eyes on Charlie. "I still have sixty seconds left."

Charlie nodded, and Françoise raised an eyebrow. "Michael and I are working late tonight. We are right there—" she gestured toward the counter—"if you need anything."

Tanner didn't wait until Françoise was out of earshot.

"Fifteen days in Moscow, Charlie. All expenses paid, plus a nice salary."

Moscow. The last place her father was seen alive.

"I violated Soviet sovereign territory by going into Hungary. The Reds would never let me in. Fifty-two seconds."

"You'll have full diplomatic immunity. Press credentials—anything you need. You can write stories. Spend the day at the Bolshoi. Look for your father. No spying required. You just have to be there."

"No. Forty seconds."

"You don't understand, the situation has changed."

"My mind hasn't. Thirty-five seconds."

Tanner pulled an envelope from his breast coat pocket and held it out to her. "Maybe this will help."

Charlie recoiled. "A *bribe*? Are you out of your mind?"

Tanner fumbled as he tore open the envelope and dumped out its contents. A watch landed on the table with a soft thud.

Charlie stared at it, stunned.

It was her father's watch, sent home with his belongings at the end of the war. She had adopted it as her own, and knew its every millimeter: the nicks in its crystal, the creases in the leather band, the red Soviet star above the number six on the dial that winked in sunlight. For years it was the first thing she reached for in the morning, and the last thing she took off at night. Eight months earlier, it disappeared behind the Iron Curtain in the pocket of Second Deputy Premier Vasily

Nikolaevich Zhirov, a Kremlin fixer who nearly managed to take her to Moscow to stand trial as a spy.

With trembling fingers, Charlie picked up her watch. Carefully, she wound its stem and then held it to her ear to hear its steady *tick-tick-tick*. She wrapped the band around her wrist, her hand shaking.

"Your watch showed up a week ago with this." Tanner pushed a brightly colored brochure across the table at her. *Sixth World Festival of Youth and Students, Moscow, U.S.S.R., July 28 - August 11, 1957*, it read in bold red letters. "Zhirov sent it with your watch for a reason. I'm asking you to go to Moscow and find out what it is."

Charlie stood so abruptly that her chair fell backward. "If and when I go to Moscow, I'll go as a journalist, not as a spy." Her fingers clenched her wrist, as if she would never let her watch go again. "Time's up, Tanner. My answer is still no."